JORDAN'S BITTER PILL

LUCA DIMATTEO DPM

SHATTERED CEILING PRESS, Inc

Jordan's Bitter Pill

ISBN-979-8-9949862-0-2

Printed in the USA

In Memory of George R. DiMatteo
July 14, 1966 – October 4, 2025

A loving son, brother, father, husband, brother-in-law, family member, and friend.
He shared his love, his attitude, and his bigger than life presence.
Among those who knew him, just saying "George" would tell all you needed to know.
We miss him.

CHAPTER 1
SHATTERED

IT HAPPENED while Andie and I sat sipping wine on a short vacation at the Biltmore Estate. I was finally unwinding after a long and stressful final six months of my residency. The blue sky mixed nicely with the wine flight I had chosen. Gone were all the demanding attendings and bewildered new residents, but all that bliss vanished in an instant. A stranger seated a few tables away crashed to the ground, clutching his left arm. The gray-haired woman who shared his table sank to her knees beside him instantly. She clutched his face and then turned to the crowd. "Help! Some-one, please, help my husband!" She begged. "Please, help! Call 911!"

Frantic fingers began pushing buttons. Other onlookers sat stunned, unable to do anything.

Andie's head whipped towards me. "You have to help!"

I stared at her. "But . . ."

"You have to!"

My heart pounded loudly in my chest. "Andie, I—I've had a lot of wine."

"Doesn't matter. Do something!"

Part of me pleaded to stay hidden. I wanted to be just Jordan Carey, anything but a doctor, just for one more minute, but Andie was right. I ran through the maze of patrons, paralyzed in place by what was unfolding. I knelt beside the stranger. Without further hesitation, I began my assessment. From his wrist to his neck, to his chest, my hands moved over him on instinct as my mind connected all the dots. “Sir. I’m Dr. Carey, and you need to get to the hospital. You’re having a heart—”

“No! Please! Don’t do this. We can’t go through this again.” The large man pleaded through clenched teeth. He struggled to inhale deeply. “Just let it happen.”

My eyes widened with disbelief. “Sir, you don’t know what you’re saying.”

From beside me, his wife cried out. “Henry, no! Don’t worry about that now.” She glanced at me, then back at the crowd. “She has to do something! For God’s sake, she’s a doctor! Tell her she has to! Tell her!” The woman turned back to her husband. “Henry! Please!”

“Please. Henry. You have to trust me. Let me help you. Your wife needs you.” I interlocked my hands atop his chest.

He placed his hand over mine and gently spoke. It seemed as though an ease came over his entire body. “Doc, don’t, please.” His voice began to weaken.

“But, Henry, you’ll di—”

He pulled me close and whispered in my ear.

I slowly removed my hands from him and raised them to my mouth. A lump in my throat nearly blocked my own breathing. My shoulders dropped as I looked at his wife. I couldn’t form a single word. I was only able to shake my head.

Henry calmly reached for his wife’s hand. “I love you.” He let go of her and closed his eyes.

Henry’s wife, tear-filled and defeated, whimpered a solitary, “No, Henry.”

The lack of music and festivities petrified time. Only the distant howling of the ambulance’s siren broke the hallowed space. Still kneeling beside him, Henry’s wife looked at me. She said nothing. Her blankness bore through me.

The EMTs hurtled themselves through the crowd and stopped alongside us. I gave a subtle nod. They gave space. I placed my hand on hers for a moment, rose, and aimlessly walked back to our table. Nothing and no one caught my eye as my mind scrutinized the horror. *I could have helped him—he didn't want my help—he had made the choice long before this day. He told me; you didn't have a choice.* The words thundered through my head, filling every possible space.

I had lost the battle for a man's life, not against death but against something far worse. Henry chose to die to spare his family. It was an unbelievably high personal price to pay.

Andie sat at the table, tears in her eyes, both hands clutched over her mouth. She waited a minute, leaned in, and questioned, "Why didn't you . . ."

I fell into my seat. I slowly folded my glasses and placed them on the table, subverting every urge to smash them. "I didn't have a choice—it all happened so fast . . . He told me . . . I couldn't—I . . ."

Andie leaned back. "What? No, why didn't you ignore him? You should have—"

I grabbed my wine glass with a stranglehold but did not lift it from the table. "Andie! Leave me alone!" The crowd shifted its gaze towards me. I ignored them.

The vibrant inner courtyard turned into a bone-chilling tomb as we watched the EMTs strap Henry's body to the gurney and wheel him away. This terrible experience would be etched into my memory forever. I didn't want just a glass of wine; I wanted a case. I needed to wash away the entire memory.

We returned to our hotel room without exchanging a single glance. Andie knew better than to force me to talk. Hours later, after a room service dinner I couldn't eat, Andie asked me what the man had whispered.

I turned my face away from her. "Andie, I still don't want to talk about it."

Andie touched my shoulder and handed me a glass of bourbon.

"You have to. You're a doctor. You know what holding in this kind of stuff can do to you."

I took a large gulp. "Fine! He told me not to help him. He told me I couldn't and that his wife didn't know, and I couldn't tell her."

"Tell her what?"

I swallowed the last of the bourbon. "He had signed a DNR." I took a deep breath. "He had a DNR not because he was done living, but because he was done paying to stay alive, because he was done putting his family into debt." Before I realized it, I had thrown the empty glass across the room, hitting the antique wallpaper. Andie saw my pain and began picking up the shards. The anguish of repeating his words and realizing their meaning burned more than the cheap bourbon. The glass wasn't the only thing that shattered that day.

"Jordan, you can't keep going on this way."

"What does that mean?"

"It means that you get too attached to ideas, to people. Do you remember when those five stray cats lived behind the school, and the school was about to have the pound come pick them up? You spent hours finding them homes and failed an exam because of it. And how about when you helped collect money for the girl with the broken eyeglasses?"

"First, they were helpless kittens, and they were cute. Second, her glasses were broken by bullies, and third, we were kids back then. None of that even comes close to what happened today."

Andie sat on the armrest of my chair and hugged me. "That's just two incidents. Jordan, unfortunately for you, it's who you were back then, who you are today, and who you will be tomorrow. You dive in and help when the system fails."

I stared back at her, heat rising higher through every cell of my body. "This was a man's life—one I could have saved!"

"You don't know that."

Tears broke through, which angered me more. "Andie, he died for all the wrong reasons!"

Andie moved to the other end of the couch and fell into it as if she was trying to outdo my anger. "It wasn't your call to make."

"But—"

Andie placed her arms around me again. "Jordan. I know it hurts. It. Wasn't. Your. Call. To. Make."

I hated Andie for asking me to take that trip and for the life-changing experience that haunts my memory. I hated that a system meant to help instead victimized so many. Most of all, I hated that I was a willing and, until that day, a blind enforcer of such a system. I didn't know it back then, but somehow, I would find a way to feed the kittens and make sure they had eyeglasses.

CHAPTER 2
POLISH TO TARNISH

For months afterward, I tried to put the experience out of my mind, but it refused to be ignored. Not so much Henry's death but the reason behind it. As a young child, I recall sitting in the back seat of my parents' car as Dad drove us through poorer areas to reach a destination, like an airport or some nice vacation spot. I saw the poverty through the window, and even then, I knew something was wrong.

Ignoring this broken healthcare system meant remaining behind the glass of that car window. I knew I had to help, so I turned down a lucrative offer in a fancy suburban office and opened a practice in an urban neighborhood near the hospital, just a few blocks from the apartment I rented as a resident. I decided to keep it.

Anticipating the second-floor elevator doors opening and seeing my name on the wall used to make me feel like I was floating two feet above the ground. Now, frustration fills the air around me. There is no enthusiasm as I take a deep breath and turn the door handle. My practice is filled with people who were versions of Henry. They have no insurance, inadequate insurance, or unaffordable "affordable" insurance.

Clara gives me her usual chipper greeting. "Good morning, Dr. Jordan."

I feign a smile and reply. "Good morning, Clara."

"It's going to be a busy day. You already have two patients waiting in the exam rooms."

Clara is from the neighborhood. She's in her mid-forties, single, and street-savvy. She refuses to marry from the neighborhood, but she rarely leaves it. She is a thin, dark-haired, five-foot-four dynamo whom I've come to rely on. Like Rebecca, the office money person, and most of my patients, Clara too has taken to calling me Dr. Jordan. I think it makes them feel more at ease with me, an outsider. "Hmm, it's only eight fifteen. I thought we started at nine o'clock today. Clara, remind me why we give patients an appointment?"

She has told me many times that the people in this neighborhood pride themselves on punctuality, among many other things, and that I'd better get used to it. "Early bird and all the rest of that jazz."

Clara hands me a chart. "Billy Weston is in Exam One. You're not going to be happy with him. Bottom of the second page. Labs show he's not taking his meds again. Oh, and he's up eleven pounds."

Two years have passed, and I wonder what that other practice would have looked like. "Eleven pounds in two months?" I shake my head. "Any chance I can get a sip of coffee before starting?"

"Better make it half a sip, Dr. Carey. Going to be a long morning." She only uses my last name when trying to get a point across.

Once inside my private office, a more pronounced huff seeps out. "I probably passed up floor-to-ceiling windows for this closet." *It's just not right. How did I get here?*

I trade my jacket for a lab coat, skip the coffee, and head for Exam One.

"Good morning, Billy. Clara tells me you're not taking your meds. And your bloodwork confirms that. What about the diet? You're up to 276 pounds. Not good." I perch on the rolling chair.

Billy places his hands on his knees and stares at the floor. "Whew . . . Well, Dr. Jordan, I think I'm going to lose my job and have to go onto COBRA insurance. It's expensive, and I'll bet the coverage isn't all that good. So, I'm rationing the meds and stress eating on top of that."

I roll closer to him. "I'm so sorry to hear that, Billy. I get it, but you have very high blood pressure, and it's not controlled. I don't want you to have a stroke. You have a family to think of." I find myself saying that last bit over and over since that day.

"I'm a fifty-eight-year-old fat, bald guy with three kids and a wife who needs every penny I bring home. They're all I'm ever thinking about. We can't afford COBRA plus my meds. If I cut back on taking the pills, I won't have to buy them every month. And—."

"Billy, we both know you can't do that. Let's make a deal. You keep taking the medication as I prescribed it, and I'll find a way to get it for you that won't stress you, your wallet, or your diet. Deal?"

Billy reaches out to shake my hand, and I feel the tautness of his skin. "I, I think I can work with that."

"You're already retaining fluid. Look at the dents my fingertips made on the back of your hand. How many doses have you skipped?"

"Four . . . maybe five days' worth. But not all in a row."

"Billy, do you still have the water pills I prescribed last month?"

"Yes. Of course. I never throw any pills out. Somebody might need them."

"Somebody? What does that mean?"

Billy pretends to look around to see if anyone is listening. "Dr. Jordan, around here, somebody always needs something."

My facial muscles tighten. "Billy, are you selling your meds?"

Billy's cold gaze is fixed on my chest as a much lower, deeper tone questions me. "You wearin' a wire, Dr. Carey?"

"What? God no. I just don't think it's safe to share or sell your meds." I'm careful not to move back or forward from the man.

Billy returns to his jolly nature. "Whoa, Dr. Jordan, you had me going there for a minute. Nah, it's not like that in this neighborhood. Sure, we got that here and there, just like everywhere else, but we help each other here. Sharing, having each other's back, and all that. You know what I mean."

I point a finger at him. "Billy, *you* need them . . . all of them. So, don't share your medications with anyone. And don't take anyone else's medication. Please."

"The fluid pills are the white ones, right?"

"Yes, remember two months ago when you were here, I wrote 'water pills' on the bottle."

Billy smiles. "Oh yeah, now I remember. Okay, but I'm still not throwing anything out. I paid good money for them. Lots of people around here keep their meds, just in case. It's how it works around . . ." He stops and stares at my chest again.

"Still no wire. Don't share and you shouldn't have any to throw out. Let's go on. Your breathing is a bit heavier than normal. That's also from the fluid. I think we should do some more tests before . . ."

The rest of the examination with Billy proceeds quietly. I urge him again not to skip meds; he half-heartedly agrees. I tell him to see me again in a month; he says okay. I have no clue if he will do either.

Back in my office, I finally take a sip of now-cold coffee and start dictating Billy's visit. "Mr. Weston has been skipping doses of . . ." I dictate recount of Billy's visit into the recorder effortlessly and without any emotion. My mind drifts as it has been for the last few months, but this time the words are loud and different. *Each patient used to be a medical challenge that you fiercely took on. Have you given up? Do you really believe this is all you are? Line Tower, System Enforcer. Why did you come here? Find a way back.* ". . . I will see Mr. Weston again in a month. End dictation for Billy Weston." I take another sip of coffee. "What the Hell was that?"

Rebecca calls as I pass her desk. "Dr. Jordan, can I have a minute?"

I can feel a headache brewing. Rebecca is a stocky redhead with a streak of—for lack of a better word—sternness that causes most patients to tremble. She handles all the payments and insurance claims, so she has to be tough. "What's up?"

Rebecca practically snarls. "Yevgeny Olenska's insurance says he doesn't have coverage. He owes you over seven hundred dollars. I tried calling him, but there is no answer."

"Aside from knowing that you should have come to me before it got this . . ." My mind hiccups. *Enforcer*. I hold up a hand. "Sorry about that. Last time he was in, he told me his wife was diagnosed with inoperable cancer. You can guess the rest. Send him a gentle reminder, giving him a month to set something up."

"Dr. Jordan, everyone has problems, and you can't make them yours. And you can't keep going on this way."

Unexpectedly, a fervor rises from under my neckline. "I keep being told that."

Rebecca scrunches her face at me. "Excuse me. I don't think I have ever . . ."

"Sorry, I know you're right. And today, the money won't break us—but it might break Mr. Olenska. So, one month."

Rebecca makes a growly throat-clearing sound, trying to hold back her dismay.

I lament in kind. "Go ahead, Rebecca. Speak your mind."

"You know he's probably not coming back. People in this neighborhood take pride in paying their bills. And when they can't, they avoid you like the plague. We have to be tougher."

I bend down next to Rebecca's ear. "By 'we,' you mean me. I hear you." I stand up straight again. I think about the words my mind is screaming at me. "Sometimes people need to know that someone is fighting for them and not merely following the rules." I lean in again. "We okay?"

She returns the whisper. "You deal with their hearts, and I'll deal with their wallets. We're good. Always." I hug her, and she fights it but softens.

Exam Room Two holds Stella Thorne, an eighty-four-year-old Medicare recipient. "Good morning, Mrs. Thorne."

"Good morning, Dr. Jordan. And, as I have told you before, it's Stella. Don't you go making me feel my age."

"Okay, Stella. How are the tremors?" There is an unsettling lightheartedness to my tone.

Stella must notice it too. She pauses before proudly holding both hands out. "Look for yourself."

I give her a large smile. Again, something I haven't felt the urge to do in a while. "I don't see anything."

"Ha! That's what I see, too." Stella bends in closer to me. "Say, did you hear that old Charlie Frazier left the neighborhood last week? No one really knows why. But I'll find out. I always do. I think you can remove him from your patient list."

"Hmm. What makes you think Charlie is a patient?"

"Dr. Jordan, I have lived in this neighborhood all my life. I make it my business to know everything. No one, including you, in this neighborhood can hide anything from Stella Thorne. I'm as old as dirt, and like dirt, I'm all over everything and everyone."

I roll back on the stool and raise my left eyebrow, an ability that impresses most. "I'm not touching that one. Can we get back to the visit now?" I check her lungs, heart, and reflexes. "All looks good, but I still want you to stay on the tremor medication."

"Dr. Jordan Carey, you very well know that I can't stay on this medication for long. I have other bills to pay."

"I know you think that. But now you have Medicaid as your secondary insurance. Do you remember that?"

Stella smirks. "Yes, I guess I recall something about that."

"Do you also recall that it picks up the balance of the medical bills that Medicare doesn't pay?" I wait to see her reaction. "Well?"

Ignoring my last question, she folds her arms and snarls. "I get what you're doing. You want to test my memory. All these insurances and numbers are confusing. I remember when the doctor came to the house for a few dollars and an apple pie. He would look at you, your kids, and the dog, if you had one. He gave you whatever pills you needed. That was what the pie was for. Now, a bottle of aspirin takes half my social security check."

I play along. "I can honestly say that I don't know anything about those days. They must have been wonderful times, but now we have to play by today's rules. Maybe someday things will change."

"Oh, Dr. Jordan, you can bet they will change, and not for the better."

Has she always been this cantankerous, or does she believe that her age earns her that right? "Stella, sometimes I believe the exact same thing."

Stella stands and, with a slight wobble, heads for the door, the bite still lingering in her voice. "As far as the rest of my memory, don't you worry, Dr. Jordan, I can tell you every important thing that has gone on in my life and in this neighborhood since I was five years old. You see if you can remember to remove old Charlie from your list."

"So, I take it we're done here?"

"You checked my shakes, my heart, my breathing, and told me to stay on the pills; what else is there to do? Besides, I've been off the streets for over an hour. God only knows what I've missed."

I nod and wink playfully in return. "Stay on the meds. See you in three months." I'm left sitting in the room contemplating how Stella Thorne always manages to leave first.

The afternoon is only slightly better. The local shop owners make their appointments then because there is a lull after lunch and before it gets busy with those traveling home from work.

At the end of the day, Rebecca, Clara, and I begin our ritual of closing out the ledgers. Rebecca declares, "Well, ladies, it was a good day. We didn't get any insurance letters asking for money back, and we even got in a few checks."

Clara adds in, "And we only had two no-shows, and almost half of the patients had at least part of their co-pays. On the other hand, quite a few said they didn't know they had a co-pay. Still, a good day."

"If the two of you say so."

"Come on, Dr. Jordan. They all manage, and you help them feel better."

I sit back in Clara's chair at the front desk. "It's hard to keep hearing patients refuse 'useless' tests, 'unnecessary' medications, and visits to 'expensive' specialists," I say, making air quotations with my fingers.

Rebecca positions herself atop the desk next to me. "They think all that is a waste of money and time. Money they don't have."

Clara nods. "She's right, Dr. Jordan. That's the way it works around here. They know you; they don't know specialists or lab tests."

"Clara and I both grew up around here. They don't trust outsiders. You're making up ground. Just stay the course."

I chuckle. "Okay, okay, thanks for the pep talk, ladies. Let's go home."

A heavy mist dampens the sidewalk, forcing Clara and Rebecca to share an umbrella. I opt for an Uber to my apartment. "Do you want to share?" Both women wave me off.

"Good evening, Dr. Jordan," the driver greets me as I open the car door. "It is a wonderful night for an Uber, is it not?"

The hopefulness of his smile temporarily wards off the gloom that surrounds me. "Good evening, Samuel. Yes, it is. How is the family?"

"All are very good. Thanks to you." His smile widens. "Those antibiotics you gave Gracie worked wonders. Thank you for your kindness."

"You are very welcome."

"Do you have a fun destination or just going home?" Like most of the people who live here, Samuel moved in as a child and never left. Now, he is the local ride-giver.

"Going home. It's been a long day."

Samuel cranes his neck to look at me. "Dr. Jordan, every day you have the opportunity to make a difference in the well-being of others. That never makes for a long day."

I exhale. "I suppose you're right."

His lips straighten. "It is only a long day when you are not doing what you were meant to do."

"How is it that you stay so upbeat?"

"I have lived in this neighborhood since coming from Nigeria twenty-three years ago. These people are my family. Most of them have my private number and call me directly. Most of the time, I don't even charge them. They couldn't pay if I did. Or, they would pay and go without something they might need. Oh, I trust you will not share that with my employer when you give me a five-star rating after the ride." The broad grin returns.

"How do you do that? Don't you worry about your family?"

"I choose to help and know that somehow, I will be rewarded for it. Like everything else, we have a choice. All I have to do is look at the wonderful community I am part of. Then, for me, the choice is simple. I like to think that I do things that make a difference here. Please don't mention any of that either."

I lament. *When did the polish on my glorious dream of private practice become nothing but tarnish?*

CHAPTER 3
A KNOCK AT THE DOOR

It has now been three years since that day at the Biltmore. Two years of witnessing the community where I practice struggle under a broken healthcare system. And a few months spent replaying Clara's, Rebecca's, and Samuel's words in my mind.

"We are having an office meeting," I announce to my office staff one morning. "I have an idea. The way I see it, we have been on the sidelines watching our patients choose between family and their health. We're just enforcing the rules of a broken system, towing the line." This is the first time I've spoken the words aloud.

Rebecca grabs my arm. "Dr. Jordan, are you okay? You're as white as a ghost."

It feels like every ounce of blood has left my body. Then something inside of me shifts. Like the Grinch holding the sled high above his head, I could feel my heart come alive. "We were part of the disease, and now we are going to be part of the cure."

Clara eyes Rebecca, then turns to me. "No offense Dr. Jordan, but that sounds a bit preachy."

Rebecca adds, "And overly dramatic. Crazy even. If you don't mind me saying so?"

Ignoring the remark, I place a hand on Rebecca's shoulder. "You once told me that the people in this neighborhood take pride in paying their bills, and if they can't, they stay away. That's basically what you said, isn't it?"

"Um, yes, that's close enough."

"Clara, you said they depend on having each other's backs, and they want me to do the same. Right?"

"Uh, okay."

"Great! Let's do both. Let's make it easier for them to pay what they owe or can without damaging their honor. Let's show them we have their backs."

Silence screams through the room. Clara and Rebecca sit there, not daring to look at me or each other. "Okay, let me explain. The idea is to place a box in the waiting room. Patients can anonymously pay what they can afford. No one will know how much they put in the box, so there is no shame."

"Dr. J., I don't think this idea will work, and patients will start coming in soon. But, and this is a big but, that 'no one' you're talking about includes us. How do I track who's paying for what?"

"Rebecca, it's not always about the money. This time it's about getting them the care they need."

Rebecca slumps back into her chair. "Doc, as your friend, I think it's a lovely, idealistic sentiment. As your bookkeeper, I think this is going to be a mess."

"It will work out . . . Just record what you can and put the rest in as a total."

Rebecca shakes her head. "You're the boss." Rebecca finally looks at Clara. "Nothing from you?"

Clara holds up her hands. "Like you said. She's the boss."

I smile. "Glad you both feel that way. I already ordered the box. It will be here tomorrow."

After a rough start, the "Money Box," as it comes to be known, becomes a welcomed friend in the waiting room. Patients laugh at the idea but fold their paper money and checks so that no one in the waiting room can see what they put into the box. They begin visiting the office more regularly, and even the atmosphere of each visit feels lighter.

"Good evening, Dr. Jordan," Samuel says from behind the wheel of his Uber. "There is a lot of talk about your 'Money Box.' Word on the street is that it's a wonderful thing you're doing."

A large smile breaks out on my face. "Good evening, Samuel. It's nice of you to say that."

"See, I told you. When you choose to do what you are meant to do, happiness is unavoidable."

"Yes, you did say that. Things are better now, but I'm still struggling to get folks to fill their prescriptions."

"You still do not fully understand how it is out here. We cannot always get our medication from a pharmacy. Most of the time, our money must go somewhere more important. Dr. Jordan, most of us just do not have the money. Someone in the neighborhood always takes the same medication that someone else may need. Secretly . . . ha! I guess, not so secretly . . . Word travels quickly. A trade, or loan, or borrow, or gift is done through several hands, and neither side is embarrassed. It works. And it has worked for years."

I can feel the wrinkle on my forehead magnifying. "Samuel, that's insane and so dangerous. There has to be a better way."

Samuel shrugs his shoulders. "You are here now, so you had better get used to how things are done."

I whisper, "Damn it, Billy!"

"What was that, Dr. Jordan?"

"I was about to repeat that's insane and very dangerous."

Samuel smirks. "You have to admit. It is very cost-effective."

I step out of the car. "Bye Samuel, and thanks."

"You're welcome, Dr. Jordan. It's been a pleasure giving you a ride home . . . and an education." He laughs.

I yell back, "Thanks for that, too." I don't laugh.

. . .

It's seven thirty in the morning when I'm unlocking the clinic's front door. The exhilaration of my new idea has made it impossible to sleep. "Okay, take a breath. Go in, sit down, and wait for them to get here. Just half an hour more. You can do this."

A half hour later, the door handle clacks as it reaches the open position. "Good morning!" I call out.

Clara nearly falls backwards out the door. "Oh, Dr. Jordan? Good morning? You're here early."

Rebecca is now holding her coffee above her head. "Whoa! Why did you stop . . . Wow! Good morning? Everything okay?"

"Come in. Come in! I have good, no, great news!"

Rebecca places her purse on the desk and sips her coffee. "Wonderful. Can you tell us the great news at a greatly lower level?"

"Rebecca," Clara chastises.

"What? It's not even eight in the morning." She takes another sip of her coffee. "Fine. Go ahead, Dr. Jordan, scream away."

The grin on my face can't be helped. "So, you know how our patients still won't get prescriptions filled? I know why. They share them on the streets."

Rebecca jumps in. "And this revelation is 'good, no, great news'?"

"That's not the news, smart ass."

"Go on," Clara insists.

"I have a new box for the waiting room. We can call this one the Pill Box. I ordered it last night, and we should have it in a few days." I explain all the details to both of them and let it sink in for a few minutes before continuing. "So, let's start talking it up with the patients."

Rebecca scowls. "What the hell. Dr. Jordan . . ."

"I know it sounds crazy. But, it's much safer with me handing out free medication than them trading pills on the streets or in back alleys."

Rebecca grabs Clara's arm. "Clara, say something, please!"

"Dr. Jordan, Rebecca is right. This is a slippery—"

"It will work. I'll handle checking the meds and handing them out. I'll control the what, and the who; I have it all planned out. It will be perfectly safe. Besides, it's too late, the box is already ordered."

Clara looks at Rebecca and mouths, "Legal?"

I answer, "It's got to be more legal than what they are doing now."

Rebecca murmurs, "At this rate, we'll have no place for the patients in the waiting room."

The new box faces as much consternation as the first. However, over time, the concept takes off, and the idea of free medication gently spreads through the neighborhood streets. Patients deposit their unused prescriptions or medications from deceased loved ones into the box for redistribution.

As the months pass, the "Money and Pill Boxes" encourage better healthcare for the community's patients. Everything appears to be running smoothly until one morning, when a loud knock on the entrance door is followed by six individuals bursting in wearing jackets with large yellow letters on their backs.

"Everyone, get to your feet! Follow that agent to the street!" a man's voice barks orders to the waiting room patients and points to a man standing in the doorway. The inner door to the reception area crashes open. "Where is Dr. Carey?" the same voice booms.

I hear Clara scream and quickly emerge from Treatment Room One. My face is pressed against the wall, and the icy steel suddenly around my wrists disorients me even more. One of the men says in a matter-of-fact way, "Dr. Jordan Carey, you are under arrest. You have the right to . . ."

The rest of his words are lost as I watch four other agents busy themselves with securing the Money and Pill Boxes.

"Dr. Carey, do you understand these rights as I have explained them to you?"

"What, yes, no, I'm not sure. Why?"

"We have a warrant for your arrest."

As we pass the office's front door, I realize that the loud knocking was not a knock at all. It was the pounding of a fist attaching a sign to the door's outer surface: CRIME SCENE. DO NOT ENTER.

"The name-to-fame, winner-takes-all, high-profile case of Dr. Jordan Carey starts today. For those of you living under a rock, this young doctor seems to have thrown caution to the wind regarding her patients. Safety be damned. Dr. Carey states that . . ." The news anchor continues before Brian Freeland asks the driver to switch off the radio.

"All rise for the Honorable Judge Constance Harris," the bailiff announces.

"As you know, we are all assembled here today to begin the trial of Dr. Jordan Carey. Attorney Freeland, does your client understand the charges against her?" Judge Harris begins without salutations or even glancing at those in Courtroom Five. She appears to be in her sixties and carries herself with poise. The judge applies just enough makeup to look respectable while still being intimidating. She isn't thin or overweight but is definitely tall, which enhances her intimidation. She has shoulder-length brown hair and gold wire-rim glasses. Judge Harris has yet to say much, though she takes numerous notes. I stop watching her write because it heightens my anxiety.

"Yes, Your Honor." Attorney Brian Freeland respectfully responds. Brian is from Freeland, Schmidt, and Van Holt. According to Brian, Schmidt and Van Holt are long gone, but the names still carry clout. Brian's a seasoned attorney who has a tough fight ahead of him.

"Will your client agree to waive the reading of the charges?"

"Yes, Your Honor, my client wishes to waive the reading of the charges into the record." The judge's mannerisms do not faze Brian Freeland.

"Well, then let's get started. Mr. Barrens, please provide the prosecution's opening statement."

"Thank you, Your Honor. The state will demonstrate that Dr. Jordan Carey knowingly and willingly committed tax evasion, drug trafficking, fraud, and dispensed narcotic and nonnarcotic medications without the proper licensing. We will show that . . ."

A fast-track start date has brought me here eight months after my arrest. In my view, Barrens's task is to depict me as a monster while Brian's job is to portray me as the heroine. The truth is, I did it. I did it all. Well, not the tax stuff. But I didn't do it with malice, as Barrens strongly suggests. Everything I've done was for the greater good. I'm sure that's been said billions of times.

I could have accepted a plea deal and ended all of this. Brian even urged me to consider it, but I couldn't. That would mean letting down my patients, and what about Henry?

Brian quietly calls to me, "Jordan, pay attention, please."

". . . Dr. Carey's creation of what she called the Money Box is a direct attempt to subvert funds and evade taxation. Furthermore, the use of the so-called Pill Box is medically irresponsible and violates pharmaceutical laws. We will demonstrate that Dr. Carey was aware of her actions; nevertheless, she continued to engage in these illegal practices, only stopping when she was arrested. Finally, the state will reveal that Dr. Carey undertook all these actions with forethought and intent. Thank you." Attorney Barrens makes eye contact with each juror as he concludes his opening statement. He then turns toward the judge and nods. This is clearly a gesture he's performed countless times before.

"Very well. We will take a break for lunch and return in one hour to hear the defense's opening statement." Judge Harris bangs her gavel.

On cue, the bailiff commands, "All rise . . ."

I was making a difference. I was really helping people, and that's what matters. I'm not an activist, a political upstart, or anything else. I wasn't trying for global change; I just wanted to help the people in my community. I was making a difference, wasn't I?

"Jordan, Jordan." Brian lightly taps my forearm with his pen.

"Yes, I'm sorry. I was just thinking about . . . never mind. What was your question?"

Brian frowns as his voice becomes gravelly. "It was a statement. We have to leave the courtroom. Let's get lunch at the diner across the street and discuss what just happened."

"Okay." I wait for Brian to get a few steps ahead of me, then whisper to myself, "Oh em gee."

"I'll have my usual," Brian says, his weathered chair teetering as he barks his order at the arriving waitress.

The diner across from the courthouse has red pleather-cushioned booths, matching chairs, and a black-and-white checkered floor, just like you would imagine in a movie. The food is subpar, but it is convenient for the time-scarce attorney and client who need to eat before rushing back to court. Location, location, location.

"All right, so turkey on rye, with L&T and a large bath. Got it. How about you, ma'am?"

I unknowingly let out a giggle at the bath comment and reply pleasantly, trying to balance Brian's warlike orders. "I'll have the same, but without the tomato."

The waitress gives me a smile. "Got it. Ditto with only one T."

Brian shakes his head. "Jordan, did you understand all of Barrens's opening statement?"

"Honestly, I was only half listening. It's hard hearing him depict me as this awful person who planned every step in advance. I'd like to think I could have found a better way to cheat the system." I glance at Brian, who is looking around the diner. "That's not a confession."

The waitress returns, placing the turkey sandwich plate in front of Brian, loudly clattering it against the metal table. She accompanies this display with a sneer and muffled, colorful expletives. I smirk as my plate gently taps the table. She leaves, dropping one final smile, knowing her message was also served.

Brian sighs but remains silent. Instead, he just continues to look at me and wait. We have played this game numerous times in the days leading up to the trial. "I understand, but it's the prosecutor's job to render you and the charges against you in the worst light possible. He will demonize you with every word."

Forcing myself to ignore Brian's last statement, I ask, "What are you going to say in your opening statement?"

"I need to make the jury understand and believe that you're a good doctor and that your heart is in the right place. I need them to see that what you were doing wasn't criminal. I have to show them that every choice you made was in your patients' best interests. You violated various distribution laws regarding the medications, but I'll massage it. I'll blame the system. We tried to select a jury that is sympathetic to the idea of fighting against the system."

"What about the tax issues? Those things scare me." My voice flutters, and my pulse pounds. "Barrens is fixated on this point. He is so certain, and that troubles me. I was very careful . . . but what if I made a mistake?"

"They have no real evidence of wrongdoing; it's merely their opinion. Every check and receipt is accounted for, and regarding the cash, there is no way to determine anything about that. Therefore, that aspect could go either way."

"Do you think we got hurt in there this morning?"

Brian sighs, causing beads of sweat to roll down my back. "Yes, but only because we didn't get our chance. Barrens knew that if he took up enough time, the judge would recess for lunch, allowing the jury to hear only his side. This means they will only see one side of the story for the next hour. I'll work hard to change their minds when we get back in there."

I lean back in the chair to prevent the sweat from running further down my back. "Are you certain you can do that?"

A sarcastic grin appears. "Finish your sandwich. I'll take care of it."

I trust Brian implicitly. I think. However, he doesn't reveal much. I imagine most attorneys don't, as it might horrify their clients to know every scenario being played out. Brian advised me to accept the plea deal. That meant losing my license and going to prison for three years. I'm not sure which part of that deal was more terrifying.

Nevertheless, he believed it was a fair deal. He wasn't the one going to prison. I clearly remember the conversation that occurred in his office just five months ago:

"Jordan, the deal is a good one. With a trial, we never know what a jury will do. The reality is that juries are a roll of the dice. We can present the best possible case, but the outcome is in their hands. Emotions are in play, and no one is ever totally impartial."

"I'm losing my license either way, right?"

"I'm not sure. Your license is an administrative action. It's up to the medical board. But since you did everything that was reported to them, probably."

"Almost everything."

"Yes, I got it. Barrens is using that as the icing on the cake. Jordan, like I just said, what the jury believes matters. And no one can really predict that."

"NO! I want to have a trial. I'm innocent, and I was only trying to help. The healthcare system is broken, and I tried to make a small part of it better!"

"Okay, okay. That's what we'll do our best to show."

At the time, my decision to go to trial seemed like a good idea. But now that I'm in the midst of it, I'm afraid, and all I can see are prison bars.

Walking back across the busy street, the sight of the courthouse steps leaves my mouth as dry as the turkey sandwich. I hope Brian works some good magic this afternoon. I promised him I would pay better attention, but all the legal jargon, Barrens's apparent hatred of me, and fear of prison make it hard to keep that promise.

". . . Lastly, Dr. Carey risked it all to do the right thing. She saw a problem that put her patients in harm's way and stepped in to help. We all understand the true meaning of the Hippocratic oath that doctors, including Dr. Carey, swear to uphold. Furthermore, the things Dr. Carey did were not selfish acts. In fact, they were just the opposite. Dr. Carey never gave a second thought to what might happen to her. She did what was right for her patients and her community." Brian speaks for about an hour and forty minutes and performs spectacularly.

"Thank you, Mr. Freeland. We will stop for the day and return tomorrow morning at 9:30 a.m. sharp." Judge Harris bangs her gavel, then stands.

"All rise," The bailiff cries out for the last time today.

Day one is over, and I do not feel any better. They should offer a sedative to help the defendant get through this. I'd think about prescribing one if my license weren't suspended. "Great thought. Put yourself in more trouble."

Brian turns towards me. "What? Did you say something?"

I shake my head. I wish I could be in the heads of the jurors to hear what they're thinking instead of what I'm thinking. Actually, that might scare me more. "Brian, your opening statement was fantastic."

"Jordan, let's step outside the courtroom and talk for a minute." His face is stoic.

"I don't like the sound of that."

"No. It's fine. I just want to go over some strategy."

"Okay." I'm wondering what changed. After all, we've gone over strategies and game plans a hundred times in the past eight months.

Brian and I walk to a small room with two chairs and a small metal table. "We will have to use this for now." He closes the door behind me. "I've been thinking. The jury will hear from some of your patients, some satisfied and some, let's say, unsatisfied. I'm telling you again because that could happen tomorrow. I don't want you to look worried or surprised when it happens. Every doctor has unhappy patients. The jury knows this."

"Too late. Okay, why now? What changed? Why are you telling me this now?"

"Nothing has changed."

My spine twitches, and that proverbial Spidey sense is on full alert. "Are you sure?"

"I just want to make sure you're ready to hear what patients might say about you. That's it. Tell me again how you saw yourself as a doctor with your patients." Brian sees my eyes begin to well up. "I just want to cover all the bases again. Nothing more. You want me to be on my A game, right?"

I exhale deeply, trying to relax. "Well, I tried to be more than just a white coat to them. I treated my patients like I would have wanted to be treated. I asked about their families, their needs, and what made them tick. I wanted to bond with them. I wanted to treat them as people, not ailments. I never gave up, even if that meant referring them to someone else for a fresh look, even though they wouldn't go. I was their advocate." The more I spoke, the more my anxiety rose, the more the level of my voice climbed. "Brian, you know, I've told you dozens of times. I didn't care about myself. I cared about them."

Brian holds up a hand. "Okay, okay, Jordan."

I pull away and start pacing the tiny cubicle-like room. "This is all BS! Corporations, big business, faces you can't see keep people from getting the care they deserve, and I, a doctor, try to give a small piece of it back, and I'm being crucified for it!"

Brian stands and moves towards me like a father consoling a child. I angrily whisper, "No, it's all BS! Am I the only one who sees it?"

Brian leads me back to the chair. "Jordan, you have to control yourself. Barrens is going to attack you with witnesses. You have to remain calm. The jury is watching every reaction you have."

I close my eyes for a few seconds. "I understand. I'm not going to lie to you. It's going to be grueling."

"Just do your best. Think of something that keeps you on an even keel."

I smile. "But you told me to pay closer attention."

Brian returns a grin. "Let's call it a day. I'll see you at the Safe Haven across the street at nine o'clock sharp. Have a good night and get some sleep. I've called an Uber for you. I need to stay here for a few more minutes."

I wave goodbye, and I mouth thank you. "How do I have a good night when I'm on trial? I haven't slept since all this started." *At least I'm going home to my bed. Thank you again, Brian. Is a fifty-thousand-dollar bond for bail a lot? Thank you, Andie.*

CHAPTER 4

BUCKFORD HMC, REBECCA, AND THE MONEY BOX

IN THE BEGINNING, my office was a wonderful workspace and a sanctuary. It gave me purpose and protection. Now, it's a sealed crime scene. Since my trial started, the media coverage has picked up again, but nothing like before. Brian does a great job of limiting my exposure. The threat of some sophisticated legal action has kept the reporters at a distance, but the trial is the next level for them. So, they wait on the courthouse steps, in the corridors, and I'm betting, even in the restrooms, for a career-furthering snippet.

Sitting in my apartment, I think about how this all started. Brian has asked me, on numerous occasions, to think about the sequence of events, the timing, and the pivotal moments that pushed me to make my choices. I don't like the word "pushed."

"Dr. Jordan Carey." Dean Kate Sanderson announces as I walk across the stage and past the lectern. Joyous cheers erupt from Joseph and Linda Carey. Cliché or not, they seem to be the proudest parents in the auditorium. I graduate just above the midline of my class, affording me a reputable residency and a bright medical career. The reception for the newly adorned doctors is filled with wide-eyed parents as they silently play out the next phase of their doctor-child's bright future.

"Welcome to Buckford Hospital and Medical Center. As you know, we pride ourselves on seeing and treating patients from every walk of life . . ." Dr. Charlene Manham repeats a speech handed down from previous senior residents. One that I eventually recited to nervous new residents in my final years. "Okay, let's get acquainted with the residents' lounge. Here at BHMC, this room is anything but a lounge. You will be working hard and now learning medicine in real time. And this is where you'll understand what you don't know. Five of you are starting today, and only one of you will make it to take my job. Occasionally, you will be asked to make difficult choices. I will watch over you for the next two years. I won't let you harm a patient. By the time you leave here, you will have seen much about medicine and patient care, but you will also learn a great deal about yourself. Up until now, you have been taught how to treat diseases. Hopefully, here, you will come to appreciate that being a doctor isn't just about treating diseases; it's about treating people. Having said all that, I'm sure your time here will be as fulfilling as mine. I will see you in the small conference room in fifteen minutes." Without another word, Dr. Manham left five young, bewildered doctors standing in an ocean of thought.

She was not wrong. Buckford Hospital and Medical Center is a small inner-city hospital primarily serving lower-middle-class and low-income patients. It allowed me to expand my knowledge and experience as a doctor. More importantly, it introduced me to a world I had never encountered. I grew up in an upper-middle-class family; poverty never knocked at our door. I did not comprehend what it meant to be poor or to experience overwhelming debt. I now categorize the debt my parents had as luxury debt. We did not use credit to survive; we used it to thrive.

BHMC brought me closer and closer to making the choices that landed me here. I decided to practice in a lower-income community during my final year as a resident. The dreams parents have about their doctor-child's future came crashing down for Joseph and Linda.

Mom jumped in first. "Darling, are you sure about this?"

"Jordan, your mother and I think you should take more time to think it over."

"I have thought about it enough. I want to work where I can make a difference. Isn't that the right thing to do?"

"What your father means is that you need to be sure about this. It's going to change everything. I mean, really change everything."

"I know it's not what you wanted for me, but this is what I want. I already signed a lease on an office close to the hospital."

I remember my dad placing his arm around me and smiling. "Jordan, your mother and I love you, and we will always support whatever it is you want to do. If this is where you think you can do the most good, then we are behind you one hundred percent."

Little did we all know how important that final thought would be. Even after my arrest and the setting of the trial date, my parents have not uttered one "I told you so." Instead, they stand firm in my corner.

"How was last night?" Brian's cheeriness is comforting as my fear rises.

"If you're asking, did I sleep? Unfortunately, the answer is only when my body gave up. And only long enough to recharge and start the process again." I want to yawn for a dramatic flair, but there isn't one waiting in the queue.

"Okay. Let's talk about today. They are going to say a lot of bad and personal things about you in that courtroom. It's crucial that you don't show any response. Do not look down like you have regret or are ashamed, especially ashamed. That's not what we're going for. Oh, and don't look arrogant."

"I'M NOT ARROGANT!" My fear and anxiety collide. It's like an iron worker standing on a steel beam fifty floors up for the first time.

"That's precisely what you can't do. We're going for a doctor who puts her patient's needs before hers. No matter the consequences."

I take a deep breath. "Got it. This is not going to be easy."

"I know, that's why I'm bringing it up now, out here."

"Please all rise for the Honorable Judge Constance Harris." The bailiff at the front of the courtroom bellows. There is uniform silence.

Judge Harris glares sternly over the courtroom as she waits for the shuffling of shoes to cease. "Mr. Barrens, is the prosecution ready to call its first witness?"

"Yes, Your Honor. The prosecution would like to call Mrs. Rebecca Nils to the stand."

After Rebecca is sworn in and all the preliminary questions are answered, Barrens begins his assault on me: "Mrs. Nils, please take us through your time working for Dr. Carey. Please start with why you were hired and end with the day Dr. Carey was arrested."

"I was hired a little over two years ago by Dr. Jordan to run her billing department. We called her Dr. Jordan . . ."

Barrens interrupts, "Please let the record show that when Mrs. Nils refers to Dr. Jordan, she actually refers to Dr. Jordan Carey. I'm sorry, Mrs. Nils. Please continue."

Rebecca frowns at the prosecutor. "As I was saying, I made sure all the patient insurance information was up-to-date and all the insurance and personal billing was done correctly and sent out on time. I also did collections. Some people had a hard time paying what they owed. Sometimes they even got angry and threatened to sue, saying our fees were too high."

Barrens again interrupts. "Did you tell Dr. Carey that people complained about her billing practices?"

"Yes, but it wasn't about our billing practices. It was about the fee amounts."

"Did you ever advise Dr. Carey on a solution for her billing problems?"

"It's not uncommon to have patients question their balances. Especially when their insurances don't pay well or at all."

Barrens looks to Judge Harris. "Your Honor, could you please advise the witness to answer the questions that I am asking?"

"The witness may embellish her answer if she wishes, but Mrs. Nils, you are required to answer the questions asked of you eventually. Do you understand this?"

"Yes, Your Honor." Rebecca stabs a look through Barrens and continues, "I told Dr. Jordan that we might need to hire a collection agency."

"And what did Dr. Carey do in response to your suggestion?"

"Hmm, I guess nothing at first. Then, one day, Dr. Carey told us about her idea of using this wooden box. She said we were going to change our billing and collection practices. I . . ."

Barrens turns and locks eyes with the jury before returning to the witness. "Mrs. Nils, can you please tell us how Dr. Carey planned to change her billing practices with this wooden box?"

"It became known as the Money Box. Dr. Jordan said that we would continue to bill the insurances for the patient, but we would now have a collection box out front, in the waiting room, where patients could make anonymous payments for their services. Dr. Jordan explained that the insurance companies set large deductibles and high co-pays, so our patients couldn't afford to come to the office. As a result, they were refusing to get the treatment they needed. Dr. Jordan said we had to do our part."

"What was your response to this news?"

Rebecca hesitates. "At first, I told her I didn't think it was a good idea, but I didn't push the issue—she is the boss. It is her office."

Barrens places his hands on his hips as he shakes his head. "Aren't you a certified medical biller?"

"Yes. I am certified."

"Mrs. Nils, it's safe to say that you are an expert in your field?"

"Um, yes."

"Did you feel that this Money Box scheme concocted solely by Dr. Carey could be a problem somewhere in the future?"

Rebecca peeks at me, then quickly shifts her eyes away. "Yes, I even thought there might be some legal implications. But I said nothing. Like I already stated, Dr. Jordan owned the practice."

Barrens places a hand over his mouth momentarily while looking directly at the jury, then continues. "I see. What happened next?"

Rebecca inhales and appears to almost refuse to exhale. Barrens demands, "Mrs. Nils, you are under oath and must answer my questions. What. Happened. Next?"

"Okay. The office income started to drop. The patients would put some cash or checks in the box, but it wasn't enough." Rebecca's complexion pales.

"So, there wasn't enough money? Did that affect the office payroll?"

"Um. It was temporary. And Dr. Jordan made it up right away."

"Let's get back to the insurance claims and the payment for those claims. How did that work out with Dr. Carey's Money Box scheme?"

"Objection!" Brian stands up. "Attorney Barrens's repeated use of the word scheme implies malice, and none has been proven."

Judge Harris looks at the prosecutor. "The court agrees with Mr. Freeland. Mr. Barrens, until you can prove malice, please refrain from using such misleading words as 'scheme.'"

"My apologies, Your Honor. Mrs. Nils, how did billing the insurance companies and receiving payments from them work with the use of Dr. Carey's Money Box, um, plan."

Brian stands again. "Your Honor!"

"Mr. Barrens, you're walking a very fine line here. The witness may now answer the question."

"We would send them out, and they would return with the patients owing all or part of the fee. This was the same as before. Dr. Jordan told us to bill the patients for the remaining amount and then give them a professional discount if they couldn't pay. We didn't collect co-pays anymore. We didn't even know if patients were paying anything at all. It was tough." Rebecca stares at the floor directly in front of her.

Barrens is now standing at the jury box. "Were you able to do your job effectively?"

Rebecca's voice shakes and the volume gets softer with each response. "Not in the traditional sense."

"Mrs. Nils, did you say anything to Dr. Carey about the confusion and chaos her system was causing?"

"I had no choice. I told Dr. Jordan that I couldn't track the money. There just was no way to keep accurate records."

A look at the jury, and I can see this isn't going well for me. I turn to Brian, who is motionless. He's just sitting there. Is he even paying attention?

"What did Dr. Carey say when you told her the new system was a disaster?"

"Objection! Your Honor, the witness never used the word disaster. She didn't even imply it!"

Judge Harris's eyes are locked on Brian. "Settle down, councilor. Sustained. Mr. Barrens, rephrase the question or move on."

"Yes, Your Honor, please accept my apologies again. Mrs. Nils, what did Dr. Carey say when you told her the system was, uh, difficult?"

Rebecca looks up only long enough to answer the question. "Dr. Jordan smiled at me and said it would all work itself out just as soon as the patients got used to it."

"Did it 'work itself out'?"

"No. I could never tell who paid what, so I just stopped."

"What do you mean, you just stopped?"

"I only recorded payments to a patient's file if the insurance paid something for that particular patient or if there was a check in the Money Box that identified who the payment was for. For the rest, we just recorded it as the daily total."

"So, you're stating there was no way to accurately account for who paid what and when?"

Rebecca takes a long time to answer and finally whispers, "Yes."

Barrens contorts his face as he leans toward the witness stand. "Can you please repeat that. And can you please speak louder, Mrs. Nils?"

Rebecca clears her throat. "I said, yes."

Barrens nods in receipt of the response. "Okay then, let's move on. Can you please take us through what happened at the end of each day regarding the money in the Money Box? And Mrs. Nils, please remember to speak up so the jury can properly hear you."

Rebecca's glare at Barrens is hollow as she lets out a defeated sigh. "The boxes were too heavy to lift. I believe Dr. Jordan made them big so no one could steal them. Anyway, each evening Dr. Jordan went to the waiting room, took the cash and checks from the Money Box, totaled them, and then told us the amount. One of us would record the amount in the computer's ledger."

"By us, you mean you or Clara Smythe, the receptionist?"

"Yes."

"Did you verify that the amount Dr. Carey gave you from the Money Box was accurate?"

"No. As I said, I recorded the checks and insurance payments. Clara, Dr. Jordan, and I trusted one another. There was, and still is, no reason for me to doubt either of them."

Barrens again waits for the jury to absorb the information. "So that's a no? You're telling the court that only Dr. Carey knew if the amount was correct? Neither you nor Miss Smythe had ever verified that amount of untraceable money coming out of the Money Box?"

Brian stands. "Objection—."

"Overruled. The money is untraceable since, other than the assumption that it came from patients who visited Dr. Carey's office, of which there is no tangible evidence, its origin is untraceable. Therefore, overruled. The witness will answer the question." Judge Harris never shifts her eyes from the papers in front of her.

"As I already said, we trusted each other."

Judge Harris looks directly at the witness and sternly interjects. "Mrs. Nils, it is your choice. Get to answering the questions or be held in contempt of my court."

Rebecca's fiery office tenacity is gone. "No, we didn't verify the amount."

"Thank you for answering my question," Barrens says. "Let's go back to the insurance claims. What happened when the insurance payment or denials came in?"

"When payments or denials came in, I placed them within the patient's account."

"Did the accounts balance with Dr. Carey's new system?"

"No."

Barrens is taking full advantage of his position as the pace of the questions increases. "Did anyone ever complain?"

"Yes."

"What were their complaints?"

Brian springs out of his seat. "OBJECTION! Hearsay!"

"Sustained."

"Did anyone ever directly complain to you?" Barrens take a quick look at me. I turn away.

"Yes. some people claimed they put money into the Money Box and still received a bill."

"How did you rectify the complaint when the patient's billing records were, by your words, so difficult?"

"Most of the time, we just took their word for it."

Barrens is now standing in front of the prosecutor's table. "As an expert, certified medical biller, is that the normal or customary way billing complaints are handled?"

"No."

"How should these types of complaints be handled?"

"By researching the payments and balances and coming to an investigative conclusion."

"You mean follow a paper trail?"

"I guess so."

"In Dr. Carey's Money Box system, was there an accurate paper trail?"

Tears begin to flow down Rebecca's cheeks as she whimpers, "No."

"Thank you, Mrs. Nils. Your Honor, I have no more questions for this witness."

Judge Harris looks at Rebecca and then at the courtroom. "We will take a ten-minute recess. The jury is dismissed to the jury room. Bailiff, please escort the witness to one of the side rooms and return with her in ten minutes. The attorneys and Dr. Carey, please remain seated in the courtroom."

"Brian, what's going on?" I ask. "That was brutal."

Brian murmurs, "Please stop reacting. She's just giving her a chance to compose herself."

Ten minutes feels like a lifetime as we sit in silence until the sound of the bailiff opening the courtroom door rumbles through the empty courtroom. Rebecca enters, followed by the chaotic undertones of the much larger crowd, hurrying to fill the gallery seats.

Brian's voice is calm and welcoming. "Mrs. Nils, as a billing and collections expert, did Dr. Carey do anything illegal?"

Rebecca has regained color and depth. "No. She was making

changes for the betterment of her patients. Knowing Dr. Jordan, she wasn't thinking about herself."

"Objection!" interjects Barrens. "The witness cannot know the defendant's mindset without direct conversations about the fact."

Judge Harris focuses a steely look at Barrens. "Sustained. The jury will disregard the witness's last statement."

Brian asks, "Did Dr. Carey willingly or knowingly commit tax fraud or evasion?"

"Objection. The witness is not a tax expert."

"Sustained."

Without the slightest reaction, Brian continues. "Did you ever indicate to Dr. Carey that she might be crossing a line?"

"Objection. The witness is not a legal expert." Barrens stands, but his voice is low and controlled.

"Sustained."

"Did Dr. Carey's system cheat or mislead anyone?"

Rebecca smiles. "Yes, I believe her system did cheat someone. It cheated Dr. Jordan, herself."

"Mrs. Nils, did the office patients seem happy with the changes made by Dr. Carey?"

"Oh yes! Word got out, and we had lots of new patients. The cash flow was eventually up again, but it was never where I thought it should have been. The patient numbers rose, and they seemed more willing to come for their visits and take their medications, which is why Dr. Jordan did it."

"Mrs. Nils, you are a certified medical biller. Are billing mistakes common in a medical office?"

"Well, I would like to say no, but the truth is, billing mistakes happen more often than anyone wants to admit."

"Do you believe Dr. Carey had any nefarious intentions when she started using the Money and Pill Boxes?"

"No. I am absolutely sure that she did not intend to harm anyone or commit any crimes at all. I believe she is a good person and a good doctor. She cares about people."

"No more questions. Thank you, Mrs. Nils." Brian smiles at Rebecca and she returns one.

Noting the interaction, Barrens quickly responds. "Redirect, Your Honor."

"Go ahead, Mr. Barrens." Judge Harris makes another note.

"Mrs. Nils, have patients ever been double billed with Dr. Carey's new system?"

"Yes. Like I said mis—"

Barrens interrupts again. "What happened when patients stated they already paid the bill?"

"I tried to handle the problem first, and if that didn't work, I would bring it to Dr. Jordan's attention, and she then took care of it."

"I see. And exactly how did Dr. Carey handle it?"

Rebecca's testimony continues for another half hour. Everyone in the courtroom loses interest as the attorneys try to make minor points seem like mountainous findings of legal and illegal activities.

Honestly, it wasn't about legal or illegal, right or wrong. I didn't have a plan. It was more of a string of ideas that tied themselves into what everyone now calls my system. I thought the idea of having the boxes was a stroke of genius. I guess in the medical world, the word "stroke" has a much different meaning. The government, or rather Prosecutor Barrens, seems to be having a stroke from my actions. The smile on my face grows, and I casually cover it with my hand.

Brian fizzes in my ear. "Jordan. Jordan!"

"I'm here. I'm listening." I look around, and the courtroom is entirely empty.

"It's time for lunch."

"Okay, but I'm not having the turkey today." I'm trying to lighten the mood, but the scowl on his face isn't leaving.

“Follow me.” My usually talkative attorney doesn’t utter another word as we walk down the cold marble corridor of the courthouse’s fifth floor.

“Brian, what’s going on? What’s wrong?”

“Not yet. Just keep quiet for a minute.” Brian doesn’t even look at me; he just keeps walking. Finally, we enter a room off the right side of the corridor. Brian closes the door with more force than I would have preferred.

A large wooden conference table and old leather-bound chairs occupy most of the floor. The wood-paneled walls are bare. It’s a place stuck in time. The room’s icy marble floor adds to its cold, lifeless expression. This is definitely a place where deals are made, or attorneys and their clients discuss unwelcome news. Either way, I didn’t want to be in here.

”First, where are you in this trial? You seem to be in some faraway trance. I need you to be present at all times. It’s like you don’t care. Second, was Rebecca Nils correct on cross-examination when she said that patients were double billed?”

“Wait, what? No, sometimes we make mistakes, but every office makes errors. They were always corrected.”

“How many mistakes, and can you prove they were corrected? It may not be enough to have Rebecca say they were mistakes. The police have a saying that every attorney and judge knows very well: Once is a mistake, twice is a coincidence, and three times is a pattern. Which one are we looking at?”

“Brian, I didn’t do anything illegal, intentionally.” Brian has never had this look before. He doubts me. I can see it.

“How many mistakes?”

“I don’t know. That was Rebecca’s job.”

“She testified that she brought them to your attention. Did some patients complain about getting billed twice?”

“Yes. In the beginning, a few patients mentioned that they had placed money in the box and then received a bill. I’m sure that we wrote the balance off. That's what we had to do. It was the only way the Money Box worked. In order to keep them coming in and getting treatment, they had to know we trusted them."

"Jordan, what does that mean?"

"It means that we couldn't prove they did or didn't put cash in the box, so we had to take their word for it. We always billed the insurance company for the patient so they could get credit towards their deductible. We always recorded payments from the insurance company first."

"What about those patients on assistance, like Title 19? Did you take money from them?"

"No. If a patient was on Medicaid, we were not allowed to collect payment from them. So instead, we billed their insurance and took only what it paid." I'm shaking now because I can see where Brian is going with this.

"How do you know they didn't put anything in the box?"

"I don't. We would tell those patients they didn't have to put anything in the box."

"Did you have any signage in the office or give them printed information explaining that they were not to contribute to the box?"

"No. I figured they would already understand their insurance. I believe it's the rule that patients are to understand their insurance plans."

"Technically, it is. This conversation is privileged, so don't share it with anyone, and let's hope the prosecutor doesn't bring it up. I won't say anything about it unless it's to defend you."

"Brian, I'm worried. I didn't mean to do anything wrong. I was trying to help."

"I know, I know. We'll work with it. I have a plan if it comes up. Don't worry about it now." Brian gives me a forced smile. "Let's get out of here."

CHAPTER 5
CLARA AND THE PILL BOX

"JORDAN, are you almost done? It's time to go back."

"I'm done." I didn't touch my lunch. Truth is, what lunch I may have eaten, I did so obliviously. I'm a million miles away, wandering through countless courtroom scenes of witnesses betraying me. What will they say or be made to say that could end everything? "Brian, maybe we should cut a deal."

"What? Now hold on! We are just getting started. I—"

"Dr. Carey. Don't you give up . . ." The waitress demands as she comes up behind me.

Brian frowns at the waitress's name tag. "Excuse me, Rachel, but I think it's my job to tell her to quit or keep going."

Rachel bends down close to Brian's face. "Where would you like me to slam tomorrow's plate first?" She returns her attention to me. "Dr. Carey. I'm not one of your patients, but my grandmother lives in that neighborhood, and she is. I've never seen her look so good. She, like a lot of others there, know you and what you were doing for them. So, don't give up. They wouldn't want you to." Rachel hugs me then drops the check in Brian's lap without the slightest glance at him.

Brian drops fifty dollars on the table. "Well, there you have it. I guess the people have spoken."

"That's a big tip."

"That's a big plate. Still want to quit?"

"Okay, well, don't get ahead of yourself. It was just a temporary bit of doubt. I'd watch how you talk to me from now on. Apparently, I have groupies."

Standing at the door to Courtroom Five, Brian turns to me and quietly grouses. "Leave any look of doubt, shame, or regret at this threshold. That's your job. You do your job well, and I'll do the same at mine. Oh, and pay attention."

"Attorney Barrens, please call your next witness."

"We call Miss Clara Smythe to the stand."

While Clara is sworn in, Brian and I sit silently. The possible loss of my license, and worse, the reality of going to prison churns inside of me, causing my gut to send out gurgling screams. My brain is playing out scenarios: *We could just run. Just leave. Move away. Do something else*. My insides are anything but silent, and now I'm fidgeting.

Brian taps my foot with his as Barrens starts his next attack. "Miss Smythe, you worked as a receptionist for Dr. Carey since day one. Is that correct?"

"Yes."

"As the receptionist, you sat looking out of the inner office window into the waiting room. Is that also correct?"

"Yes."

"So, it's safe to say that you had a clear and unobstructed view of the Money and Pill Boxes?"

"Yes. Uh, except when a patient was standing right in front of the window."

"Were you able to see patients place cash and pills in the appropriate boxes?"

"Yes. I could see patients walk up to the boxes, but I couldn't tell you how much money, if it was a check, or what medication they dropped in either box. When it came to the Money Box, most were very secretive about how much they put in. That is a very sensitive issue. Several times, there were plastic wrappers in the boxes. Some of our patients have memory issues and then there are the small kids. I'm guessing they thought the boxes were odd-looking trash cans."

The muffled giggles bouncing around the gallery are quickly deflated by one glance from Judge Harris. Clara continues. "As for the Pill Box, most of the medications were brought in those pill bottles you get from the pharmacy, so all I saw was the patient place them into the opening then the bottle hitting the bottom of the box or another plastic bottle. That's as much as I can tell you."

"Did you ever see them put little bags of pills or other substances in the 'Pill Box'?" Barrens makes air quotes.

"Objection! There has been no indication or production of evidence that anything besides unused legally prescribed medication has ever been placed in the box. The prosecution is misleading the court with extremely condemning and fantastically false commentary."

"Take it easy, Mr. Freeland. Sustained. The jury is to disregard any and all of Mr. Barrens's last commentary. Mr. Barrens, I have already told you that you are walking a fine line. You have every right to do so, but it is an arduous path you're taking."

"I solemnly apologize, Your Honor."

Judge Harris looks up from the note she has just written. "I strongly suggest you refrain from any more antics. Now move along, Mr. Barrens."

"Thank you, Your Honor. Miss Smythe, is this the Money Box you could see from your seat?" Attorney Barrens's two junior lawyers lift the actual wooden box and place it loudly onto the prosecutor's table. All eyes are now focused on the "Money Box."

"Yes."

"Is this the so-called 'Pill Box' that was placed in the waiting room by Dr. Carey?" The assistants now place the second wooden box on the table. It too makes a thud as it lands against the table's hard surface. The effect is more profound than the first time.

"Yes."

Both junior attorneys smile. They see that the jury's eyes are transfixed on the mini coffin-like boxes. Clara's answers no longer matter.

"Did patients place money, checks, or gum wrappers in the Money Box before or after their visits with Dr. Carey?"

"Some patients placed money or a check in the box after a visit, others placed it before, and some never put anything at all."

"Were you able to keep track of who was putting what in the Money Box?"

"At first, I tried. It was a game for me. Then I stopped because it was too confusing. It distracted me from my work, and I realized I was mostly guessing." Much like Rebecca, Clara doesn't look at me.

"Did you see patients place things in the Pill Box?"

"Yes . . ."

"I'll ask you again. What did they place in the Pill Box?"

"I mostly saw those orange pill bottles."

Barrens pauses for a long moment. "Hmm. You said you mostly saw. What did you mean by that?"

"I mean not all the bottles were orange."

"What other colors were there?"

"Some were white and some were blue. That's what I can remember."

"Did patients always put bottles in the Pill Box?"

Clara pauses, looks at me quickly, then turns back to Barrens. "No."

"What other types of containers did they put in the Pill Box?"

"Sometimes they were in little bags."

"These little bags, did they look like they came from a pharmacy? Were there any logos or drug . . . Strike the word drug please. Were there any medication names on these little bags?

"I'm not sure. Dr. Jordan handled the medications from the Pill Box."

"So, it's safe to say that only Dr. Carey knew what was in those bags?"

Clara sits there quietly, staring at her hands as Barrens moves closer. "Miss Smythe, you understand that you are obligated to answer my questions."

"Ye . . . yes."

Barrens is now close enough to breathe on her. "Is that yes, you understand, or yes, only Dr. Carey knew what was in the bags?"

"Both."

"You stated that you could not see the boxes when patients stood in front of the window. When did this happen and how often?"

Clara looks at me and mouths, *I'm sorry*.

Barrens nearly lunges between Clara and me. "Objection, Your Honor. Please advise the witness to refrain from making any conspiring contact with the defendant."

Brian adds to the mayhem. "Objection! Objection! Objection! Attorney Barrens is again making grossly speculative conclusions without any proven fact."

Judge Harris's gavel crashes down against the desk repeatedly.

Barrens ignores the thunder. "Your Honor, as was the case with Mrs. Nils—"

One more gavel-induced roar, a deep breath, and Judge Harris begins a slow, forceful monotone rejoinder. "Do. Not. Speak. Either one of you. Your outrageous behavior in my courtroom ends now, or this will be the last case either of you will ever have the privilege of litigating." The silence reserved only for the most prestigious of libraries carries over the courtroom. "Mr. Barrens, state your objection again, please."

"Miss Smythe is a reluctant witness, and it is merely my opinion that she is conspiring with the defendant, Dr. Carey, to protect her."

Judge Harris returns to her emotionless state. "First, I will sustain Mr. Barrens's objection. Miss Smythe, you are not permitted to communicate with the defendant in any manner. Secondly, Mr. Freeland's multi-objection response, which, sir, will never occur again, is also sustained. Lastly, Mr. Barrens, we are in a court of law, evidence and proof are the rule. Some speculation is given leeway, but personal opinions, especially by the attorneys, are never permitted. You are a seasoned attorney and know better. The ice is melting quickly beneath you. Now continue."

"Your Honor, how is the jury supposed to unhear the continued accusa—"

Judge Harris holds her gavel high in the air. "Mr. Freeland, you, too, are a seasoned trial attorney, and you also know that once I rule, there need not be any further discussion on the matter. Mr. Barrens, move along."

A male voice calls out unexpectedly from the back of the room. "Hey, Judge! That attorney is right! How is that jury going to forget that? Dr. Jordan is a good doctor, and she deserves better! Hell, she deserves a medal for helping us! It's just plain rotten to have her sit here and be told she did something wrong!"

Judge Harris's gavel strikes the sound block like cannon fire. Her voice is oddly calm and guttural—her eyes fixated on the galley intruder. "Bailiff, remove that man from my courtroom immediately."

Billy Weston stands as the bailiff ushers him to the rear door of Courtroom Five. "You got this, Dr. Jordan. And I'm taking my meds every day! And I'm not sharing them either! We love you, Dr. Jordan!"

The rear doors of the courtroom slam. "Any further outbursts from the gallery and this trial will be closed to all. Let's take a ten-minute recess. Bailiff, you know the routine with the witness.

The jury is excused to the jury room. Everyone else, remain seated."

Brian turns to me. "Friend of yours?"

"Patient."

Brian smiles, "I know. We all know."

"I didn't know he was even in the courtroom."

"I know. Let's hope that doesn't happen again."

CHAPTER 6
THE RECAP

THE SILENCE FILLING the backseat of the Uber is crushing. My eye catches Samuel's look in the rearview mirror. I give him a nod, signaling him I'm okay. A "Thank you" quietly passes through my lips.

"You're welcome," Brian responds, "but we're only getting started. There's a long way to go."

I wink at Samuel by rearview mirror, as I answer Brian. "I know. I just wanted you to know I appreciate all that you're doing."

"Again, thanks, but let's wait until the end for the thank-yous."

Samuel shoots a large, playful frown back at me but says nothing.

Brian's words set me on edge again, and I begin to murmur. "It was the right thing to do. It was the right thing to do."

"What's that?"

"I guess, it's my mantra. I say it so I won't jump off a bridge."

Samuel's eyes widen. "There is no need for that, Dr . . . I mean Miss."

Brian looks to Samuel, then to me. "Okay. Is there something I should know?"

"Fine. Samuel is . . ."

"From the neighborhood. Is he a patient too? Is he even an Uber driver?"

"Yes. No. And yes."

"This can't keep happening. Barrens will find out and it will really start to look like a conspiracy. Samuel, it's Samuel, isn't it?"

The disdain in Brian's voice has me wishing for that crushing silence to come back.

"Glad to finally meet you, Attorney Freeland. We know that you will do all that you can to make sure our wonderful young doctor comes back to us."

Brian is shaking his head. "By we, do you mean people like the fine gentleman who caused a scene in the courtroom today?"

"Ah, yes, Billy Weston. That was most unfortunate. And not what he was asked to do. Since he is currently unemployed, we thought we would give him a job. Mr. Weston was to sit in the courtroom, listen to what was said, then return to us and report what he had heard. That's all. He was not to end up on the evening news."

Brain leans forward toward the cabbie. "Well, that didn't go as planned, did it?"

"No, it did not. You know Mr. Freeland—apologies. Attorney Freeland—"

Brian's tone lightens. "Either will suffice."

Samuel returns a wink to me before continuing. "Thank you. In hindsight, perhaps sending Mr. Weston was not a well-thought-out decision."

Brian sits back. "Look, Samuel, I appreciate how much you and everyone in the community care for Dr. Carey, but we can't have any more drama like today."

"Sir, I assure you, we could not agree with you more. Truly, Attorney Freeland, we only want Dr. Jordan to return to us and for everything to be like it was before."

Brian sighs loudly. "Samuel, if there is one thing that I'm sure of, it's that Dr. Carey will not be going back to her old way of doing things. If anyone, including you, Jordan, thinks that might happen, well, then just turn this Uber around and drive us upstate to the prison now."

My voice quivers. "Brian, that's not funny!"

"I apologize, Jordan. Samuel, you need to go back and tell everyone that the circumstances that placed Dr. Carey in this predicament are never coming back."

Samuel pulls the Uber to the curb. "Mr. Freeland, we want Dr. Jordan back, however it may look. She understands us. You must ensure her return."

"I'm working on it, Samuel. So, how about you drop off Dr. Carey first, then circle around and drop me off at my office near the courthouse. And before you ask, because it's going to look better if someone is watching."

"If you believe that would be better, then we will do that."

I open the car door and turn to face Brian before stepping out. "Thank you, Samuel. Brian, you treat him well."

"Understood."

Inside my apartment, the day is not over yet. Since I won't let them come to court, my parents insist on a phone call each evening. They force me to replay every heart-crushing event.

Joseph and Linda are good parents. They aren't activists, cultists, upstarts, or anything along those lines. They are ordinary people going about their everyday middle-class lives. My childhood was neither a minefield of emotional scars nor abusive. My parents taught me to face my troubles and to choose right over wrong.

My father is an engineer for a mid-sized but very successful auto parts company. He's the kind of dad who lets you make your own mistakes but doesn't let you fall too far. The type of dad your friends wish they had. He woke up early every Saturday morning to make me breakfast until I moved out. I'm guessing he would come to my apartment to continue the tradition if I let him. He did all the right dad things, like teaching me how to ride a bike and going to father-daughter dances with me.

Mom is overprotective, in a loving way. She is an artist who channels her creativity as a mid-level executive in an advertising agency. Mom stayed home with me until I started grade school, then went back to work part-time at first, and then full-time when I entered my high school years. Linda is the mom who invites your friends over because she likes to see you having a good time and smiles as she carefully watches over you. She's the mom who welcomes your entrance into womanhood with a cake and presents —friends too, if you let her.

The phone begins ringing, and a slight panic rushes over me. My mind springs into action. *Stay positive. Sound upbeat. Smile. Smile?*

"Hi, Mom."

"Hi, Jordan. Wait, let me get your father and put you on the speaker so we can both hear."

"Hi, Jordan. Dad here." This is a routine they repeat with every phone conversation. I don't have the heart to tell them stop.

"I know. Hi, Dad." I can almost see the concerned grin on his face.

"Jordan, your mother and I have been talking, and we still think we should come to court. It would show support for you. We could tell the judge that you made honest mistakes and that you're not the bad person they say you are. We could show them photos and the awards you got as a child. You could bring in your report cards."

"Dad. Dad! Sorry, but we've been over this. Brian insists, and I agree that it wouldn't be a good idea." My thoughts begin running alongside the conversation. *Brian actually believes having you in the courtroom shows the jury I'm a family person. I, on the other hand, know both of you would be like a mother bear protecting her cub. It would make the Billy Weston fiasco seem like a fading ember next to the fires of Hell. Every ill-spoken word or dark scenario painted about me would infuriate you. You would say something, or worse, make some physical response that could outweigh any benefit Brian hopes to gain.* "Nope. No, thank you, Billy two-point-oh, no way."

"What's that, honey? Who's Billy someone, something?"

"Sorry, no, uh, I repeated a name of one of . . . never mind. Dad, you were saying?"

"Jordan, darling, it's Mom. Your father is right. We should be there. Like your father said to me just today, they don't know you like we know you. He thinks we should get up on the stand and tell the jury all the good things you did growing up." My parents are pros at casting one or the other as the author of an idea they know their child won't like.

"Linda, I didn't . . ."

"Joseph!"

"Mom, Dad, I have to go with my attorney's advice." It's a lie, but a necessary one.

"Jordan, hi again, it's Dad. How did court go today? Did your attorney do a good job? Did the other side tell disgusting lies about you?"

"It's okay, Dad. Brian did a great job. The other side didn't tell any lies about me. Brian and I have planned a good strategy, and it all seems to be falling into place."

"Jordan, your father would like you to come to stay here with us. Just until the trial is over."

"Linda, We both—"

"Joseph, please!"

"I'm fine, Mom. I like coming home to the quiet." The truth is, the silence is painful. My mind wanders in every direction. Conversely, I also have no desire to be with anyone. I just wish my mind would turn off. That would never happen if I stayed with my parents.

After replaying almost every moment of the courtroom events with my parents, they're satisfied. The phone call ends, and I'm exhausted. We're only on day two. I'm not sure which will be the longer road, the courtroom or the replays.

I now want some food and a glass or two of wine. Brian made me promise not to have more than two glasses of wine at any given time. "You have to look put together at all times. You never know who's watching." Finally, something to laugh about today. Sadness comes into play too.

I'm a reasonably good cook, so I'll whip something up in no time flat. I'm forgoing the wine. "Seems like you're supposed to drink after a hard day, but drinking alone feels more like a problem, and right now, you don't need any more problems." When you live alone, you tend to think out loud. There is no one to ridicule you for doing so.

One red pepper, one yellow onion, and half a green squash, all chopped and sautéed in low salt soy sauce, spices, and some chicken. There it is, chicken stir-fry for one. The whole time, I'm trying to figure out how the IRS caught wind of my "Money Box" idea. This question has been doing laps in my mind since the beginning. I have to stop using the words "caught wind of," since it makes it sound like a dubious action I intentionally schemed. Brian and I were told by the IRS that they received an anonymous tip. Brian said we would find out more in discovery and then in court. We have yet to revisit the question. He's now concentrating on the trial and his strategies. He keeps me informed, but I still feel like I'm just along for the ride. My fate hanging in the hands of others is incredibly overwhelming. I would run away if I could, but that's not who I am. "Ha. Thanks, Mom and Dad."

Before going to bed, I lay out my clothes for court. "Dress professionally, not too revealing, not too prudish, and not too casual." Laughter and sadness again.

I pick out a navy-blue dress with a modest neckline. I don't own overly suggestive clothing or anything that might be considered aggressive. Standing in front of the mirror in my bra and underwear brings a thought. *You're more the girl next door that no one notices.*

"Look at you. You're not overly attractive or hideous, not shapely or fat—average at five foot five, with dark shoulder-length hair. You've always been Andie's wingman. You know there's nothing wrong with that. Right?"

My thoughts interrupt the monologue. *You could be a movie star or a model. You are going to do extraordinary things someday. Everyone will know your name. All moms think their little girl is the most beautiful.* My chest heaves, and in the mirror, I can see the tears running down my cheeks. "I want to be just a wingman again."

CHAPTER 7
ATTORNEY BRIAN'S RAINY DAY

"CAN you please drop me off midway up the block, before the courthouse? I'm meeting my attorney at the diner. He doesn't want me walking alone through the mob of reporters waiting on the courthouse steps."

The Uber driver nods. "Of course, Dr. Carey. Samuel told me to do whatever you ask."

Every step closer makes me gasp for air. Across the street from the courthouse, a throng of reporters hunt for defendants. "It's just anxiety, don't panic, don't panic. They don't notice you." Apparently, talking to myself is not limited to my apartment.

The earth-toned scarf that originally sat around my neck is now pulled over my head and face. Choosing such a dull and lifeless garment is my way of hiding in plain sight. "You're blending in. No one will notice. Keep walking. And don't look towards the courthouse."

A slight drizzle begins to fall, and suddenly, there's a small herd of umbrellas traveling between the reporters and me. This offers me ample cover from the predators.

Brian is sitting at a booth in the back of the diner. I sigh, "I made it across the concrete Serengeti."

"What was that?"

I smile nervously. "Never mind."

He points to the seat across from him. "Have a seat there. If your back is to the door and an overzealous reporter dares to come in, he won't see you at first."

His somber inflection worries me. "Dares? Wait, what's wrong?"

"Everything is fine. I'm just going over my plan for today."

"Spill it."

"You're going to think it's silly . . . insane, even."

This routine is not routine at all for him. "Brian, when your attorney tells you something he is about to say makes you think he's insane, it's very unsettling."

"Fine. It's the rain."

"What?"

"The rain."

"I know; I heard that the first time. What about the rain?"

Brian sucks in a large gulp of air, then looks around the diner. I shift in my chair following his eyes around the room with my own. "What are you looking for?"

"Even though this diner is safe you never know which attorney may test the off-limits rule."

"What's the off-limits rule?"

"Anything overheard in here is off-limits, no matter what it is. It's the only way this place survives. Remember me telling you this the other day?"

"Sure. Okay, what about the rain?"

Brian looks around again. I rumble, "Stop that."

"The jury is coming to the courthouse in the rain. They'll be wet and uncomfortable, and that makes them irritable. If jurors are irritable, they listen less closely. That means I have to be extra on top of my game today. That means they are more likely to go on what they already know instead of hearing anything new or contrary."

"Well, I have to admit that does seem silly, and yet, at the same time, it also seems logical. Now I'm worried. But you have tried hundreds of cases. It had to have rained before. What do you do on rainy days, call in sick?"

Brian shakes his head. “This is why I don’t share this kind of stuff.”

“I didn’t know you were superstitious. How do you plan to control the rain?”

“Funny. I’m not trying to control the rain. I’m trying to control the jury’s emotions. I’m sitting here trying to think of an opening line to take the jury’s mind off caring only about being wet and uncomfortable.”

“So, you’re serious about the rain?”

“Look, Barrens is a good attorney. I’ve known him for years, and we have done battle countless times. I say we are dead even or close to it. Your case is high profile, so he’s going for the jugular. I think we have a mutual respect, but I’m not letting anything slip through the cracks. Not even the rain.”

“Okay. What if you directly draw the jury’s attention to the rain? Use the fact that we’re all wet to bond with them. Doctors do this all the time to gain trust. We talk to patients about their families, work, interests, anything to make us seem more human to them and to create a connection.”

“That might just work. And Barrens will never see it coming.” Brian looks at the old clock with the tarnished glass hanging behind the lunch counter. “Still works. We should get going. By the way, it’s my job to take care of you, not the other way around.” There is a long pause. “Jordan. Thank you.”

A few reporters come over and start asking questions. Brian nicely says good morning to the flock, and we make our way through it. He opens the door and allows me to pass through. “Be in in a second.”

Brian steps out from the building’s stone cornice and into the rain and looks to the sky.

Now I shake my head. “That may have been a bit too far.”

Brian wipes his face—a devious smirk reveals itself as he lowers his hands.

"All rise for the Honorable Judge Harris." The bailiff waits for the shuffling of feet to stop, then opens the door, allowing Judge Harris to enter the courtroom.

Judge Harris takes a long look at Brian. "Mr. Freeland, do you need a moment to . . . well, dry off?"

"No, Your Honor, it's as good as it's going to get."

Judge Harris turns her attention to Clara, who sits in the witness box patiently waiting. "Miss. Smythe, you understand that you are still under oath and that your testimony is to be truthful?"

"Yes, Your Honor."

Brian walks over to the jury. "Good morning, ladies and gentlemen of the jury. I trust you managed to bring some of the rain into the courtroom as I did. But don't worry, as the day goes on, our clothes will dry, and hopefully, the dampness in the air will lift. But now we have to shift our attention to uncover the matter at hand. And what is this matter we need to uncover? It is the truth. More specifically, the truth of what my client, Dr. Jordan Carey, was doing for the patients and the community she has come to care for and love."

"Mr. Freeland. Please get on with the case." Judge Harris does not like idling about.

"Yes, Your Honor." Brian gives the jury the tiniest of smiles and wipes the rain off his brow. Judge Harris clears her throat in protest. "Thank you for returning on such a rainy day, Miss Smythe. Let's get to it. In your opinion, do you believe that Dr. Carey was trying to do something illegal or dishonest?"

"Thank you. And no, not at all. I think Dr. Jordan, I mean Dr. Carey, was doing her best to help her patients."

"Did Dr. Carey try to hide what she was doing from the staff, the patients, or even the authorities?"

"Objection. Calls for speculation."

"Sustained."

"Miss Smythe, did Dr. Carey ever try to hide from you any of the money or the medications she removed from the boxes?"

"No. Not at all. She treated us like family. Dr. Carey shared everything with us."

"Did Dr. Carey keep every pill from the box?"

"No. If it was too old or it looked funny, or if she couldn't identify it, Dr. Carey threw it into the hazardous waste container in the back of the office."

"Objection! Your Honor. The witness already testified that she didn't see what Dr. Carey did with the pills."

"Overruled. The witness can testify to what she saw and to office practices in which she participated or witnessed directly. And, Mr. Barrens, there is no need to raise your voice in my courtroom."

"Understood Your Honor, my deepest apologies, please."

Brian is now leaning on the edge of the jury box. "Do you know of any instance where Dr. Carey took the prescription medications from the Pill Box and sold them to patients or anyone else?"

"No, Dr. Carey gave all the pills away to her patients for free."

"Did Dr. Carey ever sell any of the medication she bought through medical catalogs or from the pharmacy?"

"No, Dr. Carey gave those away too.

Brian walks over to the Pill Box and holds up a clear small bag. "Miss Smythe, what do you see in this clear sandwich-type bag?"

"Several oval blue and green pills."

Brian pulls out a second bag. "How about this one?"

"Small round white pills."

Brian searches through the pill box, pulling out a handful of clear bags. "Miss Smythe, you were there the day the office was raided and the two boxes were taken by the authorities, is that correct?"

Clara appears puzzled. "Um, yes."

Brian replaces the bags and picks up a page from inside the box, then walks over to Clara. "Can you read the title at the top of this page to the jury?"

"'Chain of Custody for Evidence.'"

"There is more information on that form, correct?"

"Yes."

"This information consists of a date, time, reason for collection, what was collected, and Dr. Carey's name. Is that correct?"

"Objection, Your Honor. Relevance? To save time, the prosecution stipulates that the form is a standard chain-of-custody form that was correctly executed and handled."

Judge Harris looks at Barrens again, with no indication of anything. "If that is what you wish. But the part about your objection is overruled. The witness may answer the question."

Clara now smiles. "Yes. It also has the name of the person who collected it."

"Is this all straightforward and easy for someone not in the business of law to understand?"

"Yes, I understand it. If that's what you're asking me."

Brian returns the smile. "It is. Now, according to Mr. Barrens himself . . ."

"Objection, I'm not on trial here."

"Overruled."

"According to Mr. Barrens, everything is perfect with this form. Do you know what that means?"

Clara's smile widens as Barrens's two junior attorneys sink into their chairs. "Yes, it means that everything inventoried on this form was all that there was in the Pill Box the day it was taken from the office."

"Correct. Would you say that, aside from the authorities bursting in, it was a typical day in the office?"

"I would."

"Miss Smythe, did any of the bags I held up have anything but pills in them?"

"No, they did not."

"Would it surprise you if I told you that I held up all the clear bags that were in that box?"

"No, it would not."

"You have already testified that Dr. Carey shared everything with the office staff, and that day was like any other day, so is it safe to say that you believe that what was in the Pill Box was an accurate representation of what is in that box every day?"

"Yes, I would."

"Just one more question. Did you ever see Dr. Carey take any money from either box for personal use?"

"No. She wouldn't do that."

"Thank you, Miss Smythe. No more questions, Your Honor."

Clara and I look at each other. Neither can hold back the tiniest smile. Brian walks between us, giving me a look of dismay. I almost laugh.

"Redirect, Your Honor." Attorney Barrens's anger causes the wrinkles around both eyes to protrude like large sand dunes on a vast desert plain. Even the jury can't help but notice as they await the vicious assault.

Judge Harris warns, "Proceed, with caution, Mr. Barrens."

"Miss Smythe, let me get this right. You're saying that you saw every pill bottle and every bag Dr. Carey removed from that damn Pill Box?" One of Barrens's junior attorneys tries to clear his throat loudly to mask his superior's misstep.

Judge Harris crashes her gavel down. "Attorney Barrens. Profanity is not necessary, not wanted, and not tolerated in my courtroom. Don't press me on this. It will not go well for you. This is your first and only cautioning. You know better."

"My deepest apologies, Your Honor. It will not happen again."

Judge Harris's face remains hardened. "I don't want your apologies. I want you to remember your courtroom etiquette. These rules are in place for good reason. Now move along."

"Yes, Your Honor. Miss Smythe, could you please answer my question?"

Clara leans forward like a tiger about to pounce. "What I said is that I don't believe that Dr. Carey would do anything that would hurt anyone. What I said was that Dr. Carey is honest and only has her patients' best interests in mind."

"Please answer my question, Miss Smythe. Did you actually see Dr. Carey discard pills into the medical waste container, or could she have pocketed some of them without you knowing?" Barrens is speaking calmly, but his voice now carries a sternness.

Clara's voice is getting louder and more defiant. Almost too defiant. "Yes, that might be possible, but highly unlikely. The probability of it happening is zero."

"Your Honor, I would like the last part of the witness's statement stricken from the record and the jury told to disregard it. The witness is not a mathematical expert and cannot accurately make such an assessment."

"Mr. Barrens, you asked for the witness's opinion. Your motion to strike is overruled."

Barrens first scowls at his junior-throat-clearing attorney, then turns back to Clara. "Who took the deposits to the bank at night, Miss Smythe?"

"We all did."

"You all went to the bank together to make the deposits?"

"No, that's not what I mean. At one time or another, any one of us would make a deposit."

"Was the deposit amount ever off from what was written on the deposit slip?"

"Sometimes. Why?"

"I'll ask the questions. You can be certain that I will get to the why. Were any of those 'sometimes' when Dr. Carey took the deposit to the bank?"

"Objection! The witness cannot account for every deposit ever made by anyone working in the office."

"Overruled. Please answer the question, Miss Smythe."

"I'm not sure." Clara is looking directly at me. The jury is following Clara's eyes.

"Is it possible that the deposit amount might have been off more on those days Dr. Carey dropped off the deposit at the bank?"

"Objection! Your Honor! The prosecutor is calling for speculation."

"Sustained. Mr. Freeland, while I can appreciate your tenacity to fight for your client, please also refrain from raising your voice. I can hear you perfectly fine when you use your inside voice."

"I apologize, Your Honor."

"Miss Smythe," Barrens continues. "Is it safe to say that if the deposit amount was off, there was no way of knowing if it was truly an accounting error because there was no way of accurately checking the amount that came in that day? In fact, because of Dr. Carey's deliberately deceptive system, there was no way of tracking the total or even the source of the money on any given—"

"Objection—"

Judge Harris interrupts Brian to give a subzero glare directly at the prosecutor. "Sustained. Mr. Barrens. Do I even have to explain this one to you? The jury will ignore the prosecutor's reference that Dr. Carey's system was in any way deliberately deceptive. There has been no proof of this up to this point in the matter. Mr. Barrens, the ice beneath you has a substantial crack in it, tread lightly. Miss Smythe, you will answer the questions as to if it was difficult to track the total or even the source of the money."

Clara's eyes well up as she sits there quietly. She didn't want to answer. I couldn't take seeing her in pain. I found myself standing and uttering the words, "It's okay, Clara, answer the question."

The courtroom erupts. Objections fly through the air like fighter pilots in a fierce dogfight—the judge's gavel repeatedly thuds against its block. Brian grabs at my arm to sit me down. I pull away. The jury sits slack-jawed. It's rubberneckers on a highway passing an accident, unable to look away.

Six words I spoke in less than three seconds sends the world of Courtroom Five into an apocalypse, all except for Clara and myself. Our eyes lock onto each other's. Nothing else matters. I smile to let her know it's all going to be okay. She returns a small affirming nod.

The two or three minutes of sheer pandemonium seem like hours. Finally, Judge Harris restores order. I wonder if this is one of those things you hear about that leads to a mistrial. I don't want to start over.

Judge Harris's calm demeanor is gone. Beads of sweat hang from multiple edges of overtly red face. Some may even be close to boiling. "Mr. Freeland." She takes a long pause. "We are going to take a fifteen-minute recess." Her voice grows louder and less controlled. "I want, no demand, that you explain to your client the rules of my courtroom! You are to ensure that she understands them thoroughly." Another pause. "She is to commit them to memory." This time an audible exhale. "And Mr. Freeland, I remind you, that you are held accountable for every and all of your client's action in my courtroom. Do you understand?"

Brian looks at me then the judge. "Yes, Your Honor."

"I will see counsel in my chambers in ten minutes!" Her gavel is thrown down with such force that reverberations rattle the years of soot built up on windows of the diner across the street.

"All rise." The bailiff shakes his head which draws unwanted attention from Judge Harris.

Brian says nothing to me until we reach the courthouse suite. He closes the door and paces around the room, refusing to look at me.

The dramatic effect is not wasted. “I’m not ashamed of my action. My friend needed me.”

“In that courtroom, I’m your only friend! Is that clear?”

“Brian, I didn’t think—I could only see Clara’s pain.”

“Do you understand the possible consequences of your action?” Brian’s face is flushes, and the anger makes him speak loudly. Loud enough to warrant a knock on the door from a bailiff who happened to be passing by. “All good in here.” He turns back to me. “Do you understand the possible consequences of any of your actions before you take them?”

“I’m sorry, it won’t happen again.” My thoughts scream, *You hope it won’t happen again, but the reality is, you care too much about people.* I’m not sharing the last part.

Brian starts pacing again. “Jordan, we can’t keep having these kind of theatrics in that courtroom. If you haven’t figured it out yet, Judge Harris doesn’t put up with anything. No one intentionally messes with her or her rules. Please just sit in your chair and look at the wood on the front of her bench. Don’t take your eyes off it unless I talk to you. Got it?”

“Got it. You’re the only one I can trust. Don’t take my eyes off of the judge’s bench and don’t mess with Judge Harris. Got it. Sorry.”

Brian slumps himself into the chair across from me. “Damn rainy day. I knew something was going to happen. Don’t speak to anyone about anything. And don’t leave this room until I come to get you. I have to see how bad a storm the judge is planning to bring.”

Ten long minutes later, the door to the courthouse suite opens. I ask. “How bad is it?”

Brian holds a hand up towards me as he waits for Barrens to pass by. “Wait until I close the door.”

The latch to the door clicks. “Is there going to be a mistrial?”

“No. You watch too much TV. But, if you act out again, the

judge will put all of us in jail. Hell, she might even try to put the jury and a few bailiffs in cells. A few more meetings like that and I'll be ready to retire."

"That mad? I'm so sorry." I start pacing around the table.

"That's what I've been trying to tell you. This judge is no joke. Only idiots mess with her. Let's go."

Walking back to the courtroom, I look through the corridor window; it's still raining. I whisper to myself, "Damn rainy day."

CHAPTER 8
THE SAFE HAVEN DINER

JUDGE HARRIS BEGINS with an admonishing breath. "Now that we are all settled down and everyone is planning to abide by the rules of this courtroom, I will address the jury. Ladies and gentlemen of the jury, the discord that took place earlier is not to be considered a reflection of guilt or innocence. It was merely an emotional breakdown on behalf of all parties. You are to place no weight on any of it in deciding the outcome of this case. That incident is closed and not to be discussed." Silence reigns over Courtroom Five as the judge gives a prolonged stare. "Very well, Mr. Barrens, please continue."

"Thank you, Your Honor. Your Honor, I would like the court reporter to please read back the last question I asked the witness."

"Will the court reporter please read aloud the last question asked by Mr. Barrens?" Judge Harris is staring at me.

"Miss Smythe, is it safe to say that if the deposit amount was off, there was no way of knowing if it was truly an accounting error because there was no way of accurately checking the amount of money that came in that day?" The court reporter looks directly at me. I suspect all eyes are on me. I continue to stare at the wooden bench.

Judge Harris breaks the silence. "Please answer the question, Miss Smythe."

"Yes, sorry Your Honor. That's true; knowing who paid, and for what, became difficult. The checks and insurance payments could easily be tracked. They had the patients' names on them, but the cash was impossible."

Barrens takes a quick peek at me then turns back to Clara. "Miss Smythe, with Dr. Carey's new, let's call it, plan, did you feel unsettled with the inability to account for who paid what and who owed what?"

"I don't know if I would call it unsettled. It was troublesome, and as I already stated, I just started putting down the totals for each day."

"Did anyone direct you to just put down the totals?"

Clara turns her head away from me. "Yes, Dr. Carey did."

"Did you ever think that this Money Box might be a scheme to hide money and not a plan to help the patients?"

"No. I trust Dr. Jordan. Even though we were close, she owned the office."

"You stated earlier that you were family. That's more than close, wouldn't family question something that didn't work or might be troublesome?"

"I knew Dr. Jordan's heart was in the right place, but I guess family would."

"So, then you did have doubts about the sudden change in Dr. Carey's office policy on collecting payment for her services?"

"Of course I had doubts. But not about why she did it. Just about the outcome of it."

"You're telling this court that you didn't ever wonder why Dr. Carey made it so difficult to track the money coming in?"

"Objection, asked and answered. Several times already."

"Sustained. Mr. Barrens, move it along."

"Miss Smythe. Did you or Ms. Nils take part in coming up with Dr. Carey's plans for the Money and Pill Boxes?"

"Um, no. But that—"

Barrens interjects, "So, Dr. Carey planned this all out on her own."

"Yes." Clara glances in my direction. Brian casually extends his index finger to point at the judge's bench.

"Thank you, Miss Smythe. No more questions, Your Honor."

"Your Honor, I have a few questions for this witness, please."

Judge Harris jots down something then replies. "Proceed, Mr. Freeland."

"Miss Smythe, what did Dr. Carey say the purpose of the Money Box was?"

"It was a way for patients to anonymously pay what they could afford. She said it allowed those patients who couldn't pay much to keep their dignity."

"Why did Dr. Carey put this plan into effect?"

"Because patients were refusing to come in. In most cases, I think they felt trapped. Some couldn't afford to pay their co-pays, and others had no insurance at all."

"Did the concept of the Money Box work?"

"Yes, people started coming in and getting the treatment they needed."

"A few more questions, if you don't mind? Who suffered because of this Money Box?"

Clara grins, then covers her mouth, muffling an unannounced snort. The galley follows with its own unified chortle. Clara sheep-ishly looks at the judge. "Sorry."

Brian ends the clearly unwanted folly. "Miss Smythe. If you please."

"Oh yes. That's easy. Dr. Jordan suffered. The Money Box idea was great for the patients, but made it almost impossible for Dr. Jordan to pay herself."

"What about paying you and Mrs. Nils? Did the two of you get paid?"

"Yes. Well, at first Dr Jordan did miss two of our paychecks, not in a row, but she made those up."

"How did you get paid, and how did Dr. Carey make up those two missing paychecks?"

"Dr. Jordan had a payroll service. Once the community heard about the Money Box idea, we started getting more new patients. Shortly after that, Dr. Jordan had the payroll service cut extra checks for Rebecca and me to make up for the missing checks."

"Did Dr. Carey ever cut extra checks for herself?"

"No."

"Who did the Pill Box hurt?"

"Again, if I had to say it hurt anyone, it was Dr. Jordan."

"How did Dr. Carey hurt herself, again?"

"Dr. Jordan put a lot of work into that Pill Box. She put a lot of hours into carefully sorting each medication, then rebottling them for our patients. She would come in early, skip lunch, or stay late most days. We had to remind her to eat. It was like all her free time was used up on making sure she did things right."

"Thank you, Miss Smythe. No more questions, Your Honor."

Judge Harris lifts her head and looks at the witness. "You may step down. We will stop here for lunch. Court will resume in one hour. Bailiff, please remove the jury." Judge Harris bangs her gavel.

We stand and I lean towards my attorney. "That was great, Brian."

"Let's get to lunch. We can talk there. And thanks." Brian is flaring out his chest a bit. He's a seasoned attorney, but a win is a win. Especially after your client just derailed the entire courtroom.

"Um, Brian, the reporters. They're almost double."

"The rain has stopped. Now they're willing to wait on the steps."

"Should we say something? You know what they've been writing about me."

"Calm down and just keep walking through the crowd." Brian steps fully in front of me, shielding me from the mob.

He holds my arm as we walk through the mass of intrusive

recording devices. Finally, we cross the street, and I notice that the reporters barely leave the curb on the courthouse side. It's like there is a sea of fire that they're afraid to cross.

"Why aren't they coming into the diner?"

"They can't. They're not allowed, unofficially. If they come into the diner, it's all off the record. There's a sign posted in the window and behind the counter." Brian points at both.

A friend you must be, or the lawyer's wrath you shall see.

"And they stick to that? First Amendment and all that?"

"There's where it's brilliant. The sign doesn't specifically mention reporters, just friends." Brian lets out a chuckle. "Besides, it's a room filled with lawyers. What would you do?"

"Good point."

I can't shake the image of the reporters standing at the curb, unwilling to give chase. We sit at a table; all the booths are taken.

"The diner owner has that much power?"

"Since you're obviously not letting this go, I'll explain it. By the way, no client I have ever brought here has questioned this or even noticed. The Safe Haven Diner, as it is unofficially known, is a no-fly zone for reporters. It was bought many years ago by an ambitious young attorney who ate here every day, up until the day he died. The original owner was getting on in years and the attorney, whose name I can't remember, wanted an investment. They struck a deal. Before the attorney bought the place, reporters sat in the booths, at the counter, or just stood around, waiting to overhear the latest details of court cases or strategies. Every week there was a breaking story, from an unknown source, revealing confidential information about a current headline case. That all stopped when the diner changed hands. Stockland, Jonathan Horatio Stockland, that was the attorney. Stockland's first and most brilliant move with the diner was to ban reporters from the place unless they came in as civilians. The signs were posted within two days of Stockland taking ownership and have been there ever since. At first, a few reporters tried to break the rules. They found themselves up against dozens of lawyers standing together, ready to unleash the full extent of the law. It worked, and the Safe Haven Diner was born."

"That's a great story, but why has it never made the press?"

"The reporters barely cross the street." Brian points to the haze on the dust-covered windows. "I think Stockland intentionally didn't clean the windows, just in case some jackass reporter dared test him, us."

"Maybe I should throw a few more specks of dirt on the windows?"

Brian and I both laugh as the waitress comes over. Brian orders the turkey sandwich. I grimace and order pasta. "I haven't eaten since last night. I'm starving. With all the excitement in the courtroom today, I forgot how hungry I was."

Brian merely raises his eyebrows.

There isn't an empty table or counter space, and a line is forming at the door. "Do all the attorneys eat here during the day?"

"Not every attorney; only those who aren't camera hungry. The attorneys trying to get a tagline on the news or a spot on a local network generally eat at the food trucks on the corner or one of the other eateries a block or two away. During lunch, the reporters wait there, knowing they have a good chance of getting a hot bite, and I'm not talking about the food."

"Brian, why didn't Attorney Stockland ever remodel the place?"

"What's there to remodel? It's a hidden treasure." We start laughing again.

It's good to feel the relief of laughter amid this stress. "Hey, how about I stay here, and you go to court? I'll even eat all the rubbery turkey they want me to." Our laughter attracts odd stares.

The diner is stuck in a much simpler and more inviting time. The wallpaper is faded in most spots and yellowed in others; the ancient metal fans hanging from the ceiling are old ghosts from a time before air conditioning. The counter still has the round red pleather stools bolted to the floor. Brian might be joking, but he's right; the Safe Haven is a treasure.

"Jordan, Jordan, we have to get back to court shortly. Are you almost done?"

"Um, yes. I'm sorry. I'm starting to understand why you like this place so much."

"What? No, this place is basically a dump."

"So much for my dream."

"Jordan, a lesser attorney would start taking offense from a client who continually spaces out during their conversations."

"I'm sorry, Brian. I paid full attention in court this morning. I space out because it helps me get through all of this. And by the way, this place has a special charm. You're just not seeing it. Well, except for the turkey." A smirk falls across my face.

Brian holds his hands up like he's surrendering. "If you say so."

"What's next?"

"You mean who's next? I believe Barrens will call a patient named Nathan Roberts."

"But his story isn't true." Nathan Roberts was a patient of mine for almost a year. He works at a local factory and doesn't make much money. He and his wife have three small children, so they have to watch every penny they earn. Nathan can afford only subpar insurance. His deductible is so high that he only sees the benefit in the event of a catastrophic emergency.

"That's what I'll prove. Let's go."

As we leave the diner, I feel a pang in my heart for this space. I look back at the door, almost taking a step back towards it. Brian is now pulling me along the street. Neither of us is relishing the possibility of making Judge Harris wait. We dash through the reporters and other court patrons.

Brian stares at me with great displeasure as I lag behind him. "What is going on with you? We can't afford to piss off the judge again."

"We're here, aren't we?" I wish Stockland bought the courthouse and made signs that banned prosecutors. I wish I was sitting in the Safe Haven Diner.

CHAPTER 9
NATHAN'S FIFTEEN MINUTES

HOLDING A HANDFUL OF PAPERS, Barrens rises from behind the prosecutor's table. "For the record, please state your name and relationship to Dr. Carey."

The hard-faced man sitting in the witness chair nearly snarled before speaking. "My name is Nathan Roberts, and I was a patient of Dr. Carey's."

"You stated that you *were* a patient of Dr. Carey's? So, you're not anymore?"

Nathan pauses to pull at the too-short sleeves of an obviously borrowed shirt. This time, he grunts. "No. I left Dr. Carey's practice because I felt something was wrong with her billing practices."

Barrens makes slight hand gestures signaling his witness to calm himself. "Can you explain what you mean when you say something was wrong with her billing practices?"

"Objection. The witness is not a billing expert." Brian turns slightly so his chest and torso are in full view of Nathan. He pauses before casually straightening his tie and sitting back down.

"Sustained." Judge Harris glares at Brian, then directs her attention to the witness, who is now wrestling with his necktie. "Mr. Roberts, do you need a moment?"

"No, Judge. I'm fine." Nathan paws at the straining buttons around his waist.

Barren gives Brian an odd stare, then continues. "Mr. Roberts, can you tell the court about your experience with Dr. Carey's billing tactics?"

Brian adjusts the cuff of his sleeve as he calls out, "Objection. The use of the word 'tactics' in this manner infers that Dr. Carey was engaged in a deliberate process to cheat her patients financially."

Judge Harris contemplates her answer for an extended moment. "Sustained. Mr. Barrens, please reask the question, if you wish, but use less accusatory terminology."

Barrens shoots Brian a glare and steps between the Defense's table and the witness. "Thank you, Your Honor. Mr. Roberts, can you kindly tell the court about your experience with Dr. Carey's billing procedures?"

"I received a statement in the mail; I don't have a computer or any of that email stuff. Anyway, like I said, I received a statement from Dr. Carey's office informing me I owed $128 for my last two visits, but I didn't. I placed cash in the Money Box and thought that was the end of it. So, when I received the bill, I was upset. I called Dr. Carey's office, and her billing person told me my insurance deductible had not been met. I explained that I placed cash in the Money Box because I knew my deductible was not met. The billing person, I believe her name was Rebecca, told me that she would delete the bill. She told me not to worry about it. The following month I received another statement saying I still owed $128. I called Dr. Carey's office again, and Rebecca stated that she had handled it and I should disregard the bill."

"What happened next?" The inflection in Barrens's voice makes it sound like he's hearing the story for the first time, and the jury is on board for the ride.

"I assumed this was the end of the misunderstanding. That's what they called it. Then, I received a third notice. I went down to the office and demanded that the bills stop coming to my home. I also informed Dr. Carey's office staff that I would not be coming back as a patient."

"Did Dr. Carey ever speak to you about the matter?"

"Yes, the day I went to the office. Dr. Carey asked me to come into her private office. She apologized for the mistake. She looked up my file on her computer and told me the balance had been removed and that I would not receive a bill again. She then asked that I not leave the practice. I told her I couldn't stay. I explained that I didn't like how her office handled my situation. They made me feel like a deadbeat."

"What did Dr. Carey say to that?"

"Dr. Carey said that she was sorry. That it was not their intent to make me feel bad. Then she asked me not tell anyone what happened. She called it a one-off."

Angrily, I pick up the pen and scribble the words "NOT TRUE" on Brian's legal pad. He doesn't react to me or to Nathan's comments. Instead, Brian slowly points his finger at the Judge's desk. I squash the frustrated sigh and focus on the desk.

"What did you do next?" Attorney Barrens is methodically moving back to the prosecutor's table.

"Something was wrong. I knew some of my neighbors also saw Dr. Carey, so I discussed the situation with them. I found out that a few of them were having similar problems with Dr. Carey's billing."

"Objection, Your Honor. Hearsay."

"Overruled."

Barrens gives a wave of his hand. "Thank you, Your Honor. Mr. Roberts, how many is a few?"

"Six."

"So, with you, that made seven of Dr. Carey's patients having concerns with the office's billing practices?" Barrens is holding up seven fingers.

"Yes." Nathan is looking at me like I'm a criminal.

"Your Honor, I would like to approach the witness to have him verify the names on the affidavit bearing the six other patients' names. This affidavit has already been entered into evidence." Barrens holds up what appears to be an entire ream of paper.

Not looking up, Judge Harris replies, "Go ahead."

"Mr. Roberts, are the names on the bottom of this affidavit the people you spoke with and does it include your name?"

"Yes, these are the people I spoke with, and yes, that's my name at the bottom."

"No more questions, Your Honor." Barrens drops the pile of papers he's still holding onto the prosecutor's table, allowing it to make a Bible-like thump. He has prepped the witness well and timed his action just as well. The jury is staring at the stack. "Thank you for painting such a wonderful detailed portrait of Dr. Carey's billing tact—procedures. Now I won't need to go through this pile of papers."

"Objection. Attorney Barrens is performing for the jury."

"Sustained. Mr. Barrens, please stick to the case and leave the theatrics to the actors down the street. Mr. Freeland, the witness is yours."

Brian loosens his tie. "Mr. Roberts, did the billing error get corrected after your last visit to Dr. Carey's office?"

Nathan's hands immediately start digging into his collar. His lips purse. "Yes."

Brian takes a moment to remove his jacket and roll up his sleeves. "Did you ask the six other people on the affidavit if their billing concerns with Dr. Carey's office were ever resolved?"

Nathan is now pulling at both sleeves, his collar, and the torso of his shirt. "What was the damn question?"

"Objection." Barrens barks. "Your Honor, Come on."

"To what. Me repeating the question or your witness asking me to repeat it?"

The gallery collectively snorts. Judge Harris raises her gavel. "Overruled. Just repeat the question. And, Mr. Freedland, put you jacket back on. You will stay properly dress in my court."

Brian winks at Barrens and continues. " Yes, You Honor, My apologies. Mr. Roberts, did you ask the six other people on the affidavit if their billing concerns with Dr. Carey's office were ever resolved?"

Still squirming, Nathan answers. "I did."

"What was their answer?"

"Well, yes." Nathan clears his throat. "But that doesn't mean—"

Attorney Freeland jumps in quickly. "Did you receive a letter from Dr. Carey's office explaining the cause for the billing error?"

"Yes."

Brian now holds up a single sheet of paper. "Isn't it true, sir, that each of you received the very same letter?"

Roberts slouches. "We did. But I think she was trying to cover her backside."

"Your Honor, move to strike the last part of the witness's remark. There is no basis for it. In reality there is actual evidence to the contrary. Which I will now present."

"Sustained. The jury will disregard the witness's opinion part of his reply to the previous inquiry."

"Thank you, Your Honor. Mr. Roberts, is this the letter you received from Dr. Carey? And did you sign a release to have your medical file sent to Mr. Barrens's office? Lastly, do you understand that this letter was part of that medical file, which is now evidence?"

"Yes. Yes, to all of it."

"Did you see any of the other letters?"

"I did. Uh, again, so what. None of that matters. She was trying to cheat all of us." Nathan begins to shift quickly in his chair.

Brian pushes on. "Let's hold that thought for a moment." Brian hands the witness a piece of paper. "Mr. Roberts, is this the letter you received from Dr. Carey?"

"It's a copy. I gave that man the real letter."

"Let the record show that the witness pointed to the prosecutor, Attorney Barrens. Is this copy of your letter accurate?"

"If you mean is it the same one I got, then yes."

"Is it handwritten or typed."

"Handwritten. But anyone in her office could have written it."

"Do you think that Dr. Carey didn't write this letter to you?"

"No, she wrote it. So what, I write every day."

Brian ignores Nathan. "Can you please read the letter?"

Dear Mr. Roberts,

I apologize again for the repeated mistake in the billing system in my office. We have found that the computer software we are using was updated and this caused a malfunction in the billing process. It has since been corrected, as has your account. I want you to know that our office did not intentionally mean to keep billing you. After you notified us of the billing error, as did several other patients, we took care of it immediately. Apparently, the software didn't register the command and continued to bill you. I have placed a copy of this letter in your file. Should you want to view it again, please let us know. I hope you will understand that this error was computer generated and we have made all the necessary corrections. My staff and I take full responsibility for the mistake. We hope that you will accept our deepest apology.

Sincerely,

Dr. Jordan Carey and the office staff

"Thank you for reading the letter, Mr. Roberts. You said that the six other patients all received letters from Dr. Carey. Were they also handwritten?"

"Yes, they were. So—"

"I know. So what."

Barrens rises. "Objection, Attorney Freeland is mocking the witness."

"Withdrawn."

The galley releases a round of quiet sputters. Judge Harris looks over them and silence returns.

"Do you know if the others accepted Dr. Carey's apology?" Attorney Freeland inquires.

"They did. And I told them I wasn't going to make any more trouble, but I wasn't goin' back to her."

"I don't understand. Then why are you here today, Mr. Roberts?"

Barrens stands again. "Objection. The witness's motive for being here is obvious. He is here—"

"Overruled. Mr. Barrens, if it's so obvious then why would you object? The witness may answer the question."

"I was done with this whole thing; then a guy who works for him shows up at my door and convinces me that I gotta come here today. He tells me that Dr. Carey is out of control and needs to be stopped. He makes me believe that Dr. Carey is cheating all the people in the neighborhood. That's why I'm here today."

Brian clarifies, "First, let the record show that the witness again pointed to the prosecutor. Mr. Roberts, is the man who came to your home and convinced you here today in this courtroom?"

Nathan takes a good look around the courtroom. "No, I don't see him."

"If you saw him again, would you recognize him?"

"Sure I would. The man sat in my living room for over an hour explaining all kinds of things that Dr. Carey did wrong."

The feet of Barrens's chair screech against the wooden floor as he tries to slide back. "Objection. The witness is testifying to hearsay that cannot be corroborated."

"Overruled. Mr. Barrens, the man he is testifying about works for you and the witness is yours. I don't see any conflict here. Continue Mr. Freeland."

"Thank you, Your Honor. Mr. Roberts, after sitting on the witness stand, do you still think Dr. Carey was trying to cheat her patients?"

"Objection!" Barrens fires again.

"Sustained. Mr. Freeland, you may reword the question if you wish to ask it."

"Thank you, Your Honor. Mr. Roberts, do you now believe Dr. Carey was telling the truth in her letter and do you accept her apology?"

"I guess I do."

"No more questions, Your Honor." Brian looks at me as he passes the prosecutor's table. He places the letter on the edge of the prosecutor's table and nods.

Judge Harris does not miss the gesture by either attorney. "Counsel approach at the bench, please."

Both attorneys stand in front of Judge Harris's bench and, in unison, nod their compliance to whatever admonishment she has just administered. They both turn and sit in their respective chairs. Neither gives any tell of the events.

"It is nearing four o'clock; we will stop for the day. Court will resume tomorrow morning at nine o'clock. Please be on time." Judge Harris isn't hesitating; she bangs her gavel. There aren't going to be any objections.

"All rise," The bailiff says as he moves quickly to open the judge's door.

"Do you want to grab a quick bite at the diner before we leave?" I'm hoping Brian will say yes. But I know the chances are slim.

"Jordan, it's okay for a quick lunch, but I don't need to eat dinner there. Besides, I'm having dinner with my family tonight. Don't worry, it went well today."

"Oh, I'm not worried. I think you did a great job. What did the judge say?"

"Thanks, and nothing that concerns you. Let's leave it at Barrens and I are on equal ground in the judge's eyes. Come on, I'll get us through the reporters."

I have forgotten about the reporters. Exiting the front door, we notice the reporters huddling around Nathan Roberts. He smiles widely as he tells them that he testified today against me and that there's more to me than meets the eye. I look at Brian. We walk down the steps behind the scrum. I'm spotted, and Nathan's fifteen minutes of fame ends.

The reporters won't let us by without a comment. "Come on, you don't want us to print what this guy is saying without anything from your side. It's going to make the Wicked Witch of the West look like a saint next to your client."

Brian stops. "Okay, I'm not going to tell you any specifics about the case, but I will tell you that Dr. Carey is an outstanding doctor. She is honest, and her heart is in the right place. The allegations against her are just that, allegations. Each day we prove they have no merit. Thank you and have a pleasant evening."

A mid-aged, lanky, tattered-fedora-wearing reporter fires back, "So, you're saying Barrens has nothing and is just blowing smoke to make himself look better?"

"Let's be clear. I said no such thing. I did not suggest it, nor make an inference to it. Nothing is further from my mind. Prosecutor Barrens is a very capable attorney, and he is putting on a good prosecution. We are working hard to prove Dr. Carey is innocent, and a competent medical professional. That's it. Thank you and have a nice evening."

Another reporter shouts from deep within the crowd. "It's a whopper of a case, and she did do most of it. And it's an election year. Someone's going to lose big."

Brian glares into the crowd of reporters then begins to walk down the steps again; this time his arm is around me. I'm saying nothing, but I want to call Nathan a liar. I want to call Attorney Barrens a liar. My gaze is fixated on the Safe Haven Diner. We get into the car waiting at the curb. Tears pool in my eyes, but I refuse to let them fall. I'm not sure what's worse, a courtroom filled with terrible fabrications or the front steps covered with microphone-toting trolls dreaming of a front-page byline. All this at my expense.

In the car, Brian sits quietly, waiting for me to say something. He's not on his phone or skimming through papers; he's just sitting there, waiting.

"I don't have anything to say." I can't stop the tears.

"It's okay. Just like Barrens, it's their job. So don't let them get to you."

"How do I do that? They're all looking at me like I'm a serial killer."

"Are you?"

"No!"

"Then why believe them over yourself? Over me?"

I don't say a word. I know Brian is right. Nathan Roberts cherished his fifteen minutes of fame. I don't want mine.

CHAPTER 10
IT'S NOT ABOUT THE MONEY

THE KNOCK at my door startles me. "Who's there?"

"Dr. Jordan, please open the door. We can't stand out here all night." The perfectly pronounced letters of each word with a Nigerian twist is unmistakable.

"Samuel, you heard Brian. This isn't a good idea. What if someone sees you?"

"Then you had better open the door before someone notices us."

My smile evaporates and fear fills the air. "What do you mean *us*?"

"Oh, for Pete's sake! Open the door!" A second discernable voice practically yells.

"Billy Weston?" I quickly open the door and there stand five neighborhood patients, their arms straining under the weight of grocery bags and Tupperware.

"Girl, move out of the way. You want us to get caught and then hauled into court? Not all of us can shine like good ole Samuel." Stella Thorne eyes Billy.

The groceries and homemade food get placed on the kitchen countertops. Ellie Zeiglebaum, a thin seventy-three-year-old woman with severe arthritis and nearly blinding cataracts, begins searching through my kitchen cabinets.

"Mrs. Zeiglebaum, what are you looking for?"

Ellie pushes her untamed greyish hair from her face. She reluctantly stopped wearing a wig several months ago when I told her that the rash on her scalp was from it. "My dear, didn't your mother teach you how to set up a kitchen? *Oy vey.* Where are the dishes?"

"Well, you see, I've been kind of busy so they're in the dishwasher."

Ellie slaps her hand on the counter. "Pay up, Stella. I believe you owe me a quarter."

Stella shakes her head. "Dr. Jordan, with all you got goin' on, you have to keep a clean home. It's your sanctuary. The place where you come to find peace. And there ain't no peace in bein' untidy." Stella opens the dishwasher and removes seven random plates.

Inez Guzman, the fifth member of this surprise invasion, taps Stella on the back and holds out a thick, stubby, seventy-two-year-old hand. "Mrs. Stella, I believe now you owe me a quarter, too. I told you, the girls today, they are too worried about getting the job and looking professional. They don't do the proper things to run a home. That's why so many of them get married so late, no matter how much their mother begs them."

Stella looks at me. "Didn't your mama give you a set of dishes when you moved in here? That's what mothers are supposed to do when their daughters move into their first house."

Samuel chimes in. "I believe that is supposed to happen when they get married and move into their new home."

I look at them all. "Samuel, you're not helping."

Ellie reaches into her oversized handbag to produce a pair of rubber yellow gloves. Her tiny frame allows the gloves to touch both biceps. Loud thumps repeat across the wooden floor as Ellie makes her way to the sink. "Inez, since you're the youngest, you will dry. Billy, you set the table and don't break anything. Samuel, you help Stella put the food on the table. To save time we'll skip putting anything in serving bowls."

Stella mutters, "I would have lost that bet too."

I pull Samuel to the side. "You know Brian isn't going like this. There are reporters everywhere. If they saw all of you, they'd go crazy. I'm positive one of them will write that I'm meeting with my gang to plot my escape, or to hide all the money and drugs I have. Or some other BS like that."

"Relax, Dr. Jordan, we dropped the food off at a neighbor earlier today while you were in court. We cut through her backyard and came up the back way. The super is a friend of mine. Besides, the people who live around here are on your side, remember? I had Billy close the curtains while you were talking with the ladies. No one sees us and no one knows we are here."

The rest of the evening is lighthearted, and the soul-comforting food is from at least seven different ethnicities. They share stories of first visits with me and recount how out of place I was. Each one takes a turn explaining how they took me under their wing to shape me into the doctor this neighborhood needed. The hours fly by and I don't want this to end.

After all the dishes are washed and the food is put away, Stella claps her hands. "It's gettin' late and we all have things to do. Samuel, make sure the coast is clear. Billy, help Ellie get her coat on. Inez, start saying goodbye. You take forever to leave."

It's just about seven thirty. I say nothing about the time. "Thank you for coming and for all the wonderful food. I think I needed this more than you know."

Billy chuckles. "Don't you mean, more than *you* know?" I give him a hug.

The door opens and Samuel sticks his head in. "We can go now. Good night, Dr. Jordan."

As the last of my friends leave, the emptiness of being alone hits me hard, but the playback of their visit sends a warmth through me. The welcome vibration of my phone against the countertop is startling. "Hi, Mom."

"Hi Jordan. It's Mom, you sound very cheery. Why haven't you called yet? Did court go late? Wait, let me put the phone on speaker so your father can hear, too."

The rest of the re-cap with the parents goes as expected. Of course, I don't tell them about the outburst, the courthouse steps, or the surprise dinner guests. I do tell them about the Safe Haven Diner. They aren't impressed. Mom asks why I am concentrating on a diner instead of the court case. She says that Dad told her to ask the question.

Dad's asking if I need money since I am technically without a job. The question gets me thinking about the money Andie raised to pay Brian.

Andie's a social media wiz and started a crowdfunding campaign for me on something called SupportMyCause.com. I later found out it's one of those internet fundraising platforms where people can raise money for just about anything. Andie placed my story on this site with a catchy title: "Help a Good Doctor Stop a Bad Case." Someone in Brian's office brought the campaign to his attention, and he agreed to take the case for whatever the campaign could raise. The campaign lasted sixty days and after all the customary fees, just over $126,000 remained. Brian and I have only spoken about the money one time. I signed the entire amount over to him when I agreed to let him represent me. That feels like a lifetime ago.

Before I knew better, I would have told Andie I didn't need her to raise the money because my malpractice company should cover it. Shortly after making bail, I contacted them. Apparently, MedFender is a cut-rate malpractice company. They stated that the collection and distribution of medications was beyond my scope of license. They went one step further, calling my actions deliberately criminal. A Mr. Aldrich Bentonhall, Esq. then informed me that if I had read my policy, I would have known that it clearly states, in numerous places, that criminal acts are excluded from any type of MedFender coverage or defense. He's correct, I should have read my policy better. I also should have gone with a more reputable company. When I started the Money Box, the office took a deep financial hit, forcing me to cut back where I could. My malpractice insurance policy came up for renewal and MedFender was half the price. They were also half as honest. MedFender has many more exclusion clauses and stipulations. In the end they basically pay for nothing. And I'm considered the criminal.

When Brian Freeland's office first contacted me, I thought he was this high-priced attorney in it for the glory. I remember our first meeting in Brian's eleventh-floor midtown office. There are thick, heavy wooden doors guarding access to the kingdom. Several names are engraved on the wall next to them, with Brian Freeland at the top. The doors are locked, for a reason I'm still unsure of. I press the intercom button, and a woman's voice asks, "Dr. Jordan Carey?"

My puzzled expression fades as the red light on the camera flickers. I reply, "Yes? Yes."

A loud clack signals me the door is unlocked. "Dr. Carey, please step back so the door can open."

"Oh, sorry." A tight-knit steel-blue carpet with no visible seams leads to a waiting room left of the doors. It's a space made of glass walls on three sides. I feel like I am being watched from every angle. This personal invasion is only second to sitting in the defendant's chair in the courtroom.

Attorney Brian Freeland forces me to wait ten long, silent minutes before he appears at the waiting room door. He escorts me to a spacious conference room with a mammoth table with at least twenty leather-bound chairs encircling it. This room is even more intimidating than the waiting room. I don't know Attorney Freeland, but I instantly surmise that he is like most of my teaching attendings. They too always want to have the upper hand. We waltz through the pleasantries of a first-time meeting then Brian begins to question me.

He looks directly at me over the top of his half-glasses. His graying hair sways a bit as the air conditioner kicks on. In another universe where he was about ten years younger, and a few pounds lighter, I could be attracted to him.

"I've looked over your case, extensively. I think we can defend you. But first I have a question for you. Knowing what you know now, would you do anything differently?"

The question hits me hard. I refuse to look away. Without pause I respond, "I would do it all exactly the same."

Brian's face contorts. "Hmm. Why?"

Suddenly, I want to lunge forward, claws drawn. "Having second thoughts? Sorry, that was rude. I know you think I must be insane, but I'm not. My patients needed someone to step in and help. Mr. Freeland, you have a good-paying job that allows you to buy whatever you need. Thousands of people out there have to decide whether to pay for a prescription or buy food for their families."

Brian leans back in his expensive leather chair. His arms are crossed over the girth of his well-fed belly. "Go on. I'm listening."

I fight the urge to call him smug and leave. "Imagine you have high blood pressure and need to take medication daily, but you only take it three times a week. Some weeks even less. You're doing this so you can stretch the number of days before you have to pay for the refill. Unfortunately, your insurance plan doesn't fully cover the medication you need to stay healthy or just alive. The pharmaceutical companies are implementing monetary assistance programs, but it's not enough. I did what I did because I was trying to mend a broken system. Even if it was just a small fix."

Attorney Freeland places his hand on the table and bends towards me. "Jordan, there are other ways to do that."

"In hindsight, I could have become an activist, joined a movement, or reached out to the politicians in my state. But, all of that takes too long. How many of my patients would have suffered, had serious health issues, or even died in the meantime? Instead, I decided to make a change in my little part of the world." I pause and lean back in the expensive leather chair. "I did it for all the right reasons. And I stand by it." That may have been the first time I said those words out loud.

Brian reaches into the folder in front of him, extracts a large stack of papers, and flips to the last page. He removes a silver pen from his inside-jacket pocket and signs the document. He slides the stack to me and drops the pen on top of them.

"What am I signing?"

"You're hiring me to be your attorney. And you're giving me control of the money raised for your defense. I'll take the case for the money raised. You will have to trust me with everything." Brian holds out his right hand.

My eyes circled around the wood-paneled room and then back to the attorney sitting there in a custom designer suit. "I don't know . . ."

"It's okay. But I do have one condition. You must do all that I ask and don't improvise. Do you agree to this?" Brian thumbs through the file and pulls out another page. "There is the matter of this mysterious account with eleven thousand dollars in it."

"I have no idea who did this. It just showed up in my mailbox addressed to me. The account number and password are there. Apparently, an anonymous group set up a bank account for my defense and collected the money in donations."

Brian gave me his first and, so far, only ever disbelieving look. "I'm not having you sign that account over and you're not to touch that money. Not for any reason at all. Is that clear?"

"Sure, but why? It's supposed to be for my defense."

"Imagine you answer the question, where did this money come from? You'll have to say that you don't know. Everyone will give you the same look I just did. Then the prosecutor will ask you if you have drawn on any of it. I want you to be able to answer no."

"I'm going to hate the prosecutor, aren't I?"

"He's just doing his job. And if you touch that money, he's

going to make it look like kickbacks or worse, hidden drug money." Brian paused then pointed to the contract.

"All right. But I have a condition of my own."

Brian smiled and let a curious grunt escape. "Interesting. Okay, I'll bite. What's your condition?"

"Before I sign, I want to know about you. Who is Brian Freeland?" I was frightened of every word coming of my mouth and determined not to show it. "I have to know who's in charge of saving me."

"That's a bold question from someone in your position, but I can appreciate the spirit of it. I've been an attorney for over twenty-five years—"

"From the looks of this place I can see you're no slouch. Tell me what makes you, you."

My almost-attorney plays along. "You want to know about my . . . let's call it, substance. I'm a good husband, a father of three who wishes he were home a bit more, and I'm dedicated to my friends and co-workers just as much. Which sometimes is not a good thing. Professionally, I always do my best. I have more wins than losses. And, while I might have an overpriced office space with all its outlandish flash and prestige, it's all for the clients. I learned long ago they want to feel like they're getting the best." Brian casually flails his arms in the air. "All of this is some insane proof of that. At least that's what they think. I'm not sure why I'm sharing this, but I will deny it if you bring it up again."

Wanting more, I add, "So, you're telling me you could take an office in the neighborhood I work in and be just as happy?"

Brian gives me the first real glimpse of the pearly white teeth that I will later find out are his trademark symbol of confidence. "I still remember the days of working on the second floor of a three-floor walk-up, hoping that my next client, arrested for shoplifting, for the third time, would soon walk in. I'll never forget that. Would I go back there? No, but you already know that. No one likes to struggle. That doesn't mean I don't care. It means I like nice things like everyone else in the world." He pauses, looks at the ceiling then back at me. "I guess that's who I am."

Without further thought, I lower the pen and sign.

We have not spoken of the money since that first day. I don't know how much Brian has used or if any of it is left. Like I've said before: I treat my patients knowing that someday I will be the patient. I believe that Brian has similar thoughts. I always treat, treated, my patients as more than an ailment or a monetary chit. I think under different circumstances, Brian and I could be friends. He cares about people, and that's the real reason he took my case. For people like us, it's not about the money.

CHAPTER 11
MRS. OSGOOD'S TIC

I GET to the diner before Brian. It feels like a good place to hide. The place is nearly packed with people who, I surmise, are just like me.

"Good morning, Jordan. You're early. Is everything okay?"

"Yes, Brian. Everything is fine."

"Good. Have you eaten breakfast today?" Brian looks at me like a dad speaking to his teenage daughter.

"In fact, I woke up still a little—never mind." I give telling him about last night's neighborly intervention a second thought.

Sitting in the chair across from me, Brian glares at me over his half-glasses. "I don't want you have a hangry outburst."

Like everything Brian does, it is a polished move. "Is that the Dad-look you give your kids to get them to listen?"

He pats the silk tie sitting on his slightly overstuffed mid-section. "It's the look I give clients that don't know what's good for them." Brian runs a hand through his mildly unkept grey hair. I believe the style keeps him at the corner of hip and corporate. "And yes, my children get it too."

I look him up and down and smirk. "Does it work?"

Brian lifts a pant leg to reveal designer socks, color matched to the silk tie. "It does when I give the final power move."

We both start to laugh. "I'm glad you put on your game face for me."

Brian smiles and stands. "I'm glad you approve. We need to go."

"Okay, I'm ready. Today the coffee is on me." I slide over the five-dollar bill I had tucked in my sleeve earlier.

Brian leans in and whispers, "That five didn't come from the account I told you not to touch, did it?"

"It did not. Remember I am under contract to listen to everything my attorney tells me to do or not to do?"

Brian curtly counters, "If only that were true."

The crowd on the stone steps is more extensive than usual. I look at Brian. He quietly mutters, "It's fine. I don't think they're here for you today. There's a police shooting trial starting today."

"Thank God." Brian gives me a well-deserved odd stare. "I didn't mean it like that. You know what I mean."

"Let's walk around them and quietly get inside." Brian places himself between the reporters and me. Thankfully, no one notices us. We ramble through the serpentine-like checkpoint line, removing the various articles of clothing and placing them on the conveyor belt. After only four days, this feels way too normal. It's a process that no one likes, yet we all willingly adhere to it out of necessity or a general distrust for each other.

The elevator pings as the number five displays in red above the doors. "Courtroom Five. That's our stop."

Brian is not amused. "You're overly jolly today. Is there something I should be aware of?" Brian looks at me as if to ask if I've been drinking or worse.

I almost reply, "Yes, I took some of the drugs Barrens says I've been selling," but I don't. "Nope, everything is the same. I'm just trying to have a more positive attitude."

"That's good, but I think you might want to tone it down a bit. You're on trial, remember."

At our table, Brian points to the judge's bench. I nod in agreement, but today I think I can look at the people on the stand. I don't know them, and that seems to make it less personal. I hope I'm right.

"All rise for the Honorable Judge Harris," The bailiff declares while standing at his post like a Buckingham Palace guard.

"Good morning, please be seated." Judge Harries glances around the courtroom. "Yesterday, we left off with Mr. Freeland ending his cross of Mr. Roberts. Mr. Barrens, do you have a need to question Mr. Roberts any further?"

"Yes, Your Honor, just briefly, please."

"Very well. Mr. Roberts, please retake the stand. I remind you that you are still under oath. Sir, do you understand this?"

"Yes, Your Honor." Nathan's oversized black T-shirt flows freely as he makes himself comfortable in the witness chair.

"Mr. Barrens, please proceed." Judge Harris is once again scribbling notes while calling out her orders.

Barrens flaps a sheet of paper in the air. "Mr. Roberts, what did you think when you first received this letter from Dr. Carey?"

"I thought she was being truthful and that it could have been just a big mistake."

"Did you return to Dr. Carey's practice as a patient?"

"No."

"Why?"

"The more I thought about it, the more I kept getting this gut feeling that the letter was just a way for Dr. Carey to cover her bu—backside. And now I see that I was right."

"What do you mean?"

"I think Dr. Carey wrote the letter just in case she got caught with her hand in the cookie jar. Then, she could use the letter to say it was an honest mistake."

"Objection. Calls for speculation."

"Sustained, the jury will disregard the witness's last statement."

"No more questions for this witness, Your Honor." Like yesterday, Attorney Barrens looks directly at me as he walks back to his table. It's just as unsettling today as it was yesterday. It's like he's saying, *I know what you did and I'm coming for you.*

Judge Harris nods to Nathan Roberts. "The witness is excused. Mr. Barrens, please call your next witness."

"Your Honor, we would like to call Miranda Osgood to the stand."

I scribble on Brian's pad: Who's that? Brian slowly and gently places my hand down on the table. Brian has previously asked me not to overreact and not to hastily pick up the pen and write with such a palpable urgency. He told me that the jury sees every move I make, and They will think I'm panicking because I'm guilty. I know the contract condition, but I can't help myself.

"Mrs. Osgood, please state your expertise for the court?"

"I am a CPA specializing in forensic accounting and have been a certified fraud examiner for over ten years."

"Are you being paid to testify here today?" Barrens ensures the jury is aware of the payment before it can be used against his witness. Brian has told me of this tactic during one of our planning meetings.

"Yes."

"Mrs. Osgood, did you examine Dr. Carey's accounts and tax returns?"

"Yes, I examined Dr. Carey's office and personal accounts as well as her office and personal tax returns for the past five years."

"What did you conclude?"

The jury's eyes are glued to the red-haired slender woman in the witness chair. Unfortunately, I don't think it's her fair complexion and stunning deep green eyes that have their attention. This thought makes me start fidgeting.

Brian lifts a finger ever so slightly and points at the judge's desk. As much as I hate to admit it, focusing on that damn desk does return me to calmness.

"Dr. Carey's business accounting leaves much to be desired. Before just two years ago, Dr. Carey's accounting was typical of most small medical offices. Monies received from patients and insurance companies were all recorded in the appropriate locations. Bills were paid, and the flow of money in and out of the account seemed well-defined. The totals were substantially lower than a typical office but still not out of the ordinary. Starting approximately two years ago, the recording of payments from insurance companies tapered off, and the patient payment recordings were almost nil. Instead, daily amounts were recorded as two total sums taken in. It appears that personal and insurance checks were afforded to the corresponding patients, but the cash amounts varied greatly from day to day. The numerous patient write-offs were odd to me. There were far more than normal. Then there was the creation of a second account labeled 'medication account,' which showed money coming in and being paid to a credit card or directly to various pharmacies. There was no indication of what these payments were used for other than to buy drugs."

Brian stands. "Objection, the connotational use of 'to buy drugs' is slanderous and speculative in nature and could slant the jury's opinion unjustly."

"Sustained, the witness will refrain from interchanging the words 'medications' and 'drugs' to just using the word 'medications.' Can you please restate your last sentence?"

"There was no indication of what the payments were used for other than to buy medications."

Barrens inconspicuously eyes Brian with disdain. "Please continue, Mrs. Osgood."

"While it seems that Dr. Carey was not hiding her actions, they were hard to track. As a result, there is a great deal of uncertainty regarding accountability in her record-keeping."

"Mrs. Osgood, could you please explain what that means?" Barrens's inquisitive tone even piques my interest. Fear replaces my unwanted curiosity as I start to imagine how intrigued the jury must be.

“It means there was no way to know who was paying what amount or for what reason. That usually spells trouble.”

“Objection. The witness is giving an unfounded opinion.”

Judge Harris looks up from her papers. “Overruled, but only if Mr. Barrens can have his witness clarify the answer immediately.”

Barrens nearly leaps forward. “Of course, Your Honor. Mrs. Osgood, can you tell us why you can make such an opinion?”

Miranda Osgood straightens herself in the witness chair. “During the course of many of the forensic audits I have done, I can safely say that when the numbers don’t add up, they don’t add up. In this case the numbers come out of thin air. There is no paper trail, no accountability, nor is there any reasoning of why, how, or what the money is doing in the account. It is either the poorest bookkeeping method or the dumbest money laundering scheme I have ever come across. That is not my personal opinion, it’s my professional one.”

Judge Harris waits a moment. “Objection overruled.” Brian says nothing.

Barrens has the grin of a father whose daughter just won an Olympic gold medal. “Well Mrs. Osgood, that was some clarification.” He takes a long stroll-like walk around the prosecutors table then continues. “Let’s move on. Did you speak with Dr. Carey’s office staff regarding the current accounting process, and what did you find?”

“I did. Both women stated, independently, that after Dr. Carey changed the process of collecting receivables, they were unable to figure out who paid for what. They both also stated that they were forced to trust Dr. Carey’s decisions for the overall scheme.”

“Objection. The use of the word scheme is—”

“Sustained. The witness will please use another word. The jury will give no weight to the use of the word ‘scheme.’”

Barrens looks at Mrs. Osgood, who continues. “Oh yes, sorry.

They both said they were forced to trust Dr. Carey's choice to use this, uh, plan."

"Thank you. Let's get back on track. What is your professional opinion of Dr. Carey's overall intention in using these methods?"

"I feel that Dr. Carey took reckless actions regarding her bookkeeping and financial records. These actions seem to border on some larger . . . plan . . . that was done intentionally to make her financial trail fall into a grey area. I suspect fraud is at play here, but to what degree is undeterminable because it is a puzzle missing key pieces."

"So, you feel that Dr. Carey has tried to commit fraud regarding her financial records and thus her tax returns?" Attorney Barrens is now standing next to the witness box facing the jury.

"Yes."

"No more questions for this witness, Your Honor."

Judge Harris swivels towards Brian. "Mr. Freeland, do you wish to question the witness?"

"Yes, Your Honor. Mrs. Osgood, approximately how many cases have you testified in?"

"I believe the number is getting close to one hundred."

"How many of those near one hundred testimonies were for the prosecution?"

"I would say the majority of them."

"Would you like to know that you testified ninety-three times in the past seven years and eighty-seven of those were for the prosecution?"

"Objection, relevance."

"Get to the point, Mr. Freeland." Judge Harris apparently doesn't like suspense.

"Do you know how often your professional opinion was determined to be wrong or, if I may say, biased?"

"It happens to most expert witnesses. It's part of the job. But to answer your question, I believe it has been about eight or so times."

"Would you find it surprising to hear the number is more like forty-one? I believe, as you put it, if the numbers add up, then they add up. They certainly add up here."

Barrens quickly rises. "Objection. Mr. Freeland is testifying."

Judge Harris stares at Barrens first. "Sustained. Mr. Freeland, as you so swiftly objected to earlier. Please refrain from announcing your personal opinions to the court."

"My apologies, Your Honor. Mrs. Osgood, are you sure of your findings in Dr. Carey's case?"

"I stand by my results now as I have in the past."

"Do you feel Dr. Carey was hiding anything in the numbers she and her staff recorded during their accounting?"

"It's hard to tell."

Brian moves closer to the witness stand. "So, your answer is that you really don't know."

"No, not conclusively." Mrs. Osgood is rubbing a small spot over her left eyebrow.

"Do you need a moment? Do you have something in your eye? We can stop for a minute." Brian's tone is still disapproving.

Attorney Barrens stands with both palms raised in the air but does not raise his voice. "Objection, Attorney Freeland is badgering the witness."

"I am merely asking the witness if she needs a break. How is that badgering? Your Honor, I believe that to be just the opposite of badgering."

"That will be enough out of both of you. Overruled. Mrs. Osgood, do you, in fact, need a minute?"

"Thank you, no, Your Honor."

Judge Harris's scowl further admonishes the attorneys. "Continue, Mr. Freeland."

"Yes, Your Honor. Mrs. Osgood, did Dr. Carey claim that the patient write-offs were bad debt for tax purposes?"

"No." The area above Mrs. Osgood's left eye is now visibly red and swelling.

"According to the records, did Dr. Carey and her staff record insurance checks, personal checks, and cash received every day the office was operating?"

"Yes, I believe so." Mrs. Osgood is now tightly grasping the arms of the witness chair with both hands.

"Is it possible that Dr. Carey and her staff recorded every financial transaction to the best of their abilities and without malice?"

A sigh of defeat escapes from Mrs. Osgood while her left-hand reaches, yet again, for the reddened area. "Yes. Sure, it's possible."

"No more questions for this witness, Your Honor."

Judge Harris peers at the now enormous red beacon above the witness's eye. "It is nearing the lunch hour, and I think we could all use a break. Do you agree, Mr. Prosecutor?"

"Yes, Your Honor. I too feel this would be a good place to stop." Barrens turns and stares at the two young associates sitting next to him. It is the junior attorney's job to find and vet all witnesses and experts. Attorney Barrens is not hiding his utter loathing of the now cowering junior attorneys.

The expert forensic CPA makes her way down from the witness stand and heads straight to the outermost junior attorney at the prosecutor's table. The bright red blotch over her left eye is growing by the second. "I want more money or I'm done."

A thin, greying woman is making her way to the front of the courtroom. The pounding of her shoes and cane against the marble floor overpowers us into silence. "Excuse me, Miss. I was sitting back there, in the courtroom, while you were up here, with the judge, and the jury, and the attorneys who were asking you all those questions. That's a lot of *farkakte*. If you don't mind me saying so. Anyway, honey, you don't look so good for doing it."

"Who the heck are you? You can't talk to her." The outermost junior interjects.

"Young man, you are too young to speak without being asked a question. Watch and you might learn something." Ellie turns back to Mrs. Osgood. "Like I was saying. I am Ellie and I live right around the corner from that wonderful young woman you are saying all the bad things about. She is truly a good doctor and it looks like you could really use her help. Let's hurry and catch her before your eye closes all the way." Ellie begins to pull Mrs. Osgood down the center aisle. "Are you married? I see the wedding ring on your finger. Maybe you could teach her how to keep a more tidy home."

"Bailiff? Please," the other junior attorney calls out.

The commotion behind us causes me to turn around. "Oh no."

Brian watches as I start back. "No Jordan, don't . . ."

"Mrs. Zeiglebaum, stop. Let her go. Ellie, please."

"Dr. J., she needs your help. Tell this *mashugana* in the rent-a-cop suit to let me go or—"

I place my arm around Mrs. Zeiglebaum. "Ellie, stop talking now. Come on, she'll be fine."

Brian walks over to Barrens, who is waving to the bailiffs. "No. Let it go. She had no way of knowing. Dr. Carey can't help that they love her. And that's exactly what I'll say in open court. Besides, how's it going to look, you persecuting a defendant for an old Jewish lady trying to help your witness?" Brian smiles. "They'll call you Barrens the Barbarian, or worse."

Barrens stares at me. "Just get her out of here, now."

Mrs. Osgood waits patiently for our exit. As the bailiff opens the courtroom door, loud commentary regarding the Rudolph-like affliction and the laughter that follows pour in from the corridor. Between Ellie's show and Mrs. Osgood's tic, I'm sure there will be a flurry of words in the news tonight.

CHAPTER 12
THE COURTHOUSE SUITE

"Did that go as well as I think it did? She's a train wreck. Did—"

"Jordan, please stop talking." Brian is again quietly scolding me as he, once more, grabs my arm and drags me to the cold and lifeless conference room.

"Why are you upset?" I'm willing to listen to my attorney, but this disobedient child routine is getting old. Brian and I are going to have to establish some new playground rules.

Brian's voice is low and lifeless. "I'm not upset. I don't want us to undo all the good by looking too happy. The trial isn't over yet."

"Um . . . what's going on?"

"It's best if we do not show any reaction, confident or concerned, in the courtroom or any other public space. There are reporters just waiting to use a quote they said they overheard or artists wanting to draw an absentminded expression you mistakenly made during the trial. It's best to show no reaction, at least for now." Brian pauses for a moment, then intentionally smirks. "Yes, that was a win with Mrs. Osgood, but Barrens won't let it happen that easily again. He's better than that. Right now, he's firing one or both of those junior lawyers. Don't be surprised if there are new faces at that table after lunch."

"Can he do that?"

"That's exactly the face I don't want you to make when you see the new attorneys."

"Okay. Can we head over to the diner? I'm getting hungry, and there won't be enough time to eat if we don't go soon." My stomach grumbles in concurrence.

"Actually, I texted my office to send over food. We'll eat here. Look around you. We have our very own private courthouse suite."

"Why? The diner is safe. You told me so yourself." I realize how desperate I sound, but that diner is becoming a much-needed emotional release valve.

"I'm changing it up for today. We need to talk about some things and get some details straight."

"What details, what things?" My frustration is not hidden.

"First, how common were the addition errors on the deposits?"

"I don't know. A few here and there at best. Why does that matter?"

"Barrens will try to show that you took cash from the deposits before taking them to the bank." Brain takes out his cell phone and begins speaking a text. "Erin, carefully go over all the bank statements to see how many deposit corrections there were in the past two years. See how many of them have totaling errors. Then compare the number of errors to the previous two years' errors."

"Why wouldn't I just take the cash out before the deposit slip was written? Or, why wouldn't I just write a new deposit slip with the correct total on it?" Disgust and anger replace frustration. "I'm not an idiot!"

"Okay, that's exactly what I don't want you to say. I think Barrens will revisit this matter when you get on the witness stand, so I'll ask questions about it first. We better have our facts straight." Brian begins to dial another number on his phone when there's a knock at the door.

He gives me a wave to answer the door. I point to myself. "Who, me? When did I become your—"

The second set of knocks is less patient. Erin, a mid-level attorney at his law firm, is standing there, a scowl on her face. Mid-level means she does whatever is needed, from making copies to delivering food. Erin is in her late twenties or early thirties. She is also a thin redhead, but her skin is almost luminescent except for the freckles that seem to dash across it. She could be mistaken for a high schooler if it were not for the depth of her character and poise. Erin is a tough one with ice in her veins. We have met many times since the firm took my case. She is ambitious but controlled. Although in the past few weeks, I have seen more playfulness in her. I was nothing like her growing up or even as a resident at Buckford Hospital. I volunteered to take just about any case and came in early or stayed late. I wanted to be noticed. I don't believe Erin needs to be seen. She seems more confident playing the tigress lying in the grass, waiting to make her move. I envy that in her. She also takes too much from Brian.

"Hi, Erin, what's for lunch?" My shoulders drop as I see the diner's logo on the large brown bag.

"Hi Jordan, Brian had me pick up turkey sandwiches from the diner." Erin sees my shoulders drop and starts to laugh. "No, I'm joking. Brian wanted me to say that. I got you both BLTs and some apple pie."

I shoot Brian a dirty look. He is ignoring both of us. "Thanks, Erin. Is there anything I should tell the great and powerful attorney?"

Erin gives me a sneer as she turns to leave the suite. "No, just tell him to call if he needs anything else."

I hold up the lunch bag so Brian can see that Erin has completed her task. He motions for me to start eating. This order I'm glad to follow. The warmth and smell emanating from the bag has me already: the salty bacon, the sweet tomato, and the crisp lettuce. The rustling of the paper bag forces Brian to turn his back.

Reaching into the bag makes me remember the Money and Pill Boxes. They were always in view of at least one staff member. The boxes were made of wood and too heavy and cumbersome to move. I counted the money or took out the pills from the boxes right there in the waiting room. I was always in plain sight. I never tried to hide any of it. I counted the money and then handed it through the sliding glass window. I went through the pills, put those to be discarded into a blue container, and those we kept into a yellow one. Then I handed those through the window. Clara or Rebecca was behind the glass. At least one of them could see me going through the same process every day.

I can feel the electricity of vindication coursing through my veins. The hair on my arms is at attention. "Brian. Brian!"

The tapping of his shoulder inadvertently frustrates him. "I'll have to call you back." Brian turns from his phone to me. "What? What's wrong?"

"No, listen. I was opening the bag; your back was turned, forget that. The important thing is that I never, and I mean never, opened either box anywhere else than in the waiting room."

"What, exactly, does that mean?" Brian is now sitting, holding his BLT, but his eyes are focused on me.

"Because of the layout of the office, the waiting room is in full view of the reception area through panes of glass. The Boxes are made of wood and too heavy to lift. So, both boxes were always emptied in the waiting room. In full view of my staff." I'm speaking rapidly and gleefully pacing around the Goliath table.

"I'm not following the logic here." Brian unwraps his sandwich and is about to take a bite.

I place my hand over his BLT. He gives me a concerned look. "Brian, both Clara and Rebecca could see me the entire time I emptied the boxes. There was no chance to steal money or hide pills, even if I wanted to." I go through all the details again, much slower this time. "Clara and Rebecca can swear to it."

"Are you telling me that you actually had a reproducible system that your office used daily to handle both boxes?" Brian removes my hand from his sandwich and places it on a napkin. His thumbs begin to hammer away at the letters of his cell phone.

"More work for Erin?"

"Let me finish." Ignoring my question, he finishes his text and places the phone on the table next to his BLT. "Okay, I'll have the office draw up a motion to recall Clara and Rebecca so they can verify what you just told me. Let's move on. Barrens's next expert is a big pharma guy named James Connor, PhD. His expertise is in pharmaceutical safety. This is going to be a tough one for us, but I have some ideas. First, I need to go over how you determined which pills to save and which to throw out. Try to remember everything."

Brian and I spend the next thirty minutes retracing every waiting room step, every deposit slip step, and every pill collection and distribution step. After the third time through I break. "Brian, we've gone over this a million times. Nothing is going to change. What are you looking for? I can't do it again."

Brian places his half-glasses on the table before speaking. "Jordan, I'm looking for you to not stop to think about what you are stating. There can be no 'ums' or unexpected pauses. You have to be one hundred percent confident about the process."

I can feel the anger and fear bubbling. "I am sure of it. All of it."

"It has to be like lifting a fork to your mouth to eat. You have to be relaxed and controlled when you answer Barrens's questions. And mine. It has to feel natural."

I wait a moment to let the words sink in. "I understand. And I will be." I wish I could believe that.

Brian's phone alarm pings. "It's time to go back."

Back in the courtroom, I look over at Attorney Barrens's table. Brian was right. Both junior attorneys have been replaced. The new team is slightly older and, I'm guessing, a bit more seasoned. They appear to be the aces you bring in to secure the game's victory. This thought comes with enormous amounts of anxiety. Brian is busy preparing something for the next witness. I return my focus to the judge's bench almost instinctively. The calmness is slow to return.

I'm thinking about the courthouse suite. That's what I now call it in my mind. The space is cold at its heart, yet it continues to serve a purpose. A purpose that only Brian knows before entering it.

CHAPTER 13
PHD BIG PHARMA

"DR. JAMES CONNOR, would you please state your expertise for the court?" Attorney Barrens's determination is palpable. The two new litigators appear less stiff but still alert, waiting for any order that their fearless leader commands. Their suits look more tailored and less off-the-rack than their predecessors.

"My expertise is in pharmaceutical quality assurance and control. I have twenty years of experience in developing safety systems and assessing the pharmaceutical industry." Dr. Connor's bravado has the jury's full attention.

Barrens returns to standing next to the jury box. "Dr. Connor, can you tell us the difference between quality assurance and quality control?"

"Yes. Simply put, quality assurance is a process in which mechanisms are designed to establish that a product does exactly what it is said to do. These assurance mechanisms are put into place before the production of a product. Quality control tests the end product to make sure that it does what it is supposed to do, and it also tests for consistency of the product."

"Dr. Connor, how does all this fit into the pharmaceutical industry?"

"Experts like myself are hired to help make sure that a drug has all the proper safeguards in place to ensure the best possible version of that drug is given to people. We assist in the development of protocols before the process of pill-making starts, and then we test the pills at the end to make sure they perform as indicated." Dr. Connor is a tall, slender man with the slightest of graying in his tightly trimmed beard. His black-framed glasses and dark suit only add to the highly educated, polished look he portrays.

"Could you please explain how all this relates to Dr. Carey and her Pill Box?" The turning of Attorney Barrens's gaze in my direction has created a monkey-see-monkey-do effect with the jurors. My eyes are fixed on the grain pattern of the judge's bench.

"Dr. Carey's actions regarding the so-called 'Pill Box' were reckless and endangered the lives of everyone who received the medications." James Connor, PhD, might as well have been wagging his finger right at me when he said this. Everyone in the courtroom lets out a tiny gasp.

A quick thud of Judge Harris's gavel brings the courtroom back under control. "Order. There will be none of that."

"How is this so?" Barrens is prodding his expert to stick the knife in deeper.

"Regarding quality assurance, Dr. Carey had no process to truly ensure the medications were dosed correctly or untampered with. Lastly, she had no one checking any procedure she might think she was using to sort the pills. From a quality control standpoint, it was a deadly hazard biding its time."

"As an expert in your field of pharmaceuticals, what would you have told Dr. Carey to do if she came to you with the Pill Box idea?"

"I would have emphatically told her not to do it. I would have told her that she could kill someone or even many with this idea." Connors is nearly yelling this point. The only thing that could add more credibility to his testimony is a white lab coat.

Barrens first looks at the jury and then back to the witness. "I can see you are very passionate about your work and your opinion. Did you confer with other colleagues regarding this matter before you testified today?"

"I did."

"What did they say?"

"Objection, hearsay, and those other colleagues are not here to corroborate the witness's statement or to be cross-examined."

"Sustained." Judge Harris is giving attorney Barrens the "over the line" look that neither attorney wishes to see.

"I apologize, Your Honor. No more questions."

Judge Harris raises her gavel like a pointer. "Your witness, Mr. Freeland."

"Thank you, Your Honor." Brian stands and looks down at a small stack of papers piled in front of him. "Dr. Connors, you stated that your expertise is in the pharmaceutical industry, is that correct?"

"Yes, it is."

"You also stated that you have worked with pharmaceutical companies to create methodologies and assessments for the production of medications. More specifically for pills, is that correct?"

"Yes, that's correct."

"Do all pharmaceutical companies have experts like you involved in some part of the process and the assessment of the end product?"

"Yes. They are required by law."

"Would it be safe to assume that the pills that Dr. Carey was taking in through her Pill Box were manufactured by pharmaceutical companies?"

"Yes."

"Therefore, those pills would have gone through the required scrutiny that you have been describing well before they reached Dr. Carey and her Pill Box?"

"Yes. I suppose so. But—"

"So, if the pill was made incorrectly in any way and accidentally made it to the public and then into Dr. Carey's Pill Box, the fault would be that of the pharmaceutical company, and by your own testimony, yours or someone in your same position, by extrapolation, is that also correct?" Brian is flipping the pages on the table as if he has one question per page. Connors is watching the pages, perhaps wondering how many pages there are in total.

"Yes, but—"

"Thank you, let's continue. Do you know if any of Dr. Carey's patients, those who received medication from her Pill Box, took ill, or might have even died, as a result of taking those medications?"

"I was not made aware of any such incidents."

"Didn't you emphatically state that this would happen?"

"Objection."

"Sustained."

Brian looks back to the witness and continues. "Would it surprise you to know that it didn't happen? I'm letting you know for your records."

"Objection, Mr. Freeland is making statements and introducing unvetted evidence."

"Sustained. Mr. Freeland, please just ask questions of the witness and save your statements for your closing."

"Yes, Your Honor. Dr. Connors, can you explain what a PDR is?"

"PDR stands for physician's desk reference and is a compilation of all known drugs to date. It lists the drug, with its image, its indications and contraindications, its drug interactions, its dosing, and its side effects." Dr. Connors's voice is slightly softer. The bravado is gone.

Brian is holding up a thick book. "Is this the book, and can you also view it online?"

"Yes, to both."

"Is it accurate?"

"Yes, very accurate."

"Can a doctor verify a pill with it?"

"Yes."

"Do you know if Dr. Carey used the PDR in her office?" The large book sends a tremor through the courtroom as Brian drops it onto the table. Judge Harris admonishes Brian with a single look.

"I was not made aware of whether she did or didn't."

"She did. If Dr. Carey used both versions, could she successfully identify the pills from the Pill Box and therefore reduce the chances of killing any of her patients to almost zero?"

"I suppose so."

"Yes or no, please."

"Yes."

"No more questions, Your Honor." Brian walks past the prosecutor's table without even the tiniest of glances towards the three attorneys sitting there. The junior attorneys are making themselves appear busy looking for rebuttal points. Attorney Barrens is watching Brian walk past the table, waiting for his chance to stand and salvage what might be left of his expert.

"Dr. Connors, as an expert in quality assurance and quality control, do you feel that there could be a higher possibility of tampering with the pills in the so-called Pill Box since the handling of these pills is not being monitored like they would in a large pharmaceutical company?"

"Objection, calls for unjust speculation."

Judge Harris speaks clearly and sternly. "Overruled. Mr. Barrens, you have the shortest of ropes here."

"Thank you, Your Honor. Dr. Connors, can you please answer the question?"

"In a company setting like the manufacturing plants for medications, everything is closely monitored for various obvious and also not so obvious reasons. One of the most obvious reasons is tampering with the product. That is one of the main concerns of quality-control checks. It's how most tampering is found out. In Dr.

Carey's model, no one can definitively determine if the pills have been tampered with, and that's a dangerous game to be playing." Dr. Connors is once again sitting tall and speaking with authority as he overpronounces his words for dramatic effect.

"Thank you, Dr. Connors. No more questions, Your Honor."

Judge Harris peers at the clock on the courtroom wall. "Once again we have reached the hour at which it may be good to stop for the day. Do either of the attorneys have an objection to this?"

"Actually, Your Honor, I do have a few quick questions for the witness that will take under five minutes, and then the witness will not have to return tomorrow." Brian is playing with fire.

Attorney Barrens rises to his feet. "I am not opposed to finishing with this witness today if it only takes five minutes." Barrens is shielding his fellow attorney from the wrath of a common foe. I don't know if it is out of respect for Brian or the profession, but it is honorable either way. Erin has told me that attorneys will stick together out of respect. It's why the Safe Haven diner exists.

Judge Harris eyes both attorneys as they stand almost shoulder to shoulder between their respective tables. "Well, far be it from me to override such solidarity. Very well, Mr. Freeland, you have about five minutes."

"Thank you, Your Honor. Dr. Connors, was Dr. Carey manufacturing the medications?"

"No, of course not."

"Then how was Dr. Carey to perform quality assurance on a product already produced?"

Behind his beard, Dr. Connors takes his time clearing his throat. "I guess . . . she couldn't."

"Didn't Dr. Carey perform quality control on the pills by throwing away anything she thought looked odd, was expired, or she couldn't identify?"

"In a very crude manner, I would have to say she was performing quality control. It's still dangerous."

"Is your expertise to assess patient danger in addition to quality control and assurance of medications, Dr. Connors?"

"No." Dr. James Connors's shoulders are once again slumped.

"Then is it safe to say that Dr. Carey's method was, in essence, a double check of Big Pharma's already in-depth process, and as far as the patient danger assessment, that was merely a guess, I'm sorry, an opinion on your part?"

Dr. Connors throws in the towel. "I guess so. Sure, you could say that."

"No more questions, Your Honor." Attorney Freeland sits down, staring straight ahead at Judge Harris.

"Court will resume at nine thirty sharp tomorrow morning." Judge Harris bangs her gavel for the last time today and we all stand as she and jury exit.

"Thanks for backing me up on that one." Brian reaches his right hand out to shake Attorney Barrens's hand.

"Honestly, I'm second-guessing the gesture." Barrens smirks, but he knows that Brian would have done the same with a judge like Judge Harris. "Nicely played."

Brian lets out a big smile. "If you get the nerve to stand up to her, I've got your back. Just make sure it's not flagrant enough to make us bunkmates for a night in the tank." The two seasoned veterans are laughing as they walk out of the courtroom together.

"Will we see new partners sitting at your table in the morning?"

"No. So much for Mr. PhD. Big Pharma. I am getting a bit of a reputation. Better that I behave and play with my new toys quietly." Barrens let out a boisterous laugh, and Brian follows suit.

Brian looks around to make sure no one is watching, then pulls me to the side to say that we had a good day and I should go home happy. I think he wants to meet with his cronies in some lawyer bar to blow off some steam and maybe gloat.

He turns to walk away as he gives me his final order for the day. "I'll see you in the diner by nine sharp."

I guess he does deserve to go out and play with the gang tonight. He owned that courtroom today. I'm glad for him. I'm glad for me.

CHAPTER 14
LEON'S UNDERWORLD

"Hello Andie, I was just thinking of calling you. Do you want to grab a quick drink and catch up?" I can already hear Brian's voice in my head. "Do not divulge anything about the case to anyone. I am your only friend." I don't intend to come near the subject.

"Leon's Underworld in about an hour?" Andie's cheeriness is always welcome.

Andrea Sullivan is my oldest friend. Although she now goes by Andie Tanner. She's a year older than me, married, and has six-year-old twin boys. Andie and I met at Saint Agnes, a private elementary school that both our parents demanded we attend. Andie's public-school performance in fourth grade was not up to Saint Agnes's standards, so she was forced to repeat it when she entered the private school. We became friends immediately. I was the girl who played baseball and wanted to know how things worked, and Andie was the new kid with no friends. Andie was a bit on the mischievous side, still is, while I was the shy one in a crowd. We have always been a good balance for each other. Andie's flowing blond hair and her slightly-taller-than-all-the-other-kids stature made her stand out just about everywhere. When the movie *Twins* came out, people joked that it was about Andie and me. We didn't appreciate the comments, but they were accurate.

Andie went on to open her own successful catering business. She met her husband, Sebastian Tanner, while catering a very lucrative, formal dinner for millionaire Tovia Thornton. Mrs. Thornton was running for Congress. She was soundly defeated in that year's election. Sebbi, as he is known, comes from a family that made its money in wineries. They own three, but Sebbi has no interest in the family business. His love is politics, although Sebbi prefers to be behind the scenes. Their lightning-fast courtship led to twins, Allister and Stanton, just over a year later. I'm known as Aunt Jordan to them. The boys are in school full-time now, and Andie is planning to return to her catering business.

A sarcastic chuckle appears at the thought that at least I'll have a job if I need one after all of this.

Leon's is a bar and grill that has served as Andie's and my meetup place for the last eight years. I'm not sure there is a Leon anymore, but the name and the décor remain the same. Leon's is a major leap up from the Safe Haven Diner. The floors are dark wood, perhaps mahogany, with a high gloss finish. They remain sturdy and unblemished from the years of evils they have endured. The table-tops have been created to carry the darkness upward, but they have been unable to hide the wrinkles that come with age. The lights that hang in the bar area cast a low but warm glimmer, maybe to keep the identities of patrons seeking a refuge from the daily grind a secret. The bar itself creates a dark wooden barrier separating its four barkeeps from the herds that stampede towards it every night. Behind the bar is a mirrored wall, fronted by inlaid glass shelving, with bottles of spirits standing in soldier-esque rows, waiting to be sent into battle.

The darker bar area is separated from the lighter, more family-like dining space, housing bleached wooden tables, matching chairs, and bright overhead illumination. The shoulder-high partition with its glass windows is still in place, a throwback to when smoking was allowed in public spaces. If it were not for the shared entryway into the establishment, most would think these were two totally different businesses.

Andie and I have been coming here so long that we don't notice the differences anymore. I'm waiting at a bar-height table for Andie to show up. She's late, as usual.

"Sorry, Sebbi got delayed." Andie rolls her eyes. He makes her happy, so I'm happy.

"It's okay. I'm used to it by now. In fact, I would have shown up fifteen minutes late myself if I weren't already nearby. Let me guess. Some big meeting regarding his next major client."

"Of course. I expected you to look, I don't know, more run-down. You know, from everything that's going on. I wish you'd let me come to court." Andie's loving hug hello feels more welcome now than ever before.

"Andie, what would your kids think if, sometime in the future, they found a picture or video of you in the courtroom or on the courthouse steps with a mob of reporters asking you God knows what about me? Or worse, something they found in your closet or Sebbi's. Better they see me getting all that unwanted attention."

"Tell me what's going on. How's the trial going? Are you winning or losing? Is Attorney Brian what's his name any good?" Andie ignores me and bounces up and down with the anticipation of a young child on Christmas morning.

I'm talking in a low voice. "Andie, please sit down. My attorney told me not to share anything about the courtroom activities." Even though the din of the other patrons carries in all directions, I still look around to make sure no one is listening. I don't want anyone overhearing me. "Brian continually harps that the press could be lurking anywhere."

"Jordan, it's me. I'm not going to tell anyone anything. Not even Sebbi. Okay, maybe Sebbi."

"All I'm going to say is that I'm doing well personally." I give her something, hoping to satisfy her.

"I can't imagine what you're going through."

I place my hand on Andie's hand, silently pleading with her to move on. "It's been a good day, and I just want to spend the end of it with my best friend. Can we change the subject? How are the boys?"

"The boys are great. The catering business is getting off to a slow start, but I remember that was the case . . . wow, almost seven years ago." Andie takes a sip of the Barolo I had taken the liberty of ordering for both of us when I first arrived.

Traditionally, Andie and I start with a glass of red wine; if the night is going well, we will end with a much stronger spirit, the variety not yet determined. "Do you remember how many nights during my residency you made me come over and taste-test food for new recipes you brainstormed? I swear, I must have gained twenty pounds in six months." I'm happy to accept the soreness in my cheeks from smiling.

"Do you remember coming to help me with my first real catering job and spilling almost half the soup onto the floor of my car on the way there?" Andie is laughing now, but that day almost ended our friendship.

"Yes, and there was still enough for twice the number of people. Didn't you lose money on that job?"

Andie wags a finger at me while she defends herself. "Okay, I'll admit it, portion control has been my nemesis, but I'm not going to ever get caught empty-handed. Even if it lowers my profit margin."

The wine is starting to have its effect on both of us. A heavy sigh escapes me. "Andie, it's good to be here with you. Truthfully, I needed to see you."

"Jordan, we have been through a lot over the years. We have always been there for each other, and that's never going to change."

Whether it is the wine or the company, I begin to speak freely. "Andie, this court case is turning out to be a rollercoaster ride. It feels like the prosecutor is just making up stuff, the judge scares me, and I don't know if the jury will see through all of the legal smoke and mirrors." I continue for a few more minutes, unburdening my fears to the only person I know will not repeat any of it.

We continue to enjoy Leon's Underworld, drinking and reminiscing for the next several hours—laughing and lamenting through our past and present. It's what we do. For me, the present woes are very obvious. For Andie, it's a bit more complicated, as she feels pressure to return to a career she left at its peak. Going back means pulling herself away from the boys and the man she loves dearly.

It's nearly eleven, and Andie and I have been drinking and fine dining on chicken wings, potato skins, and even nachos with extra cheese. This is not unusual when we get together at Leon's. We have an understanding: Whenever one of us calls and requests Leon's, we show up, no judgments made.

Andie makes several attempts to focus on the hands of her watch, an old analog, gifted to her by her grandmother. She smiles as she announces the last round. "Tonight's parting drink is an orange martini." It's her turn to order the last drink of the night, and the rule states that there can be no questioning the choice—just part of our Leon's tradition.

After one final toast and a duo of very audible slurps, another tradition, we each open the Uber app on our phones to plan a safe trip home. I smile at Andie. "That's all I need at this moment. Can you imagine how long I would be locked up in that courthouse suite if I got pulled over for driving while under the influence now? They might as well bring that uptight Judge Harris into the suite. She could sentence me to do my time right there in that damn room."

Andie is confused by the flurry of terms I just threw at her. "Can you have visitors at the courthouse whenever?"

We both laugh as we start our customary hugs and kisses goodbye. A quirky "Love you, sis" is exchanged as we climb into our Ubers.

Many glasses of wine and one orange martini later, I'm home and in need of sleep. I drink two large glasses of water, hoping to ward off any post-drinking hangover that might try to accompany me to court tomorrow. It would still be worth it. We haven't been to Leon's since before all my legal troubles started. I hit the pillow, carefree, something that has not happened for a long time. A strange thought gallops through my mind. I wonder if Judge Harris ever goes to Leon's Underworld.

CHAPTER 15
MEDIA MAYHEM

IT'S seven thirty in the morning, and my cell phone squawks for attention. After last night's Underworld experience, the hot shower feels too good to leave. Since the customary recap didn't happen, I'm sure that Mom and Dad waited as long as they could before feverishly pressing number after number to find out if I'm okay. I had decided to skip it somewhere around the middle of the third glass of Malbec. The wine seemed a better option than reliving even a good day as a defendant.

The cell on my nightstand bounces hastily, wailing like it's in utter pain. I grab my phone. "Hmm, not the 'rents, Brian." Seven missed calls, and just as many texts. *CALL NOW, NEED TO TALK NOW, WHERE ARE YOU? CALL ME BACK NOW.* A nervous sweat negates the shower. "What the hell is going on?"

I'm about to hit redial when my phone screams again. "Where have you been?" Brian shouts. I can almost see the steam rising from his ears.

"I was in the shower. What's the problem?" I'm standing in my bedroom naked and only half dried off. I didn't plan this call well.

"Have you seen the morning news?"

"No." The sweat is now a river down my back.

Brian's breathing is loud, almost at seething. "Your fans from the crowdsourcing site are furious at the treatment you have been getting in the courtroom."

"What?"

"The morning news is reporting that social media has been

exploding regarding the 'ups and downs' you have been forced to endure during your trial. Some anonymous informant posted on the SupportMyCause update page with inside information coming from a close friend of yours. I told you not to comment in any way! Exactly what did you say and to whom did you say it?"

"Brian, slow down. I don't know what you're talking about. I went out with Andie last night. She asked about how the case was going, but I said nothing. In fact, I changed the subject." There is a long pause before I continue. "Wait, I did tell Andie that I was glad to be out and that the case was like a rollercoaster ride. I may have said something like, some days it feels like it's going well, and others it feels like it's all over. What could she glean from that?"

His huffing increases in volume. "Apparently, your friend Andie went home last night and posted an update or told someone else about your conversation. Then it was posted on the website. The people who donated to you are upset. They fired back attacks at everyone. Turn on the news, watch it, and then meet me at the diner at nine. Jordan, this is bad, and we have to get ahead of it." Brian hung up the phone.

I press the button on my phone. "Call Andie." I press the button again to cancel the call. "It will only get worse. How could you, Andie?" The television remote shakes in my hand—tears flow as fear spins out of control within me.

The news anchor drones on about this and that, and finally, the story about me comes on.

"Supporters of Dr. Jordan Carey are outraged at the treatment this local hero is receiving during her trial. A source close to Dr. Carey posted yesterday that she spoke with the doctor personally. SupportMyCause, the website that originally hosted Dr. Carey's campaign, is withholding the name of the source at this time. According to the posting, Dr. Carey appears to be well, but she is tired and stated that the trial is like a rollercoaster ride. The source also states that Dr. Carey is forced to sit there staring straight

ahead. What she thought were loyal employees and patients are testifying against her. Her attorney, Brian Freeland, shows glimmers of greatness and at other times allows the fallen doctor to take hit after hit. Lastly, the source says Dr. Carey noted that Judge Harris and the jury look at her as if she has already been found guilty. Stay tuned as we await more from this source on what is now being looked at as a landmark case in the fight against healthcare injustice in the United States."

"NO, NO, NO! Andie, what have you done?" The chiming of a ringtone interrupts my horrified outburst. It's Andie. "No effing way." Rage replaces fear. "Inhale, exhale, inhale, exhale. Andie—"

"I'm so, so sorry. I must have been more drunk than I thought last night. I got home, and Sebbi asked—you know how he is. I told him, and he said I should try to help you. He said you needed emotional support." Tears and short, choked breaths make it difficult for Andie to speak. "I . . . I couldn't sleep. Sebbi was asleep, and I thought about what he said. I got up and went to the computer. I couldn't help myself, and now it's out of control."

"Andie, I can't right now. I have to deal with this. Brian is already trying to get ahead of it." Click. "How did she think she was helping?"

Ping. A text from Andie. *Sorry, I know you're mad. What can I do? I'm so sorry.*

I start to text a response, but think better of it. "I don't have time for this now."

I can see Brian sitting at a table, glaring at the door, anticipating my entrance. All the clanging of silverware, the pounding of coffee mugs, and the clambering of voices aren't going to hide me from his backlash. The Safe Haven Diner has lost its mystique at this moment.

"Sit, please." Brian's voice is cold and lifeless.

I remove the scarf and hat camouflage. "Brian, I'm sorry. I handled Andie—"

"Judge Harris wants to see everyone in her chambers before court. This is not going to go well. I hope that she doesn't hold you or us in contempt of court. Did you have to mention her and the jury last night? What were you thinking? When we get into the judge's chamber, you are going to apologize and explain that you didn't exactly say what was printed. You're going to tell the judge it will never happen again and apologize once more. Am I clear?"

Ashamed of myself, I answer quietly, "Yes, I understand and will do exactly as you say."

Brian picks up the files scattered across the table and starts reading them. For the next twenty minutes, we sit in silence, except for the occasional sipping sound Brian accidentally makes while drinking his coffee. The quiet is broken by Brian telling me it's time to go.

"The number of reporters will be at least double today. You're an even hotter commodity than the cop shooting trial. And I don't mean that in a good way. Say nothing, look straight ahead, don't look shameful or cocky. Just don't do or say anything."

"Okay, Brian."

I take the hat and scarf out. Brian shakes his head. "The reporters are going to know it's you either way, so I don't want you to hide yourself. You'll look guilty. Remember, look straight ahead—"

"Okay, I hear you. Please don't repeat it again."

The reporters have decided that the yellow line in the road is no longer an unpassable barrier. Microphones and taping devices of every kind are shoved into my face as we leave the Safe Haven's protection. I'm about to turn and head back into the diner when Brian grabs my arm. Stepping in front of me, he clears a path for us with his briefcase in hand, and we cross the street, head up the courthouse steps, and enter the building. He whispers to the guard at the door to give us a few seconds head start. The guard nods and winks. It's like a bad old movie, and yet I'm grateful for it.

Once we're through the metal detectors and into the elevator, the guard releases his grip on the outer doors of the courthouse. Brian looks at me, and I mouth a thank-you. There is no response from him.

Fighting back tears and shame, I lean in. "Brian, I didn't know—"

"You can apologize to me later. Right now, we need to concentrate on the judge and jury. Let me do the talking until I tell you to speak." Brian sounds softer and more fatherlike again.

Speaking of fathers. I didn't call my parents. "Brian, I need to call my parents. They need to know I'm okay. They must be going—"

"There's no time for that. If there's time before court, you can call them then." The doors open. "Remember, don't say anything until I say so."

I nod.

"Please be seated," Judge Harris sharply commands. "This meeting is off the record and is for fact-finding and clarification of the news hitting the airwaves regarding this trial. I'm sure that none of this comes as a surprise to any of you." Judge Harris is standing with her hands on her hips. She is not wearing her robe, but is no less intimidating.

"Your Honor—"

"Mr. Freeland, I would like it if you could wait just a moment longer so that I might finish my thoughts."

"Yes, of course, Your Honor. My apologies."

"Thank you. I am very disturbed by the turn of events in this morning's news reports. Dr. Carey, do you feel that you have been treated poorly or unjustly in my courtroom?"

"Your Honor . . ."

"Mr. Freeland, as we are here unofficially, I would like to hear from Dr. Carey directly. Do you have a problem with my request? If so, we can do this on the record."

"No, Your Honor."

Barrens leans forward. "Your Honor, perhaps it is best if we get this on the record. The prosecution does not want to participate in anything that might feel unjust to Dr. Carey or her due process."

"Mr. Barrens, I would like to first find out if Dr. Carey feels there is any unjust treatment. If Dr. Carey feels that she is being treated unjustly, I'll bring in the court reporter, and we'll go on the record. Does that work for you?"

"Yes, Your Honor." Attorney Barrens looks at me, then leans back in his chair.

Judge Harris is now more perturbed. "I will ask again. Dr. Carey, do you feel that you are being treated poorly and/or unjustly in my courtroom?"

"No, Your Honor." Staring at the conference table is all I can manage.

"Then why the comments to this mysterious close source?"

"I was out with a friend last night, and she asked if I was okay. I answered yes and told her that some days it feels like we're winning and others it feels like it's all over."

"That's it?" Judge Harris is looking at me with considerable skepticism.

"No, as the night wore on and we drank a bit more, I may have let it slip out that I feel like you and the jury look at me as if I'm already found guilty." Any thought of making eye contact with Judge Harris fades quickly.

"What about the comments about your attorney and Mr. Barrens?"

"Honestly, Your Honor, I don't recall saying anything that even comes close to those comments. But that doesn't mean I didn't imply them."

"Mr. Freeland, Mr. Barrens, do either of you have anything to add to this mess?"

"Your Honor, my client made an innocent mistake. One she will not repeat. I can assure this." Everyone in the room is looking at me.

"I have nothing to add, Your Honor, except that the jury may be looked at as tainted in the end, and whatever decision they make may be under scrutiny." Barrens continues to fan the flames, shaking his head for added effect. "I just don't know how we come back from this without a mistrial."

"Mr. Barrens is correct; the jury will be under scrutiny. This trial is now truly a high-profile case, and the jury will be under fire no matter what decision they make. Dr. Carey, I believe you did not mean for this to occur, but if it happens again, I will hold you in contempt of court. And you will watch the rest of this trial from one of my jail cells. As for the jury, I will advise them that the media is sensationalizing the facts and that they are to disregard any reports they have heard or read. As for a mistrial, Mr. Barrens, I'll advise you not to overplay your position. Bailiff, please." Judge Harris gives a hand gesture to the bailiff at the door, signaling that the meeting is now concluded.

In the corridor, I pull Brian aside. "Do I have a minute to call my parents?"

"Make it quick. And say nothing that the media can use to cause more of a mess. Understand?"

All eyes are focused on me. Brian stands between the crowd and me as he pretends not to eavesdrop. I exhale and try not to think about Andie as I call my parents.

"Jordan, are you okay? The press, the court, that Judge, we have to come today. We can make sure you're not getting railroaded."

"Dad, it's o—"

"Jordan, your father is right. We are coming down to the court, and we'll show them—"

"Mom, stop, please. It's all been handled. Everything is fine. I can't go into it right now. Please, stay home. I promise I'll call you later."

Brian touches my shoulder. "We have to go in."

The packed corridor is a frenzy of murmurs and overt questions. "Brian, it's chaos." My voice crumbles a bit. "Which are the reporters and which are just nosey?"

"It's not like on television, but media mayhem is real. Just focus on getting to Courtroom Five."

I look at Brian. "Media mayhem?"

CHAPTER 16
JUDGE HARRIS'S LITTLE SISTER

"PLEASE BE SEATED. We start today with an interesting but disturbing dilemma. Good morning, ladies and gentlemen of the jury. As you have probably heard or read, Dr. Carey confided in a close friend last evening."

A restlessness runs through the jury. Judge Harris continues. "As I was saying. I sat with Dr. Carey and both attorneys this morning to discuss the comments that Dr. Carey allegedly made to her friend. Dr. Carey stated that the comments on the website were inaccurate and did not accurately reflect her feelings. After considerable thought, I concluded that she was telling me the truth. I believe Dr. Carey's remarks were misunderstood or taken out of context by the individual who posted the comments. It is also my belief that social media sites may have taken some liberties with their commentaries. It is not my place to speculate on the news being reported other than to inform you, the jury, to disregard any information from this morning's pre-court events. This trial is going to receive a great deal of news coverage as we move forward, so please remain vigilant and only consider what is said inside this courtroom. If this becomes an impossibility, I will have no choice but to sequester you." Judge Harris is facing the jury, but her peripheral gaze is locked on me. Instinctively, the jury members' heads turn, almost in unison, in my direction.

Judge Harris waits for a moment, then continues. "We will now proceed with this trial. Mr. Barrens, please call your next witness."

"Thank you, Your Honor. The prosecution would like to call Catherine Hawthorne."

Barrens waits for the witness to be sworn in. "Ms. Hawthorne, can you tell us where you work and what your specialty is?"

"I work for the FDA, and my specialty is investigating drug trafficking of all kinds. Sometimes—"

Brian lets out a sigh of disgust. "Objection, Your Honor. Again, the use of the word 'drug' incriminates my client on many levels."

"Overruled. Ms. Hawthorne is referring to the specialty of her occupation and not to the defendant. The witness may finish her statement."

Like Judge Harris, Ms. Hawthorne shows no emotion in her delivery. "Thank you, Your Honor. Sometimes I'm called in to testify on matters of the legality of how a medication is dispensed by a pharmaceutical company, a pharmacy, or, like here, by a doctor."

"Thank you, Ms. Hawthorne. Have you reviewed Dr. Carey's case?" Barrens points to a large stack of papers sitting on the prosecutor's table.

"Yes, I have."

Attorney Barrens's previous tablemates have done well in choosing Catherine Hawthorne. She is a younger version of Judge Harris. She wears gold wire-rimmed glasses. Her hair is shoulder-length, although sandy in color compared to Judge Harris's deeper brown. Ms. Hawthorne speaks with a nearly identical slow, deliberate cadence and tone to the judge. Both have this foreboding dominance that would make muggers turn and run if they met in a dark alley. Their names even share the same initials: Constance Harris versus Catherine Hawthorne.

All this must scream instant credibility to the jury. It makes me recall when I first opened my practice, I advertised in the local Catholic church bulletin. It was like God was recommending me.

"Can you share what you determined regarding Dr. Carey's collection and dispensing of drugs, sorry, medications in her office?" Barrens looks at Brian.

"Yes. Dr. Carey did not follow safety regulations, nor did she obtain any special permits for dispensing the medications. Dr. Carey did not write a prescription for the medication she was dispensing, and there is no evidence that her patients signed any documents stating that they knew they were receiving medication that had already been prescribed to someone else or that they had the right to purchase newly prescribed medications elsewhere."

"Ms. Hawthorne, aren't doctors allowed to give medications out from their offices?"

"Yes, but those medications are samples, and they should have been clearly marked as such and with 'not for resale' printed on them."

Barrens holds up a photo marked Exhibit Three. "Ms. Hawthorne, do you recognize this photo?"

"Yes, that's a photograph of the unsecured cabinet where Dr. Carey stored the medication she collected. It should have been able to be locked when not in use."

"Did Dr. Carey violate state and FDA safety laws or rules with the process of collecting and distributing medications she, without proper preparation, implemented?"

"Yes. Most certainly."

"Lastly, is it your expert opinion that because Dr. Carey was not well versed on these safety processes and laws, which she violated, she placed her patients in harm's way?"

"Objection, Your Honor. The prosecutor is being overly dramatic in this verbose and convoluted manner of questioning. He is obviously trying to curry favor with the jury."

Judge Harris removes her gold-rimmed glasses, looks at them as if to notice the similarity to the witness's eyewear, and then places them on the bench. "Sustained. Mr. Barrens, just ask the questions, and leave the theatrics at the door."

"Yes, Your Honor. My apologies. Ms. Hawthorne, is it your opinion that Dr. Carey placed her patients in, or rather, at risk by creating her medication distribution method?"

"Most definitely." The witness says without pause.

"Thank you, Ms. Hawthorne. No more questions, Your Honor."

I look at the jury, and they appear to believe every word. Hell, I would if I were them.

"Mr. Freeland, if you please?"

Brian nods at the judge. "Ms. Hawthorne, did Dr. Carey ever sell any of the medications she collected, or any of the medication she bought herself, to any of her patients?"

"I did not see any evidence that she sold the medications."

"Then, that's a no. She didn't ever sell the medications, did she?"

"I guess that's correct."

"The violations you previously stated while Attorney Barrens was questioning you. Were they for the resale of medications or just medication distribution in general?"

"I think, technically, they were created regarding the resale of medications by physicians."

"Therefore, Dr. Carey did not violate any law or rule you suggested earlier, technically or otherwise?"

"I, um, still believe that she was wrong."

"Ms. Hawthorne, your opinion here is as an expert and is based on the understanding of the facts presented and the law and rules that accompany them, is that correct?"

"Yes."

"Then I'll ask you again. If the rules and facts are geared towards the resale of medications by a physician, and Dr. Carey did not sell the medications to her patients, did she violate those rules and laws you stated?"

"No, but that's a technicality. She shouldn't have been handing them out so freely."

Brian gives a look of utter surprise. "Ms. Hawthorne, are you suggesting that Dr. Carey *should* have been selling the medications she collected?"

"No, of course not. If she charged for them, that would be against the law."

"So, you're now stating that her carefully collecting, verifying, and responsibly, but free of charge, giving the medications to her patients is not breaking the law?"

Catherine Hawthorne wrings her hands, almost stomping her feet. "Yes, no. I'm not sure."

"That's okay, Ms. Hawthorne. No more questions." Brian starts his return to the table.

"Redirect, Your Honor."

"Proceed, Mr. Barrens."

"Ms. Hawthorne, as a seasoned FDA investigator, can you please tell us what the dangers of Dr. Carey's actions are? What should she have done differently to protect her patients with regard to the collection and distribution of medications?"

"Objection. The witness, by her own testimony, stated that she is an expert in the rules and laws governing physicians' resale of medications. Since that did not occur here, her opinion is not of an expert nature."

Judge Harris sits quietly for a moment. "Overruled. I will allow the witness to answer, but I will intervene if I think the response strays too far. Please answer the question."

"Yes. Okay. It does seem like a reckless process. Before starting her collection and distribution plan, Dr. Carey should have obtained further training and knowledge on how to proceed safely and correctly."

Barrens tries to calm her down. "Ms. Hawthorne, what about the security of the medication in the cabinet in Dr. Carey's office?"

"Uh, yes. Dr. Carey took a risk by leaving the medications in an unsecured location. Every pharmaceutical site, whether a pharmacy, distribution center, hospital, or manufacturing facility, stores medications in a secure space. I don't think Dr. Carey made it as safe as she could have."

"Ms. Hawthorne, there has already been testimony that patients placed various forms of money into the so-called 'Pill Box.' Would this constitute patients illegally paying for medications?"

"Objection. Come on, Your Honor. There isn't any law anywhere that says it's illegal to put money in a box. Nor does it constitute prepayment for medication. It's not even inferred anywhere."

"Sustained. Mr. Freeland, you may make objections, but you will not give attitude with them. Continue, Mr. Barrens."

"Again, Ms. Hawthorne, what is the protocol for storing medications?"

"They must be locked up and be secure at all times."

"Thank you again, Ms. Hawthorne. No more questions." Attorney Barrens's glance at the jury causes Judge Harris to clear her throat.

"Your Honor, I have just a few more questions, please." Brian waits for Judge Harris's approval before continuing. "Ms. Hawthorne, doctors have samples in their office all the time, correct?"

"Yes."

"Those samples are kept in a room or cabinet where patients are not allowed access to them. Is that correct also?"

"Yes, I suppose."

"In Dr. Carey's case, were the medications stored in a room or cabinet that patients were not allowed to access?"

An audible sigh escapes from the witness. "Again, technically, yes."

"Can doctors buy medications from medical catalogues and dispense them?"

"Yes, but—"

"Could the money the doctor used, whether it's on a credit card or by check, come from monies that patients paid, either directly through co-pays or indirectly from the patient's insurance company? Technically speaking."

"Well . . . yes, when you put it that way."

"So, is there a difference between the money those doctors used and the money Dr. Carey used?"

Another heavy sigh, this time from one of the second stringers at the prosecutor's table. Catherine Hawthorne glares at Attorney Barrens. "No, there certainly is not."

"So, then the laws and rules you stated earlier don't apply to dispensing these medications to patients?"

The witness's eyes are locked on Barrens. "No, I can see that I was mistaken."

"Did Dr. Carey sell any of the medication she dispensed to her patients?"

Ms. Hawthorne shakes her head and lets out her own sigh. "No. I can now see no actual evidence of Dr. Carey selling the medications."

Brian pushes the point home. "Therefore, Dr. Carey, like thousands of other doctors, did not violate any laws. Is that correct too?"

"Yes, that is totally correct." Catherine Hawthorne's final answer is filled with vile contention, but not for Brian. Her unwavering gaze into Barrens's soul tells the entire story.

"Thank you, Ms. Hawthorne. No more questions."

"The witness may step down. We will break for lunch." The bang of Judge Harris's gavel is a rescue beacon for Attorney Barrens, but not for his team.

"All rise," the bailiff says right on cue.

Brian says nothing as he packs his notes away. We stand and

walk towards the door when Attorney Barrens stops us. "Brian, I would like to ask the judge for a continuance until tomorrow. I just found out my last witness will not be able to get here in time because he's tied up in another matter. Will you back me up on this?"

"Yes, not a problem." Brian smiles; the attorney code is at play. Now they are square.

"Thanks. Besides, I can't take another round like the last one." Barrens is looking at the new team at his table.

"I did have more, but I thought you had enough for today." Brian laughs. "I'm sure you'll find a way to get me back."

This time Barrens chuckles. "That's how it works. No hard feelings, right?"

I pull Brian into our courthouse suite. "Why are we letting them get away? If they can't produce a witness, it's their problem!"

"This is not a courtroom TV drama. Besides, Judge Harris would grant it anyway."

I slump into a chair. "Then why did he ask you to help him?"

"It's the right thing to do, on both sides." Brian sits down beside me. "Look, we are doing well. This isn't a personal war for the attorneys. It's business, and business has rules and etiquette that need to be followed. Let's sit here and wait for Erin to bring lunch."

The expression on my face is one of only half surprise. "Why are we staying here for lunch again?"

"Do you really want to face the ever-growing mob waiting outside? Do you want to be hit with a barrage of questions about this morning's news?" Brian isn't really looking for an answer.

I question. "By the way, why are we the only ones who use this room?"

Brian smiles, flashing his big white teeth. "Oh, we're not. I just reserved it from eleven to one every day for the next two weeks." There's a knock at the door, and he gets up to let Erin into the room.

He steps aside, and Erin and I make eye contact. "Hi, Erin."

"Hi, Jordan." Erin is her pleasant self.

"What's it like out there?" Brian asks.

"Let's just say, it's better to eat lunch here today."

Brian grins as he looks at me. "Playing one show here, in this room, every day from eleven to one for the next two weeks. Sold out!"

CHAPTER 17
AN OFF AFTERNOON

BRIAN and I are back at our table. Judge Harris is settling in. Mr. Barrens stands, clears his throat, and looks to Judge Harris. "Your Honor, unfortunately, my next expert is delayed in another court matter. He has informed me that he cannot make it here today. He assures me that this issue is out of his control and he wishes to extend his deepest apologies. I, too, apologize to the court as I ask for a continuance until tomorrow morning. He promises he will be here."

Judge Harris is not concealing her dismay. "Mr. Freeland, were you made aware of this development, and do you have any objection to Mr. Barrens's request?"

"Yes, Your Honor, I am aware, and no, I haven't any objection."

"Mr. Barrens, just to satisfy my own curiosity, when did you find out that your expert was not going to be here in time?"

"Just after court broke for lunch, Your Honor."

"In the future, if any such developments come up, please bring them to my attention immediately." Judge Harris is scowling at both attorneys. "Court is dismissed until tomorrow at 9:30 a.m. sharp. On behalf of both Mr. Barrens and Mr. Freeland, I apologize to the court for their keeping us all here without cause." With that last bit of venom, Judge Harris bangs her gavel, places it loudly on the bench, and leaves the courtroom. The poor bailiff is barely able to play his part on time.

We decide to call it a day, too, and that means I'm free, at least for today. During our escape from the courthouse and the reporters, I debate asking Brian if I can return Andie's call, but I think better of it. He said I can't mention anything about the trial. He didn't say anything about visiting friends.

Andie is close to tears. "Jordan, come in. I'm so sorry. I want you to know that I deleted my SupportMyCause account this morning, Jordan. I've also banned myself from any social media until the end of your trial. And Jordan, you should also know—"

"Andie, Andie! Stop saying my name, calm down. I'm not mad anymore. I came over here with much more to say, but let's leave it alone; it's done. Talking about the trial or anything related to it is dangerous. So, let's just drop it."

"It was a mistake, a bad, bad mistake."

I sigh. "Andie, I won't stay if we continue to talk about it."

"All right, all right. How about a late lunch or early dinner? Will you stay for that?" Andie begs.

"No. I just wanted to come here and tell you that I understand and that we're fine."

"But I want to show you how sorry I am."

I haven't even taken off my jacket, and I'm already heading back toward the front door. Staying would be the good friend thing to do, but I'm too worried that I'll begin saying things I'll regret later. "Honestly, Andie, everything should be fine in a few days or so. Stop worrying about it."

"Jordan. Jordan! Wait, please." Andie hugs me from behind. I step through the threshold. She yells, "I love you."

I keep walking. "I know." Turning to look would be the beginning of a terrible mistake.

The ride home is filled with thoughts of everything I wanted to say to Andie about her actions and about the trial. It's Thursday at three thirty in the afternoon. Typically, there would be three more hours of treating patients, writing charts, and oh yes, hiding the pills stolen from the "Pill Box" and the cash from the "Money Box." Sitting there in my sparse apartment, the anger flourishes. I practiced medicine in one of the most impoverished areas in town. Can anyone really think I was doing it for the pills and the money? Now I might lose my license and my freedom. I stare at the mirror hanging down the short hallway. "Stop! Stop it now!" A deep breath. "Your patients needed you, and you stepped up. You were making a difference. Pity is not a good color on you. Stop it right now!"

My cell phone rings. It's time to give a recap of today. "How long have I been standing in front of that mirror?"

Thankfully, my parents don't have social media accounts. Imagine how angry Brian would be if he knew how much detail I have shared with them. "Hi, Mom, I'll wait until you put the phone on speaker."

"Hi honey, it's your father."

"Yes, I know. Hi, Dad."

"Is everything okay? We saw the news. Who told the people on the webby thing about you? Did they also call the news stations? Did you lawyer, Bobby—"

"It's Brian with an *i* or Byran with a *y*. It's definitely not Bobby."

"Okay, Brian or Byran. Is he going to sue them for lying about you? They could hurt your trial. Has he thought about that?"

"Everything is fine. It's been handled and no one is getting sued or hurt. We were let out early for good behavior."

"Jordan, that only happens after you get to prison." Mom scoffs.

I had no witty comeback. "The prosecutor's next expert was delayed, so the judge ended court early today."

Dad waffles. "Are you sure you're okay, honey? Should we come over, or do you want to come over here?"

"I'm fine . . ." I realize that I'm about to go down the Andie rabbit hole again and stop mid-sentence.

"Jordan dear, you don't sound okay. What aren't you telling us?" Mothers can always tell.

"It's only four o'clock, I'll take an Uber to your house and have dinner with the two of you. Does that work? Wait, why did you call me so early?"

"The reporter said your trial ended suddenly. We got worried, so we called."

"Linda, he said it ended suddenly for the day."

Mom ignores Dad. She speaks over the sounds of clanging pots. "Darling, yes, of course. Come over, I'm already starting an early dinner."

Dad's volume is low and muffled. "Jordan, it's your father. Mom is starting dinner. She can't hear us now. We want you to know, it wasn't us. We would never tell anyone anything."

"It's okay, Dad. I know who it was. It's all done. Nothing came of it. I'll fill you in over dinner."

"It should be ready by the time you get here. We'll see you soon. I'll tell your mother you're on your way. Love you. Bye." The phone call ends with the sounds of a meal well underway.

Dinner with my parents goes as expected. They practically trip over one another as they spend two hours doting on me. Being an only child does have its perks. I, like most adults with a busy life, don't visit them enough. They spent eighteen years making me the center of their universe, and then I left. I promise that when this is all over, I will visit them more often. After a day that started with my bones being pecked at by vultures, it was nice to end on a good note.

Eight o'clock and I have nothing to do. No charts to review, no emails or phone calls to return, and yet that overwhelmed feeling is still present. Thoughts of Barrens only having one more witness to put on the stand and Brian showing the jury the truth about me and my intentions brings me some relief.

For the first time I notice my hand trembling as it holds the remote. The television awakens to the same local cable news channel from this morning. The news anchor is covering stories from around town. Finally, he gets to the court cases. The police shooting is being discussed first. I'm happy about that. Next, a large and not very flattering photo of me is flashed on the screen. My hair appears windblown, and not in a good way. They must have doctored the photo to make me appear withered and sleep-deprived. "Do I really look like that?"

The trial against Dr. Carey came to an unexpected early recess today as the prosecution was unable to present its final witness. This is probably a good thing for the young doctor. She certainly did not help her situation with the previous evening's comments of mistreatment by just about everyone flooding the internet. For more, let's go to Sherman Watts.

The station puts a copy of what Andie posted up on the screen for their viewers to read along.

Thanks, Bob. According to the source, whose name the hosting site SupportMyCause, will not release, Dr. Carey stated that Judge Harris and the jury have already found her guilty. It sounds like Dr. Carey feels she is being railroaded and the trial is just a formality. I spoke to my contact in the prosecutor's office today, and he assured me that this is not the case at all. My contact went on to say that this is another example of poor judgment on Dr. Carey's part. We can only sit back and wait for the trial to unfold. Bob, back to you.

Apparently fake news has taken an interest in my life. Another tap of the remote and the television falls dormant. The newscast spirals me downward. I'm uncertain if it's minutes or hours later when my phone rings.

"Hi, Jordan. It's Dad. Mom is here too. We just saw that Sherman guy say all kinds of lies about you. Did you see it?"

"Yes, I happened to be watching it too." I roll my eyes, pull the phone away from my mouth, and let out a deep sigh.

"Jordan, don't you believe a word of what that man said. Your father and I didn't teach you to make poor judgments." My parents are just as good at tag-team statements as they are making it about themselves.

That's what they thought was the worst part of the story. I'm not surprised, but they mean well. "It's okay. I know I did it for the right reasons." Without consideration, my mantra escapes from my lips causing me to smirk.

Dad unloads rapid-fire. "Jordan, are you being railroaded? Do they have it in for you? I see this happening all the time. Is your lawyer good enough? They always go after the little guy."

"Dad, it's fine. Actually, we're winning. Like I told you at dinner, Brian has been knocking out every witness they put on the stand."

"Maybe I should come down to the courthouse and do some knocking out myself!" I'm confident that Dad is pacing the living room floor throwing punches in the air.

"Dad, that won't help, and you know it. Please stay home and let Brian do his job." Visions of Joseph Carey getting physical force me to quickly mute the phone to blurt out laughs. My Dad is a nerd. He's never thrown a punch. I'm fairly certain that a knockout blow is not in his wheelhouse.

Mom chimes in, "Only if you're sure you're okay."

"Yes, I'm okay. I'll call you tomorrow after court." I hang up the phone. One more laugh escapes at the vision.

My cell phone rings again. "Andie, it's late, and I don't have the energy to go over this again. We're fine, really."

"Jordan, please, you have to hear me out. I want to tell—"

"Andie, I love you, but today has been a long one. After the trial, I'll let you apologize however you want, for however long you want. Good night, Andie."

Another eruption from the cell phone—Andie again. I let it go to voicemail. Last night's drinking is starting to catch up with me.

One more glance at the mirror. “First Andie, then my parents, and now Andie again. Don’t forget Sherman Watts; this afternoon off has really been an off afternoon.”

CHAPTER 18
MR. DIAZ DOES US A SOLID

BRIAN IS ALREADY at the Safe Haven Diner. He doesn't like to be outdone.

"Good morning, Brian. You're here early."

"Good morning, Jordan. I trust that there are no surprises from last night?"

"No. I had dinner with my parents, stopped at Andie's for a brief moment, and then went home to watch Sherman Watts degrade me. How about you?"

Brian presses his lips. "Andie's"

"Just to tell her we're okay and that we'll talk about it when this is all over. She wanted me to stay, but I didn't."

"Well, I didn't have as much fun as you, but it was nice to spend a little extra time with my family."

I take a seat across from Brian. "So, how do we look for today?"

Brian folds his hands in front of him. His gold wedding band clangs against the aged metal table. "I'm not going to lie to you. Today's witness might be a tough one to break. He's giving testimony on how and why medical licenses are revoked. He'll talk about the concerns the state licensing board has with out-of-line doctors. I'll look for some way to stop him, but there isn't much I'm going to be able to do to refute him. Revoking of a medical license is up to the state board, and their decision is on a case-by-case basis. We may have to ride this one out."

"Thanks for the heads-up. I think I know what you're going to say, so I'll say it for you. You want me to study the grain on the judge's bench."

"Actually, no. Today, I want you to look at the witness and show remorse, and maybe a slight bit of shock. Today, it's your career you're fighting for. Show him you're passionate about what you do. That's really why you stuck your neck out for your patients. Don't oversell it, but show commitment."

Heat rises from my neck into my face. I grit my teeth trying not to yell. "I won't be selling anything! I *am* passionate about my patients and their well-being!"

Brian holds his hands in the air. "That's overselling."

The walk up the courthouse steps is uneventful. The reporters are chewing on the bones of the police shooting trial. Brian whispers, "That trial ends today. Word at the diner is the guy might walk. The prosecutor is young, and he's made a number of bad choices that caused crucial evidence to be tossed out."

"I wish he were on my case."

Brian snorts. "Me, too."

"All rise for the Honorable Judge Harris." The bailiff calls out.

"Good morning, everyone. Mr. Barrens, I trust your witness is here and ready to take the stand?"

"Yes, Your Honor."

"Very well. I would like to remind the jury that we are still under the orders and conditions I set forth yesterday. Mr. Barrens, please call your witness."

"Thank you, Your Honor. I call Mr. Horatio Diaz to the stand."

Diaz, in his late fifties, approaches the stand in a dark gray suit that fits his toned but average height frame well. His walk is confident with a pace that screams authority. Diaz is clean-shaven, with a chiseled chin and black hair neatly trimmed around his ear. Only the wrinkles on his face give away his age. He might be a bureaucrat, but I'm guessing there is definitely a military background in his history. The jury intently watches every move he makes.

Barrens stands behind the prosecutor's table. "Mr. Diaz, could you please state what you do and why I have brought you here today?"

"My name is Horatio Diaz; I sit on the state licensing board. You brought me here today to testify as an expert witness regarding medical licensure and the guidelines for revoking a medical license."

"Mr. Diaz, are you in any way involved in Dr. Carey's medical licensure investigation?"

"Not at this time. But I will be involved in the final decision after the ongoing investigation of Dr. Carey is completed."

"Is it fair to assume that the answers you give today are as an expert on medical licensing and not on the specifics of Dr. Carey's licensure investigation?" Barrens words are precisely chosen and practiced.

"That is correct, sir."

"Mr. Diaz, how many years have you been part of the medical licensing board?"

"For over nine years."

"In those nine-plus years, have you ever run across cases similar to Dr. Carey's?"

"Objection, the prosecution has already stated that the witness will only give expert statements of a general nature." Brian's voice is uncharacteristically loud.

Judge Harris looks at Brian as if to warn him and then turns to Barrens. "Sustained. Mr. Barrens, you did state that the testimony of this witness would be for general purposes only."

"Yes, and thank you, Your Honor. Mr. Diaz, in cases where doctors have shown flagrant disregard for their patients' well-being or for the safety of the community, how has the board responded?"

"In such cases, we have sought revocation of the doctor's medical license."

"Why?"

"Generally, it's the board's opinion that if a doctor is brazen in his or her actions, thus putting patients in harm's way, we have no choice but to revoke that doctor's medical license."

"In your opinion, would dispensing used medication and double-charging patients be flagrant enough to revoke a medical license?"

"Objection!" Brian roars.

"Mr. Freeland, your tone is noted . . . again. The objection is sustained. The jury will refrain from making any association between Mr. Barrens's last question and the previous answer given by the witness. We will take a ten-minute break, and I will see counsel in my chambers." The banging of the gavel shouts louder than Brian's objection.

"Brian, please keep your cool." I'm concerned that the strikes against us aren't just coming from the prosecutor's table."

"I'm fine. I'll be back in five minutes. Just sit here, don't say or do anything."

When they come back to the courtroom, Brian leans on the prosecutor's table. "That was low. We've kept it clean until now. Why?"

"I know. I'm sorry. Because of that idiot on the cop shooting trial, this has become a much bigger deal to everyone above me." Barrens shakes his head. "He's too green, and he came out of nowhere. He's probably some bigwig's nephew. He made a shit show of the whole thing, and now I'm expected to save face. Won't happen again."

Brian turns and mutters. "I hope so. Let's not make this fight in the mud."

Brian sits. I whisper, "What was that all about?"

"Let's just leave it at Barrens and I are very close to sharing a room at the Harris Hotel if he doesn't stop the games and if I keep yelling at him for doing it."

I reply a bit too quickly. "Sounds like stupid kid crap." Brian gives me a stare down. "Sorry."

"All rise—"

"Please, sit down. Mr. Diaz, you are still under oath. Mr. Barrens, continue."

"Thank you, Mr. Diaz. Your Honor, I have no more questions." Barrens states without even standing.

Judge Harris, like the rest of us, I'm sure, is stunned by Barrens's ending his questioning of the witness so abruptly. "Well . . . Mr. Freeland . . . your witness."

Brian's dumbfounded look is obvious. "Mr. Diaz . . . does the state licensing board revoke . . . most licenses they investigate?"

Horatio Diaz is staring at the three attorneys sitting at the prosecutor's table. "No, uh, most of the time there is a suspension with some limitation or retraining."

"Do you know that Dr. Carey's license is only suspended?"

"Yes."

"We have heard from Ms. Hawthorne, of the FDA, that there is training that Dr. Carey could take to improve her process of medication handling and distribution, and that she could also obtain special permits. Is it possible that with the proper training, Dr. Carey could keep her medical license?"

Diaz appears to be firing bullets with his eyes at Barrens. "Yes, it is possible. It would be my opinion that the board might look favorably at those efforts."

"Mr. Diaz, does the licensing board have specific criteria it follows, or does it review each incident individually and on its own merits?" Brian is fishing for the first time in the trial since Barrens made no real points for him to rebuke.

Diaz, clearly now agitated, responds quickly. "Of course there are criteria! Every case is looked at independently. Like I basically already said. The severity of the incident is definitely taken into consideration."

"If this were your case—"

"Objection, Your Honor. Attorney Freeland has already stipulated that we must speak in generalities regarding this witness."

"Sustained. Mr. Freeland, those were the rules you demanded with your earlier objection. Do you wish to amend the rules for this witness?"

Brian pauses—his glasses dangling from his left hand. "Withdrawn. Thank you, Mr. Diaz. No more questions, Your Honor."

"Mr. Barrens, do you wish to redirect?" Judge Harris glares at both attorneys, letting them know that this cat-and-mouse sport they are playing is getting close to the line.

"Yes, Your Honor. Mr. Diaz, does the licensing board take practicing medicine beyond the scope of a license seriously?"

Diaz straightens his tie just before his delivery. "Quite seriously. There are many different types of licenses, and each has its limitations. The board also considers factors such as the judgment used to make the decision to practice beyond the scope of a license and the intention for doing so. Was that doctor acting in poor judgment, or was there no other choice for the incident? We also look at how many times the incident occurred."

"Let's talk about poor judgment for a moment. What constitutes poor judgment for a doctor regarding a medical license?"

"Well, there are many factors, but simply put, if a doctor makes reckless choices or choices that put their own interests before those of his or her patients. That constitutes poor judgment."

"What constitutes a single incident? Does repeating the same act over and over constitute a single incident?"

"Objection. The prosecutor is indirectly making an inference about the particulars of this trial." Brian's objection is controlled.

Judge Harris does not look up. "Sustained. Mr. Barrens, please reword your question or move on."

"Mr. Diaz, hypothetically, if a doctor repeatedly creates false documentation in charts. Would that be considered one or multiple incidents?"

"Each charting incident would stand on its own and therefore be considered a separate infraction."

Barrens waits for the response to sink in. "So that would be a great deal of bad judgment. Might the board look more harshly upon this type of behavior? Is that correct?"

"Objection. Mr. Bar—"

"Overruled. But you're close to the line, Mr. Barrens. The witness may answer."

"Yes, that kind of behavior would show repeated bad judgement."

"Obj—"

Judge Harris points the head of her gavel at Brian. "Overruled and noted for the record. Mr. Freeland, this is a trial, and the guidelines are being followed. Neither the prosecutor nor the witness made an actual reference to your client. Stop objecting unless it has real merit. Mr. Barrens, please continue."

"Mr. Diaz, what do you, the board, look for besides bad judgement?"

"We look very closely at the doctor to see if she . . . or he, is repeatedly doing things that are not consistent with the norms associated with their license."

Barrens looks at me, then Brian, and finally at the jury. "So, if a doctor creates schemes or gimmicks to bend the medical system and then implements them—"

"Objection!"

"Withdrawn. My apologies, Your Honor. I truly was trying to be general."

Barrens returns to the prosecution's table. "No more questions, Your Honor."

Brian stands. "Your Honor, I have just a few questions for this witness. If I may?"

"Very well, go ahead, Mr. Freeland."

"Mr. Diaz, does the licensing board look at the real reasons a doctor acts the way they do in each instance, or do they pit the doctor's actions against . . . what did you call them—the norms?"

Diaz again looks to Barrens. "Well, to clarify, yes, we try hard to figure out the circumstances and the motives behind the doctor's actions. Then we act accordingly."

Brian speaks slowly as he continues to press Diaz. "Does the licensing board . . . do you . . . thoroughly and impartially investigate every incident before taking action?"

Diaz leans forward, clenching his right hand into a fist atop the front edge of the witness box. "I just said we always do a thorough job. I do a thorough job." Diaz stands. "And this case is no different. I don't even have to be on the case to know your client, Dr. Carey, crossed the line hundreds of times!"

"Objection, Your Honor." Brian keeps eye contact with Diaz—daring him to take the first swing.

An incensed Diaz bites. "If I could, I would take your client's license right now, right here, and right in front of you."

The gavel strikes its base several times as Judge Harris yells, "Sustained!" By the third explosion, quiet blankets the courtroom. Judge Harris demands, "The jury must disregard the witness's last two statements in their entirety. Mr. Freeland, finish up."

"Just one more question, Your Honor. Mr. Diaz, you stated that each case is investigated thoroughly and without bias. Oh, and considered individually, given the circumstances involved. What were the words? Ah, they were something like—'Did the doctor have no choice for their actions?'"

Barrens looks up from the yellow pad on his table. "Objection. Is there a question or is Attorney Freeland merely giving a closing statement?"

"Sustained. Ask a question or call it a day, Mr. Freeland."

"Mr. Diaz, if the doctor were to become aware of a medically dangerous process in the community, wouldn't they have no choice but to act to help in whatever way possible?"

Diaz smirks. "They would have to take action."

"Sir, that doctor, like I'm sure many others all around us, would then meet your standard of care. How can you say that my client, Dr. Jordan Carey, should lose her medical license here and now, if she has satisfied the very criteria you yourself have set forth?"

Diaz brushes the lapels of his suit jacket, takes a deep breath, and then looks at Brian, and slowly extends both middle fingers over the witness stand railing. "You're good and you're right. She wouldn't."

Unflustered by the witness, Brian responds, "Thank you, Your Honor. No more questions."

"Mr. Diaz, for the record, I will be notifying your employer of your unprofessional conduct. You are lucky that I don't hold you in contempt." Judge Harris turns to the jury and softens. "Ladies and gentlemen, we will break for lunch and return at one o'clock sharp." The disgusted thumping of her gavel shakes the walls of the courtroom again.

"Brian, did that really just happen?" I whisper.

"Yes, we just showed the jury that the licensing board is not impartial and not rational. Let's go to the diner." Brian walks quickly. "I don't want to run into Barrens in the corridor."

"Okay, but why?"

Brian's longer strides are hard to keep up with. "Because Barrens held back. He probably feels that we're even now. That's how I would feel. And, I don't want to give him the chance to say it."

"What does all that even mean? Is this another one of those unspoken rules from the lawyer's secret codebook?"

"I'll explain at the diner."

We're barreling through the crowd at the exit, and Brian is acting like an offensive guard blocking for his running back. The reporters are back onto our case, but giving way to my attorney's deliberate pace. We reach the front door of the diner, and Brian peeks inside. "Good, no Barrens." We sit at a table. Brian takes a deep breath.

"What's going on, Brian?"

"I'm going with a gut feeling." Brian is talking about his stomach, yet he's pointing to his head. I'm worried my attorney is having a breakdown.

The fact that we are in the Safe Haven Diner slips my mind. I lean in and mutter, "What are you talking about?"

"Barrens caved too quickly. Even if it was a mea culpa cave."

"Do you realize that you're the only one able to follow you at this moment?"

Brian hisses and shakes his head. "Look, Barrens has something up his sleeve, and I didn't want to give him the chance to spring it on us in the corridor with hundreds of reporters watching. I believe he had a number of questions to ask Diaz. I would have asked about twenty more questions. I could see it on Diaz's face. Diaz got pissed off, so I pushed him over the edge. Barrens should have fired back. He didn't. He was more interested in that yellow legal pad. My gut is saying something is coming."

"Brian, you sound a little paranoid."

Brian runs his fingers through his salt-and-pepper hair. "Maybe you're right. But I'll keep it in the back of my mind. Let's order lunch."

My appetite is quickly disappearing; Brian has yet to be wrong, and his little meltdown is really out of character. "Brian, do we need to figure this out before we get back to court?"

"Now who sounds paranoid? No, and it's my job to manage the trial. Don't worry about it. I shouldn't have said anything."

"That's like telling the jury to unhear what they just heard." The familiar buzzing of my cell phone against the metal table distracts me. I reach for it. "It's Andie."

Brian places his hand over mine. "Don't answer that. We don't need Andie getting any more information."

"I'm not . . . never mind; I won't answer it." I pull my hand from under Brian's hand as the phone goes through another rumbling cycle. Brian begins searching through his pockets.

"What are you looking for?" I ask.

"Damn it. My cell phone. I must have left it on the table in the courtroom." Brian's fingers tap the table as he stares off into the distance.

"Are you okay? Do you want to use mine? Should we go back to get it?"

Brian looks at me. "What? No, let's eat our lunch. I just wanted to check in with the office. Everything is fine. Besides, Mr. Diaz getting angry did us a solid. Let's go with that." Brian forces a smile.

CHAPTER 19
BARRENS'S SURPRISE

Brian picks up his cell phone sitting on the defense table. "Damn it!"

"What's wrong?"

"My office has called seven times, and there's a call from the courthouse. Wait, there's a text." Brian goes silent for a moment. "Damn it."

"What? What is it? What's wrong? Brian, answer me."

Brian presses a button on his phone. "My office wants me to call immediately."

The bailiff announces. "All rise for the Honorable Judge Constance Harris."

"Damn it!" Brian curses quietly.

"Please be seated." Judge Harris appears disturbed. "Mr. Freeland, is it your habit not to answer your cell phone when a member of the court calls you?"

"No, Your Honor. I accidentally left my phone here on the table. I didn't know that anyone called me. I am very sorry."

"I'm glad to hear that it is a misunderstanding, but we are now forced to continue with our case. I will allow you to object if you please."

"Your Honor, since I don't know what I would be objecting to, I'm not sure I can object at this time. I would like to reserve my objection for a later time if needed."

"I believe that to be a fair request." Judge Harris may be impressed, but shows no life towards it.

"Mr. Barrens, is the prosecution finished at this time?"

Barrens cannot control his smirk. "Actually, no, Your Honor. We want to call one more witness."

Brian erupts. "Your Honor, the prosecution has gone through all the witnesses it listed, and there has been no mention of any additional witnesses before this moment." Brian breaths deeply before continuing. "It appears that I will be activating that reserve objection sooner than I thought."

"Yes, I thought you might. The court will take a short recess as counsel and Dr. Carey meet with me in my chamber." Judge Harris waves to the bailiff, directing him to remove the jury. She then bangs her gavel and leaves Courtroom Five.

"I knew that SOB was up to something," Brian rants under his breath.

"What's this all about?"

"I don't know, and I don't like it. Let's go."

"Okay." I can feel beads of sweat forming on my face. My mind is racing. *I told my parents everything that happened yesterday. Did they tell someone who said something? Is this Andie all over again?* "Stop!" I say this a bit too loudly, and the courtroom's low-pitched warbles suddenly disappear. All eyes are on me, and I want to run.

Judge Harris removes her robe. She must not believe this will be a short meeting. "This will be on the record. Dr. Carey, I allowed you to be here as a courtesy; please don't speak unless I direct a question to you. Let's get to it. Mr. Barrens, please explain."

"Your Honor. In light of yesterday's release of Dr. Carey's now very public commentary, the prosecution has decided to call one more witness. This witness was not on the original witness list submitted to Mr. Freeland. In fairness, we didn't know she existed until we dug deeper into yesterday's events."

"Who is this witness?" Brian's anger and frustration fill the room.

"Have a seat, Mr. Freeland, and let's keep calm." Judge Harris quips.

"Andrea Tanner. Or Andie, as Dr. Carey calls her." Barrens adds the last part just for effect.

"Who is Andie Tanner, and what is her significance in this case?" The judge looks at the stenographer, then to Barrens.

Brian jumps in. "Andie is Dr. Carey's closest friend and confidant. She is like a sister to my client. Mrs. Tanner is the woman who posted the comments that my client allegedly said."

"Mr. Freeland, your client admitted to having the conversation that led to those comments. I don't feel they are alleged anymore."

"Your Honor, that conversation, here in your chambers, was off-the-record, as you wished. No disrespect intended." Brian knows he's treading on thin ice.

Barrens steps in quickly. "The off-the-record conversation doesn't matter. We started compiling our information before the meeting and independently of it. Therefore, off-the-record or on-the-record, it didn't affect anything."

Brian barks at Barrens. "So, you're saying you started your search for Andie before we met, and you didn't see fit to mention her as a possible new witness during the meeting or any time afterward. Until now?"

"There was nothing to mention. We didn't have a name. The website host wasn't releasing the name, and until yesterday afternoon, it was a dead end."

Judge Harris questions, "Mr. Barrens, what happened yesterday afternoon?"

"Our investigator followed Dr. Carey to Andie's home. He pulled the public land record to see who owned the home, and the story started to unfold immediately after that." Barrens sports a pleased look.

Brian's face almost blisters from the rage. "You followed my client? Your Honor, this a gross misconduct by Attorney Barrens and his office!"

"Mr. Freeland, sit down! I understand your anger. You can file a complaint with the bar later. For now, I find that the use of this witness is valid, and she may shed some light on Dr. Carey's mindset, one way or another. The prosecution may present this witness first thing Monday morning. We will return to the courtroom now, where I will adjourn court for the day." Judge Harris begins putting her robe back on. "Mr. Barrens, the disclosure of all proper documents will happen immediately."

Barrens calmly replies, "Your Honor, my office has already sent over the documents to Mr. Freeland's office."

Brian pleads, "Your Honor, we have not had any time to prepare for this witness."

"You have the rest of today and all weekend if you need it. I've made my decision." Judge Harris points to the door.

The bailiff chimes, "All rise for the Honorable Judge Constance Harris."

"I have met with both sides in my chambers, and I have decided to allow Mr. Barrens to call his extra witness. In fairness to Mr. Freeland and Dr. Carey, I am adjourning court until Monday morning. I want to remind the members of the jury that all the guidelines I have stated to you are still in place." The gavel is struck, the bailiff plays his part, and court is adjourned.

Brian heads for the courthouse suite. It's going to be a long afternoon. Once inside, Brian punches a button on his cell phone. A flurry of loud commands ends with Brian shouting that someone should have raced to the courthouse to find him. There is a momentary silence, then the barrage restarts. "Send out an office-wide email. There is a new policy: If it's urgent, find the partner no matter what! That means send someone to find them if need be, physically." There is a pause. "I don't care if the other partners think it's a waste of time. It's my name at the top!" Another pause and a deep sigh. "Just bring me the documents, now, please."

The coolness of lingering sweat sends a chill as I look at Brian, waiting for details. "What's this all about?"

"Barrens put an investigator on you when that website wouldn't release the source of your comments."

"That's crazy. I didn't do anything wrong."

"You went to Andie's house, and they must have questioned her about the website posting and maybe more. Anyway, now she's Barrens's witness on Monday."

"Damn it! Andie called me late last night, again this morning, and then at lunch. She was trying to warn me. I blew her off. Wait, she left a voicemail."

"Don't play it!" Brian practically grabs the cell phone from my hand.

"Why not? It could be important."

"It could be seen as witness tampering. Just leave it on your phone, unheard. Don't listen to it and don't delete it. Just leave it alone. Clear?"

"Okay, I got it!"

Brian places my cell phone on the table next to him. Fifteen minutes later, there's a knock at the door, and Erin appears with the documents Brian demanded. She leaves without saying much. I'm guessing she may have been the recipient of Brian's outrage. Brian and I spend the next three hours going over the documents and discussing every tedious detail of my conversations with Andie. We cover every word spoken at Leon's B&G, at Andie's home, and on the phone last night. I'm mentally and physically worn.

"We'll call it quits here. Don't, and I mean don't, contact Andie during this weekend. Barrens might have you followed again. No contact with Andie, at all."

"Brian, you know Andie is going to call me."

"Don't answer. I don't care if she calls you one hundred times."

Brian picks up my cell, stares at it, then hesitantly hands it to me. "You call me if she tries to come over, got it?"

"Got it. I do. No contact with Andie."

I call my parents, knowing that they will be glad to see me two days in a row. I'll go there for dinner and fake being too tired to go home. I'll spend the night. Andie won't come looking for me there, and if she does, my parents will cover for me.

My phone rings as I get into the Uber. It's Andie. I let it go to voicemail. Andie tries four more times while I'm in the Uber. Each call is more painful than the previous one. I know Andie; she is suffering, but I can't answer. My phone continues to buzz and I wonder about Mr. Barrens's surprise. *I hope you think all this pain is worth it, Prosecutor Barrens.* My entire body fills with fire as I picture Barrens sitting at home enjoying his weekend. I call Brian in hopes of relieving the anger. "Brian, it's Jordan. Andie has called five times in the past ten minutes. I don't think I can hold out."

"Jordan, you don't have a choice. Give me a couple of other numbers where you can be reached, then turn your phone off."

I give Brian my parents' number. I don't have a home phone. I tell him I'll turn my phone back on when I get home tomorrow afternoon. I hate Mr. Barrens's surprise.

CHAPTER 20
DOERS OF THE DISTASTEFUL

After a couple of hours of my parents treating me like I'm a newborn, I realize I can't use them as a shield from the world. In the Uber, I turn my phone on. A storm of pings informs me of the countless emails, voicemails, and texts, all from Andie.

Ignoring them, I text Brian, letting him know my phone is back on and I'm getting out of town for the weekend. The phone starts its next round of dings, chimes, and beeps. This time it's Brian. How can he text, IM, and call me all at the same time? "Hello, Brian. That was very fast and somewhat overwhelming."

"Where are you going? You're not doing anything foolish, right?"

I snap, "I'm just going to a hotel one town over."

"Jordan, take a hotel here. Remember you're out on bail. If you leave town with a suitcase, it might look like you're on the run."

"Is there nothing I can do to get some peace? Andie keeps trying to reach me. I'm probably being followed by . . . who knows, and my parents had a million questions. I just want to go someplace quiet for a few days." Tears flow freely, and the Uber driver looks at me through the rearview mirror. I slant a smile. He's not buying it. His eyes widen as he recognizes me, he turns back to the road. I want to believe he's being respectful but he's probably just protecting his job. "Brian, everyone's out for their damn self, aren't they?"

"Jordan, take a deep breath. I've got a better idea. I'll book you a hotel here in town, through the office. That way, if anyone asks, we can verify that it was my idea to put you in a hotel to keep the press away from you."

My brain hears Brian's words, but it takes a moment for them to register through my fit of self-pity. "Okay, that might work. I'll go home to pack a bag. Text me the hotel info when you've booked it."

"Jordan, go straight there. I'll have Erin meet you there. She'll get the keys to your apartment and pick up some clothes for you. Remember to have her get clothes for court on Monday." There's clicking in the background. "Okay, you're all set at the Marriott on Third Ave. Have the driver drop you off there. Erin is on her way."

"How did you do that so fast? This isn't the first time you, your office, has done this is it?"

Brian chuckles. "Think of it as the wonders of computers and multitasking."

The phone goes dead. "Change of plans. Take me to the Marriott on . . ."

The driver eyes me through the rearview mirror again. "On Third Ave. I know. Your phone was on speaker."

"Oh, okay, and please hurry." I leave him a good tip and five stars.

Erin is already waiting in the lobby. She gives me the same slanted smile Brian gets and waves a key card.

"Hi, Erin. Thanks for doing this."

Sarcasm rolls from Erin's lips. "Hi, Jordan. Apparently, it's part of my job. You probably shouldn't tell him I said that."

"I won't. I made a list of what I need. Can you give me your number so I can text it to you? Better yet, why don't I go with you? He'll never know."

"I'm not supposed to give out my number, but I don't want to rewrite the entire list. I'll call you, then you'll have it. Go with me? I don't think so. If some idiot snaps a pic of us together and it ends up anywhere, Brian will know. Then we'll both be fried. So go upstairs and relax."

"Erin, I appreciate this so much."

"You know if you want to quietly tell him it's wrong to treat me as an errand girl, I won't object," Erin blusters in disgust. "Nope, don't do that. Just forget I said anything. I'll be back soon. Room 264."

"Erin, just so you know, I do think it's wrong too."

"Room 264, now go."

Room 264 is much more than one person needs. It has a spacious sitting area with a larger desk than my office had. There are two cloth chairs with modern jade and grey patterns. The bedroom area houses two queen beds and is separated from the sitting area by a bookshelf atop the desk that doubles as a wall. All the wood has a light finish, making the two rooms look more expansive. The bathroom is made private by an enormous, frosted sliding glass door. This may be the most glamorous room I've ever stayed in.

"Brian, this room is lovely, but I can't afford this."

"You don't have to worry about it. The firm leases the room to clients and their families, or to a witness who may need to be housed during a trial. It just happens to be vacant for the weekend." Brian snorts. "It's not coming out of your pocket. I'm going to expense it to the account that pays for me."

"What about the quick computer and multitasking bit?"

"I have to keep you believing I'm the superstar you think I am."

"Hmm. Like I said . . . everyone's just looking out for themselves."

Brian lets a long silence pass before continuing. "Jordan, I know this is difficult, but you can't become hardened to the world. There are good people out there."

Now it's my turn to wait. "Speaking of good people, Brian, I don't think Erin is happy with you. I can see it on her face. It's not right to use her as an errand girl."

Brian nearly growls. "Did Erin tell you to say that? How about you worry about the trial, and I'll handle my staff."

"Brian . . ."

"Jordan, I apologize. I will consider your . . . observation. Thank you for sharing it. Enjoy your weekend." The phone call ends.

The next hour is spent surfing the 48" flat screen that hangs on the wall in front of my bed. Brian's reaction worries me, and I'm hoping I didn't put Erin at risk. The hotel phone rings; it's the front desk letting me know Erin is on her way up.

"Thanks for going to my apartment. Would you like to get something to eat? It's on me."

Erin throws herself down onto one of the cloth chairs. I can see that she is tired of the world using her too. "Thanks, Jordan, but I can't. I have other plans, and I'm already late."

I'm slightly older than Erin and understand being abused by your mentors. I sit in the twin chair next to her. "Erin, when I was a resident, which is a fancy name for the doer of the distasteful, it seemed like it was never going to end. It does and it will for you too."

Erin smiles and gives me a hug. "Thanks, Jordan. I know that. I'm okay." A furrowed brow appears. "One of us, probably me, will check in on you during the weekend." At the door Erin gives a pensive look. "We shouldn't continue this conversation. It's not professional."

Heat rise to my face. "Did Brian say something to you?"

Erin lets out that smile again. "Jordan, just let it go. Please."

"It won't be you who checks up on me. That's a promise. Have a good weekend, Erin." The cylinders of the lock clack.

The feelings of being mistreated or unseen for my potential from my residency days rush in like a tidal wave. I pick up my cell phone and dial. "Brian, Erin just left and I told her she is not going to be the one checking up on me this weekend. Understand?"

A woman's laughter is in the background. Brian quickly answers. "Sorry about that." A low-grade hiss sounds through the phone. "I understand."

Now only muffled sounds pass through. "Do you have me on speaker? Was that your wife?"

Brian Freeland is used to being in charge and doesn't play the subordinate well. Agitation and shortness accompany his response. "I said—I understand." He hangs up.

I look at my reflection in the blackness of the idle television. "That felt good. Really good." Oddly, I'm not worried about Brian's response. Room 264 is my world for the next forty-eight hours. It's a good time to relearn a few things.

CHAPTER 21
NO MORE HONOR AMONG THIEVES

BRIAN GIVES A HALF-HEARTED SMILE. “Did you enjoy the hotel?”

“I did, and when this is all over, we’re having a conversation.” I want to sound like a mother getting ready to scold her child. “You didn’t call.”

Brian lets out a belly laugh. “You told me not to have Erin call.”

“Funny. Talk afterwards. Don’t forget, because I won’t.”

Courtroom Five feels like an old acquaintance you don’t really want to run into. We take our seats behind the defense table. The Barrens group is already seated. The B team is thumbing through stacks of papers. I’m guessing to avoid any conversation with the boss. The bailiff stands at the ready.

Brian’s tone is stern. He holds up his index finger. “Jordan, focus on the bench. This could be a rough one.”

Attorney Barrens walks over to our table. I catch his eye following Brian’s finger to the judge’s bench. “Good morning, Brian. I know you know this isn’t personal. It’s just business. I have no choice.”

“You always have a choice. Good luck.” Brian extends his hand.

“Thanks, good luck to you.” Barrens’s hand clenches Brian’s aggressively.

With my face now only inches from Brian’s, I grind out, “What the hell was that?”

“Not now. Besides, we’ll know exactly what in a few seconds. We’re the ones without a choice.” Brian points again. “Don’t forget. No matter what.”

"No matter what . . . really?"

"All rise . . ." The bailiff is right on cue. It's 9:30 a.m. sharp. Judge Harris does not disappoint.

"Good morning, I believe we left off with Mr. Barrens about to call his last witness. Would you please go ahead, Mr. Barrens?"

"Thank you, Your Honor. I would like to call Andrea Tanner to the stand."

Andie's eyes are puffy and red, and she has a death grip on the tissue in her right hand. I know Andie never thought she would be in this position; then again, neither did I. I follow Brian's orders; I cannot watch my best friend, my sister, up there.

"Mrs. Tanner, can you state your full name for the record?" Barrens's icy timbre causes Andie to shiver.

"My . . ." Andie clears her throat. "I am Andrea Tanner, but I go by Andie."

"Mrs. Tanner, how do you know Dr. Carey?"

"We're best friends. We have been since childhood." Andie looks in my direction. Her pale face is now red around the nose, and tears run down both cheeks.

Barrens steps into Andie's line of vision. He looks at me before moving to one side. It's like he wants me to see her in pain. "Mrs. Tanner, can you tell us about Leon's Underground?"

"Leon's is a bar and grill where Jordan, um, Dr. Carey, and I meet when one of us needs to blow off some steam."

"What do you mean by 'blow off some steam'?"

"It's where Jordan and I go to help each other through tough times or to unravel together."

"The last time you went to Leon's, who initiated the meeting?"

"Um . . . Jordan did. She called me and asked if we could meet at Leon's."

"So, the person who needs to talk or 'unravel' calls for the meeting?"

"Yes."

"What is the meaning of unravel for you and Dr. Carey?"

Andie looks toward me again. I do nothing. "It means that we can unpack, talk about whatever it is that's bothering us, and there is no judgment."

"Dr. Carey called the meeting, so you assumed she needed to 'unpack' something?"

"Objection. The witness is being asked to make an assumption as to my client's state of mind."

"Overruled. Mr. Barrens has already established the specific criteria that make up the foundation for calling a meeting." Judge Harris peers at Barrens. "Continue, please."

"What happened at Leon's last time you were there with Dr. Carey?"

"We started out drinking wine, like we always do. We made small talk to catch up, and then we ordered bar food. Then, when I had had enough to drink, I ordered a martini to signal that it was our last round."

"Can you explain the 'signal' part to us?"

"It's a scheme we came up with. When one of us has had enough to drink, that person orders one last drink that isn't wine. This drink is our last-call drink."

"Mrs. Tanner, you used the word 'scheme.' This scheme is used to hide the fact that one of you is too drunk or just too afraid to admit defeat."

"No, it's not a scheme. It's more of a signal. And no one is being defeated. Jordan and I don't compete like that."

"Is Dr. Carey good at coming up with schemes?"

"Objection."

Andie blurts out, "It was just a game."

The Judge's gavel strikes its base. "Sustained. The jury will disregard the witness's response. Mrs. Tanner, when an objection is entered, you must wait for my ruling before proceeding. Do you understand?"

"Yes. Sorry, Your Honor."

Barrens nods to Judge Harris, then continues. "You said that you were the one to order the last-call drink, correct? Does that mean Dr. Carey was willing to continue drinking?"

"Objection, speculation." Brian bellows effortlessly.

"Sustained."

"Mrs. Tanner, you stated that you and Dr. Carey are friends since grade school and that you don't compete. You attended high school together, is that correct?"

"Yes."

"Close friends often fall for the same boy. Did you and Dr. Carey ever compete for the same boy's attention?"

Andie stops to think. "I'm not sure, maybe."

Barrens walks to the witness stand. "Did Dr. Carey win or lose that competition?"

"I don't recall."

Barrens grins. "So, there is competition. Does Dr. Carey like to lose or feel defeated?"

"I suppose not. Who does?" Andie looks at me. Barrens steps between us.

"Before ordering this last drink, did you and Dr. Carey talk about her court case?"

"Yes, but . . ."

"What did Dr. Carey say about her trial?"

Andie is crying freely again, both cheeks now striped with black streaks from an eyeliner that has failed the saltwater siege. She is looking directly at me. Her pain is becoming overwhelming to me. Andie takes a deep breath. "She said she felt everyone was against her and it was just a show, and she had already lost the trial."

"NO! ANDIE, THAT'S NOT WHAT I SAID!"

Repeating bangs of the gavel, whispers from the gallery, a look of shock from the jury, and the stern painful grasp on my shoulder by Brian tell it all. Judge Harris regains control of the courtroom except for Andie and I, who are in tears. I don't care; I can't stop at this point. "We will take an immediate recess. Bailiff, escort the jury out now, and place the witness in a secure area. I will see everyone else in my chambers immediately."

Brian calmly places his glasses on the table and turns to me. "You have a minute to compose yourself."

Tears still cascade freely. "Brian, I want to change my plea to guilty. I want all of this to be over. I want it to be over, now!"

"Jordan, we're winning. Don't let Barrens beat you now. This is dirty, and I will file a complaint with the bar as soon as we're done. Don't give up now. It's what Barrens wants."

"I can't go see the judge. I just can't. I know I'm in big trouble, and it will be worse if I don't go, but I can't." My entire body is trembling uncontrollably.

"There isn't much of a choice here. Let's stand and walk slowly to give you a few extra seconds."

"I want it to be over!"

Brian stands in front of me, his stout torso only inches from me. "It will be soon. Just don't make it today. Please."

I see Barrens juniors sitting at the table, grinning and grotesquely proud of the pain they have just inflicted. Hatred boils within me. "I don't quit. They need to pay."

Brian turns to see the juniors trying to suppress their joy. "Don't say that here. Let's go."

Judge Harris stands with her arms folded across her chest. "Mr. Freeland, this is the second time you have not controlled your client. Dr. Carey, you are giving me no choice but to hold you in contempt of court. And you will be along with her."

"Judge Harris, please don't do that. My client is watching a woman, a sister to her, be forced to betray her. It's dirty, and it's wrong." Brian pleads as he scowls at Barrens.

"Mr. Freeland! Control yourself. I agree, but we are here now and moving forward. You can take it up with the bar later. Mr. Barrens, you are making a mess of my courtroom. I suggest you find a way to get your points across quickly."

"Your Honor, I would like to keep my client out of the courtroom for the rest of the prosecution's questioning of Andie Tanner. If she wishes to return during my questioning, I will bring her back in. Is that okay with you?"

Judge Harris is contemplating the request; she is a shrewd courtroom veteran. "Actually, I am going to agree to it and stay the contempt. Mr. Barrens, you can record an objection in court if you wish."

"No, Your Honor, I have no objection." Barrens knows that an objection of this nature in front of the jury will paint him as a monster.

"No! That's not fair! I have to know what Andie says! I have to hear my best friend be forced to throw me under the bus!" The tone of my voice brings two bailiffs hurrying into the judge's chamber. Judge Harris waves them off. "None of you has the right to make that choice for me!"

Judge Harris ignores my drama. "Mr. Freeland, would you like a minute to confer with your client?"

"It doesn't look like I'm going to change her mind, so no."

"Fine, Dr. Carey, I admire your perseverance. But know this. An order of contempt is just inches from my reach. I will walk you down to a cell myself. Let's return to the courtroom in fifteen minutes."

In the corridor, Brian places his glasses in the breast pocket of his suit and pulls me to the side. "Jordan, this is a mistake. I can't stop you, but I don't think it's a good idea."

"What part of any of this was a good idea from the beginning!"

"I texted Erin. She will be sitting beside you to make sure you remain in control. It's not a request."

"How is she supposed to do that if I can't?"

Brian thinks for a moment. "Girl power."

"Really. That's all you could come up with. A sexist remark."

Brian sneers. "Think about that for a while."

"All rise for the Honorable Judge Constance Harris," the bailiff once again announces.

"We have had some excitement again this morning. I can assure you that if we have any more, the culprit will be dealt with quite severely." The judge has not taken her eyes off me. "Mrs. Tanner, you are still under oath. Mr. Barrens, please continue."

"Mrs. Tanner, you stated before the recess . . . that Dr. Carey thought the trial was already decided . . . that everyone was against her, and that she lost . . . is that correct?" Attorney Barrens's long pauses are deliberate.

"Yes."

"When did Dr. Carey tell you this, before the two of you started drinking or after both of you had been drinking for a while?"

"After we had been drinking for a while?" Andie answers. She is still crying and appears to be wandering in the dark.

"What did Dr. Carey tell you about the trial when you first met at Leon's?"

"She told me that her attorney told her not to say anything about it."

"Did you believe that Dr. Carey wanted to talk about the trial?" Barrens asks, just a bit louder. This gets a look from the judge.

"Yes."

"Did Dr. Carey tell you anything else about the trial as the night went on?"

Andie whimpers and gathers herself. "Dr. Carey, Jordan, told me that deep down, she may have known she might get in trouble for doing what she did." Andie brings her hands to her face. "Jordan, I'm sorry!"

"Objection." Barrens tries to stop Andie before she says anything else.

"Sustained. Mrs. Tanner, you are not allowed to address the defendant directly. Please do not do it again. The jury will disregard the last part of the witness's statement."

"Mrs. Tanner, can you tell us what you posted on the Support-MyCause website right after your night out with Dr. Carey?"

"I posted that Dr. Carey was not happy with the way her trial was going."

"In my hand, I have a copy of what you posted on the website. Can you please read the post so the court can hear the exact wording?"

Andie whimpers, takes a deep breath, and begins. "'To all of you who donated to Jordan's cause, I believe you deserve a true update. Dr. Jordan Carey is not getting a fair deal. She believes that the judge and jury have already made up their minds, and the trial is just a sham. Jordan is being made to look like a villain, and everyone, including her own attorney, treats her like a criminal. The system is tainted against her. I have known Jordan for most of my life and she is not the monster that the legal system and the press are making her out to be. Thanks for your continued support. I'll keep you posted.'

Barrens rubs his face, allowing the words to sink in before moving forward. "Did Dr. Carey discuss all the points you posted on the website?"

"Yes, but not in so many words." Andie continues to sob as she shreds me to pieces.

"Would you say that you know Dr. Carey well enough to understand what she is trying to tell you?"

"Objection. Speculation."

"Sustained."

"Mrs. Tanner, in your opinion, as a lifelong friend of Dr. Carey, would you say this may just be another case of poor judgment on—"

Brian stands. His voice rises. "Objection. The witness is not an expert in psychology or internal medicine, nor should she be asked to speculate about my client."

"Your Honor, Mrs. Tanner has known Dr. Carey a long time and has seen her make many choices in life. Surely, she should be able to have an opinion about a lifelong friend?"

"Sustained. Please move on, Mr. Barrens."

"Thank you, Your Honor. No more questions." Barrens makes his way back to the prosecutor's table, once again dropping the exhibit in his hand on our table for dramatic effect.

I remember during my education, a professor once told us that if something is to stick in your memory, you have to hear it three times. I am sure Barrens will come back to my poor judgment at least once more.

Judge Harris finishes a long notation and then looks out over her courtroom. "I think that we have had a full morning. It is time for a break. We will return at 1:00 p.m. for the afternoon." The gavel sounds.

"Wait here. I'll be back in a minute." Brian turns to Barrens. "Can we have a word?"

It's obvious that Barrens is confused by the request, but he beams. "Sure. Ready to give up?"

The two attorneys walk down the center aisle of the courtroom and sit down in a row, just within my earshot. "What happened in here was offensive. There used to be a code of honor or maybe moral ethics that we, as attorneys, adhered to, but in today's world of lies and fake this and fake that, the only thing evident is that everyone is out for themselves. What you put that poor woman through was uncalled for. It was dirty and just—"

Barrens places his hand on the backrest and interrupts. "I did what I had to. I will continue to do what it takes to see that your client, a rogue doctor, stops risking patients' lives."

Brian runs a hand through his graying hair. "Who have you become? There is no more honor among thieves."

Brian returns to the table where I'm waiting for him. "Let's go to lunch at the diner. I can't sit in this courthouse right now." Brian makes sure he has his cell phone and heads for the door.

CHAPTER 22
BARRENS WILL PAY

The reporters swarm around Barrens and his teams, almost forcing them to retreat into the courthouse. Questions fire at them from every direction like it's a sharpshooter's convention. Andie emerges, and they frantically migrate to her. Sebbi is doing his best to shield her, but he's outnumbered. I look at Brian, who knows what I'm asking. He waves a hand. "No. Keep moving towards the street."

I look over my shoulder and see Andie. Her eyes are red and swollen. Our gaze connects, and I can see she's lost and desperate.

"Brian, please."

"No, I'm sorry, we can't. Keep moving. Please."

Sebbi manages to pull her away from the reporters and into their blue SUV. I don't know who's driving but it's neither of them. She used to use the SUV for catering business; now she shuttles the twins around in it. Brian has me by the arm, pulling hard, and trying to get into the Safe Haven Diner before the reporters have a chance to refocus.

Inside the diner, he finds an isolated table near the back. We sit. My tears begin anew. The picture of Andie standing on those steps, asking for my help, and me turning my back will never leave my thoughts.

"Jordan, Jordan, I need you to find a way to hold it together. Appearances." Brian whispers through clenched teeth.

"I'm trying! Sorry. I'm really trying."

Brian hands me one of the Safe Haven's menus and pushes it up to my face. Thankfully, they are large enough to hide behind. Some say that the menus were made intentionally large by old man Stockland to protect conversations. Brian explains that there are rumors of some attorneys overhearing conversations or reading lips and getting paid a handsome fee to disclose the information. According to Brian, no such instance has ever been proven.

"Try to find something to eat. Food will help. And keep the menu up in front of you until you are calm again."

I peer over the cardboard tower. "Brian, are you going to do the same thing to Andie? If so, I don't want you to ask her any questions."

"No. And, if it makes you feel any better . . . normally, I don't share information like this with a client. This is not a normal situation. One of my contacts told Erin that Judge Harris is flabbergasted with Barrens's theatrics today and she is planning to address it with the bar."

"It does make me feel better. Does anyone still use the word 'flabbergasted'?"

Brian's arms strain to loosen his red and yellow paisley tie. "That's what you took from what I just told you?"

"Is that an old suit? The color is nice. Grayish-blue works well with your complexion but the arms appear a bit too tight."

It's one of the few times Brian gives that blank stare of confusion. This also causes his crow's feet to become very pronounced. "What are you doing?"

I heave an overly dramatic sigh. "I'm trying to take my mind off Andie and this morning."

"Wonderful. Can you not do it at my expense?"

I give a devilish smile. "Isn't everything else at my expense? If I'm paying for it anyway, I might as well have some fun with it."

"Not the time or the place." Brian softens. "Although I'll admit it, that was a good one."

"So, you think Barrens will get in trouble for this morning?"

"My guess is he will get a fine and a reprimand, but Barrens didn't really step too far over the line. It was just enough over." Brian is shaking his head. "I've known attorney Barrens for years; he has never done this before. I don't know why he is now." Brian pulls the menu over his face trying to conceal some untruth he may have just told me. I don't ask.

We finish lunch without saying much more. Brian gives me the space I need to recover. I give him the room to sit with his lie. Knowing that Barrens will pay for his treatment of Andie in some way is no real comfort.

On the courthouse steps, the reporters are poised like large cats waiting on the Serengeti. "Brian, this doesn't look good."

"Just stay behind me and don't say a word."

An anonymous question from the herd catches my attention. "Dr. Carey, did you know Andie Tanner was going to do it?"

"Jordan, do you take any responsibility for what happened?" This question is thrown at me every day, and every day it makes me want to fight back.

Brian pushes us through the reporters. Two bailiffs meet us at the top of the steps and escort us into the building. With the bailiffs at our sides, we are allowed to bypass the metal detectors. A third bailiff holds the elevator doors open. The look of concern on Brian's face is matched by the confusion on mine.

"Brian . . ."

"I don't know. Don't say anything."

Bailiff number three hurries us past Courtroom Five—we exchange bewildered glances again. Inside Judge Harris's chambers are Barrens and his two juniors, all with confused looks. All seated waiting for us.

"Thank you, bailiff, I'll take it from here." Judge Harris sounds more official than usual. She directs us to empty chairs. "Please, sit down."

"Your Honor, is there a problem?" Barrens questions.

"Yes. Andrea Tanner—Andie, as you call her, Dr. Carey—is in the hospital. She left the courthouse with her husband during the lunch break and returned home. She then decided to take a handful of muscle relaxers. Her husband found her in time. He called 911, and they rushed her to the hospital. She is still unconscious, but she will survive. The muscle relaxers did stop her breathing for a short time, so doctors don't know if there will be any permanent damage."

I stand up, sending my chair crashing to the floor. I'm staring at Barrens as I move towards him, my fists at the ready. "You did this! You pushed her too far!"

"Jordan! Stop, now." Brian is standing between Barrens and me.

"Dr. Carey! Sit down! There is another problem."

I glare at the judge. "What? What could possibly be worse than Andie trying to kill herself because of me?" Rage is filling me, not allowing sorrow or tears any space.

Judge Harris ignores my outburst. Her voice is low and uniform. "Jordan, the prescription bottle that Andie removed the pills from has your name on it."

Silence explodes into the room. The Judge waits for the implication to sink in, then continues. "Did you prescribe the pills to her?"

I'm frozen, trying to gather my thoughts. "Yes. But that was over a year ago. Andie hurt her back lifting one of her twins. She should have finished the prescription long before today."

Brian strongly interjects. "Jordan, don't say any more."

"Mr. Freeland, I am not accusing Dr. Carey of anything," Judge Harris quickly interrupts.

"With all due respect, Your Honor, you may not be, but I'm certain Attorney Barrens will find a way to work it into the trial. I need a moment with my client."

"Fine, you can go out to the corridor if you wish."

"Thank you, Your Honor."

Angrily, I wait for the door to click. "Brian, I didn't hurt Andie; Barrens did. I need to get to the hospital to see her!"

"We have to handle things here first. Then I will tell Judge Harris that you need to go to the hospital. Let me handle everything from here on."

My fists instinctively rise to chest level. "If Andie dies, I will make it my life's work to see that Barrens pays for it."

Brian snaps, "Don't say things like that. In fact, don't say anything at all."

We reenter the judge's chambers, where all the players await silently. Judge Harris has demanded that no one speak so that nothing could be confused as collusion.

"Judge, my client is not going to answer any more questions at this time. She did nothing wrong. The prescription is legal, and Mrs. Tanner's treatment was complete at that time. Mrs. Tanner recovered from her injury, and Dr. Carey assumed she had taken the medication as prescribed. There is no way Dr. Carey could have known that Mrs. Tanner still had the medication and that she would use it as she did today. I ask that nothing of this matter be admissible in court."

"It's okay, Brian. I agree. For all the faults that Dr. Carey may have in the eyes of the law, we do not see how she could have foreseen this happening." Barrens's comment is humble and brings the room to a standstill, again. My rage is not quelled.

Judge Harris thumps her palms on the table and gives her orders for the afternoon. "We will return to court as planned. I will adjourn the court for the day. I will have to think about how to proceed. I will let you all know tomorrow morning before court. Please be back in my chambers at 9:00 a.m."

"Your Honor, I would like to note that my client has every intention of visiting Andie at the hospital as soon as court is adjourned. Since Andie is unconscious, there should be no conflict."

"I will agree to it only if you accompany her, and if Mrs. Tanner wakes, your client must leave immediately. As an officer of the court, you are bound to adhere to these orders. Do you agree, Mr. Freeland? Any objections, Mr. Barrens?"

"I agree."

Barrens responds. "No objections, Your Honor."

The bailiff announces Judge Harris, and the jury settles in for another session. Barrens says very little to anyone. I know this because I cannot take my eyes off the man. He abused Andie to get to me. I will never forgive him.

"There has been yet another turn in our courtroom today. It seems that the witness, Mrs. Tanner, has taken ill. She is unable to continue at this time. I am forced to postpone this trial yet again. We will return to this court tomorrow at nine thirty sharp."

For me, Judge Harris couldn't bang her gavel fast enough. I take my first steps towards the door before the bailiff finishes his verbal dance. Brian catches up with me in the corridor. "Jordan, I have a car waiting for us."

"Fine, let's get going." I'm leading the race to the street.

"Jordan, wait, there's going to be a lot of questions on the other side of that door."

"I don't care."

The courthouse door opens to flashes of light and an army of microphones. I'm in no mood to deal with the hounds. We push through. This time I'm at Brian's side. At the edge of the street, in front of the open door of the Uber, I'm struck with the courage of an entire platoon. "You want something to print? Here it is. My best friend, a mother of twins, a wife, a woman who is like a sister to me, was mercilessly humiliated this morning. Andie Tanner was so stricken with grief that she took pills to forget how she was forced to betray her lifelong friend. Her words were bent and twisted to make me look like a monster. That happened inside those walls. Out here, you stand waiting to sensationalize the grief that almost took the life of this woman. Is it worth it? I'm off to the hospital to sit next to my unconscious friend and hope that she survives. And when Andie does, I'm going to tell her that I'm sorry for what she had to endure because of me, and because of Attorney Barrens, and because of a system that allowed it. If you use her for your glory, I will tell her that her suffering continues because of you. Finally, I will spend the rest of my life trying to make it up to her. I ask you, no, I demand that you stay away! Let Andie heal in peace."

From the back of the crowd came a low clapping; it was Erin. Her clapping is joined by some bailiffs standing near the door and also by two younger attorneys, the juniors. The crowd of reporters turns to see who is clapping. Questions are now flying in their direction. Brian seizes the opportunity and shoves me into the car. The clappers return back into the courthouse without answering a question.

Brian stares and smiles. "While I don't usually condone speaking to the press, I can see why you had to. If you do half as well on the stand as you just did out there, we have it in the bag. That's not on the record, and you can't hold me to it."

"Thanks Brian, but I'm so angry and so worried. What if Andie has lasting effects from all of this?"

Brian invokes his fatherly tone. "I believe she will pull through. However that might look, she is going to need you when all this is over."

"I'm going to be right by her side."

The sight of BHMC doesn't bring tears but more rage. "Barrens has to pay! You have to make him pay for this. I want him to suffer like Andie and her family are suffering." My eyes begin to swell. "No! I won't cry!"

"Jordan, it's okay. Let's get inside."

"Brian!"

"I know. Barrens will pay."

CHAPTER 23
VINDICATION

ANDIE IS IN THE ICU, still critical. Sebbi stands there, holding her hand. The whooshing of the ventilator and beeping from various monitors make for an eerie orchestra. I look at Brian, signaling I'm ready. I take one last deep breath before entering. My sister's body lies motionless, multiple tubes exiting her, and her lungs rise and fall in a mechanical cadence. All the medical training in the world cannot prepare a person to see a loved one like this.

Barely audible and with my hands covering my mouth, I say, "Sebbi, I'm so sorry. I had no idea . . ." Brian is frozen in the doorway with a far-off gaze. Perhaps a bad memory of a family member or friend is running an unchecked flashback loop. "Brian, Brian, it's okay, come in."

Brian refocuses on Sebbi. "Yes, uh, sorry. Sebbi, right?" Brian wipes beads of sweat from his forehead. Sebbi and I exchange glances but remain quiet.

Sebbi extends a hand. "Yes. Uh, you must be Jordan's attorney, Brian, right?"

Brian's head bobs repeatedly. "I'm sorry to, um, intrude." His eyes begin darting around the room. "It's the only way Jordan could see Andie. Judge's . . . orders."

Sebbi eyes me. I shrug. "I'll explain it to you later."

"Jordan, this is not your fault. It's mine." Sebbi turns away in apparent shame. "She was panicking in the car. She couldn't sit still or stop talking. When we got home, she suddenly became serene. I didn't think anything of it. I figured she may have just worn herself out. Then she said she had to take a nap and asked not to be woken for the next thirty minutes. That seemed to confirm my assumption."

"What are you talking about? This is my fault, and it's that damn prosecutor's fault."

"No, Jordan, it's mine." Sebbi erratically strides around the hospital room like one of those new robotic vacuums. "I told Andie to put the post up. Andie found the unused pills in the back of her nightstand about two weeks ago. She wanted to throw them away, but I told her to save them. I convinced her we never know when we might need them. I set all of this in motion." Sebbi sobs uncontrollably. The pacing stops as he stands in front of Andie's bed, shaking.

A low throat clearing comes from the doorway. "I'm going to wait in the hallway." Brian steps out.

"Andie, this is not on you; it's on me. Come back. We need you." I gently steer Sebbi back to Andie's side. "Sebbi, none of this is your fault. Andie was pushed too far in court, that's the truth. It's also true that she chose to take the pills. You didn't force her. Hold her hand. Trust me, she'll know."

Sebbi's grip blanches Andie's hand. "Why did you do this?"

"Sebbi! Let go."

He follows my eyes down to the bed and quickly lets go. "I'm sorry for that too."

"Andie, I'm sorry too." I shift my attention to Sebbi. "I knew she was nervous and stressed about going back to work, but I didn't see this coming. I should have seen it!"

"No this is my fault. I didn't take care of her. I should have watched her more closely after this morning. It's all my fault. I made her do the post." Sebbi begins to cry.

"How could you see her being forced to testify against me?

That's insane. There's only one person to blame for this. I will make sure he gets what he deserves. That's a promise."

Several tense minutes pass when the call of "Code Blue" echoes through the hall. My knowledge of the severity of its meaning causes me to break the stillness. "Sebbi! Tell the doctors it's okay to talk to me!"

Sebbi sighs, and his shoulders drop. "I knew you would come, so I already tried. The doctors said they can't."

Ignoring him, I ask, "What have the doctors told you?"

"Not much. It's a wait-and-see situation. The tests show there is brain function. I don't know the names of the tests."

"CT and EEG, that's not important. It's good news."

"Jordan, she has to wake up, she has to be okay. What will the boys and I do without her?"

The hole in my stomach grows larger. "I'm going to stay as long as it takes for her to wake up."

Sebbi begins pacing again, this time he's also pulling at the buttons of his shirt. "You know you can't. You're already on trial for trying to help. I don't think you can afford more trouble."

I grab him and hold him close. "Stop, Sebbi, stop. She's going to be okay."

Sebbi is surprised by the physical contact and pulls away. "Jordan, you don't know that. No one does. You can't even be her doctor."

For a solitary moment, I forgot about the trial and that Brian is waiting patiently on the other side of the door. I'm speechless, holding a vigil at Andie's side. Sebbi sobs quietly. I run through the checklists I learned as a resident, but it's futile. I don't have enough information. "I'll be right back."

Strange looks and stares are directed at me as I walk to the nurses' station. The smug attitudes and the backing away from me on their rolling chairs say it all—Pariah. No matter, I still have privileges at this hospital, at least I think I do. No letter has been sent to my home, and the office is closed. It's a technicality I'm willing to risk.

"Hi, I'm Dr. Carey. I'd like to see the chart for bed eight, Andrea Tanner." I'm smiling, exuding confidence, and acting like I belong here.

The nurse behind the counter intervenes. "Hello, Dr. Carey. I don't think I can give you the chart. I know she's your friend. Dr. Milner said you might be coming. He told us to call him if you came to the desk."

My choices are limited, so I smile wider and nod. Dr. Milner appears from around the corner. He is a bit older and keeps himself in good shape by using the hospital gym every day. He was an attending during my residency and is now a colleague. "Hi, Doug."

"Hi Jordan, let's go into the doctor's lounge and talk." He's not even waiting for a response.

"Doug, I know you can't officially tell me anything, but she is like a sister to me."

"Jordan, we've known each other for some time now. So, I'm considering this a favor. Andrea Tanner is going to survive. You probably already know this. If or what degree of brain injury she may have suffered is unknown. She has brain activity, but she isn't breathing on her own yet. We just have to wait. There isn't anything else in her chart that will help you." Dr. Milner rubs the back of his bald head and neck. "You know it takes time. Give the meds some time to do their job."

I exhale. "Thanks, Doug. I appreciate it."

Milner whispers, "For what it's worth, Jordan, there are a ton of us here that wish we had the nerve to do what you did for your patients." Doug is peering through the glass of the doctor's lounge. "Jordan, I shouldn't be telling you this, but a number of the doctors and nurses here at Buckford anonymously donated to your defense fund. No one knows exactly who, but someone got a call from a friend of yours about this campaign. Most of us were afraid of the repercussions of publicly donating, so we created a second, more secret way to help. As you know, we raised eleven thousand dollars. You're kind of a celebrity around here. Please don't share any of that."

"That was you guys? I didn't know where it came from."

"That's why it's called anonymous. We're pulling for you." Doug Milner shakes my hand and leaves the lounge.

Vindication, finally! Win or lose in Courtroom Five, I've won out here. This is where it starts and where it counts. I reset myself back to the somberness of the situation.

Brian is back in the room and not pleased. "What did you do?"

Another forced white lie. The truth is not important right now. "Nothing, I had a conversation with a colleague." There is no follow-up question. Brian is definitely out of his element.

We sit in Andie's room for the next two hours. Brian busies himself typing and texting on his phone. There is no change in Andie's condition. Her body lies there, still motionless. The doctor in me knows she doesn't feel pain. The sister in me hopes it's true.

In the Uber, Samuel's friend goes unnoticed by Brian. Very little is said about our experience in Andie's room. Brian reminds me to be in front of the judge's door at nine tomorrow morning. The Uber pulls up to my apartment. The driver was never given an address, and again Brian doesn't take notice. As I'm getting out of the car, Brian insists I promise not to go back to the hospital or call Sebbi or anyone there. I hug him goodbye. He accepts my embrace. The Uber driver pulls away, leaving me entirely alone for the first time today. It's as if I've just been dumped on a deserted island. The loneliness is overwhelming. I wish I had a volley ball.

"Hi, Mom, I'll wait. Put me on speaker." I say as cheerfully as possible. I should have checked the news before calling.

"Hi Jordan, it's Dad. We saw you on the news. Terrible about Andie. We didn't know she had a drug problem, oh, and those dear boys of hers. What about her husband? Does he do drugs, too?"

"Hi Jordan. Mom here. Has she been sent to a rehab center? Are they going to take turns going to rehab? Your father and I heard those places can do wonders for people."

"Jordan, it's Dad again. Are the kids safe? Did they get all the drugs out of the house?"

"Andie is still in the hospital. Neither of them is a . . . never mind." I sigh.

"Jordan, it's Dad again. What you said on the TV was very powerful. We have been getting phone calls from the neighbors ever since it aired. Don't worry, we're telling everyone you didn't know that Andie and her husband were into drugs. Your mother is getting a sore ear from answering all the calls."

"Then tell her to stop answering all the calls."

Mom cuts in. "Then we might have missed your call."

"Jordan, your mother has a point."

My parents don't have caller ID. If they did, it would only make matters worse. "That's a good point, Mom. Listen, I just called to let you know I'm okay. I said what I said because Andie is my best friend."

"Your mother and I always say that if we had a second child, it would have been Andie. She's like a sister to you. We would have sent her to rehab early on if she were ours." Dad's words bring a tornado of emotions—anger, frustration, and remorse.

"Okay, I'll check in again tomorrow. Love both of you." I hang the phone up and sob. I'm tired of all this. Sitting in my apartment, the world seems light-years away. If only the sorrow I feel for Andie and for myself could be checked at the door, too. My mind has no desire to eat, but my stomach screams out in hunger. The continued grumblings are hard to ignore, and I make my way to the kitchen. Grocery shopping has not been high on my list. Luckily, I still have leftovers from the *Golden Girls* gathering.

A shower is next, and then I'll crawl into bed and hope the night absorbs me. Dr. Milner's words play back. In all the misery of today, there is still a hidden shimmer of joy. I close my eyes with a final thought: *I am vindicated.*

CHAPTER 24
ELLIOT FERN, PHARMD, RPH

THE LIMESTONE GREEK REVIVAL–ERA courthouse is adorned with iconic sentinels that protect against unwanted visitors. Come to think of it, how many people, other than lawyers, might actually want to break into this building? The many large marble steps challenge even those in decent physical shape. Ancient Greece would be proud of this fortress's ability to ward off unwanted intruders. Only a handful of dedicated reporters show up early, and they are too busy readying themselves to notice me maneuvering behind the outer columns at the far end of the courthouse.

The door-locks clunk, and a towering bailiff, a living column himself, opens the door to signal they are ready for business. The reporters turn, as if a dinner bell has been rung, and my invisibility is gone. The microphone-clad crowd moves like a school of piranha. I squeeze past the bailiff, avoiding any questions.

In the empty lobby, thoughts of Andie retake the stage. I have fought back every urge, both as a friend and a doctor, to call or go to the hospital. I mutter, "Concentrate on the moment." Only two bailiffs await at the metal detector. They have seen me here every day and no longer go through the routine of telling me what to remove or where to place my belongings.

Brian catches up with me at the elevators. "You walked past the reporters without me?"

I shrug. "I got here before them and hid behind a column until the doors were unlocked."

"Have you heard anything about Andie?"

"Oh, not funny. Have you? You and the judge told me I couldn't go near her without you."

He rolls his eyes. "Just checking."

The elevator pings are followed by the opening of the polished golden doors. Brian extends his arm. "Manners and such."

Barrens and the B team are standing in front of the judge's chamber. "Good morning."

"Good morning, Attorney Barrens." Brian's response is extremely formal.

Judge Harris opens the door. "Good morning, please come in and sit down."

"Your Honor, have you heard anything about Andie?" I can't wait any longer. The four attorneys glower at me.

The judge exhales loudly before starting. "Yes, I have already called over to the hospital. Mrs. Tanner, Andie, is in and out of consciousness. She is breathing on her own now. The doctors have taken her off the ventilator. They are hopeful." A collective sigh ripples through the room.

A large grin appears on my face. I'm unwilling to hide it. "Thank you."

"The doctors also stated that Mrs. Tanner will not be able to resume her place on the witness stand anytime soon. I have decided to order the jury to disregard her entire testimony. Are there any objections? Mr. Barrens, if you're thinking mistrial, I suggest you keep it to yourself."

The breath of the room sits on Barrens's shoulders. He stands there quietly shaking his head.

"Good, then this matter is settled. I'll see you in court at nine thirty." For the first time, I think I see a slight upward turn at the edges of Judge Harris's lips.

"Brian, I'm calling Sebbi. I'll be right in."

Brian taps the face of his wristwatch. "Don't be late. Nothing about the trial."

The conversation with Sebbi isn't as bright as I'd like. He confirms Judge Harris's report. He adds that Andie's words are slurred, and she is unable to form coherent sentences. Sebbi further relays that the doctors said Andie needs more time to heal. As a doctor, I know that this's doctor-ese for 'We don't really know yet.' They're hoping to buy time to see if Andie will have permanent damage.

Sebbi asks, "Jordan, you're family. Don't lie. Are they telling me the truth?"

"This is all good news. I'm confident Andie will make a full recovery. Sebbi, I have to go into the courtroom now." A not-so-white lie, but I don't think he can handle hearing that no one truly knows.

"All rise for the Honorable Judge Harris."

"Please be seated. It is with great displeasure that I must inform you that Mrs. Tanner will be unable to return to finish her testimony. Therefore, the defense will not have its chance to question her. Members of the jury, I instruct you to disregard any and all testimony from Mrs. Tanner. This means you cannot give any weight to her testimony when you make your final decision on the matter before you. While this is highly unusual, it is quite necessary. We will now proceed with this trial." Judge Harris surveys the jury before continuing. "Am I correct in saying that the prosecution is done with its presentation?"

"Yes, Your Honor. The prosecution rests."

Judge Harris makes a notation. "Okay, Mr. Freeland, please begin."

As Brian gets ready to call our first witness, I'm reminded of our conversation about whether I should testify or not.

"Do I have to get up there?"

"In a criminal trial, we don't have to put you on the stand. But, let's hold off on that, for now."

"No! Sorry, I don't want to testify. All the others will prove I didn't mean any harm."

"Okay, we'll come back to it later."

Brian didn't push me. He let me sit with the idea. After yesterday, with Andie and then the reporters on the steps, I realize I need to be heard.

Brian rises, looks at the jury, and presents the pearly whites. His signature move. "Thank you, Your Honor. The defense calls our first witness, Elliot Fern, PharmD, RPh, to the stand."

Elliot is the pharmacist who ran one of the local pharmacies I dealt with daily. He's in his mid-sixties and probably wishes he had retired long before the big hitters started flooding the pharmacy industry. This neighborhood prides itself on supporting the local merchants. But it won't be long before some large chain moves in and offers better prices and fancier items. Sooner or later, the cost of medications will force them to choose the large chains, and Elliot will be done.

"Mr. Fern, can you tell us what the initials after your name mean?"

"PharmD is the degree I obtained. It means Doctor of Pharmacy. The initials 'RPh' indicate that I'm a registered pharmacist." After almost thirty years in the business, Elliot still says this with great pride. He is the first in his family to obtain initials after his name.

"Mr. Fern, I'm sorry, should I address you as Dr. Fern?"

"No, that isn't necessary."

"Okay, Mr. Fern, can you tell us about your dealings with Dr. Carey and her patients?"

"I can as long as you aren't asking me about patient specifics. That would violate a bunch of privacy laws."

"Just the information about Dr. Carey's interaction with you and your pharmacy, please."

"Well, Dr. Carey is always very careful with her prescriptions. She is very thorough. She constantly calls with questions about medication, reactions to medications, or interactions with medications. If she is unsure about a medication, for any reason, she calls. Dr. Carey is also cautious. She even calls to double-check answers she already knows. I remember one time, it was raining . . ." Brian gives Elliot a look. Most of the time, witnesses are prepped by the attorneys they testify for. Brian knows that Elliot rambles on, so he must have come up with some signal to keep him on point.

". . . Yes, um. Dr. Carey never overprescribes. Some doctors will give five refills to avoid having to reorder. That's good for me, but it's not always necessary or good for the patient. Dr. Carey only orders, ordered, what she thought the patient needed. Like I said, cautious and prudent. I'm guessing she's that way with everything in her office."

"Objection. Speculation," Barrens chimes in.

"Sustained."

"Mr. Fern, did Dr. Carey ever pay for prescriptions for patients?"

"Yes. Often."

"Did Dr. Carey or anyone from her office ever pick up any of the medications that she prescribed for patients?"

"No, the patient picked them up, or we delivered them to the patient's home."

"When Dr. Carey bought medications for patients, how did she pay for them?"

"We charged an office credit card we had on file."

"Did Dr. Carey ever pay in cash for any of the prescriptions for patients?"

"No, never. And I wouldn't allow it. That would raise too many questions."

"Did you know that Dr. Carey had started a medication collection process to help those patients who couldn't afford their medications?"

"Yes, she would call if she couldn't identify a pill. She would send me a photo of the pill from her phone. If I couldn't identify it, I would tell her to dispose of it."

"As a pharmacist, do you know other pharmacists?"

"Yes, many." There's a puzzled look on the witness's face.

Brian steps between the witness stand and the prosecutor's table. "Can you tell those pharmacists who know their field well and those who don't?"

Now understanding, Mr. Fern smiles and delivers his answer. "Oh, yes, definitely. When you have been in the business as long as I have, you can tell the good from the bad, from the mediocre."

"What can you tell us about Dr. Carey? More specifically, what can you tell us about her knowledge of medications?"

Barrens stands, places both hands on his hips. "Objection! Your Honor! Mr. Fern is not qualified to rate doctors. Mr. Freeland continues to skirt the line here, and this court should not tolerate any more of it."

Brian turns towards Barrens and calmly replies, "I'm not asking the witness to rate all doctors. I'm asking him to rate Dr. Carey's knowledge of medications. As a pharmacist for almost thirty years, he's more than qualified."

Judge Harris clearly conveys her answer. "Overruled. Mr. Barrens, sit down, and do not speak for the court again. The witness will answer the question."

"Dr. Carey was like most other doctors, but with time, her skill and knowledge of identifying medications by sight became almost that of a seasoned pharmacist."

"Was Dr. Carey careful in her process of collecting the unused medications?"

Barrens quietly growls. "Objection. The witness was not present at the time of the collection of the medications; therefore, his answer would be no more than a guess."

"Sustained. Mr. Freeland, stick to the facts."

"Thank you, Mr. Fern. No more questions, Your Honor." Brian manages to keep Elliot on point, and the questioning is swift.

Barrens starts his questioning. "Mr. Fern, did Dr. Carey's amount of prescribing drop off when she began her Pill Box?'

Elliot hesitates. "Yes, come to think of it."

"Did the number of sales charged to her credit card go down?"

Elliot squirms for a moment, then answers, "I'm sorry, I don't know."

"Would it surprise you to know that the number of credit card transactions from Dr. Carey to your pharmacy didn't go down? In fact, there is an increase since the start of the Pill Box."

Elliot's tone rises. "I already said that I didn't know either way."

"Mr. Fern, did you help Dr. Carey set up or continue her Pill Box process?"

"No, I only answered questions regarding medications when she called." Elliot's lips purse, draining the pink from them. He tries to wipe the sweat from his forehead casually.

"Did you tell Dr. Carey that the Pill Box idea was a bad one?"

"I did not. Look! I didn't do anything wrong. Dr. Carey wrote prescriptions, and I filled them. That's my job, and that's all that I did. I answer questions for patients and doc—"

"Objection," Brian interrupts.

"On what grounds?" Barrens spats.

Brian smirks. "Withdrawn."

The pounding of the gavel rattles the courtroom. "Both attorneys to the bench." With the courtroom silent, the plaster walls echo the whispers from the bench. "Enough of the tallywagging around. Mr. Freeland and Mr. Barrens, you are both looking to become roommates for the night. No more erroneous objections from either. Back to your places and let's continue."

Barrens clears his throat and pauses just long enough to receive a glare from the judge. "Sir, do you have an obligation to report any misuse of medications?"

Brian continues his assault on Barrens's questions. This time, in a low, monotone manner. "Objection, there has been no determination of misuse of medication."

"Sustained. Mr. Barrens, please reword your question."

"Yes, Your Honor. Mr. Fern, are you obligated to report any suspicious use of medications?"

"Yes. Pharmacists have the opportunity to do it anonymously." Elliot's face cools.

"Mr. Fern, were you the anonymous source that called the authorities?"

"Objection. The question violates the very purpose of the law of anonymity." Brian's loudness draws an intense, dark look from the judge.

Judge Harris remains fixated on Brian as she responds. "Sustained, the witness will not answer the question."

I can't believe that Elliot turned me in. Now I sound like the criminal they want me to be. I've known Elliot ever since I opened my practice. When I first decided to be in the neighborhood, I made the rounds. I introduced myself to the local merchants, the various clergy, and anyone else who would listen. I thought Elliot and I had a bond. He knew I was trying to help, trying to make a difference. *Damn it! Everyone is looking out for themselves!* Thankfully, this time it's only an outburst in my mind.

Barrens flips through his notes, then continues. "Mr. Fern, do a lot of doctors pay for their patients' prescriptions?"

"No."

"Do you have any other doctors who pay for patient prescriptions with their own credit cards?"

"Objection. The credit card is a business card and not Dr. Carey's personal credit card."

Judge Harris peers over her glasses at Barrens. "Sustained. Mr. Barrens, you may reask the question if you clarify the credit card issue."

Barrens nods at Brian. "Mr. Fern, do you have any other doctors who use a business credit card or any other type of payment to buy patient prescriptions?"

"Well, now that you ask. No, I don't. But—"

Barrens intervenes. "No more questions, Your Honor."

"We will take a lunch break. Be back at 1:00 p.m., please." Judge Harris raises her gavel.

"Excuse me. I'm sorry, but I have a question before the witness is let go." Brian dispenses with the formalities. "I was not asked if I had any questions for the witness."

Judge Harris's scowl causes the courtroom windows to shutter. "Mr. Freeland, you are correct . . . I did not ask you if you wished to question the witness yet. You will have your chance after lunch. The hour is already late, and we have an obligation to let these fine jurors have a midday meal. Wouldn't you agree? Good." The thunder from Judge Harris's gavel sends a shockwave throughout the entire courthouse.

The bailiff mutters, "Yes, uh, all rise . . ." Judge Harris pushes past him.

Brian cracks from the repetitive clicking. "What are you typing?"

"I'm ordering an Uber?" I reply.

"Where are you going? Wait, Jordan."

"She's not part of the trial anymore. That means all bets are off."

"Jordan."

"Brian, I have just enough time. The directions say it takes sixteen minutes to get there. That means I'll make it in twelve. I'll grab something in the cafeteria and eat in Andie's room. I promise I'll leave at twelve thirty. That gives me half an hour to go twelve minutes."

"If you're late, Harris will crucify both of us."

"It's worth it." I hug Brian and dash past him, already deciding to take the stairs to the lobby. Fighting through the large crowd of reporters on the front steps is going to be a challenge, but I've got a better idea. "Quiet. Please, I don't have time to make a statement now. I'm on my way to the hospital to see Andie Tanner. Time permitting, I will give you a full report when I get back. If not, I will make a statement at the end of the day. I promise. Just let me through, please."

Like the parting of the Red Sea, the reporters separate. I high-five outstretched hands as I make my way to the Uber.

"You worry too much, Dr. Carey. Get in quickly." Samuel smiles before closing the door. "Like you text stated to me, we only have a short period of time. Who else is going to care about that?" Samuel hands me a plastic container with a red lid.

"What's this?" I ask.

A bigger smile appears in the rearview mirror. "It's your lunch."

"How? When did you have time . . ."

"You still don't get it, do you? We are all family. Alberta Carter was in the courtroom. She called Stella Thorne, as did I."

My face contorts from the confusion. "No, I mean, where did the lunch come from?"

Samuel laughs. "What do mothers always say? Ah yes. Your face is going to freeze like that. Ellie Zeiglebaum was in my car when you texted me. She was going to give me that food as a gift for the ride. I explained your dilemma, and she came up with the idea of making it your lunch. Jordan, you are part of us now. You had better get used to it."

I push it back towards him. "But it's your lunch?"

"No, my wife already packed me a lunch. Good woman." Samuel holds up a second container.

I eat four perfectly crisp potato latkes by the time we pull into the hospital's entrance, only ten minutes later. "Can you pick me back up at twelve thirty sharp?" A small chuckle rumbles through my mind. *I sound like Judge Harris.*

"I am not leaving. I'll eat my lunch in the parking lot across the street and be back here by 12:20." Samuel lets out a boisterous laugh. "But I want a five-star review."

I hold up all ten fingers. "Five for getting me here and five for the return trip, if we're not late." We both laugh.

Sebbi isn't here. His earlier text explains that their children are not in a condition to attend school. The twins don't understand why mommy isn't home. They just know she's very sick and in the hospital. Indignation courses through my lips. "Barrens, you self-serving, pompous ass!"

Andie is asleep. I sit beside her, taking the liberty to sip some of her ice water to wash down the latkes. "I know you won't mind." The tubes, pinging monitors, and ventilator are all gone. Time is running out. A hopeful prayer and a gentle nudge, followed by a whisper, "Andie, I only have a few minutes. Please . . ."

Andie turns her head towards me. Her voice is low, gravelly—almost inaudible. "What the hell are you doing? I'm sleeping." A tiny smirk rises from her as she squints an eye open. "Took you long enough to get here. How about some water, please?" A forced laugh.

"Might have to get some more." I wait, staring at her. "Andie, why? Was it so terrible? You were done with the hard part." There is no response. The doctor in me didn't expect one; the loving sister begs for one. I shift away from Andie; I didn't want her to see me cry. My left foot taps the bottom of the bed, jarring it.

"Aren't I hurt enough? How about that water?" Both her eyes are open, but a haze is still apparent.

I am unable to control myself. Tears fly as I fling my arms around her weak, limp body. "I love you, you jerk! What were you thinking? What—"

Andie's words are forced, and her breathing is labored. "The pills didn't kill me, but you're going to if you don't let go. Get off me."

She takes the plastic pink cup from me. "Why is there lipstick . . ." Andie looks at my face, more precisely, my lips. "You drank my water? You drank water meant for someone on their deathbed?"

"Not funny." My phone pings to let me know it's time to leave. "I have to go, or I won't make it back to court in time."

Andie tries to lift her arms, but she is too weak. "You're leaving?"

I pass through the ICU curtain and look back at her. "I love you, and I'll explain later when I come back."

Samuel is waiting as promised. "How is she?"

"She's awake. Let's go."

"On it."

CHAPTER 25

WISHING THAT TRIP NEVER HAPPENED

"All Rise for the Honorable Judge Constance Harris."

"How is Andie?" Brian quickly mouths.

I'm still out of breath from running up the stairs. I take a deep breath and mouth back "Awake, alert, and—"

Brian slants his eyes toward Judge Harris sitting on the bench. "Better tell me later."

"Got it."

Judge Harris catches our little exchange. "Mr. Freeland, is there a problem?"

"No, Your Honor." Brian reveals nothing about Andie's current condition.

The Judge returns a glare of distrust. "If my memory is accurate, Mr. Freeland, you have more questions for this witness. Now is your time to continue."

"Yes, Your Honor. Mr. Fern, did Dr. Carey ever write a prescription for herself or any of her staff members?"

"Yes, but very rarely, and only for things like antibiotics or anti-inflammatories."

"Did Dr. Carey or her staff pay for any of those prescriptions with the office credit card?"

"No, I don't believe so." Elliot tries hard not to smile.

He thinks he's helping. He may be the sole reason I'm here today.

Brian continues, "As a pharmacist, do you think Dr. Carey was misusing medication?"

"Objection, the witness is not a medical doctor or a law enforcement agent and cannot make that determination."

Brian interjects, "He is a pharmacist with many years of experience dealing with doctors and medications. Mr. Fern's opinion is valid."

"Overruled. The witness may answer." Judge Harris again does not look up from her notes.

"No. I don't."

"Thank you, Mr. Fern, for your testimony today." Brian walks back to his seat when Barrens stands to ask another question.

"Mr. Fern, as a pharmacist, was Dr. Carey's medication collection a dangerous process that did not conform to the norms of the pharmacy world?"

Elliot Fern, PharmD, RPh, stares at his shoes before answering. "Um, as a pharmacist, I would have to answer, yes, I believe so. But—"

Barrens smartly dispatches the rest of Elliot Fern's answer. "No more questions for this witness. I'm done, Your Honor."

"Objection, Your Honor. The witness was asked a question about his professional opinion, and as an expert, he should be allowed to give it in its entirety."

Judge Harris peers over the top of her glasses at Barrens. "Sustained. I, too, would like to hear the full answer. Please finish your statement, Mr. Fern."

"Thank you, Your Honor." Elliot smiles as he mimics the attorney. "I was going to say that Dr. Carey is a rare breed. Not too many people, let alone doctors, would stick out their neck; heck, she put it all on the line for her patients." Elliot gains bravado as he continues. "She was helping others, and the risk to her patients was low. I understood why she was doing it. I believe that Dr. Carey's heart and her intent were in the right place. It is for these reasons that I didn't report her."

Judge Harris quietly exhales. "The witness may step down. Mr. Freeland, call your next witness."

"Your Honor, we call Lana Robski to the stand."

I didn't know Lana Robski until Brian told me who she was and how she's tied into my case. In fact, I've only spoken to Mrs. Robski one time, and that didn't go very well.

"Mrs. Robski, you have been sworn in and are bound to tell the truth. Do you understand?" Judge Harris has said these words so many times, there's no feeling left behind them.

"Yes, uh, Your Honor," Lana nervously replies.

Brian begins, "Mrs. Robski, how do you know Dr. Carey?"

"I really don't know her. I've only met her once, in Asheville, North Carolina. She wanted to save my husband's life."

"Can you tell us about yourself and your family?"

"We have three children, the oldest is now nineteen, and the youngest is sixteen. My husband and I both work. I guess now, it's just me. We were married for twenty-one years. We like, liked all the same things. He was my soulmate." The once pale complexion of Lana Robski has reddened and there is puffiness under both eyes.

Judge Harris holds a hand up, signally Brian to wait. "Mrs. Robski, do you need a moment?"

"No, Your Honor. It won't matter. If you don't mind, I will just continue." Lana sat with her hands folded across her lap and the whites of her knuckles could be seen from as far back as the last row of the courtroom. No one spoke a word or made a sound.

"I work in an office for a small real estate group five days a week and if I can pick up extra hours on the weekend at an open house, I take it. The kids and I miss my husband so much." Lana rubs her eyes; her emotions are on full display.

Brian places his hand on the jury box's front rail. "Could you please explain what happened to your husband?"

"Henry, that's my husband's name. Henry and I were at the Biltmore Estate the same day as Dr. Carey. This was the first real trip for just the two of us since the kids came along. It was just supposed to be a few days. We roamed the gardens holding hands and laughing. The smell of fresh air and the mild breeze gave Henry and me a break from our everyday life. We toured the estate like many of the other folks there, but for me, it was a private outing, no one but Henry and myself. We sat on the large verandas overlooking the green rolling hills. I wanted to stay there with him forever." Even with tears in her eyes, a smile passes over Lana's face.

"We ended our trip—I can't call it a vacation anymore. Sorry. We ended our trip at the estate vineyard with a wine tasting. It's an old cattle barn that was converted into fancy shops filled with every imaginable logoed trinket. We really couldn't afford many of the things in the stores, but Henry wouldn't let me go home without something. We picked out some cheeses to try and two bottles of wine. He was like that when it came to me. The warm mid-September breeze was blowing through this courtyard, making the flowers smell heavenly. A two-piece band played old tunes just loud enough to be noticed. We were having the most wonderful time tasting wine and eating delicious food. It was like we didn't have a care in the world. Henry always tried hard to make us feel that way. He didn't want me to worry about anything."

Lana takes a long heaving breath, then removes a man's handkerchief from her purse, and wipes her tears. "Out of nowhere, Henry was lying on the ground. I thought his chair broke, so I started to laugh. Henry was a large man. He was about six-foot-one, and weighed over 275 pounds. It turned out to be much worse than a broken chair. Henry had a couple of scares with his heart before, but nothing like this. His doctor told him to lose a few pounds, but I don't think he ever pushed Henry on it. Anyway, the place was filled with people, but no one tried to help. No one, except for Dr. Carey."

Brian interrupts, "What did Dr. Carey try to do?"

"Everything a doctor is supposed to do. I think. She wanted to help, but my husband refused. I didn't know it then, but Henry had a DNR. He must have told Dr. Carey this when she bent down to hear what he was saying. She pleaded with Henry to let her help, but he continued to refuse. He died lying on the ground in my arms. I know she didn't get to do much, but she wanted to."

Lana Robski looks down at her hands and falls silent for a long moment. Her voice quivers. "It wouldn't have mattered anyway. Turns out Henry had an aortic aneurysm . . . and it . . . it let go. He was dying . . . no one could save him."

Brian reluctantly breaks the stillness. "Mrs. Robski, sorry to ask, but did you know that Dr. Carey was bound by law not to treat your husband?"

Lana looks up at the ceiling before answering. "That's the first time I've admitted that out loud. To answer your question; no, not at the time. That damn DNR. I still wish she would have broken the rules to help Henry. Even if it gave me just a few more minutes with my husband."

Brian waits for the darkness of the scene to embed into the jury's mind. "Mrs. Robski, I'm sorry for your loss. And again, I apologize that I must continue to prolong your pain with more questions." Brian inhales loudly. "Can you tell us what your financial situation was at the time your husband died?"

"We were living paycheck to paycheck. Like I said, we hadn't had a vacation in years, then Henry won a contest at work that gave us one night at a hotel outside the Biltmore and tickets to the estate and the wine tasting. That's why we were there. We decided to pay for a second night and enjoy ourselves." Lana releases a large heave. "I wish Henry had never won that stupid contest."

Brian speaks slowly and gently. "Again, I'm sorry to keep

asking questions, but I have no choice. What was the situation with your health insurance?"

"All we could afford was this terrible policy with an extremely high deductible. We didn't go to the doctor unless it was an emergency. Henry had been told that he had a heart condition. The medication was expensive, even with help from the pharmaceutical company. I found out later that Henry had only been taking his pills every other day so he could stretch them out."

A collective groan rumbles through the courtroom. Judge Harris raises her gavel but decides against it. Brian gingerly continues. "Can you tell us what your opinion is of Dr. Carey?"

Barrens stands to object, hesitates, and sits back down.

"I think there should be more doctors like Dr. Carey. When I heard what she did to put her here and why she did it, I was proud of her. Then when your people contacted me, I was glad to come here to help her. She wanted to help my Henry. I think she did all of this to help and not for any other reason. There are a lot of Henrys in the world, I wish there were a lot more Dr. Careys."

"Thank you, Mrs. Robski. No more questions, Your Honor." Brian returns to his seat. The silence in the courtroom is broken by repeated muffled sniffles.

Barrens stands. "Your Honor, Mrs. Robski has endured enough pain having to relive her family's tragedy through the multitude of questions the defense has just made her answer. The prosecution does not wish to add to her suffering. We compassionately decline to ask any questions of her."

"Thank you, Mrs. Robski, you may step down." Judge Harris's cheeks and eyes are rose colored. "We could all use a break. Please be back at nine thirty tomorrow morning." A half-hearted banging of the gavel closes the court session for today.

Brian and I leave Courtroom Five and enter the elevator. I pat him gently on the back, he smiles. "That was a tough testimony to hear. Brian, I have to let you know that the reporters are waiting downstairs for me. I owe them an update on Andie."

Brian shakes his head. "You owe them?"

"I'll fill you in later. I just owe them. Let's just do this and go home." Even I'm feeling exhausted from Lana's unearthing of the painful details.

The reporters patiently wait and only a few microphones are thrust at me. The rest respectfully hold their distance.

"How's Andie?" A female reporter shouts as she shoves her microphone in my face. The intrusion of my personal space makes me want to take action; I resist.

"How did you feel in Asheville?" A second reporter hollers from the indiscernible crowd.

I need to regain my composure or I'll be giving them more to tell in tonight's sensationalized rendition of my life. "I'm only going to give you an update about Andie. After I was sitting with her in her hospital room for a short while, Andie woke up and spoke with me. She was tired but able to speak softly and clearly. She is in no condition to even get out of the hospital bed. She didn't explain anything about what happened. The doctors will be watching her for any signs of trouble. Now you know everything I do. I'm relieved that she is awake and able to speak with some coherency. I again will tell you more as I find out. Thank you again for earlier. Have a good night."

Some reporters continue to shout questions, but most abide by our agreement. "What about the witness's story today? Is it all true? Did you let her husband die?"

Brian steps up. "That's enough questions for today."

I move out from behind Brian. "A woman poured her heart out in front of complete strangers today. She painfully relived every moment. She did that for me. She did that because, no matter how much suffering it caused her, it was the right thing to do. She didn't do it so you could get a ten-second bite on tonight's local news. I'm sorry that you feel it's okay to take another person's misery and turn it into your glory."

Brian gently pushes me behind him again. "Okay, there will be no more comments today."

There rest of the steps are taken in silence except for the camera clicks.

Inside the Uber, I look at Brian, my brows climbing almost to the top of my forehead. "I think that went well."

"We'll see."

"You don't approve?"

Brian is motionless. "We'll see."

"We'll see? That's all you have to say?"

Brian shifts his weight so he's facing me. "Jordan, it's been a rough day for reasons I'm not willing to share. Let's just call it a day."

"Uh, sure? I'm going to shower then head back to the hospital. You go home and . . . rest."

Brian turns to me. "Please be careful. We're making headway."

I sit back in the Uber. "One thing that Lana Robski and I have in common: We both wish that trip never happened."

CHAPTER 26
ALL THE GOODBYES

Andie's face is drawn, and the blond hair that usually completes the model-like ensemble is matted and desperately in need of a wash. I make a hesitant motion towards Andie's head. "Now that's the ultimate bed head."

Andie half smiles, and turns away. "I deserve to look bad."

"Andie, don't do that. We have to talk, but now is not the time. We're family. When you're ready, we'll discuss it. For now, let's just be happy together." I lower the side rail of her bed so I can be closer to her.

Andie squeezes my hand tight—tighter than I would have expected. "Jordan, it all got to be too much."

I place my free hand on her cheek. "Hey, what did the doctors say?"

"I'm going to be fine. I have to go through some more tests, and then there's therapy." Andie rolls her eyes.

"After the last few days, let's see if we can get a group rate."

Andie's voice cracks. "I know you didn't need this on top of everything else."

I move a bit closer to her. "We'll help each other like we always do. Where's Sebbi?"

"He was here earlier. I sent him home to be with the twins. His guilt is too much to handle right now." Andie looks away again.

"I know. I spoke with him yesterday. He told me how he made you keep the pills."

Andie turns back to me, her eyes squinting and her brow

furrowing. “First of all, no one makes me do anything, especially Sebbi. You think that’s why he’s feeling guilty? Oh, no, no, no. That’s not it at all.”

“What are you talking about? You’re acting really weird. Sebbi can do a lot of things that make you mad, but never this angry. Wait, is Sebbi having an affair? It can’t be . . .”

“No. That would be easy to deal with. He was offered a job in London, and he took it without even talking to me. Two years out of the country, and he just took it . . . no conversation about it. No ‘Let’s weigh the pros and cons.’ He just said yes.”

Andie looks at me. She’s waiting for a response. “I . . . I think he should have talked to you about it.”

She ignores me and rants on. “The twins just started school, and I’m reviving my business. And you, you could go to prison. Everything is being turned upside down.”

I’m not sure what the correct response is. *I’ll be fine? The kids will be fine?*

Andie’s hands are balled into fists. “There’s more. Then, Sebbi suggests that the twins and I stay here while he goes to London. He promises he’ll fly home at least once a month. The twins and I don’t want a long-distance relationship. They need to grow up with their father, and I need my husband. What is he thinking . . . ‘stay here.’”

“That’s outrageous!” I shake my head in disapproval. “What. Was. He. Thinking?”

Andie gives me an inquisitive once-over. “I know.”

“When did he tell—”

The rage makes her cut me off. “The night we went to Leon’s. I came home half drunk. I told him about our night, and right in the middle of it, he decides it’s a good idea to spring this on me. He follows it up by convincing me to write the post. I think he was trying to get my mind off the whole job thing. I have no clue why I listened to him. What was I thinking?”

I reply, "The alcohol." Andie appears puzzled. "The reason was the alcohol. Forget it. So, have you decided?"

Andie begins to cry. "No. That's why I'm here. Sebbi's starting in three days, moving, the twins, my career, and you being on trial. The stress of it all made it impossible to rest. So, I took two pills hoping they would relax me enough to sleep. A few hours later and still no sleep, I got this dumb idea, if I took just two more, it wouldn't kill me, but it would delay having to choose. Then I could be here for you, and Sebbi would have time to reconsider."

"Andie, I love you, but that was the worst idea anyone's ever had. And, according to Barrens, I'm the queen of bad ideas." We both start laughing. "Andie, go to London. I'll be fine."

"You don't know that. What if it all goes to shit?"

I smirk. "It won't. Thanks to you, the reporters love me now."

Andie fluffs her hair. "Jordan, I'm not going to try to kill myself every time you need to get on someone's good side."

We're laughing so hard that Andie almost falls out of bed. After raising the side rail, I tell Andie to call Sebbi and let him know the whole family is moving to London.

Andie picks up the phone, and I step out of the room. There's a hollow in my stomach. *It's only for two years.*

Andie's voice quiets as the call ends. I reenter. She is brushing her hair. "That won't help. Shampoo is the only antidote."

Andie gives me a dirty look. "Antidote—really? I told him you thought I was being silly."

"I said no such thing. You really have to stop putting words in my mouth."

She produces a devilish grin. "You did now. And we have a great idea. Since we'll only be gone for two years and don't want to sell the house, we'd like you to house-sit."

"Andie, are you sure?"

"Yes, what's the chance of you having a second trial in the next two years? Too soon?"

I hold up a hand to pretend to slap her. "Funny. Thank God, because I don't think I'll be able to afford my apartment after all of this. I was dreading the thought of having to move back in with Mom and Dad."

Andie leans back in her bed, placing her arms behind her head. "Sebbi is being paid a fortune to run this campaign. So, we'll throw in the utilities. By the way, house sitters don't pay; they get paid. That last part won't be happening."

We make small talk about the details for the next ten minutes, and I feel it's time to discuss Andie's testimony. I don't know if I'll get another chance. I fill her in on how the judge threw it out and how the jury can't count it. I explain the pact with the reporters. She pleads with me not to share her going home. "I'll have to tell them something. Got it. I'll say that you're recovering slowly and under close observation."

Andie nervously nods. "Will that be enough?"

"It's a quote directly from the defendant. I am at the epicenter of the hottest story, after all."

We giggle like schoolgirls and continue to talk like old times. Like before there was a husband, twins, and a trial. Andie starts to tire, and we say good night.

The walk home reminds me of my residency days. For the first time in a long while, I feel whole. My office is just a few blocks away, and for some unknown reason, I get the notion to head over there. I know I'm not allowed inside, but there is comfort in seeing that it's still mine. My heart begins to race as the elevator reaches my floor. The doors open, and there, on my front door and strewn across the walls on both sides, is a montage of letters and notes from patients and their family members. Each one wishing me well or thanking me for trying to help. Others tell me I was making a difference. One note breaks me:

. . .

Dear Dr. J.,

My name is Gabby, short for Gabriella. I'm fourteen years old. You don't know me, but you knew my abuela. *If you don't know, that means 'grandmother.' Her name was Maria Ortez. She was 84 years old when she started coming to you last year. My abuela found out you were honest and really cared about helping people. She said she had a good feeling about you. She worked hard all her life and raised 7 children. She was diabetic and couldn't always afford all the different medications she had to take. She told us you were keeping her alive. You gave her the medications she needed and didn't make her feel bad about taking your help. She always looked forward to visiting you. My abuela passed away about two months after the police closed your office. She had no choice but to go back to her old way of dealing with the diabetes. I wish there were more doctors like you in the world. When I grow up, I want to be strong like you. I want to be brave enough to stand up for those who can't, just like you. Thank you for taking such good care of my abuela. She missed you, and now I miss her.*

Gabby.

Uncontrollable tears are followed by my entire body shaking, not from overwhelming sadness but from seething anger. I remember sweet Maria. Like Henry Robski, she didn't need to die. I place Gabby's letter in my pocket, then carefully remove the rest and take them with me. "All the good I've accomplished is in jeopardy of being erased. Why did I stop here?"

Sitting on my bed at home, reading and rereading each one, I contemplate all the goodbyes I've endured, and all the goodbyes that will soon come. Tears fall. "Andie."

The ringtone from my cell phone pulls me out of the sadness. "Brian? Is everything okay?" An unexpected sniffle wafts into play.

"Jordan, what's wrong?"

I give a long pause followed by an even longer inhale. “Nothing, just silliness.”

This time it is Brian who pauses. “If you say so.” Brian waits again. I don’t respond.

“Be at the courthouse half an hour earlier tomorrow. Barrens asked to meet with us.”

“About what? Why?” I fire back quickly.

“Relax, I don’t know. But it’s unofficial. He said just the two sides, no judge in the conference room before court.”

“Is that legal?”

“In a shady backroom kind of deal,” Brian replies. “No, it’s not legal, and he’s willing to risk a mistrial, so I’m intrigued. We’re taking the meeting.”

“Are you sure?”

Brian’s voice strengthens. “Half an hour early and don’t be late.” The call ends.

CHAPTER 27
BARRENS'S ULTIMATUM

BRIAN MEETS up with me a few yards from the courthouse steps. "Please don't play with the reporters today."

"Sure, I'll just wave hello and say good morning." A surprising disappointment seeps through me.

As expected, the reporters are parked on the steps. Brian looks at me, I smile at him, and address the crowd. "Good morning, sorry we're running late. Perhaps later."

What would I say? Maybe something about the letters. "The letters! Brian, wait, we need to stop before we get to the courthouse suite."

"The what?"

"The conference room, the one we're racing to. It's important!"

"No, I know what you meant about the room. What letters? No, wait until we're inside."

I tell him about going to the office last night after seeing Andie. Then, I explain all the letters on the door and walls.

Brian blurts out, "You should have led with Andie. Is she well enough for Barrens to make her testify?"

"I don't think so. But . . ."

Brian picks up the pace. "Good, tell me the rest later."

I give him a perplexed look. "Good?"

"You know what I mean. Keep moving, we're late." Brian pushes the elevator button several times.

"Brian, what could they possibly want?"

"I have no idea. Just get into the elevator. Barrens and his crew took the previous one and are probably positioning themselves for some kind of stand-off."

The elevator doors close, and I face Brian. "It feels like we're heading to the Alamo or the O.K. Corral."

Brian laughs as he steps out of the elevator and heads down the corridor, nearly jogging. In front of the door, he stops to catch his breath. "Don't be so dramatic." A deep inhale followed by an exhale, followed by another inhale. "Remember, a no-lose situation."

"You need to exercise more."

He ignores me and turns the knob. "Well, I see you've made yourselves comfortable." The truth is that Barrens and his team have taken seats in the middle of the table. This is a relatively weak position, strategy-wise.

"Look, I don't want to play around. The case is not going our way, so I'm prepared to offer a deal." Barrens is direct as his juniors wait, watching for any reaction we may have.

Brian, unfazed, asks, "What are you thinking?"

"If your client agrees to plead guilty to tax evasion, I'll let go of the rest of it. I'll recommend three years of probation, and we're done." The offer is well-rehearsed.

Brian stalls, searching for any backhandedness within the offer. "Why now?"

"Like I said, you're winning. The truth is, the prosecutor's office doesn't want egg on its face again." Barrens slowly stands and holds out his right hand. "Oh yes. This deal is only on the table until we head back to court."

Brian exaggerates the dragging out of a chair before sitting in it. "Why should we take this deal if, according to you, we're winning?" The two gunslingers are in a standoff in the middle of the corral. "I don't buy it. What's really going on?"

Barrens turns his head to stare at me. "I'm going to lay all the cards on the table. Brian, did you know Dr. Carey went back to the hospital last night to visit Andie Tanner?"

"No. But why does that matter? Andie is no longer part of this trial. My client can visit her friend in the hospital if she wants to."

"Did you know that Mrs. Tanner has made a full recovery and is about to leave the hospital in a day or so?"

Brian looks directly at Barrens and only at Barrens. "Again, no. And again, why does this matter?" I suspect Brian knows why it matters.

Barrens smiles; he even lets out a slight laugh. "We both know you're not that dumb, but I'll say it anyway. It means that I might ask Judge Harris to reinstate Andrea Tanner as a witness and haul her back in here. It means that I can use everything she said in court again. And she said a great deal." Barrens is no longer smiling.

Brian rises from the chair, once again he starts a slow, methodical sliding of the chair across the floor, allowing it to squeal. "Well, that's some performance you just put on. My client and I are not worried. Since we are so far ahead, I think we'll take our chances." Brian mimics Barrens's disappearing smile.

"I think you might want to ask your client if she wants to put her dear friend, Andie, through that whole ordeal again." Barrens is now looking at me. "Is she is willing to take the chance of maybe going to prison for a long time? You know, if anything seems odd with Mrs. Tanner's testimony when she returns to the stand, it's going to look like witness tampering by your client." Barrens sits and places his highly polished shoe upon the table. "Worse yet, who knows what Mrs. Tanner might do after I'm finished with her this time."

I step forward, fists drawn. Brian steps in front of me. "Let's go, Jordan." At the door, Brian turns back to Barrens. "Please remove all the trash you brought into the room when you leave."

The coldness of the marble corridor hits almost as hard as the thought of Andie back on the witness stand. "Brian, you can't—"

"Don't worry. It's never going to happen."

The thought of putting Andie through more time on the stand is too much for me. I look at Brian and turn, bursting through the conference room door. This time, there is no outburst, no raised volume; there is only a deep, slow cadence as I stand eye to eye with the enemy. "Attorney Barrens, I have watched you perform in that courtroom for some time now. I'll admit that at first, I was afraid of you. Now I feel pity for you. Each time you question a witness, you find yourself severely outgunned by my attorney. You are on your second round of table slaves, and they, too, fear Brian Freeland. So, I don't need to confer with my attorney. In fact, I don't even need to think about it. Whatever it is you think you can bring, bring. As far as Andie Tanner goes, I will testify that we spoke of no particulars regarding my trial other than the mockery you're making of it and yourself. Try whatever sort of underhandedness you think is necessary and both Attorney Freeland and the judge—"

"That's enough, Jordan," Brian interrupts.

I look at both attorneys. "This was a negotiation meeting, correct?"

"Yes, why?" Barrens answers.

"I read online that negotiation meetings are not admissible in court. Is that true?"

Brian lets out a loud snort. "You knew that, didn't you? Yes, you're right. You also know that Barrens can't repeat or use any of that in court." Brian, still cackling, grabs my arm and pulls me out of the courthouse suite.

We are standing outside Courtroom Five with a few minutes to spare. Brian excuses himself to call his office. I hear him say hello to Erin as he's walking away. I enter the courtroom alone, and the grin on my face is undeniable. What is more surprising to me is the ease I feel.

Brian comes into the courtroom to tell me to go with him. We are once again called to the Principal's office. It seems that attorney Barrens will make good on his threat.

"Brian, I need to fill you in on Andie. You need to know. You can't go in there without understanding why Andie tried to commit suicide."

"Okay, Jordan, quickly, what is it?"

"Andie tried to commit suicide because her husband, Sebbi, told her he is taking a job in London and she was trying to buy time. She told me she wanted to take just enough to knock her out, not kill her. She said it was an accident. A mistake."

"Will Andie say this in court?"

"I don't know. We didn't talk about that. Brian, don't bring her back here, please."

Brian enters the judge's chambers on the offensive. "Judge Harris, this is highly irregular. Attorney Barrens is already on shaky ground, and this makes his footing more dangerous."

"Mr. Freeland, first, close the door. Second, I am the presiding judge in this trial; therefore, I will determine how shaky Mr. Barrens's footing is. Mr. Barrens, what is the meaning of all of this?"

"Your Honor, this is about Andie Tanner. She is awake and will be going home from the hospital. There is no sign of brain damage. She can testify. She is crucial to the prosecution's case." Barrens is standing, and junior lawyer number one is trying to get him to sit down, like a child tugging on a parent's coattail.

"Mr. Freeland, did you know about Mrs. Tanner's improvement?"

"Not until Attorney Barrens told me, and then not until just before coming in here. Dr. Carey filled me in on Mrs. Tanner." Brian signals me to tell the judge what I know.

For some reason, I stand up and, for the second time today, explain the painful details of Andie's mistake.

"Please sit down, Dr. Carey. Are you able to make a medical

determination objectively about Andie Tanner?" Judge Harris is sincere in her question.

Barrens is unable to control himself. "Judge, that's like asking the fox if he can guard the chickens while the farmer goes to town."

"Mr. Barrens, if you wish to stay in my chambers, you will remain silent until I ask you to speak. Which will it be?"

Barrens makes no effort to speak. He merely points to the floor silently.

"Dr. Carey, before you answer, this is all off the record. A witness's well-being may be at stake here." Judge Harris's eyes are fixed on me.

"I think I can." I'm not really sure what the judge wants from me, but I'm willing to try.

"Do you think that Mrs. Tanner is mentally sound to sit in my courtroom and be asked difficult questions about you without later trying a repeat of the other day?"

"Your Honor, I honestly don't know. Medically speaking, the fact that she almost killed herself to keep from leaving me brings up a lot of unanswered questions regarding her mental status. No sane person would go to those lengths. That is my medical opinion. If I were you, Your Honor, I mean no disrespect. I would ask the doctors who are treating her. My answer is what I believe to be true without regard for myself, my friendship with Andie Tanner, or this trial."

"Dr. Carey, thank you for your honesty. I believe you are correct, but I will call the hospital to confirm your medical opinion. I expect this to take only a short time. Please all wait in the courtroom. I will make the necessary inquiries and call you back here when I'm done."

"Your Honor. Mrs. Tanner's testimony carries a lot of weight and must be allowed either way," junior number one chimes from behind Barrens.

Barrens points to the door. "Sorry, Your Honor. We will wait for your decision." The junior attorney leaves without further fuss.

In the courtroom, Barrens is whispering to his remaining underling while Brian is on his cell phone. Both sides are hard at work jockeying for position. I'm trying to figure out how to warn Andie. *I can't call her*. Sebbi! "Brian, I need the restroom." Brian waves me off.

After checking to make sure the restroom is empty, I call my parents, telling them not to speak and to follow my directions precisely. I make sure they understand exactly what to tell Sebbi.

Within less than a minute, my phone rings. "Jordan, it's Dad. Real quick, Sebbi's phone went to voicemail. We didn't leave a message. On TV, they never want to leave a trail."

I can feel my mouth hanging open. "Okay, let it go. I'll figure something else out. Thanks, Dad, I have to go." The restroom door swings shut behind me, knocking me into an oncoming bailiff's shoulder.

The pencil thin bailiff begins to yammer. "I'm sorry. Are you okay? Do you need to see a doctor? I mean, another doctor. If so, let me know, I don't want to get in trouble later. Oh God."

Obviously, the poor bailiff has had an altercation or two before and is clearly rattled by them. "No, it's okay, I'm fine. Please don't worry. Thanks for asking." His offer to send for a doctor makes me realize I can go to the hospital after court today and warn Andie.

Brian is waiting at the courtroom door. "Where have you been? The judge is ready to see us."

I lean in close to Brian. "What do you think will happen?"

"I don't know. I do think that we scored big when the judge asked for your opinion. Just continue to be honest and respectful in there."

Judge Harris is not alone in her chambers. This startles all of us. Barrens and Brian are staring at each other while the remaining junior busies himself with the floor tiles. "I have asked the court stenographer to come in so that my decision can be entered into the court record. I already filled him in regarding our earlier conversation. That too is on the record. I feel it is important that there be documentation of why we are in my chambers. Is there any objection?" The court stenographer records no objection. "I spoke with Dr. Milner, Andie's physician, and Dr. Fuller, the psychiatrist evaluating her. Both are very concerned about her ability to cope with being on the stand again. I must consider the safety of the witness in this situation. I am also concerned about Mrs. Tanner's credibility. I asked both doctors if there was a strong possibility that Mrs. Tanner might be prone to perjury, either knowingly or otherwise, to protect her own mental stability. Both doctors agree there is an excellent chance this will happen. Mrs. Tanner's testimony has no direct bearing on what occurred to bring this case to trial, and her instability may only further confuse matters. This could be detrimental to the prosecutor's case, and in addition, lead to a mistrial. It is my opinion that Andrea Tanner is not able to testify due to a mental defect. This ruling is final and not open for discussion or revisitation. Thank you all for your patience in this matter. We will reconvene in Courtroom Five in ten minutes." Judge Harris turns her back to us. On cue, the bailiff opens the door.

Barrens shakes his head in disbelief. The remaining junior lawyer gives him a wide girth. Brian and I walk behind them. Brian gently pats me on the back. Inside, I'm making a cheerleader's move look catatonic. Barrens's ultimatum is dead.

CHAPTER 28
THERE'S ALWAYS A FASTER GUNSLINGER

THE BAILIFF REACHES for the door behind him. "All rise . . ."

Judge Harris gets right to business today. "Mr. Freeland, please call your next witness."

"We would like to call Dr. Mark Copeland, Your Honor."

Brian stands patiently as Copeland is sworn in. "Dr. Copeland, can you please state your credentials and expertise?"

"I am a medical doctor who was part of a large medical group for over ten years. I have advanced training in multiple disciplines within the medical field. I am board-certified in internal medicine, general surgery, orthopedics, and medical practice management and assessment. I also hold an MBA, which helps me evaluate the business model of a medical practice." Dr. Copeland's speech is quite forceful and measured. He is older but has the pecs of a young dad who still goes to the gym three times a week. He has just the right amount of gray in his hair that says *I'm distinguished and still very virile*.

"Dr. Copeland, have you testified as an expert witness before?"

All the sex appeal is lost in his pretentious answer. "Yes. And I might add, successfully over twenty times this year alone, with too many times to count in the past eleven years."

Brian continues, "Have you had a chance to evaluate Dr. Carey's practice and the choices she made both as a doctor and as a businessperson?"

"Yes, I most certainly have."

Brian waits for the witness to continue. He does not. "Dr. Copeland, what did you discover about Dr. Carey's medical knowledge and her ability to practice medicine?"

"I have read all the reviews she received as a resident and interviewed numerous patients of hers. She is a stellar doctor when it comes to her medical decision-making. She may be—"

Brian butts in, "So, Dr. Carey is both a competent and good doctor according to your findings?"

Copeland repositions himself in the witness chair and clears his throat. He doesn't like to be interrupted. "As I was saying, Dr. Carey is what I would diagnose as overly compassionate. She is prone to overextending herself when it comes to the needs of her patients."

Brian's face contorts as though he is perplexed by the response. "You seem to be irritated by these findings. Why is that? Didn't you find that Dr. Carey took good care of her patients?"

"Yes. The service to her patients was quite excellent. But this came at her own personal expense. As a doctor myself, I know that you have to draw a line somewhere. At some point, you have to look out for yourself."

"So, to recap. You're stating that Dr. Carey always put her patients first?"

Copeland releases a disapproving huff, then replies, "Yes. And I'm positive it must have been exhausting."

"Can you tell us about Dr. Carey's business acumen?"

"Dr. Carey is no different than most of the doctors I evaluate. She may be a good doctor, but at best she is an average to below-average businessperson. The accounting was adequate. She recorded everything she could, but her choice to change the way she collected receivables was a business disaster." The condescending tone is back.

"By a disaster, do you mean anything underhanded or detrimental to Dr. Carey's patients?"

Copeland releases a loud huff. "No, nothing like that. Dr. Carey's actions were only disastrous to her own finances. It made no business sense to change her collection model. She was making a decent living for a young doctor. She jeopardized it all for a principle. Not something I would have done, but then again, I'm not that kind of doctor."

"Do you feel that Dr. Carey committed any wrongdoings in the matter?"

Barrens stands. "Objection, the witness is an expert. His role here is not as a juror. If he answers that question, it could bias the jury."

Brian retorts, "Every question here biases the jury one way or another. It's their job to sort through each answer and each bias to come up with a verdict."

Judge Harris again remains emotionless with her response. "Overruled, Mr. Freeland makes a good point. The witness is an expert in the field of medical assessment; therefore, his opinion is a valid resource."

Attorney Barrens remains standing. All eyes are now on him. "Your Honor, I am outraged at your hasty and carefree response. There was no consideration or impetus given to my objection and the potential—"

Brian quickly jumps in. "Your Honor, the defense would like to ask for an immediate recess for personal reasons."

"Mr. Freeland, while I appreciate your willingness to save a fellow attorney, whether friend or foe, I must ask you one question before you proceed. Is it your intention to join Mr. Barrens in his new accommodations for this evening?" Judge Harris's harshness is unsurpassed as every syllable is clearly and concisely pronounced.

Brian looks towards Barrens and shrugs. "Your Honor, it is not my intention to be Mr. Barrens's roommate for the night."

"Mr. Barrens, do you wish to finish your, well, statement?"

Barrens's hands press flat atop the prosecutor's tables as his face contorts to deliver a gritted response. "Hmm. Well, Your Honor. I believe, yes—"

"Art, don't. . ." Brian whispers.

"I also think you should not go any further. Mr. Barrens, I find you in contempt of court and highly disrespectful to these court proceedings. I, therefore, recommend that you spend the remainder of this day and night as a guest of this courthouse. I will see you at 9:30 a.m. sharp, in this courtroom. I expect that by then you will be ready to remedy this matter with a full apology to the court. Bailiff, show our esteemed guest to his room." Judge Harris rises and crashes her gavel down. She does not wait for a response or for the bailiff's exit call. She swiftly passes through the door behind the bailiff, leaving all of us stunned into silence.

One bailiff shuttles the petrified jury from their seats to a side door exit, while a second bailiff shakes his head and grabs hold of the prosecutor's arm. "Mr. Barrens, I have been here a long time, and I have never seen anyone get under Judge Harris's skin like that. If I were you, I would spend all night writing that apology and praying that the judge isn't out back building a gallows."

Brian grabs Barrens by the other arm before the bailiff has the chance to remove him. "Do you need me to talk to the judge for you?"

"Thanks, I'll be fine. Not my first time being an idiot. Maybe, when this is over, I'll tell you about it." There's a smile on his face as he disappears beyond the door.

"Brian, now what happens?" I ask.

"Barrens spends the night in jail, and we all come back tomorrow. Want to get a bite to eat? I'm hungry."

I stop walking. "That's it? And it's only 4:00 p.m. How does none of that phase you?"

"Let's go to dinner, and I'll explain it to you." Brian opens the doors of the courtroom.

I stop in the corridor. "No, I'm going to see Andie."

Brian points to Barrens's junior eyeing us from just beyond the courtroom doors. "Don't say anything else."

News of Barrens's incarceration hits the front steps before we make it to the first floor. Outside, the reporters are huddled around the junior attorney, whose blank stare and inability to form a coherent sentence only prompt a barrage of questions. I look at Brian. "He doesn't deserve this."

Brian returns a sarcastic glare. "Are you kidding? Besides, he should learn how to defend himself before he commits to being a prosecutor." A chuckle escapes.

"Not funny. One of us is going to help. You decide which one it's going to be."

A second sarcastic glare. "Fine. Stay behind me and say nothing." Brian steps in front of the terrified attorney. "Okay, okay. Settle down. Yes, it is true. Even attorneys can lose their patience from time to time. Attorney Barrens is a passionate man. The law is his ward, and he doesn't want any harm to come to her. Nothing more. Have a good afternoon." Brian pulls the young attorney away from the cluster of microphones and phones set on record.

Erin is waiting at the curb, holding the rear door open. I say hello and dive into the back seat. Brian slides in behind me after releasing the still trembling attorney on the sidewalk. Erin climbs into the driver's seat, mockingly tips an imaginary chauffeur's cap. Brian is oblivious to it. Our eyes meet in the rearview mirror. I hide my grin from Brian, but I make sure that Erin catches it. We speed away.

I can't wait any longer. "Okay, spill it. What's going on? What did I miss?"

"That Barrens is a shrewd man and an even shrewder attorney." Brian is sitting there in admiration.

"What are you talking about? Have you lost your mind along with Barrens? Is there some special type of attorney virus going around that makes all of you crazy?"

Brian and Erin laugh. "Erin, after what I described to you, please tell our client what you think happened in Courtroom Five today."

Erin gleefully shares. "Jordan, from what Brian has already told, I would say it was all a well-played ruse by Attorney Barrens. When his objection was overruled, he realized that if he let Dr. Copeland answer that question, the trial was as good as over for the prosecution. Attorney Barrens was right. The jury will defer to an expert when they answer an absolute question like the one Brian asked him."

"That's correct. Barrens had to find a way to prevent Copeland from answering the question. He had to find a way to take attention away from Dr. Copeland. He's arrogant, but he's also very credible. He makes people want to believe him. I asked the overarching question of whether you did any wrongdoings at all; whatever he answers, most of the jury will buy it as fact and not an opinion. Barrens couldn't have that."

Erin pulls the car up to The Camino. "We're here. The atmosphere is okay, but the food is an excellent mesh of Mexican and American cuisines. Around here, it's known as the Southern Border Alliance, where both sides are happy to eat."

"I'm going to the hospital."

Brian allows Erin to answer. "Jordan, if you go to the hospital right now, you'll bring every reporter under the sun directly into Andie's lap. They will follow you in just trying to get the photo of the day. You will be the headline instead of a deranged prosecutor. Just wait several hours until they have had enough time to run the current story. Then no one will have the urge."

I think about Erin's words. "Erin, will you be joining us?"

"No, I have too much work to do at the office. Thanks anyway."

Brian and I get out of the car, and Erin pulls away. "When this is all over, you and I are going to talk about Erin. You know that, right?"

Brian smirks. "Everyone has to pay their dues. Don't worry, Erin will be rewarded in the very near future. And, no, you don't need to know."

The white linen tablecloths and the dark wooden chairs complement each other. It's fine dining meets café. The lighting is set to just the right lumens to allow business and pleasure to be conducted in the same space. Unlike Leon's dark, hidden nature, The Camino is inviting and warm.

A waiter comes over to take our drink order. Brian orders a mojito. Not what I expect. My confusion makes him chuckle. "What? It was a busy day, and we're in a Mexican restaurant."

I order the same. I've never had a mojito, but now it makes sense. "No offense Brian, but I don't want to spend a lot of time here. Just long enough not to make Andie or me a headline."

"That's fine. Let's have a drink, perhaps an appetizer or two, and be done with it."

"Great. You know, telling your client that you think the opposing attorney is very clever doesn't bode well for you."

Brian lets out a booming laugh. "A faster gunslinger will always come along. You just have to know when to stand in the middle of the street and when to hop on your horse and ride away without looking back."

CHAPTER 29
IT'S BEEN A GOOD DAY

Andie props herself up in bed and gives me a defiant stare. "Oh, Jordan. What a surprise." Andie, like a real sister, can be a bit of a jerk at times. "I'm feeling fine. Thanks for asking."

"Okay, drop the sarcasm, I'm here."

"Now."

I sit on the edge of Andie's bed and calmly hold her hand. "Why are you so angry?"

Andie pulls her hand away. "I don't know. I think I'm still outraged with Sebbi, that stupid prosecutor, and you for getting in trouble."

I move a bit closer. "Andie, I wasn't trying to get in trouble, and the other stuff will work out. You know it will."

Andie begins to sob. "I know. I'm mad at myself for being so stupid; I almost died. I could have left my boys without a mother."

I hug her. "You didn't die, and the boys are fine. It's okay."

Andie pushes back from me. "Why does your breath smell like minty alcohol?"

"I had a drink with my attorney."

Andie leans back and pretends to be angry again. "I almost killed myself for you, and you go out drinking instead of being here with me."

I return the look. "You almost killed yourself for you. Don't use me as an excuse to justify what you did. Besides, it was business."

Andie rolls her eyes. "Oh. Business drinks."

"Ew, he's married, and he's old enough to be our dad."

Andie smiles. "Funny you didn't lead with the dad part."

I ignore her. "Where's Sebbi?"

"He's getting the kids some snacks in the cafeteria. He's leaving in two days. Jordan, we're all leaving soon." I can feel her pain through the heavy sigh.

"I know. It will be okay. We'll visit each other, and I'll be living in your home." I start laughing. "I'll send you photos of all the changes I make."

Andie banters back, "You better not touch one thing. Think of it as a museum. Everything is priceless."

"What would I replace anything with? I'm jobless right now, remember."

Andie ignores my response. "How did court go today?"

I know I'm not supposed to say anything, but Andie isn't coming back to testify, so I blurt out, "Barrens offered me a plea deal today. I refused. Then he told the judge he knew you were making a full recovery and wanted to drag you into court. I—"

"What? I'm not going back in there!" Andie's eyes are now wide. Her face turns pale. Her body sinks deep into the hospital bed.

"It's okay. I refused on both counts. Then I stood in Barrens's face and went on this rant. Telling him how despicable he is. Later on, Judge Harris ruled that you didn't need to come back to court. It's all good!" I'm sparing Andie the details of being determined unfit to testify.

Sebbi walks back into the room and sees the death grip fear has on Andie. "What's wrong?"

The color returns to her face. "Nothing. I thought they were going to make me get up on the stand again, but Jordan got me out of it."

Two hours later and without incident, I leave Sebbi standing beside Andie's bed, and the boys are each curled into kitten-like balls, asleep in the oversized chairs. Andie wants them there. She wants all of us there.

The hallways are quiet, and I wonder how many patients will be saddled with extreme debt, how many will have to sell cars, homes, or be forced to take out second mortgages. It's all so wrong. I'm glad I tried to help. Maybe others will find the courage, and together we can make a difference. It may cost me everything, but it has to start somewhere and with someone.

The hospital's outer doors whoosh open, and the feel of the brisk air on my face is welcome. The walk home will ensure a good sleep.

"Dr. Carey, is that you?" A woman calls out to me. It's Stella.

"Hi, Stella, what are you doing out here?"

"I'm not so well. My new doctor, well, he's not you. The walking helps. We all miss you. I was talking to Frank and Tanya Johnson the other day, and they said the neighborhood isn't the same without you. Everyone thinks that." Her hands tremble slightly as she reaches for my arm.

"Where is your cane?"

"That thing only makes me feel older than I already am. Besides, when I drop it, there's no one to pick it up. I'll forget it's lying there on the ground, trip over it, and then what?" Stella declares this with absolute conviction.

"Stella, your hands are shaking again. Are you taking your Parkinson's medication?"

"Dr. Carey, you know, that box of yours sure did help a lot of people around here. I was doing better when you could find the medication for me. This new doctor sends in prescriptions, but I only pick them up when I can afford them. I take the pills about every other day."

I stop and turn to face Stella. "I told you that you have insurance that makes it so you don't have to pay for the prescription."

Stella holds out her hand. She's making a poor attempt at fighting off the tremors. "See? Not so bad. I'm doing okay."

"How much medicine do you have left?" I know the danger of what I'm asking.

"None. Haven't had any left for about four days now." Stella is unable to look at me. She tries quickly to change the conversation. "Do you remember Old Man Thomas? He and his son got into a scuffle last week. Right in the middle of the street. Something about putting him in a home. Can you imagine that? Bad enough he is going ahead and putting his father in a home, but to make it public like that, in the street. Sharing his poor father's business out in the open, I felt so bad for Old Man Thomas. Children nowadays don't know how to keep things private. I blame it all on that inter-thing, just type it in and send it out. Everybody knows everybody's laundry. What a mess." Stella's monologue agitates her and increases the tremors.

I take out my cell phone and call Borlin's Rx to see if they are still open. "Stella, let's go to the pharmacy now." I know what I'm about to do may finish me, but I can't watch Stella get worse right before my eyes.

Stella's fingers tremble against my arm as we slowly walk along the sidewalk. She looks at me. "It's because you're making me nervous. I don't like owing anyone money."

I open the door to Borlin's, whispering to Stella, "You won't owe anything." I step through first. "Hi Roz, is Tom here?"

Roslin and Tom Borlin are now the owners of Borlin's Rx. The pharmacy was started by Tom's father. Roslin runs the store, while Tom is the pharmacist.

"Hi, Jordan. Sure, I'll get him." She gives me a nod as she heads back behind the half wall separating the medications from the rest of the store.

A man enters the store while Stella and I wait for the pharmacist to come to the counter. He is browsing the aisles, picking up an item here and there. I watch his movements carefully as some time back, during one of her visits to my office, Stella shared Borlin's Rx's history. He catches me observing him, smiles, and continues his browsing. Borlin's Rx has been robbed only a few times during its sixty-year history. The locals protect their own. During the second robbery, Borlin Senior suffered a mild heart attack. The store was closed for three weeks. According to Stella, none of the neighbors knew if it would reopen, so she took the bus to the Borlins' home and didn't leave until she got a straight answer from Borlin Senior himself.

From behind the half wall, Tom nods at us, picks up a small bag, and comes to the front counter. He's no rookie and spots the unfamiliar man immediately, eyeing his every move. "Can I help you, sir?"

The man is filling one of the small handbaskets with items. "No, I'm okay. I'm just picking up some things my wife asked me to get. I'll be up at the counter in a few minutes."

"Hi, Jordan. Stella, you haven't come by to pick up your medication. You're almost a week overdue." His attention is still on the stranger as he hands Stella a pill bottle.

Stella holds up her right hand, refusing the medication. "Now, Tom, you know I can't pick those up for two more weeks. I need to get my check first. This new doctor makes me take medicine that isn't covered."

"Why did he change your medication?" I ask.

"Dr. Jordan, he's not like you. He don't care which ones are covered. He said this one is better. I don't see any difference. Probably getting paid to give me this one." Stella's tremors increase.

I open my wallet and remove a credit card. Tom places his hand over mine. "No need for that." He's a good man and knows the neighborhood and how it works.

The unknown shopper comes to the counter as Stella hurries to put the pill bottle into her purse. "Can I help you, sir?" Tom follows the stranger's every hand movement. From behind the half wall,

Roz has the phone receiver pressed against her ear. I'm guessing she has the nine and the one of 911 already dialed.

The man spoke politely. "Yes, but I can wait for these fine ladies to finish. I'm sure it won't take but a minute more for the young woman to pay for her grandmother's medication."

Stella sneers. "Grandmother! Do we look like we're related?" I nudge Stella.

The gray-haired man gives a slight bow, catching his glasses before they fall off his face. "My apologies. I can wait until the young woman finishes paying for her friend's medication."

Tom quickly inserts himself with as much politeness as he can muster. "They're old friends, and we're catching up a bit. I'm sure they won't mind if I help you first."

The man places the handbasket on the counter and reaches into his front pocket. Tom reaches under the counter. "Okay, I'd like to buy these things." The man removes a wad of money from his pocket, and Tom emerges with a paper bag to place the items in. A loud sigh comes from behind the half wall, followed by the clicking of the phone receiver being placed back on its cradle. The transaction is over, and the stranger returns to the darkness of the street.

Stella walks over to a chair at the end of the counter and sits down. "Whoof! I'm telling you. I have lived in this neighborhood for most of my eighty-plus years, and I have never been that close to a robbery."

"Not a robbery, just a sale," Roz yells back to her. "Don't you go telling people that we were almost robbed. That didn't happen. Not even close, Stella!"

"I hear you, Roz. It's getting harder and harder to just survive. Maybe I ought to go with Old Man Thomas to the home. If I could afford it."

"Tom, I can really pay you for Stella's meds," I whisper so Stella can't hear me.

Tom shakes his head and points to the door. "Go on and get out of here. It's late, and Roz and I have had enough for today."

Stella and I leave Borlin's Rx, both happy that our adventure was successful. "Dr. Carey, thank you for your help. I will keep quiet about it. Well, maybe I might tell a few people. You know me. Did you know that some folks around here think I'm a busybody?" Stella lets out a hearty laugh as she holds onto my arm.

"Stella, you have to keep totally quiet about this. I'm in enough trouble already." I know Stella will be unable to keep quiet, but I knew that before I decided to help her.

As we walk to Stella's home, she continues to tell me story after story about every house and its owners as we pass them. I drop Stella off in front of her apartment building and continue home. The adrenaline rush from what we all thought was robbery has me wide awake. I sit down at the computer and begin to bang away on keys, looking for any news reports about Barrens.

The local news sites are filled with Barrens's incarceration. "Ha. Genius. I'm the one sleeping in my bed tonight." I click on a site with a catchy headline that makes me chuckle.

Prosecutor's Proclamation Puts Him in the Pokey

The trial of Dr. Jordan Carey took an odd turn today as the prosecutor, Attorney Artemus Barrens, lost his mind in court. It seems that Barrens told the presiding Judge Harris that she was cold and didn't think her decisions through. Attorney Barrens is currently spending the night in the courthouse's jail contemplating his choice of words. An associate of Attorney Barrens was questioned on the courthouse steps only minutes later. His only comment was that Attorney Barrens is a great attorney and that he will fight for justice and the rule of law no matter the personal cost.

"Hmm, Barrens is in jail, Andie is okay, and Stella has her meds. It's been a good day."

CHAPTER 30
THAT'S MY EXPERT OPINION

THE ELEVATOR DOORS open and a bailiff is standing there waiting for us. "Judge Harris would like a word before court." Sweat starts pooling in the usual spots.

I look at Brian and he shrugs. "I don't have a clue."

"Good morning, all." Judge Harris is sitting behind her desk with two uniformed officers standing behind her. Barrens, still in yesterday's suit, sits in a chair to the left of the desk, a new, older lawyer stands beside him. There is a familiarity about him.

My thoughts take over. *Perhaps it's Barrens's boss who I've noticed sitting in the gallery, observing. Could Barrens be removed from the trial? Is Judge Harris granting a mistrial?* I fight every urge to scream these thoughts.

Judge Harris extends a hand. "Everyone, please take a seat. There has been an interesting new twist in our drama. Dr. Carey, do you recognize the man seated next to Mr. Barrens?"

I look at Brian, confused. Brian okays me to answer the question. "He does look familiar, but I can't really place him anywhere." The tall, balding man then places a gray wig on his head and glasses on his face. My jaw drops. It's the would-be robber from Borlin's Rx. "Yes, I recognize him now." My entire body tightens.

Brian grasps my hand. "Jordan, don't say anything else. What is the meaning of this?"

Barrens rises and pats the man on the back. "This is Lawrence Downs. He's a private investigator I hire from time to time. Last night my office hired him to follow Dr. Carey to see if she went to the hospital. She did." Barrens sits back down, then appears to be trying to recline in the leather straight back chair; his hands folded over his belly in pure delight.

"So? Andie Tanner has nothing to do with this case anymore, and she is a lifelong friend of Dr. Carey's." It's obvious that Brian is outraged.

"Go on, Mr. Barrens." Judge Harris is only patient to a point.

"Mr. Downs followed Dr. Carey on her stroll from the hospital to her home. On the way, she met an old patient by the name of Stella Thorne. I'll let Mr. Downs explain the rest."

Downs clears his throat and begins to detail last night's events. "I saw Dr. Carey examine her patient right there on the street and then make a phone call. I believe it was to Borlin's Rx to order a prescription for her patient. They then walked there. While inside, I observed Dr. Carey pay for her patient's prescription with a credit card. Since all her office funds have been frozen, I can comfortably assume this was a personal credit card."

Barrens interrupts. "We all know that Dr. Carey's license is currently suspended, therefore, she cannot prescribe any medication. We interviewed the pharmacist, Tom Borlin, regarding the matter and he admits that Dr. Carey did bring Mrs. Thorne to the pharmacy and did try to pay him." Barrens pats Downs on the back again. "Sorry Larry, go on, please."

Downs pulls a chair away from the table and sits. "While in the store, I noticed the pharmacist eyeing me and squirming a bit too much. His wife was crouching down behind the wall, probably getting ready to call the cops. It's a bad neighborhood and I didn't want to accidentally get shot, so I made my way to the counter and paid for a few of the things in the basket. I had already seen enough to put us here today."

Barrens straightens up in the chair. "It seems Dr. Carey continues to have a blatant disregard for the law. We are preparing additional charges to bring against Dr. Carey at this very moment. The prosecutor's office wants to make sure that everything is above board. So, we are informing all of you of this new development." Barrens places his hands behind his head and smiles. Judge Harris shoots him a glare.

I fire back, "You don't have the facts correct."

"Jordan, don't say anything." Brian is trying to get me to stop.

"No, it's okay, Brian."

"Dr. Carey, I think you should listen to your attorney." Barrens is baiting me and I'm willing to take it.

Judge Harris chimes in, "Dr. Carey, I strongly advise not to say anything more at this time."

I push my chair back firmly sending it crashing to the floor. Bailiffs flank me immediately. "Your Honor, I apologize for the chair. I know that every action I take, every intention I have is under extreme scrutiny, but that was an accident." I move away from the bailiffs, they follow closely until Judge Harris waves them off. "I appreciate the concern you and my attorney have, but I will continue. Stella and I ran into each other on the street. She told me she didn't like her new doctor. She said he just kept calling in prescriptions for her and she couldn't pick them up because she couldn't pay for them. Stella is in her eighties, and doesn't understand her insurance. I called the pharmacy to see if they were still open."

Brian pleads, "Jordan, please stop."

"It's okay, Brian. The only thing I'm guilty of is helping an old lady."

Barrens chimes in, "Please Brian, let her continue."

Judge Harris snipes, "Has yesterday taught you nothing, Mr. Barrens?"

"I wanted to pay for Stella's medication. I don't believe it's a crime to pay for someone's legal prescription if they let you." I spend the next ten minutes covering every detail, working hard to choke down the distain I feel for Barrens and Downs and the entire system.

When I finish Downs suddenly starts clapping his hands. Barrens turns to look at him before starting his offensive. "A quickly spun tale filled with convincing untruths that are just too convenient. We checked with the pharmacy. Mrs. Thorne didn't pick for three weeks. Oddly, she wouldn't show us the bottle. She didn't even let us in her apartment. It's strange how you were able to convince her to pick it up without any mention of paying for it beforehand. Wouldn't you agree, Dr. Carey?"

Brian leaps in. "Jordan, that's enough. Don't answer that."

I ignore him. "Stella lives in a neighborhood where it's dangerous to talk to strangers. I know, my office was right around the corner. Do you remember my office, the one you closed only after turning it upside down and finding nothing? That's probably why Stella didn't let your people in. She went to the pharmacy with me because she knows and trusts that I will do right by her."

Barrens' eyebrow climb upward. "Your Honor, this matter needs further investigation. I want the opportunity to reopen the prosecution's examination."

"I have no reason not to believe Dr. Carey at her word. She has been honest and sincere throughout this entire trial. But the prosecution has the right to pursue new evidence and this could be deemed new evidence. I will allow you to put one witness on the stand."

Brian yells, "This is highly irregular! We were at the point where Your Honor was contemplating a mistrial and now this."

"Mr. Freeland, the thought of a mistrial has long passed. I have made my decision regarding the new evidence. Don't make me decide to place you in my hotel." Judge Harris then looks at the stenographer. "I'm sure you caught all of that." In all the excitement, I didn't see the court stenographer hiding in the corner. "Any further comments, Mr. Freeland?"

"No, Your Honor. I believe we are done here." Brian stands to leave.

"No, we are not." I hear the words come from my mouth; my mind is on autopilot with indignation as its fuel. "Your Honor, I do not wish to be followed anymore by any of Attorney Barrens's henchmen. Attorney Barrens is hoping that he might find something to save his sinking ship. There is no reasonable cause. I've given no indication of being up to nefarious acts, nor am I attempting to skip town."

Judge Harris face softens just the slightest bit. "Dr. Carey, while I do agree with you, I cannot side with you. You are on trial, and quite honestly, you have walked too close to the line a few times. I would suggest that you stick to a normal routine without any variations."

"Thank you, Your Honor." Brian is practically pushing me out of room.

"We will be in court in five minutes. Mr. Barrens, will you be spending another night at our hotel downstairs?"

"No, Your Honor, I'm ready," Barrens says sheepishly.

Brian and I make our way to the courthouse suite. I'm not looking forward to this conversation. Once inside, I start to speak. "Brian, I know what you're going to say. You have to understand, Stella was a just in the right place at the wrong time, and she needed my help. On trial or not, I'm still me. I'm still a doctor."

"Jordan, it's okay. You did well in there. You might even have a future in law." Brian rubs his eyes with the palms of his hands. "That was a lot for first thing in the morning. I just wanted to come in here to reset for today. Let Barrens chase his tail with this pharmacy thing. It's going to be playing in the back of his mind all day. He's going to massage it to his favor. I'll deal with it when he does. We're good."

Courtroom Five is crowded with reporters and courtroom

junkies, all waiting to see a prosecutor bend a knee. “Mr. Barrens, do you wish to address the court before we start?” Judge Harris has her palm resting on the handle of the gavel.

“Yes, Your Honor. I have had a bit of time to reflect on my actions in this courtroom yesterday. I see that I was way out of line and extremely rude to the court and all its participants. I deeply regret my actions and wholeheartedly apologize. I ask for forgiveness in the hopes that we can start anew today. I hope that all those in this courtroom can look past my flaws to see who I really am and allow me to present the prosecution’s case without prejudice for yesterday’s fall from grace. Thank you, Your Honor, for giving me this chance to make amends.” Barrens is overacting, giving his audience everything they bought a ticket to see.

Judge Harris sits quietly, a small frown oozes out from around the hand holding her chin. “Thank you, Mr. Barrens. The court accepts your apology and is willing to now move forward with this trial. Dr. Copeland, will you please retake the stand. And remember that you are still under oath.”

Brian straightens his jacket, glances quickly over to Barrens, and finally addresses the witness. “Good morning, Dr. Copeland. Yesterday, we left off with you about to answer the question: Do you feel that Dr. Carey committed any wrongdoings in this matter? Could you please answer that question now?”

“Sure. As an expert in medical practice and medical business management, it is my opinion that Dr. Carey did no wrongdoings in the way of legal terms.”

Copeland proceeds because he just can’t help his arrogant self. “It’s also my opinion, as an expert, that Dr. Carey’s actions were irresponsible to her business and to her employees. I would never have recommended the course of action she took if she had consulted me. As far as the Pill Box, I found this to be highly unorthodox and risky, but not illegal. Again, if Dr. Carey had consulted me, I would have advised against it. The Money Box was a noble gesture, but again, had she consulted with an expert of my caliber, she would have been told it was not a feasible or sustainable concept." Dr. Pompous fully transforms into Dr. Peacock, with all his colors on full display. The jury stares blankly in all directions except at the witness.

Brian stares at the witness, waiting for him to stop pontificating. "Dr. Copeland, if other doctors started taking similar actions as Dr. Carey, should they face the same prosecution?"

Copeland's bursts into a full-blown, ear-to-ear smile with perfectly rowed, virgin, snow-white teeth. The kind bought with an expensive price tag. "Again, my expertise in this matter leads me to believe that there is no merit for prosecution here. Yes, it is not customary, but it is not illegal either." Copeland widens his smile and delivers a line he has polished more than his teeth. "The system does have its cracks, and sometimes doctors let their better selves overtake what is better for themselves."

Brian hurdles in. "So, your opinion is that Dr. Carey's actions were not the problem; the system is the problem. Is that correct?"

"Well, I guess you could say it that way." Dr. Pompous's lips stiffen.

"Is that your expert opinion?" Brian is trying to sound sincere. A few jurors chuckle. Judge Harris clears her throat.

"Yes, this is my absolute expert opinion."

"No more questions, Your Honor." Brian turns and walks back to the table.

"Your witness, Mr. Barrens."

"Thank you, Your Honor. Dr. Copeland, you used the word 'customary' a few minutes ago. Isn't one of the tenets of legal medicine to look at what is customary to the standard of care when treating a patient?"

"Yes."

"As an expert, can you explain this to the court?"

"In medicine, there is what is known as a 'standard of care.' Every doctor must adhere to a level of excellence in the performance of their duties. The concept is that every doctor must have a certain level of expertise in his field and make decisions concerning patient care similar to what other doctors with a comparable background would make."

Barrens leans his backside against the front edge of the prosecutor's table, looking very at ease. "Does that include choices that would affect patients directly and indirectly?"

"Yes, I will repeat it for you. A doctor must make choices consistent with what other doctors would make in the same situation. The doctor must ensure that those choices do not put a patient at greater risk than other options. That would be directly or indirectly."

Barrens looks at the jury again. They appear lost. One juror is playing with his watch. "Would you please state that again in simpler terms for me?"

Copeland glances at the ceiling before speaking. "I will make it simple enough for everyone to follow. A doctor can't treat a patient in a manner that other doctors wouldn't do. A doctor can't pick a treatment that puts the patient in more danger than they are already in. Is that simple enough for all of you to understand?"

Judge Harris's words are sharp. "Dr. Copeland, please answer the question that is asked and keep the commentary to yourself. Do you understand my simple rules?"

"I do sincerely apologize, Your Honor. My intellect got the better of me."

Judge Harris ignores the witness. "Mr. Barrens, please continue."

"Thank you, Your Honor." Barrens fires again. "In your expert opinion, did Dr. Carey put her patients at greater risk and therefore violate the standard of care?"

"If you mean, did she risk her patients' health by handing out used medication? Technically, yes, but since there were no reported harms in the evidence presented, in actuality, I must conclude that my expert answer is actually no."

There is a collective sigh from the entire courtroom. Judge Harris taps her gavel to signal silence. There doesn't seem to be much vigor behind it.

Barrens watches Brian as he asks his next question. "Dr. Copeland, if Dr. Carey, who has a suspended medical license, walks into a pharmacy with a patient and appears to be ordering and paying for a prescription for that patient, do you find her actions to be unethical and perhaps illegal?"

"Objection!" Brian is on his feet and screeching just below a full-blown yell.

Judge Harris rages back, "Mr. Freeland, I have warned you about your tone! This is your last warning. Mr. Barrens, I will allow you to present this question as a hypothetical if you can restructure it. Don't make me rent you a room downstairs again tonight." Judge Harris is looking directly at Brian. He knows better than to object again.

"I can do that, Your Honor," Barrens agrees.

"Ladies and gentlemen of the jury, please disregard the prosecution's last question. I have instructed the prosecutor to reword his question. Please understand that the question about to be asked is hypothetical and is being presented for a fact of law only." Judge Harris nods to Barrens to continue.

"Dr. Copeland, is it illegal for a doctor with a suspended license to order a prescription?

Copeland looks at Brian, who merely raises his eyebrows. "Yes, it's illegal."

"Is it illegal for a doctor to buy a patient's medication?"

"In my expert opinion, it is not illegal, but it is highly suspicious. I would never do it. Why would I put myself at such risk?"

Barrens begins to shake his head. "Your Honor . . . the prosecution joyfully wishes to not ask any more questions of this witness."

Judge Harris waves her gavel at the bailiff to remove the witness from the stand, and possibly from the courtroom, the building, and the state.

Barrens rises slowly. "Judge Harris, per our conversation earlier this morning, and the development of new evidence, the prosecution wishes to reopen its case."

Brian fires back. "Objection. The prosecution has already rested. This is highly unusual and breaks with the normal proceedings of a trial."

Barrens zips back, "Your Honor, this evidence and this witness are not only new. The evidence is nearly in real time and extremely pertinent to the matter at hand. It didn't even exist until yesterday. Besides, it comes from the defendant's own doing."

The judge ponders her response for a moment. Since she already knows of the incident, I assume it is to look impartial to the jury. "Mr. Barrens, I appreciate your candor in not actually sharing the evidence. Mr. Freeland, I do agree with your objection; however, Mr. Barrens is correct on all counts. Therefore, as a prosecutor, it is his duty to bring it before the court. It is my duty to be impartial and ensure fairness to both sides. I will allow it. Mr. Barrens, call this witness tomorrow."

"Thank you, Your Honor," Barrens replies.

"Mr. Barrens, I know that you will give Mr. Freeland all the appropriate disclosures regarding this new witness, along with any evidence."

Barrens gives a thumbs up. "Already done."

"The court will adjourn until tomorrow morning at the usual time." Judge Harris's gavel rams down, and the courtroom exit begins.

I lean over to Brian, who is on his phone. "Who are you texting? Why didn't you object?"

Brian puts his cell phone down. "Don't worry about my texts. What would you have me object to? She decided before we even walked in here. Have you seen her reverse herself yet? We already know what he is going to do. That's my expert opinion." He expels a tiny laugh. I return an ugly smirk.

CHAPTER 31
JUST A GENTLE LEAK

THE COURTHOUSE STEPS are covered with the regular newsmongers waiting for their chance at the next sensational headline. I'm getting used to it.

"Dr. Carey, how's it going this morning? How are you holding up?"

A second voice flares overhead. "Jordan, rumor has it you tried to write a prescription illegally. Is that true?" A hush tramples the crowd.

Brian is about to speak, but I quickly jump in. "While I can guess where you obtained that tidbit, I assure you that I have never written an illegal prescription and I have no intention of ever doing so. Sir, please return to your source and ask him for the truth, then come back to me if you have a real question. As far as how it's going this morning, I'm stronger now than I have ever been. Thank you for all your concern." I grab Brian's arm and lead him into the courthouse.

"Nicely done. I must admit, my fear of you speaking is getting less with each event." Brian is frowning; it's obvious he didn't enjoy being led into the courthouse.

Courtroom Five is flooded with reporters jockeying for a good seat in the gallery. The notion of yet another wrongful act always brings them running. The decibels in the room are tenfold the norm. Even the jury members have a look of concern on their faces. I turn to Brian with a bit of glee. "You know, they're here to see me."

. . .

BANG, BANG—Judge Harris has already entered the courtroom unnoticed and unannounced. The bailiff looks depressed. After all, his moment to shine has just been ripped from him.

"Be seated and quiet down. There will be no disruption from those in the gallery, or I will clear it. This is your only warning." The courtroom returns to its library-esque atmosphere. "If you plan to return in the days to come, this is the tone to be had from the beginning. I hope that you understand. Very well. Mr. Freeland, I trust you received the information from Mr. Barrens and have had time to review it and prepare."

"Yes, Your Honor."

"Good. Mr. Barrens, please call the witness you wish to present."

"We would like to call Stella Thorne to the stand. Your Honor, we would like her deemed a reluctant witness."

"So noted."

Stella, being Stella, takes her time getting to the witness stand. She stops to whisper who knows what to gallery attendees and reporters alike. If Stella doesn't want to be here, she is making the best of it.

Barrens gives Stella a belittling smile. "Mrs. Thorne, do you understand that you just swore an oath to tell the truth?"

"Young man, I always tell the truth, no matter if it hurts or not. Better that you hear the truth than be told a lie and have the other shoe come crashing down on you like the wrath of Our Lord. And in light of always telling the truth, I will remind you that the smile you try to hide behind is very disrespectful and you're not foolin' anyone."

Barrens shakes his head. "Object—Never mind, I'll just take that as a yes."

Stella leans towards the judge but keeps her focus on Barrens. "Judge, how do you let a horse's backside like this in your courtroom?"

Barrens barks, "Your Honor, now I object."

Stella calmly turns to Judge Harris. "Judge, he told me to tell the truth."

The courtroom body lets out muffled snorts and hushed *oh*s. Judge Harris grins as she taps her gavel, but her heart isn't in it.

Judge Harris faces Stella. "Mrs. Thorne."

Stella places a hand on the bench next to Judge Harris. "Judge, you can call me Stella."

"Thank you, but I'll stick with Mrs. Thorne, for court reasons. Please try not to talk to me unless I ask you to."

"Sure thing, Judge."

"Your Honor, I would like to change the status of this witness from reluctant to hostile."

Barrens's request brings a roar of laughter throughout the courtroom. Judge Harris raises her gavel. This time, her contemplation over the landing is clearly more serious. The courtroom noise is quickly quelled.

"Mr. Barrens, she is your witness. You may declare her whatever you wish, but let's move on to some questioning or relinquish her."

Barrens scowls at his junior attorney before returning to Judge Harris. "Yes, Your Honor. Stella."

"You can call me Mrs. Thorne."

"My apologies. Mrs. Thorne, two nights ago you ran into Dr. Carey on the street. Did she make you go to Borlin's Rx?"

"No. No one can make me do anything I don't want to. Dr. Jordan suggested that she help me get over to the pharmacy." Stella looks at the jury. "I'm an old lady. I can always use a little extra help."

Barrens steps between Stella and the jury box. "Mrs. Thorne, please don't direct your responses to the jury. Did Dr. Carey try to pay for your prescription?"

"No. I have this insurance called Medicaid. It takes care of the part my Medicare doesn't pay for. She told Mr. Borlin to use her credit card to settle my account. But that was for other items I put on a tab at the pharmacy. I live on a fixed income. That means I get the same amount in my Social Security check each month, and I have to wait until it comes in to pay my bills. Anyway. Tom refused to take the card. I would have said no, if I had the chance, but it was a bit crazy in the store because—"

"Mrs. Thorne, please just answer the questions I ask. So, Dr. Carey used her money to pay for other drugs?"

Brian quickly stands. "Objection, the prosecutor is willfully interchanging the words 'prescription' and 'drugs' to give the impression that something illicit was going on, again."

"Your Honor, that was not my intent. It was merely a slip of the tongue. I withdraw the use of the word 'drugs.'"

The wrinkles around Stella's lip tighten. "Sir, if your mother lived in my neighborhood, as soon as I was done here, I would march right on over to her home and tell her how you are bringing shame down on her name and your entire family."

The courtroom once again erupts into boisterous discord. Judge Harris raps the gavel twice. "I will clear my courtroom if this continues. Mr. Barrens, control your witness."

"Your Honor, I'm trying."

Judge Harris realizes the opportunity for another outburst and scowls at the gallery. "Mr. Barrens, continue."

"Yes, Your Honor. Mrs. Thorne, in the past, did Dr. Carey buy or give you prescriptions?"

Brian quickly stands. "Objection. The prosecutor's questions are limited to only the new evidence he stated he had."

"Sustained. Mr. Barrens, stay within the lines."

Barrens again looks at the junior attorney, who now looks anywhere but in his superior's direction. "Mrs. Thorne, did Dr.

Carey examine you when the two of you were on the street two nights ago?"

"Sure, she held my hand, so she could check my pulse. She walked with me to see if I was unsteady. She even had me hold out my hands to see if I had washed them. Sir, when you go into a store, do you see things that don't conform to the law? Sure you do. It's part of your nature to do so. That's the same with Dr. Carey. She does it because she cares. You, sir, look because it could mean another visit to the limelight of the courtroom."

Barrens face begins to redden. "Madam, I'm not the one on trial here. Is that a yes or no?"

"Sir, I told you that I don't lie. You are a fool. Yes, she checked me out, and I'm glad she did." Stella holds out her hands. "Look, two days on the medication and the shakes are almost gone. Dr. Carey did that. Because she is a good doctor, and because she cares about people. What do you care about, Mr. Big Prosecutor?"

The gallery begins to rumble. Judge Harris raises her head. "Mrs. Thorne, your dislike of Mr. Barrens is obvious, but please refrain from calling him names or even posing questions to him."

Stella twists her whole body towards the judge. "Miss Your Honor, I will try my best, but I'm an old lady set in her ways. And what is going on here just ain't right."

Barrens practically stomps his feet. "Objection."

Judge Harris can't hide her smile. "Sustained, I guess."

"Your Honor!"

Judge Harris hides her mouth with her hands. "I know. I know. I apologize, Mr. Barrens. Truly, I do. Do you have any more questions for the witness?"

Barrens slams the legal pad in his hand down on the prosecutor's table. "I do not. Your Honor."

"Mr. Freeland, do you have any questions for this witness?"

Brian looks first to Barrens, then back to Judge Harris. "Well,

Your Honor, at first I was going to say I do not, but now a few come to mind. May I?"

Judge Harris is not amused. "Move along."

"Mrs. Thorne."

"You can also call me Stella." There is a chuckle from the gallery.

"Thank you, but for consistency in the court records, and if you don't mind, I'll keep using Mrs. Thorne."

"I understand." Stella looks at Barrens. "You see, he has manners. His momma taught him well, and it stuck. I don't know who's to blame for your behavior."

Barrens manages only a half-hearted retort. "Objection."

"Sustained. Please, Mrs. Thorne, leave Mr. Barrens alone. I really don't want to put a nice old lady like you in jail for contempt." The gallery can no longer contain itself, and the deafening boom of cackles and even some whistles shake the walls of Courtroom Five. Judge Harris allows the release for a moment, then raises both hands. Quiet is restored.

"That's the first time anyone may have called me nice . . . it has been some time since I have seen the inside of a jail. I wonder how much they have changed."

Judge Harris gives Stella a smirk as she looks at her through her brow.

Stella holds up her hands. "I'm sorry. Just the wandering thoughts of an old woman. Please accept my regret for offending you, Miss Your Honor."

Brian politely asks his next question. "Mrs. Thorne, how did you get here today?"

"Samuel brought me over."

"Is that Samuel the neighborhood Uber driver?"

"Oh sir, he's much more than an Uber driver. He's an angel on wheels."

Brian returns to his table. "Mrs. Thorne, the prosecution wanted you to come here today; didn't they offer you a ride?"

"Humph, they strong-armed me into coming here. I could fall down and die at any minute. No, he didn't offer a ride. I already said he doesn't care about people, especially ones who stand in his way."

"Objection." Barrens turns to his underling and whispers something. The young attorney immediately leaves the courtroom.

"Sustained. Mrs. Thorne."

"I know, Miss Your Honor. My age makes me forget and I tend to get, let's say, noisy at times. I'm truly sorry, to you."

Barrens stands. "Your Honor, I would personally like to say I'm sorry to Mrs. Thorne. She is correct. I told my young and inexperienced attorney to offer, or go himself, to pick up Mrs. Thorne. He is obviously still green and does not understand how things work around a trial."

Judge Harris sits silently. "Okay, go ahead and apologize." The gallery stirs loudly again. The judge ignores them.

Barrens walks over to the witness stand and quietly begins speaking. "Sorry."

Stella releases a devilish smile. "I'm also a bit deaf. Can't afford those hearing aid things. Can you please talk louder?"

Barrens exhales. "Mrs. Thorne, I am deeply sorry for the misunderstanding. Please accept my most sincere apologies for making you Uber here today. I will personally reimburse you." Barrens pulls out several large bills.

"I don't want your money. I'm a God-fearing woman. The Lord teaches us to forgive, so I forgive you." Stella points to the prosecutor's table. "Now go sit down, please." The gallery erupts again, Judge Harris included. Barrens returns to his chair, ignoring the laughter. Judge Harris tells Brian to continue.

Brian throws his signature move at the jury and continues. "Mrs. Thorne, why did Mr. Borlin write off the money you owed him?"

"Because that's how it works where I'm from." She again looks at Barrens. "We work to help each other, not to tear each other down."

"Stella, would you consider Mr. Borlin and Dr. Carey angels like you do Samuel?"

"The Lord gave all three of them good hearts, so yes, I would." Stella looks at Judge Harris and uses her head to point to Barrens. "You know, He tries, but sometimes the Devil gets his win too."

"Okay Stella, just a few more questions. Why was it so crazy in Borlin's Rx when you and Dr. Carey were there?"

"This strange man was sneaking around the store. I know just about everyone from the neighborhood and he wasn't from there. He kept looking up at the counter, making all of us very nervous. Dr. Jordan had her purse open. I never open my purse until the very last minute. He finally comes up to the counter. He places a few items on it, looks directly at Dr. Carey like he's studying her face, smiles at her, and then calls me her grandmother. I ask you. Do we look related when you first look at us? Don't get me wrong. I would love to have Dr. Jordan as a daughter. He had on glasses, but it was obvious he needed a new prescription. I was so angry and scared that I didn't even know what he bought. He leaves, and we finish our business shortly after. I remember telling Dr. Carey that we should take our time leaving the store just in case he was waiting outside."

"I am so sorry that happened to all of you. Was the man waiting outside when you left the pharmacy?"

"Thank the Lord no, he was nowhere to be found."

Brian extends his left hand and waves over the gallery. "Finally, Mrs. Thorne, I want you to look around the courtroom. Do you see that man here today?

Stella spans the courtroom and stops suddenly and points. "Sir, I've been around a long time, and I've learned to look for the little details that tell people apart. Yes, minus the gray hair and the glasses, I see the man. He's sitting right behind the man who forced me to come here today. I can tell because I remember the wrinkles around his eyes and the way his nose is bent to the left. Maybe a bad job resetting a broken nose or something. Anyway, that's him."

Brian clasps his hands together and raises them to his lips before he speaks. "Let the record show that the witness identified one Lawrence Downs. A private investigator hired by Mr. Barrens, the prosecutor, during the trial to dig up more alleged dirt on my client, Dr. Carey."

Barrens slams a hand on the table. "Objection! Objection! Objection!"

Judge Harris crashes her gavel down with the fury of an uncontrolled fire. "Overruled all three times! Mr. Barrens, your witness opened this door, and now you will walk through it."

Brian steps in. "Your Honor, I have no more questions for this witness. I would like to amend my witness list and add a new witness now. One that was not on my original list, but given the circumstances that occurred earlier on the courthouse steps with reporters, and now here, I feel it necessary to add this new witness. Also, today is the only time this witness can appear as his wife is scheduled for a medical procedure tomorrow." Brian is rambling on a bit.

Judge Harris stops Brian. "Before this gets out of hand, I would like to see both parties in my chambers, now. Mr. Freeland, bring Dr. Carey."

Judge Harris doesn't even sit down before demanding, "Who is your new witness and what happened on the steps?"

"Dr. Carey and I were questioned on the steps about the pharmacy incident. One reporter even asked if Dr. Carey illegally wrote a prescription."

Judge Harris is nearly strangling the sleeve of her robe. "Mr.

Barrens, did you or any of your associates leak this information to the press? Choose your words carefully. My jail has enough spare rooms for your entire office."

Barrens is holding his left hand to his chest and his right in the air. "Your Honor, I had nothing to do with it. This is the first I'm hearing of it."

"Your Honor, respectfully, right now that doesn't matter. What matters is that the jury will hear it on the news tonight. They can't help but be biased against my client. I ask that you let me put Tom Borlin on the stand to tell the truth about the matter and put it to rest quickly." Brian places both palms on the judge's desk as he waits for her response.

Judge Harris's voice is low and deliberate. "Brian Freeland, Remove your hands from my desk, now." Brian backs away.

"Your Honor, the prosecution won't have time to prepare a cross."

Judge Harris takes a pensive breath. "Mr. Barrens, you put this whole mess in motion. Go ahead, Mr. Freeland. Mr. Barrens, you, me, and the bar are going to have a long discussion after this trial. Dr. Carey, I apologize that you are present for all of this, but I think you have the right to know firsthand. Everyone, get back to court, now."

Brian reads from a pad in his hand, "The defense would like to call Thomas Borlin, PharmD."

After being sworn in, Brian begins, "Mr. Borlin, you are here to give truthful testimony on the events that took place in your pharmacy, Borlin's Rx, two nights ago, is that correct?"

"Yes, sir. That is what the woman lawyer who called me told me." He's not used to being called in to testify. Tom's world is a small pharmacy for the locals. This is a far leap for the aging pharmacist.

"You and your wife own Borlin's Rx, correct? By the way, good luck with her surgery tomorrow."

"Objec—no, withdrawn." Barrens must have thought better to object to a mature woman having surgery.

"Thank you, and yes, my wife, Roz, and I have owned Borlin's ever since we took it over from my father in 1998."

"Did Dr. Carey and a Mrs. Stella Thorne come in last night to pick up a prescription?"

"Yes. Stella had a prescription that she needed to pick up, and Dr. Carey was making sure she came in to get it." Tom is fidgeting in the witness chair.

Brian asks, "Are you okay, Mr. Borlin?"

"Yes, I'm not used to all of this." Tom lets out a hesitant smile.

"Take your time, sir. Can you tell us what happened in the pharmacy in regards to Dr. Carey?"

"As I said, Dr. Carey and Stella came in. I saw them from behind the half wall and grabbed Stella's prescription. I came up front with the prescription and handed it to Stella. At that time, I noticed a strange man in the store. He was lurking around from aisle to aisle. Something seemed out of place about him. Then Dr. Carey tried to pay Stella's balance, but I refused. I had already written it off. I knew Stella couldn't afford to pay for the things she picked up off the shelves. Roz and I have a close relationship with the community. We know just about everyone and their situations. We try to help where we can." Tom seems more at ease now. His shoulders are relaxed, and there is less squirming.

"Can you tell us if Dr. Carey ordered the prescription for Stella Thorne?" Brian's tone is clear and slow, allowing the courtroom to absorb every word.

"No, Stella's insurances fully pay for covered prescriptions, but this one wasn't on her formulary. That's a fancy word for the list of medications an insurance company covers."

Brian takes a step closer to Mr. Borlin. "Why didn't Dr. Carey write the prescription?"

"Because she can't. Since this whole court mess started, Dr. Carey has been unable to write a prescription. The prescription was from Stella's new doctor. Dr. Carey would never step over that line." Tom was now looking directly at the jury. "You people have to let Dr. Carey get back to work. A lot of people are counting on her. She's a good doctor."

"Objection!"

"Sustained. The jury will disregard Mr. Borlin's request. Mr. Borlin, speak to the person asking the question." Judge Harris's voice is a tad louder than it needs to be.

Tom is back to fidgeting, and his fingers are trying to strangle each other as his clasped hands sit on his lap. "I'm sorry, Your Honor. It won't happen again."

Brian moves closer to the witness stand. "Mr. Borlin, what happened to the suspicious man in the store?"

Tom stares at Brian and settles. "He bought a few items and left the store. We all took a deep breath when he left. I still think he was going to rob us but got cold feet."

"Would it bother you to know that the man was—"

"Objection. Attorney Freeland is about to reveal the particulars of an ongoing investigation." Barrens walks around the front of his table.

Judge Harris stands. The bailiffs all move closer. "Mr. Barrens, return to your seat, now. Sustained. Mr. Freeland, you may not proceed along that line again."

"Wait, am I being investigated?" Tom's outcry changes the entire demeanor of the courtroom. I stand. Judge Harris fires a glare at me. I sit.

"No one is to answer that question! The court is adjourned for today. Bailiff, remove the jury and send them home. I will see counsel and Dr. Carey in my chambers, now." On her way out,

Judge Harris whispers something to the bailiff. No bang of the gavel. No bailiff's proclamation.

There is a thunderous stampede for the doors as the reporters make for the corridor and the elevators to deliver what they believe has just occurred.

In the corridor, I'm side-stepping beside my attorney to yet another meeting to save my ass. "Brian, they're going to have a field day with this."

Brian replies effortlessly. "I know. I can already see the headline: 'Prescription Drug Ring Just What the Doctor Ordered.' They'll write a whole story about how a local pharmacist allegedly teams up with a doctor to illegally fill fake prescriptions to defraud someone or something. Let them write it. They'll have to recant it later."

"Why are you so casual about this? Judge Harris is breathing fire! Aren't you worried?"

A soft sigh threads through Brian's lips. "Why? It's not me she wants to scorch."

"Everyone, sit down and shut up!" The judge is pacing behind her desk. "This case has made a sham of my courtroom. I have had many high-profile cases before me. None of them have had two attorneys acting as such damn buffoons like the two of you. I asked the bailiff to bring Mr. Borlin back here to explain that he is not under investigation. Before I bring him in, Mr. Barrens, am I correct in stating this?"

Barrens eyes widen. "Your Honor, we have no reason to believe that he is involved in any way. Am I missing something here?"

Judge Harris ignores the question. "Bailiff, bring in Mr. Borlin."

Tom Borlin is trembling. "Am I in trouble? I told Mr. Freeland's assistant, I didn't want to get involved, but she told me that Jordan really needed me to tell the truth. That's what I did. I told the truth."

Judge Harris holds the man's hand. "Mr. Borlin, you are not in any trouble. No one is investigating you or your pharmacy, and no one will be either. You are dismissed. Go be with your wife. Roz, is that her name?"

"Yes, and thank you. Jordan, I tried to do my best." Tom is nearly sprinting for the door.

"You did great Tom, thanks."

Judge Harris has removed her robe. Her black-on-black blouse and skirt make her just as scary as her black robe. "Now you two idiots. And this is all off the record, so I'm just going to say it plain and simple. That's enough of the penis parade in my courtroom. Stick to the trial and the facts and stop the rest, or both of you will be in a basement cell for at least a week, together. Mr. Borlin's testimony will be thrown out. The Borlin's Rx story is dead. Mr. Barrens, if there are any more leaks to the press, you will find yourself in hearings not only trying to save your license but also keeping yourself out of prison. Mr. Freeland, no more end arounds, or you will be joining Mr. Barrens. Now, everyone, get the hell out of my office." Judge Constance Harris's grimacing red face needs no explanation.

Barrens walks shoulder to shoulder with Brian as he quietly makes his plea. "Brian, you have to believe me. My office didn't tell the press anything."

Brian nods incessantly. "I believe you. Sometimes, these things just get out."

Barrens stops walking. "You son of a bitch. It was you. You leaked the story. But why?"

"I don't know what you're talking about. That would be crazy on my part." Brian holds steady. I wait for it. There it is, his signature move.

The elevator bell dings, the doors open, and Barrens is frozen in place. Brian grabs my forearm. "We'll take this one. You can have the next." Attorney Freeland gestures a wave for good measure.

The doors snap close. "Why?"

"That was me saving your butt. Never put yourself in a situation like that again while I'm representing you. You could have blown our whole case. Stay away from anyone who could harm your case. Are we clear?" No smile, no pearly teeth, just a direct order.

My back is pressed tightly against the elevator wall. "Okay, we're clear. Can you tell me what that was?"

"Yes, once we're in the car. Erin should be waiting downstairs." A second ding and the elevator doors open.

The courthouse steps are filled again with the newshounds. "I'll do the talking this time." Brian commands the reporters' attention. "Today, we found out that Dr. Carey was accused of further alleged acts of illegal activity regarding prescriptions. We investigated these allegations and found them to be false. An earlier question from a reporter sparked a flurry of doubt about my client's integrity. Once again, we have shown that Dr. Carey is the honest and forthright doctor you believe her to be. We hope that when you report the news tonight, you will be as honest as Dr. Carey. Thank you. Now, please allow us to pass." Brian shows no emotion. The reporters part like we are royalty or untouchables, I'm not sure which, but it's impressive.

We enter the car. Erin is waiting behind the wheel. Brian insists, "Take Jordan home, please."

I can't wait any longer. "Okay, spill it. Tell me what I missed today."

"All this is client-attorney privilege, so don't share it. I called Erin and had her create just a gentle leak. A drop here and a drip there. The rest unfolded on its own. I must admit, it went better than I planned." Brian's pearly grin returns.

"What about Barrens? The judge thinks he did it."

Erin chimes in, "We made sure there was no proof and no trail leading back to him. It might have caused him a slight headache, nothing he couldn't handle. Don't worry, we protected him."

Slack-jawed, I protest, "That seems so under—"

"Underhanded?" Brian scoffs. "It may seem that way, but

Barrens has set the bar, and it's lower than Erin and I normally like it. Let's just say, we beat him at a game of limbo."

"That, that was incredible. How did you even think of it?"

Erin adds, "Jordan, you are our main concern. Saving you is our job. Barrens is a big boy and nothing will come of this. Brian and I promise you that we made sure of it."

"We're here. See you tomorrow, Jordan. Safe Haven, 9:00 a.m. Please don't worry about today." Brian waves goodbye as Erin pulls away from the curb.

CHAPTER 32
SPINELLI

The Safe Haven Diner is unusually somber this morning. I see Brian sitting at a table in the back. As I sit down, he hands me a letter. It's from the licensing board. "I can't open it. You do it, please.

"As your attorney, I receive a copy. It's not good news. I have Erin sending a letter asking them not to make it public until the trial is over. I don't want it to influence the jury. We can worry about fighting the decision after the trial ends. A win in court will go a long way."

"You're right. One battle at a time." I'm putting on a good face; on the inside, a piece of me has just died.

"Jordan, I can ask Judge Harris for a recess today." Brian is trying hard to be more than just my attorney, and I love him for it.

"No, we knew this might happen. Really, I'm fine. I'll meet you in the courtroom."

Brian fumbles through his pockets. "Where are you going? Give me a second to pay the bill, and I'll go with you."

"I'm good. I'm going over to the conference room. I want to call Andie. She's leaving soon, and I don't know if I'll get to see her." I begin to walk to the door, look back, and fake a smile.

"Jordan, wait. Uh, you should eat something. We should talk about this. Jordan . . . Jor . . ." His voice trails off as I step through the doorway.

The courthouse suite door closes behind me. I sit down in the chair farthest from it. I sit for what seems like hours. "I lost my license, soon my best friend will be gone, and my freedom could be next. Was it really worth it? Right now, I would have to say, NO." A few more minutes crawl by before I dial. "Andie, it's Jordan."

Andie is laughing. "Yes, I know, I have caller ID, we all do."

"Funny. How's the packing going?" I try to sound normal.

"I can't say I love it. How's everything on your end?"

"The trial is moving along. Brian says we're winning." A small whimper breaks free. "Andie . . . they took away my license today." I needed to tell someone close to me.

"Jordan, I'm so sorry. Let me get dressed. I'll be there within the hour."

"No, I'm okay. I just wanted to tell you that I'm sorry." My voice trembles more. "I know I haven't been there as much as you wanted. And, I know I should be helping you with the move . . ."

Her playful tone is gone. "Jordan, it's okay. I understand. Really, I do. I'll be there soon."

Repeated heaves can't be helped. "No, please don't. The judge has me on a short leash. Barrens has people following me, and I've been told not to step out of line. I'm supposed to follow my normal routine. Nowadays, what the hell is my normal routine? Andie . . . please . . . just talk to me."

"I'm here, Jordan. I'll always be." Andie begins to sob.

"I love you, sis."

"Jordan, I love you too. You are going to win this. Just hold on. Don't let them get to you. Just for a little longer."

I snort back my runny nose. "Thanks. It's good to hear your voice right now."

Andie laughs. "Nice sound. If you pick your nose now, I can say I had triplets. Two boys and a grown-woman-baby."

I snicker, causing a second snort. "That one wasn't intentional, and I'd be happy to play with my brothers, but they would have to wash their hands first."

"Not when I know you're going to be with them. Hey, I can't

pack all day and all night. Would a trip to Leon's be considered part of your normal routine?"

"I'd better not. I'll swing by before you leave and go over any house stuff we need to cover. We can say goodbye then." Tears begin to flow at the thought.

Andie is crying too. "Did you have to say that word?"

"Sorry."

Andie takes a deep breath and continues. "Jordan, we're both scared. I'm afraid of hating London, and you're afraid of going to prison."

"Is that what you call helping? And you're going to love London."

"Whatever happens in our lives? We're Andie and Jordan, a team ever since day one. That's never going to change. It doesn't matter if I'm in London or if you're in prison."

"That is not funny."

Andie giggles. "It is, and you know it."

"I know. I'm so glad I called." There's a knock on the door. "Andie, I have to go. Someone is at the door." I swallow the large lump in my throat. "I love you," I choke out as I hang up.

"Jordan, It's Brian. Can I come in?"

I quickly wipe my eyes. "Yes, come in."

Brian opens the door slowly as if I'm standing behind it again.

"Why are you knocking? It's your room." I feign a laugh and try to mimic his big teeth.

"I brought you a muffin, in case you get hungry, but now we need to get to court."

"Just a sec. I'll meet you there." Brian closes the door, and I reapply makeup.

"All rise for the Honorable Judge Constance Harris." At least the bailiff is gleaming today.

"Be seated. Good morning. Well, it seems that I once again find myself in a position to give directions. The jury will disregard any and all testimony involving Mr. Thomas Borlin from yesterday. Mr. Borlin will not be able to return to court today, and the jury will not consider his testimony. Furthermore, it should be noted that Mr. Borlin is not the subject of any investigation, nor was he involved in any illegal activities. The jury members will not be permitted to review any of Mr. Borlin's testimony when they are deliberating. At this time, I ask Mr. Freeland to call his next witness." Reporter's fingers begin to rapidly tap on tiny keypads, sending updates into the ether, hoping they are the first to break the news.

Brian addresses the court. "Your Honor, the defense calls Gina Spinelli to the stand."

Gina Spinelli is in her late seventies, with stark white hair and a mildly rotund build. She has a slight limp from arthritis in her left hip that she makes every effort to hide while walking. Transitioning from sitting to standing and the reverse is met with audible groans that Gina is unable to conceal.

Brian launches a base question. "Mrs. Spinelli, can you please restate your full name and how you know Dr. Carey?"

She constantly shifts her weight around the arthritic hip while sitting in the witness chair. "Sure, my name is Gina Spinelli, and my husband, Charles, was a patient of Dr. Carey's before he died."

"Can you tell us how your husband died?" Brian's voice is soft in tone but loud enough to carry the question throughout the courtroom.

"My husband died with dignity and comfort. It was cancer that took him from us." There is a hint of pride mixed in with the sadness.

"What do you mean he 'died with dignity and comfort'?"

"We were seeing another doctor when Charles was diagnosed. He just wanted to give my husband expensive medications that our insurance company wouldn't cover. Charles had stage 4 pancreatic cancer, and there was no cure. A friend told us that there was a Dr. Carey around the corner who found a way to help with medications. Charles was in a lot of pain, so we made an appointment with her." The strength in Gina's words vanishes; only the pain of her experience remains. Her body is now sunken into the chair. Even the shifting has halted. The entire courtroom is hushed as Mrs. Spinelli paints her story.

"What did Dr. Carey do for your husband?" Brian asks the question gently; he is careful not to break the atmosphere.

"Dr. Carey told us what we already knew about the outcome. She offered to keep Charles as pain-free as possible. We told her we couldn't afford the medications, and she told us about the Pill Box in her office. It was a miracle. Dr. Carey treated Charles like a person; she never pitied him. She never made him feel less than for having to take the free pills. She cared about him." Mrs. Spinelli sobs a bit.

I look over at the jury and see that some of them have puddles in their eyes. Barrens refuses to look in my direction, but I know he can feel my contempt for him.

"Mrs. Spinelli, did your husband say anything to you before he died?" Brian has prepped the witness and already knows her answer.

Gina Spinelli's tears create rivers down her cheeks. She takes a deep breath and begins. "My husband's condition worsened quickly, and yet there was a smile on his face. Charles told me that the last three months of his life had been some of the best because Dr. Carey allowed him to make peace without pain and suffering. He told me that he could leave this world knowing that if I ever needed medical help, she would be there. He told me that when his last breath came, he would imagine holding me in his arms for eternity. As he was passing, he asked me to tell Dr. Carey thank you. He then said he would love me forever. Charles left this world in peace and with dignity. That was because of Dr. Carey."

The only sounds in the courtroom are sniffles and heaves. Brian removes a handkerchief from his pocket and wipes his eyes. "Thank you, Mrs. Spinelli, for sharing that with us. I'm so sorry for your loss." He slowly returns to the defense table, looks at the jury, and then to Judge Harris. "No more questions, Your Honor."

She silently nods first at Brian and then in the direction of Barrens.

Barrens stands quietly, his eyes reddened. He is not making eye contact with anyone in Courtroom Five. "Hmm . . . Your Honor, I do not have any questions for this witness."

Judge Harris dabs her eyes with a tissue from under the bench. "Mrs. Spinelli, you may step down. Court is adjourned until 9:30 a.m. tomorrow." She gently taps her gavel. The bailiff is about to begin his duty when Judge Harris raises her hand to wave him off. He does not rebuke her.

There is no urgency among the reporters to fill columns with this story. Courtroom Five empties slowly and with only a few whispers. Gina Spinelli's testimony has drained all of us. Barrens and his lone subordinate leave without a word. The stunned jurors stagger out, staring at the floor.

Brian looks at me as we are the last to leave the courtroom. "Jordan, let's meet in the conference room at 9:00 a.m. tomorrow. We've had enough for today."

I am about to agree when I see Gina Spinelli standing with Ellie Zeiglebaum off to the side of the elevators. "Brian, I have to say something."

"Go ahead, I'll come with you, but won't interrupt unless I have to."

"Thanks."

"Gina?" I approach her cautiously. I don't want to startle the two women.

Gina holds a small white handkerchief to her cheek. "Dr. Carey, reliving all that was terrible. The shadows inside me are all back. I'm so lost without him. We were together for fifty-seven years."

Ellie interjects, "I remember when we lost my brother. What a mess I was for a month. I couldn't even sit Shiva."

After eyeing Ellie, I continue. "Call me Jordan. I'm so sorry you had to go through that again."

"It's what Charles would have wanted me to do for you. You helped him like no other person could. I loved him and took care of him, but you showed him how to die. He would have been in so much pain and suffered dreadfully if it weren't for you."

Ellie reaches for Gina's hand. "Your love for your husband brings you pain now. Someday it will allow you to recall all the good times. Give me your address. We will bring you food."

I look at Brian. He escorts Ellie to the elevator. I put my arms around Gina and pulled her close. "We took good care of him together." Both our faces are now filled with tears.

The elevator pings; I look around, and we are the only two left. I help Gina Spinelli into the elevator, and we hold onto each other until the elevator doors open on the ground floor.

"I'll never forget him," I tell Gina this between swells of large inhales and throat clearings.

"Neither will I, Jordan. Neither will I." Gina Spinelli hugs me one last time before heading down the courthouse steps.

CHAPTER 33
WHEN THINGS GO A RYE

THE APARTMENT IS QUIET, too quiet. I flip on the television, hoping not to catch a midday news anchor recapping my morning. The weather is being displayed on the screen. "I can handle that."

After way too many commercials, a news anchor returns.

Breaking news at the state level. State's Attorney Jack Zane will run for governor next year. That means the senior staff at the prosecutor's office will all be vying for the open seat. Rumor has it that there are only two likely candidates . . . We're sorry to interrupt with more breaking news. Dr. Jordan Carey's trial today was filled with the heartbreaking testimony of a Mrs. Gina Spinelli. According to our reporter in the courtroom, Mrs. Spinelli's husband, who died of cancer, was a patient of Dr. Carey's. The tragic story of his death was replayed by the grief-stricken widow, who was seen leaving the courtroom with Dr. Carey. The tragedy doesn't end there. Report has it that remorse-filled Gina Spinelli walked around the corner from the courthouse and, accidentally or on purpose, stepped in front of an oncoming bus. Mrs. Spinelli was pronounced dead at the scene. More on this dreadful incident as we get the facts in.

I am frozen on the couch, unable to move and barely able to breathe. My phone rings; it's Brian. I can't answer. There are no tears, not a sound. I can only think that I put all of this in motion. I got into medicine to save lives, not end them.

The doorbell rings, and three different female voices take turns shouting through the door. "Dr. Jordan, we know you're in there. We saw you come home. Let us in."

I open the door. "Not today, ladies."

They don't take no for an answer. "Hello, Dr. Jordan. You look like you could use a friend or three." Ellie holds out a Tupperware container overfilled with some ethnic concoction. The lid is only seconds away from turning the whole thing into a jack-in-the-box.

A silent *Shit* screams inside of me. "Hello, Ellie. Hello, ladies. This really isn't a good time."

Stella Thorne is leaning against the wall, her legs teetering. "Well, are you just going to stand there? Let us in."

I'm too emotionally spent. And I know it's futile to refuse. I step aside. "Sure, come in."

The process of rifling through my kitchen while insulting my homemaking skills starts immediately with Inez. "I see your mother still hasn't been here to help you set up your kitchen. I should get her number from you and call her."

"Inez! You're being rude. The poor girl is fighting for her life."

I gasp. "Stella, I don't think I'll be getting the chair or a needle."

Ellie squawks. "Don't even think such things. My family didn't think those Nazis could do such things and, well, we all know what those damn Krauts did."

I dare not comment on the use of such language. Instead, I change the subject. "So, what's for dinner?"

Stella pulls a bottle of rye from her purse, unscrews the cap, and takes a swig. "First you tell us how the trial is going. Is that bastard of a prosecutor still fucking with your personal life?"

The other two ladies look at Stella and start laughing. Inez reaches over to Stella and snatches the bottle from her skeleton-like fingers. "You start at home? I think you have had enough."

Stella purses her lips, making the tiny hairs above her upper lip stand at attention. She yanks hard on the bottle, but Inez's grip is too much to overcome. "Old woman, you better take your taste and pass that bottle back, or I'll crack you one." Stella raises a boney fist.

Inez runs her hands down the black dress that squares out her body, smiles and then slowly fires back, "*Mamacita*, that's a lot of noise for a tiny old church going woman. If you try to get this bottle, you're gonna be explaining to Saint Peter why he should let you through those gates after talking like that."

Stella places her hands on her hips. "I wasn't always a saint, you know? Back in my day, I was considered fast. There wasn't a blind pig that didn't know my name. But two husbands later and a lot of aching body parts change a person."

All three women start laughing. I ask, "A blind pig?"

Stella sits down beside me. "During the days when drinkin' wasn't legal, you had two choices: don't drink, or take your chances and go to these hush-hush places to get your fix."

"You mean a speakeasy. I've read about them."

The three of them burst into laughter again. Ellie manages to stop long enough to reply. "You read about them? You don't know anything until you've been to one."

Inez finally takes her taste and the three of them move the rye bottle between them like they have been doing it for ages. They continue to prepare dinner as I sit and watch. Ellie canes over to the table and offers me a turn.

I hold a hand over my mouth. "Oh, no. I don't think that's a good idea."

Ellie frowns and, in unison, all three shrug their shoulders. Ellie makes one more attempt. I hold my ground. Inez takes a large gulp and garbles. "More for us."

Dinner starts with some soup from the Tupperware container. It has an odd but intoxicating appeal. Stella reveals that it's Ellie's old family recipe. She adds the she just doctored up to heal my soul. Inez follows with a meat dish that she assures me is mind-altering. I believe it's some pork dish. The dinner is rounded out by Ellie serving a platter of rugelach and chocolate-covered macaroons. "I made these myself this morning. You're not going to find anything better anywhere."

Stella tries to stand, but the rye is now in control. "Old Mr. Kirby told me he saw you coming out of the Jewish deli on Market Street with a box of pastries earlier this morning."

Ellie grins. "Stella darling, you truly are an old yenta."

I ask, "What's a yenta?"

Ellie replies, "A gossiper."

"She has been calling me that for years. Now, it's an honor."

Feeling a bit lighter and freer, I ask Ellie, "What's in your past?"

Ellie huffs. "Sure, why not. My parents owned a furniture store in the old country. It was a pretend furniture store with the real business in the back. The stupid Germans never caught on that the furniture in the store was always the same. So many wanted to bet that the Nazi couldn't be stopped. My mother didn't allow my father to take bets on such things. You would be betting against the Jews, against us, my mother told him. Ahh, where we would be today if she had let my father take those bets. Today we could be in a house, probably like the one your fancy lawyer lives in. Anyway, I met my Maurice three months before the war ended. He actually came in to buy some furniture. We fell in love; I was just sixteen. A month later, the Germans burned our town to the ground. Two years later, Maurice and I moved here and opened a new furniture store. We tried to restart the numbers business, but there was too much local heat, if you know what I mean. That's okay. We made an honest living, and my heart was still pure."

Inez starts in. "After all that rye, your heart isn't pure, it's pickled." We all laugh.

"I'm feeling a little dizzy." I look at the rye bottle sitting on the kitchen counter. It's empty.

Stella smiles. "We put it in the dang food. That was the 'healing of the soul' part." The other ladies give fiendish grin before bursting into wild cackling.

Inez adds, "Don't forget the mind-altering part."

I place my hands on the table to steady myself. Their faces blur. "Funny, very funny," I mutter. "Sure, of course. Everyone else is fucking with me, why not you guys too."

Inez slurs, "Jordan, I think we, eh, can drop the doctor. Jordan, you have to loosen up. One day, we will all be joking about this mess. You have to trust us. We have been through so much worse, and we're still here."

Stella places her glass down on the table with a thud, then looks up at me. "I have to agree, you gotta lose that stick up your ass once and a while."

"No one should walk around with a stick up their ass all the time." Ellie shakes so hard with laughter that her alcohol-drenched body nearly falls out of the chair. "I think I may have just peed a little." This starts another round of hoots and hollers.

I slump back in my chair. "Sure. What the hell. And speaking of Hell. To Hell with that jerk Barrens. He thinks I'm the worst thing since . . . since . . . since taxes."

Inez slaps her hand on the table. "Girl, that's the best you can do?"

"No. I can do better, much better. That motherfu—"

Stella screeches. "No, no girl. That's too far." Stella makes the sign of the cross, and the laughing starts again.

"Okay. I got it. That butthead is acting like I committed murder. Someone should murder him. Does that work?" All three ladies nod.

The rest of the night is a blur except for one of them telling me I can sleep in tomorrow because it's Saturday and there's no court.

Saturday morning greets me like a toothache. Getting off the couch happens only to pee. I flip on the TV, lowering the volume to near mute. My eyes upsettingly open wide at the words scrolling across the bottom of the screen.

Prosecutor Artimus Barrens fought off three muggers last night in front of his residence.

I turn up the volume.

Late last night, Artimus Barrens, the prosecutor in the Dr. Jordan Carey trial, was attacked while standing in front of his three-story walk-up. According to the preliminary police report, Barrens stated he Ubered home from a short night out with some colleagues and decided to catch some fresh air before going into his home. Out of the corner of his eye, he saw three large black men running towards him. He further detailed that one of the men was waving an object. Barrens recounted that the man swung the object, possibly a clear bottle, at him. According to police, the bottle grazed Barrens's left temple and head, causing a minor laceration. Police say that Barrens trained as a boxer while in law school. This training allowed him to avoid a direct strike quickly. Barrens offered that he instinctively returned fire with a right cross that landed somewhere on the bottle-wielding attacker's face. He then punched the second attacker in the gut. The third, seeing his partners get bettered, helped them up, and they turned and ran. Dazed by the blow from the bottle, the prosecutor thought it best not to give chase. Police say that the signet ring Barrens wears had blood on it, leading them to the conclusion that one attacker was cut during the prosecutor's counteroffensive. Police also added that a street camera and one located on a local building were of no use. The dense fog combined with the glow from the streetlights created a haze too strong for any useful identification. If you have information about the attack, please call the number at the bottom of the screen.

The T-shirt I'm wearing is suddenly soaked with sweat. I grab my cell phone. Somehow the ringer was turned off. There are hundreds of calls, emails, texts, and voicemails from everyone who knows me. Switching the ringer on allows pings, chirps, and musical alerts to attack me. Poor choice of words. I turn the sound off again. "Fuck!"

I dial Brian.

"Where in God's name are you? Why haven't you answered your phone? Have you seen the news? As soon as we hang up, I'm sending Erin over to pick you up. Don't talk to anyone. Jordan, no one at all." Brian finally takes a breath.

I'm subconsciously twisting the bottom of the T-shirt. "I was asleep. Brian, you know this has nothing to do with me. Right?"

There's silence for an eternity. "You tell me. No, don't answer that. Don't answer anything. Just wait for Erin." The phone goes dead.

My head pounds as questions and answers stampede through. *I didn't leave last night, did I? No, I couldn't. I wished him dead—no, they couldn't, could they? No. It's all a coincidence, right? Yes, that's it. I had nothing to do with it.* I pace back and forth so quickly that my bare feet are starting to hurt from the friction against the rug. The barrage continues. *We finished dinner, Stella called Samuel, who picked them up. I went straight to bed. Okay, I think that's correct. That's it, I never left. This has nothing to do with me. Shit. I wished him dead.*

I look over at the kitchen counter. "Where's the rye bottle? They said it was a bottle. Where's the damn rye bottle?" I search the kitchen, the trash bin, inside the closets and under the couch, the entire apartment. Nothing.

The knock on my door shakes me from my mind's crime scene. I yank the door open. "Erin, I didn't . . ."

"No, Ms. Jordan. It is me, Samuel." He looks at me and turns his head away. "Do you often open your door with your privates exposed?"

"No." I slam the door shut. "What are you doing here?"

Samuel whispers through the door. "I have to talk to you."

I open the door again. "Stop looking down there. What are you talking about?" I take hold of his arm and drag him in, slamming the door behind him. "Wait here." After putting on a pair of sweatpants, I return. "Now is not a good time. What are you looking at?"

Samuel points humbly to the sweat-drenched tee, which is now clearly see-through. I grab a throw from the couch. "Speak!"

"You may not remember, but last night I picked up the ladies from here. By the way, I have never seen them like that."

"Samuel, that's not funny, nor is the time. And it's very inappropriate."

"What? My God. The ladies. What did you give them?"

I grab Samuel's jacket with my throw-covered hands. "I didn't give them anything. It was just the opposite. What do you want?"

Samuel steps back, confusion on his face as he unruffles his classic navy Members Only jacket. "When I picked up the ladies last night, all of you were very intoxicated and, well, you told me I was extremely attractive. Anyway, I picked them up, they were laughing and talking about what happened here and how you told them that you wanted that prosecutor dead. I dropped each one of them off and went on my way. Later that night, I got a call to pick up a man, and I did. He was a very rude man, but I recognized him. I guess the ladies dropped an empty rye bottle on the floor of my car. He found it, threw it on the front seat, and began yelling at me. He told me I was a drunk and that he was going to send me to jail right after he finished sending a crazy doctor to jail. I already told you I recognized him. We got to his place. He got out and lit a cigarette. I drove around the corner and parked the car. I looked around the corner and he was still out there. It was very foggy, and I thought, why not, you know, two birds, one stone. I ran down the sidewalk at him. I tried to hit him with the rye bottle, but I didn't get off a good blow. Then he hit me back, and I ran away."

It is at this point that I notice a small cut on Samuel's chin and step back from him. "I never asked them . . . I never told them . . . I never really wanted that."

Samuel begins to panic and pace back and forth to the front door. "That's not why I'm here. My chin won't stop bleeding. I need to know what to do. You're our doctor. You must fix me up."

"Hold on. Who was with you? Barrens said there were three of you."

Samuel stands motionless. "There was no one else, just me. Why would he say there were three of us? I hit him, he hit me, and then I ran away. That's all." Blood from Samuel's chin drips onto the wood floor. "No one can ever know. I'm scared for me, for you, but mostly for my family." He wipes the blood up with a wad of bloody tissues from his pocket and heads for the door.

Standing there, my hands tightly clutching the ends of the throw, I scream. "Wait!" I can't let him go to prison for trying to protect me. "We only have a few minutes. One of my attorneys is on her way over here." I get the first aid kit from the closet and remove the liquid bandage tube. I clean the cut and apply the colorless adherent. "Don't touch it until it's dry."

Samuel, now calm, smiles. "I knew you would help me. You are one of us now." He leans in and hugs me.

His words are gratifying and at the same time, absolutely terrifying. "Samuel, you have to leave, now."

Only seconds after he leaves, Erin knocks and shouts to be let in. "Why is there a man running down your hallway, covering his face? Are you having sex now? With all this going on? What's wrong with you?"

I wrap the throw even tighter around my upper body. "Get in here. And, no, I'm not."

Erin looks back at the stairs and chuckles. "Come to think of it, I might have been impressed that you could have, under the circumstances."

After closing the door, I drop the throw as my sweating has started again. "I think I'm losing my mind. This can't be happening."

Erin looks at my T-shirt. "You sure you weren't? Just kidding. Get dressed, maybe shower first. We have to get you to the office. The reporters are already lined up downstairs."

The news anchor mentioning Barrens's name makes Erin and I turn toward the TV.

. . . vows that he will serve justice with a heavy hand when the police arrest his attackers. Reporters outside Dr. Carey's apartment say they saw a red-haired woman enter the building and, shortly afterwards, a large black man, his face hidden, exit. Speculation is that the doctor may have had a tryst last night and that she may be in the middle of a second round. Friends and family of Dr. Carey could not be reached to determine her promiscuity or her preferences.

Erin and I look at each other. "Erin, are they kidding? Why is this happening?"

Erin grins. "It could be worse. We could have been in a threesome. Look at the bright side, at least now you have an alibi."

CHAPTER 34
CONNIE AND THE DEAL

Erin and I arrive to find Brian leaning against the outermost corner of the conference room. "What the hell were you thinking? Samuel?"

"Hold on, it's not—"

"Yes, I recognized him, Jordan. You didn't what? Know reporters would be camped outside your door? Didn't know it was a bad idea to fuck the local, married cabby? Is that why he just happens to be always around? How long have you been—"

"Go to—." I turn and start heading out of the conference room.

Erin blocks the threshold. "Stop, just stop for one minute. I'll handle this." Erin's rage turns her naturally goth-like appearance to chili pepper red.

I move to the side but don't face him. Instead, I stare through the glass wall at the waiting area, carefully wiping tears so the bastard can't see me do it.

From behind me, Erin speaks slowly and concisely to Brian. "Okay, I'm going to say this as respectfully as I possibly can. Since when do you automatically believe the media over your own client? You're being a goddamn chauvinistic pig right now. She didn't sleep with anyone. I don't know why Samuel was there. We didn't get a chance to cover that. If you make one comment about Jordan and me sleeping together, I will eat you for breakfast. You had better understand me clearly." The heat from Erin reaches Carolina Reaper intensity.

That last part forces me to let out an unwanted snort. I turn around. "No, not just a pig, but a huge asshole too."

Brian sits down at the head of the conference table. "You're both right. I apologize. I lost my mind for a moment. Not an excuse, but fellow attorneys, the media, and the police have been hounding me all morning. Judge Harris herself called right before you came in. She wants me to bring you in as soon as I have eyes on you. Please tell me you have good proof of your whereabouts last night."

Now I sit at the table. "I do, and I don't."

Brian throws his glasses onto the table and rubs his eyes. He looks at Erin, who nods to proceed. "Jordan, don't play games right now."

"I was in my apartment with three old ladies from the neighborhood last night. They brought dinner over and then spiked my food to get me drunk along with themselves."

Brian sits back and waits. "Let me have it."

"Have what?"

"The bad part. You're holding back. You implied it was good and bad. That was obviously the good."

I sigh. "You're not going to like it."

Erin taps her empty coffee cup on the table—now directing her fury at me. "Jordan!"

"All right, but first, is this privileged information. You can't share it, right?"

Brian looks at Erin, who returns the look. "Jordan, if you tell Brian or myself that you or someone you know was involved in assaulting a member of the court, we are obligated to report it. It's not a choice."

An uncomfortable quiet fills the room as they wait for me to reply. "Stella Thorne brought over a bottle of alcohol, rye to be exact, and the four of us decided to get drunk. We started talking about our lives. Then they asked me about Barrens, and I may have said he's treating me like a murderer and that someone should murder him. But that was just drunken chatter." I pause.

Brian folds his arms across his chest. "Continue."

"The ladies were unable to walk home, so we called Samuel to drive them. When he got there, they coerced him into having a few shots. Apparently, he, like me, is a lightweight. He fell asleep on the floor while I passed out on the couch. I don't know when the three-some left. I woke up when my cell phone rang. You told me Erin was on her way over, so I woke up Samuel and quickly shoved him out. That's the whole story."

Brian and Erin exchange looks again before Brian begins. "That's what you're going with?"

Perspiration pools on my back and under my breasts. "I'm not going with anything. That's what I remember happening last night."

Erin probes, "And you're sure Samuel spent the entire night?"

I answer too quickly. "Yes. He didn't leave."

Now it's Brian's turn. "But you said you were passed out on the couch. How do you know he didn't leave?"

There is a crack in my voice. "I just know."

Brian continues, "You just know. Hmm. You said you didn't wake up until I called you. Can you look at your cell phone? How many times did I call you this morning?"

"Seventeen," I say with a tad of frustration.

Erin begins to tap her coffee cup again. "So, you didn't wake up for the first sixteen calls, but you were lucid enough to know Samuel didn't leave during the night, when the alcohol in your system was at its highest level?"

Brian picks up his glasses from the table and places them in his breast pocket. He then lets out a loud sigh. "We suggest you just say you weren't involved and that you were at home all night last night. Don't say any more to us or anyone else. Am I clear?"

I nod. "I didn't have anything to do with attacking Barrens. I'm on trial for trying to help people, not hurt them."

Brian firmly clarifies, “You’re on trial for stepping out of bounds. Let’s leave it at that and get to Judge Harris.”

Judge Harris is standing in front of her desk. It’s odd to see her in a button-down shirt and jeans. I wouldn’t have guessed she was a sneaker wearer. My perplexed look must be more obvious than I hoped for. “Dr. Carey, it’s a Saturday, and we’re here totally off the record.” She looks around at all of us. “Do you hear me. Off the record.”

Judge Harris doesn’t wait for a response. “Barrens is on his way. This whole case has turned into a shit show.” My eyebrows raise, and the judge takes notice. “Yes, I called it a shit show. From outbursts in my courtroom to someone trying to take out the Prosecutor. It’s a damn shit show. And I’m tired of the whole fucking thing.” Erin looks at Brian. “Oh, get over yourself.” Judge Harris quips.

Brian gingerly steps forward. “Your Honor . . .”

Judge Harris interrupts. “Wait for Barrens.”

On cue, Barrens crashes through the chamber door. “You bitch, I know you got one of your neighborhood thugs to try and take me out.” Barrens lunges for me.

Brian steps between us. “Artemus. She had nothing to do with it. Besides, you’ve been a prosecutor for many years. There’s a long list of people who want to even the score.”

“That might be true, but the timing is too coincidental. It has to have something to do with her.”

Judge Harris raises her objection. “Put your dicks away and sit down. I’ve had enough crap from all of you.” This time, it’s not her tone that stops us.

Erin begins, “Judge Harris . . .”

“It’s Saturday, and we are off the record. For Christ’s sake let’s drop the formalities, I can’t deal with them today. Call me Connie. Does it even actually matter at this point?” Again, we are all stunned.

Brian takes over. "We have spoken with Dr. Carey, sorry, Jordan, and she was at home all night last night. She never left."

Barrens fires, "She didn't have to leave last night. She probably hired the thugs before she got home. Then she sat back all night, waiting for it to happen. It's a perfect alibi, for now."

Connie softens her voice. "Artemus, you know the law. You can't prove any of that. Let me handle this, please."

Barrens sits down on the leather couch and begins fumbling with the dressing on his head. "Fine, but I know she had a hand in it."

Connie points a finger at him while pressing her lips. "Jordan, tell me about your night last night."

I avoid looking at anyone but Judge Harris. "I got home last night, and a few of the neighborhood ladies were waiting for me outside my door. They brought me dinner. We had some drinks and ate the meal. They left, and me being a lightweight, fell asleep right after they were gone. I didn't wake up until this morning when Brian rang my phone. Actually, when he rang my phone for the seventeenth time."

Barrens interrupts. "That's a very specific number. Like you rehearsed it."

Brian growls. "No, more like I made her count the number of times because I was pissed it took her so long to answer."

Connie clears her throat. "Dicks down. What time did the ladies leave?"

I shrug. "I don't really know. The last time they brought over dinner, they left around eight o'clock. That's late for them; they are pretty old."

Barrens again attacks me. "So, getting drunk with old ladies is a habit."

I turn to Barrens. "No, Arty. The first time, there was no alcohol. And what business is it of yours who my friends are?"

"Everything you do is my business."

Brian stands. "Okay, Connie, I think that Artemus may be too emotionally invested in this trial to continue. I suggest he step down and someone else from his office take it over."

Barrens now stands. "Fuck you, Brian. It's my case and no one is taking it from me."

Brian smiles. "He's proving my point. Furthermore, I'll bet the prosecutor's office will ask for a continuance so the new attorney can get up to speed. That would be an infringement on my client's right to due process." Brian pauses for a second. "Connie, let's just go straight to a mistrial."

Barrens's face is so red the bandage on his head might catch fire. "There it is, Your Honor. These pricks set this whole thing up to ask for a Goddamn mistrial. They should be disbarred and she should go to prison for a long time."

"Everyone, settle down. Brian, are you officially asking for a mistrial?"

"Connie! Are you insane? You're actually going to entertain this crap?"

I swear I see the judge cock back a fisted hand. "Artemus. You're going to want to keep quiet now."

Brian looks at Barrens. "Since it's already on the table, sure."

Judge Harris walks over to the door and opens it. "I'll give you my decision by Monday. You can all leave now."

In the corridor, Barrens rubs the dressing on his head. "Brian, I know you had something to do with this. It's just like the whole leak thing."

Brian pushes the elevator button. "The two are miles apart. You honestly think I would hire someone to kill you and miss out on the pleasure of doing it myself?" Barrens turns and walks in the other direction. "Arty, I was kidding."

"I have to use the men's room."

The elevator bell pings. I turn around. "That reminds me. I have to use the ladies' room. I'll meet you and Erin downstairs."

Once the elevator doors close, I head for the restroom, the men's restroom. Barrens is standing at the urinal. "What are you doing in here? Did you come to finish the job yourself?"

I smile. "Sort of."

Still facing the urinal, Barrens holds up his fists. "I know how to fight. I just won a three-on-one."

I lean against a sink. "Yeah, about that. I know as well as you do that it was a one-on-one. I'm not sure why you lied to the police, but you did. So, it's time for you to cut a deal."

Barrens zips up. "I don't care what you know, I'm not letting you go."

"Oh, that's not the ultimatum. You're going to continue your made-up story with a few more details to throw the cops in the wrong direction, and even if they catch suspects, you're going to say it's not them. You're never going to identify anyone. Or, I go to the police and tell them you lied and that you're interfering with a police investigation. The headlines alone will sink you."

Barrens walks towards me. "What's in it for you? There's no piece about you in your deal."

I square off in front of him. "You can continue to come after me for what you think you already have. We'll play that one out to the end. We good?" Barrens agrees. I turn on the faucet. "Don't forget to wash. After all, I am a doctor." I leave the men's room with a smile so big it hurts.

Ping. The elevator doors open. I step out. Brian and Erin are waiting. I put on my game face. "All good, can we get out of here, please?"

CHAPTER 35
AN OPEN-DOOR POLICY

"I'M worried that Barrens is somehow going to blame you for Gina Spinelli. We don't need Barrens trying to draw a line connecting your so-called reckless actions and the grief that Mrs. Spinelli was experiencing."

"He wouldn't do that." My voice remains too casual.

Brian must have noticed. "Are you okay?"

"Yes, why?"

"You're very calm, too calm."

I sit down at the head of the table in the courthouse suite. "I had . . . let's say . . . an epiphany over the weekend."

Brian sits down next to me. "And what was this . . . epiphany?"

"Brian, just about everything I knew to be solid in my life has been taken from me. Some might say that I did it to myself, and that may be true. What's also true is that I'm going to survive Barrens's wrath and this trial. And when it's all over, I'll move on. I used to be afraid of the future, of change; and now, after all this? Somehow, I'm not."

Brian leans back and flashes his pearly whites. "I don't know if you're really brave or having a mental breakdown."

A muffled ruckus comes through the closed door. Brian stands. "Wait here. I'll check it out."

He returns five minutes later. "It's just a squabble between reporters and spectators. It seems that there isn't enough room in the gallery for both. The bailiffs are working it out. They've asked that we wait in here until it's settled down."

I place my hands on my cheeks. "Judge Harris isn't going to like not starting at nine thirty sharp."

Brian peers around the suite, pretending to see if the judge is listening. "Even the great Judge Connie Harris can't control everything." We laugh.

There's a knock on the door, and a bailiff wants to escort us to Courtroom Four. I look at Brian. The bailiff interrupts. "It has a bigger gallery. Don't worry, Judge Harris approved the move." Brian and I try to fight back the chuckles.

The bailiff understands and joins in. "This never happened."

The doors to the larger courtroom are closed as we arrive. Apparently, the noise from such a large and unruly crowd is disrupting other court proceedings on the floor. The bailiff opens the door, and the rush of sound is like standing behind a plane taking off. Courtroom Four's gallery is two or three times that of Courtroom Five. The bailiff smiles. "Divorce court gets more spectators."

As we enter the courtroom, I notice that the gallery is filled with familiar faces: patients, fellow doctors, my old staff, and in the front row are my parents and Andie. "Brian. Is this a good idea?"

Andie leans over and stops me as I'm passing her. "You know we weren't going to let you do this alone. These are all the people who love and care for you. These are all the people who know who you really are, Dr. Jordan Carey. Sis."

"But how?" The lump in my throat prevents me from speaking clearly.

"I reached out to Carla and Rebecca. They invited every patient they could find. The doctors spread the word too. Your parents were easy." Andie reaches out and hugs me.

Brian tugs at my arm. "No sense in worrying about this now. Jordan, we have to take our seats before the judge comes in."

"Did you know?"

"Yes, Andie called me last night and asked if it was a good idea.

I thought it was, and she made it happen." Brian deliberately performs his signature move. "I know you like it when I do it."

I think about raising a middle finger, but instead flash an exaggerated smile back at him.

"All rise for the Honorable Judge Constance Harris." A new bailiff is reading from a paper in his hand. He is much younger and taller. Perhaps the next generation of bailiffs. Judge Harris enters the courtroom, looking around as if it's her first time in the larger room. "As you can see, we have been upgraded to accommodate the influx of interest in this trial. I will only give one warning, and here it is. I require that the gallery remain absolutely silent during these proceedings. Any outbursts, and we won't need but a broom closet to finish this case. Thank you for your cooperation in advance." And with that opening statement, Judge Harris looks at the strange gavel, bangs it, and contorts her face, giving the impression she isn't impressed. The gallery bursts into laughter, and Judge Harris raises the gavel again. "Okay. I guess I'm to blame for that one. Neither of us will let it happen again."

Quiet returns to the courtroom. "Mr. Freeland, I have taken your motion for a mistrial under consideration. At this time, I find there are insufficient grounds to declare a mistrial. We will continue."

Brian stands. "Thank you, Your Honor."

"I understand that you are prepared to call your final witness. Is that correct?"

Barrens clears his throat. "Your Honor, before we begin, I would like to request that the gallery be cleared, as there may be some indirect bias placed on the jury with such an unusual increase in spectators. Also, I do not want the jury to feel pressured into acting in any particular manner by the increase in this trial's popularity." Barrens's request is bold. Asking Judge Harris to give up her new luxury accommodations. He's begging for another overnight stay at the Harris Motel.

"Mr. Barrens, while I can see your sympathetic point for the jury, I am inclined to disagree. The members of the jury are grown adults and are not in any danger from the gallery. Your motion is denied. Can we get on with the trial now?" With only the slightest shift in her eyes, Judge Harris redirects her attention. "Mr. Freeland, your final witness, please."

"Thank you, Your Honor. I would like to call Dr. Jordan Carey to the stand, please."

There is a mild rumbling from the gallery, which makes Judge Harris pick up her adopted gavel. The chatter settles, and I am sworn in. Oddly, Judge Harris looks at me, smiles, and asks if I'm comfortable.

"Yes? Thank you, Your Honor."

"Dr. Carey, why are you here today?" Brian has already explained that he will ask open-ended questions, giving me the chance to elaborate in detail. He wants the jury to hear as much as possible from me.

"I'm here because I saw my patients suffering. I saw them having to choose between buying the medication they needed and buying food for their family. I'm here because I chose not to be part of the problem, but actively create a solution. I chose to change a broken system. I am here because those in power would rather smother me than help the people they promised to take care of."

Barrens hits the floor fast. "Objection. Your Honor, the witness is pontificating. She is grandstanding for the larger gallery crowd. I again request that the gallery be removed."

Judge Harris removes her glasses. "Well, Mr. Barrens, I see we are going to start early today, aren't we? Overruled on both counts. Continue, Mr. Freeland."

"Thank you, Judge. Dr. Carey, do you admit to coming up with the Money Box idea?"

"Yes."

"Why did you take such an action?"

"I did it because most of my patients have poor insurance plans with deductibles so high that it's like free money for the insurance companies. My patients were never going to reach their deductible amounts." My emotions are boiling over, making me go off script. Brian's eyes widen. I continue. "We live in times that make catastrophic insurance the norm. Patients have to have a life-threatening emergency surgery to even come close to reaching their deductible limit. Even if they do, it leaves them in so much debt that most are forced to declare bankruptcy or enter loan repayment plans that impose further financial hardship on them and their families. I had to do something." I'm now standing in the witness box.

Judge Harris looks at me. "Dr. Carey, please sit down."

I want to remain standing, defy the Judge, the rules, but that's what got me here, so I sit, slowly. Judge Harris does notice and gives me the tiniest of smirks.

Brian walks back to the defense table and ruffles some papers. I think he's trying to buy me time. He looks at me over the top of his glasses. I blink twice. This is the code Erin set up so I can let Brian know I'm okay. One blink and Brian requests a five-minute bathroom break. "Dr. Carey, why did you create the Pill Box?"

"I created the Pill Box because most of my patients are on a fixed income, don't earn enough, or have terrible prescription plans. They're forced to share their medications or take them sporadically so they last longer. As a doctor, I know how dangerous this is. The Pill Box was my fix to help the people of the neighborhood be safer."

Brian questions me for almost three hours. I'm tired and need a break. I look to Judge Harris, who understands what I'm asking. "We have run late, and now it's time for a recess. We will break for lunch and return at 2:00 p.m. sharp."

Brian sees I'm heading for the gallery and stops me. "Please just sit here, Jordan. I'll explain later. Don't turn around. Just look straight ahead, please." Brian places his hand on my shoulder.

I know I sound like a disappointed child, but I can't help it. "Brian, come on, they're leaving."

"Just let them go. You can speak with them later." His grip tightens just enough to draw my attention back to it.

Barrens and his young associates are still seated at the table. The last of the gallery members exit the doors and Barrens lets out a deep sigh. He motions to his third pair of juniors; they rise and all three head for the doors. As the courtroom doors open, I can hear recognizable voices still in the corridor. I look at Brian, who signals me to continue waiting.

As the Barrens's gang closes the door behind them, Brian turns to make sure the doors are closed. "Jordan, I'm sorry about that. Barrens and his team were waiting to see who you spoke with."

My face flushes. "So what! Why does that matter?"

"It matters because the judge inadvertently gave Barrens an open-door policy. She told him on the record that he could reopen the prosecution's case if there was any new evidence."

"But that was regarding the pharmacy incident." I'm almost in tears again. How could Brian miss that point? "You made me miss a chance to speak with everyone who came out to support me."

Brian sighs again. "No, Jordan, she only inferred it was just about the pharmacy issue. Judge Harris was never explicit in her order. That gives Barrens an opening for any opportunity he sees. And he knows it. Erin and I checked the transcript last night. If you had spoken to anyone in the gallery, Barrens could have taken it as pending new evidence and reopened his argument."

"I'm getting so tired of this, so tired of Barrens."

Brian opens the corridor door to make sure it's empty. Erin is waiting with sandwiches from a deli. "Have either of you seen the update feed about Barrens's attack?"

Brian pulls out his phone and begins to read. "'Prosecutor Artemus Barrens told police late last night that he has had a few days to recuperate and now remembers more details. According to the attorney, the attacker with the bottle had dreadlocks and was very light skinned. Barrens also told the police that he thought the third attacker may have been white. Barrens recalled the second attacker, who punched him in the stomach, yelled something in a foreign language, possibly from South America. Police still have no leads.'"

Erin looks at me. "Wow, that's a lot of very specific remembering."

I reply, "Medically speaking, memory loss and its return are very difficult to determine. You never know what will come flooding back in."

CHAPTER 36
TAKING THE BAIT

BRIAN LOOKS at me and places a hand on my shoulder. "It's going to be okay. Just stick to what we went over. You're ready."

Erin sits down beside me at the defense table. "I wouldn't miss this. Barrens is desperate, use that." She bumps her shoulder into mine. "You can do this."

I didn't realize how much she has come to mean to me. "Thanks, Erin. I'm glad he didn't send you off somewhere."

Erin smiles. "Don't worry about any of that now."

I lock eyes with Barrens as if to tell him, *Do your worst.* He returns a slight smirk as if to say, *I'm coming for you.* I continue my cold stare, and he looks away.

Judge Harris goes through her usual pre-session warnings and calls me to the stand. "Dr. Carey, are you ready to continue?"

Again, her kindness is unexpected. "Yes?"

"Dr. Carey, you are still under oath. Mr. Barrens, please begin."

"Dr. Carey, you did a hospital residency at Buckford Hospital, is that correct?"

"Actually, it's called Buckford Hospital and Medical Center. And yes, I did."

Barrens sneers at me. "Your private practice was located just a few blocks from the hospital. Is that also correct?"

"Yes."

"Did you treat patients during your residency?"

"Yes."

"Is it safe to assume that some of those patients in your private practice may have also been treated at Buckford Hospital and Medical Center?"

"Yes."

"Did you order tests and write prescriptions for those patients you treated during your residency?"

"Objection. Relevance?"

Barrens jumps in. "I'm just establishing a base for my questions, Your Honor."

"Overruled. Dr. Carey may answer the question. Get to the point, Mr. Barrens."

"Yes, I ordered tests and wrote prescriptions."

Barrens lets out a loud nostril exhale. "Did it matter to you then if the patients, who, according to you, may have been the same patients in your private practice, could afford to pay for those tests or prescriptions?"

I hesitate. "I'm not sure I knew enough to even think that way."

"So suddenly, one morning during private practice, you decided that your patients could no longer afford to pay for healthcare."

Brian shrieks, "Objection! The prosecutor is leading the witness."

"Withdrawn."

Judge Harris grits her teeth. "Mr. Freeland, you are close, very close."

"Dr. Carey, let's get back to your practice. Was your practice doing well financially, that is, prior to your decision to create the Money Box?" Barrens stands at the prosecutor's table with a small stack of papers in his hand and makes no effort to even look at me as he fires his question.

"Yes, we were doing okay," I answer calmly.

"Dr. Carey, I'm going to remind you, as Judge Harris did earlier, that you are under oath and lying is a punishable crime. So, I'll ask you again. Was your practice doing well financially prior to your creation of the Money Box?" Barrens is looking at me and holding a rolled set of pages in the air next to his head.

"I'm not sure what you're asking me? Can you be more specific, please?"

Barrens unrolls the pages. "Were you behind on the rent? Were you having difficulty collecting from patients? Did you owe money?"

"I was half a month behind on the rent because it was February. We're always short on cash flow during the first three months of the year. My Medicare patients hadn't reached their out-of-pocket portion yet, and patient payments always lag. We always catch up in the fourth or fifth month of the year."

"Did you catch up with the rent?" Barrens moves to the front of the prosecutor's table with his hands folded across his chest.

"Yes. I don't under—"

Barrens quickly interjects with his next question. "In fact, when your office was closed down by the police, you were all caught up, and all your bills had been paid. Isn't that true?"

"Yes, I believe so."

Barrens returns to the curled pages on the table. "Dr. Carey, before the creation of the Money and Pill Boxes, you were struggling to pay your bills. You even skipped a few paychecks for yourself, correct?"

I squeeze my lips and shift my weight so I'm sitting at the front edge of the witness chair. "You obviously have my financials in front of you. Yes, and before you ask your next question, let me answer it. Yes, after nearly bankrupting myself with the two boxes, patients started to understand the concept and stopped being skeptical. They willingly came in for treatment and to get free medication, if I had it. I never charged them for the medication. My finances improved because the neighborhood began to trust me. I never stole, embezzled, or hid money. And finally, I never sold medications to anyone."

The gallery's cheers force Judge Harris to slam the gavel repeatedly until the order is restored. "That will not happen again, or I will grant Mr. Barrens's request."

Barrens gives the judge an "I told you so" look.

"Mr. Barrens, you too, are very close. Continue."

"Dr. Carey, how do your finances look now?"

"Mr. Barrens, I have no finances. I can't work, and I'm running through what little savings I have left. If it weren't for the generosity of the ladies in my neighborhood, I might starve. But you know all that already."

Barrens ignores the last part of my comment. "So, you went from struggling before the boxes, to being ahead while running the boxes, back to struggling without the boxes. Doesn't it seem that those boxes played a bigger role than meets the eye?"

Brian slowly rises. "Objection. Attorney Barrens is trying to draw a direct line where none exists. There is no proof of anything he is intimating."

"Sustained. Mr. Barrens, show proof or move on."

Attorney Barrens shoots a smile towards Brian then returns to his assault. "Dr. Carey, did your patient load increase when word got out about the Pill Box?"

"Yes."

"Dr. Carey, I'm holding a copy of your patient appointment ledger from the computer program you use. Would you be surprised to know that just two weeks into your use of the Pill Box, your overall patient load doubled?"

"I didn't realize that, but thanks for letting me know I was on the right track for helping my patients." The gallery stirs again. Judge Harris glares at them.

Barrens again ignores my callousness. "In fact, sixty-four percent of that increase was due to new patient appointments. Your practice is located in a community riddled with crime. Is it possible that the sixty-four percent included drug dealers who might help you with your financial woes?"

Brian stands quickly, sending his chair crashing into the rail behind him. "Objection! Your Honor, that was so far over the line. There is absolutely no proof—"

"All right, all right, Mr. Freeland. Sustained. Dr. Carey, don't answer that question. Mr. Barrens, that just earned you a letter from me to the bar. The jury will not read anything into that heinous display of misconduct."

I turn to face Judge Harris. "Your Honor, I will answer the question. But only if you allow me to give my full answer without the prosecution interrupting me." My voice is calm and confident. It even surprises me.

"Objection. The witness cannot make demands of the court. Dr. Carey is a criminal on trial, and I am questioning her." Barrens's objection is challenging and dismissive of the judge.

The single banging of the gavel is followed by nothing. Judge Harris is sitting behind the bench, staring down at whatever lies across the surface. After what seems like hours, she raises her head and begins to speak in a low and monotone voice. "Mr. Barrens, I have allowed you great leeway in my courtroom, but I cannot and will not allow you to diminish my authority here. I find you in contempt of court again. Dr. Carey is not considered a criminal at this time; she is a witness on the stand. She is under oath and must testify honestly. Her request is granted. You will allow her to finish her response. Any interruption and I will have you removed and declare a mistrial."

"Yes, Your Honor, I—"

"I do not wish to hear your apologies anymore today." Judge Harris is again looking down. "Go ahead, Dr. Carey."

"Yes, looking back at the situation, it would have been easy to steal the money. The notion of stealing never entered my mind. If I were stealing pills to make money, don't you think a neighborhood that fights every day to keep its streets clean would have turned me in? I stole nothing! I hid nothing! I didn't do anything but be the best doctor to my patients! I didn't risk everything to create some self-serving criminal enterprise. I did it because during my residency, I saw pain I never knew existed. I opened my office in a strange neighborhood that I wasn't sure would accept me and found good people who were victims of a broken system. A system I helped to perpetuate. I had to do something to help. That's why I did all of this." I lean back in the witness chair, hold my head high, and stare at the jury. "The only crime here is the one of putting me on trial for doing what doctors are supposed to do. I'm a doctor, and I'm part of that community, and I'm always going to fight for them."

The gallery no longer cares about what might happen to them. Thunderous shouts arise from behind the tables. The words are too many and too varied to understand, but the tone is clear. They are cheering for me. The clapping that follows rattles the windows. Judge Harris holds her gavel in the air and realizes there is no point. She waits until they're done.

Order finally returns to the courtroom. Only the scribbling on reporters' and sketch artists' notepads can be heard from the gallery.

"Mr. Barrens, do you have any other questions for this witness?" There is a slight, but noticeable smile illuminating the judge's face.

"No, Your Honor. The prosecution is done." Barrens is walking back to his table.

"Mr. Freeland, would you like to ask the witness any further questions?"

"No, Your Honor. I would not." Brian turns and faces Barrens; his white pearlies shine like a lighthouse beacon.

"Very well. Dr. Carey, you may step down. Tomorrow we will start closing arguments. The court is adjourned for the day. We will return here in Courtroom Four at 9:30 a.m. sharp." Judge Harris bangs the gavel.

The courtroom empties into the corridor quickly as reporters race to give details of the day's proceedings. My fans wait at the exit of the courtroom, hoping to speak with me. I'm anxious to greet them. I think it's almost over.

Brian summons me to the table. "Jordan, that was great and we can celebrate it shortly. For now, nothing has changed. Eyes straight ahead, do not speak nor look at anyone. I know you want to stand proud right now, but don't. Let's go over to the conference room."

I can feel the joy leaving me, but Brian is correct.

The courthouse suite is cold as usual. "Brian, I have to say something to them. They came and they stood up for me, and I'm giving them nothing."

"I know, but we're coming down to the end and we have to stay focused."

Erin taps my hand. "You did a wonderful job."

Brian fake claps. "You baited Barrens better than I anticipated. The jury can't help but be swayed by the gallery's reaction. Even Judge Harris was taken in."

"How did you know Barrens would bite?" I ask.

Erin leans back. "Because Barrens's ego can't allow him to lose."

"I still don't understand how you knew to link the appointment book and the Pill box."

Brian gets up and walks over to a windowsill. He places his hand on it. "Right here. It all started right here."

"Still not clear."

Brian sits back down. "I'll lay it all out for you. The prosecutor's office loses the cop shooting case, and Barrens's boss, Jack Zane, turns the heat up on him to win. Then Zane announces that he's leaving. Barrens is one of two senior prosecutors up for the position. This pushes Barrens over the edge. He's willing to do anything to be in charge. If you remember, I booked the courthouse suite for the entire trial. I noticed that things in the room had been moved, as if someone had been searching through them. So, I left a stack of papers with highlighted sections on that windowsill about a week ago. When we came in the next day, the stack was gone."

I stand up, grab the back of the chair, and lean in. "No."

Brian grins. "Yup, the very stack Barrens was using in court today."

"No."

Erin whines at me, "Why do you keep saying no?"

"I don't know."

Brian tilts his head and squints his eyes. "Anyway, you were the hook, and the stack of papers was the bait." Brian does a drum roll with his hands on the conference table. "The rest was pure magic." He basks in the glory for a moment, then continues. "It was perfect. Let's get out of here."

CHAPTER 37
HELLFIRE

I FOLLOWED Brian's orders for last night and spoke to no one, almost. I texted Andie to explain my silence. I asked her to call my parents and do the same. Strange, how the excitement of noise becomes a comfort you miss when it's not there.

The next morning Samuel picks me up at the back of my building. It's a free ride, and no one can see through the tinted windows. As we near the courthouse, blaring sirens quickly wash away the quiet from the night before.

He pulls over to the curb. "Traffic is much heavier than usual. It appears that we can't go any further. The police are redirecting traffic. I can try a different route, or you can walk the last three blocks from here. What do you want to do, Dr. Jordan?"

"I'll get out and walk from here."

There is a heavy scent of smoke in the air as I exit the car. The closer I get to the courthouse, the more prevalent the burning smell becomes. At one block away, flecks of black cinder begin to coat cars and building window sills. Firetrucks and police cars block the street to the courthouse, hastily parked in various directions. The air is warmer, and I can taste the ash. Water runs down the gutters of the street like the aftermath of a major rainstorm. A crowd is gathered at either end of the block.

I find Brian standing among the masses. "Brian, is the courthouse on fire?"

A policeman blurts out, "No, it's the diner."

"What happened? How did it start? Was anyone hurt?" I ask the policeman. He doesn't respond. I ask again.

The policeman looks over his shoulder at me, obviously annoyed at being asked so many questions twice. "We don't know anything yet." He takes several steps down the street, but not before one more disapproving look in my direction.

Brian laughs. "Making friends, I see." I don't say anything.

Soot-covered firefighters continue to stagger back to their trucks, and others take their place to endure the heat. A fire chief walks too close to the crowd and is immediately hit by a barrage of questions from a team of reporters.

"No one was in the building when it caught fire. No, we don't know where or how it started. We don't even have it under control yet." He starts walking back towards the blaze while reporters launch a second round of questions at him.

Brian starts walking. I follow. "There's no sense in standing here. Let's go around to the other side of the courthouse and see if we can go in through the back."

I don't want to leave, but then I realize that if we can get into the courthouse, we could get a better look at the diner. "Okay."

We push our way back out of the growing crowd and through a parking lot whose gates have been left open to allow the firetrucks faster access. In minutes, we're standing at a back entrance. I look at Brian. "Why didn't we use this entrance during the early days of my trial?"

Brian smirks. "Because it would have looked like we were trying to hide something."

A security officer guards the doorway. "Good morning, Attorney Freeland. The courthouse is open, but you have to stay away from the front doors. We also have to take your cell phone number in case we have to find you."

"Sure, that's fine." Brian signs us in and scribbles his cell phone number next to his name. "She will be with me the entire time." The security officer waves us through.

"He knows you by name? And where are the metal detectors? I could have avoided a lot of grief if you had just taken me into the courthouse this way."

"Jordan, I have been coming to this courthouse for many years. I have earned some of the perks." No smile, no big white teeth, just a sense of righteousness. He then opens the door to the stairwell and ushers me in.

"Are we going to climb the stairs all the way to Courtroom Five?"

Brian stops at the door with a big "1" on it. "Just follow me."

The main concourse of the first floor is empty except for two guards who stand idle at the metal detectors. "Mind if we take a look through a window?" Neither guard responds to Brian's ask.

We move to a window to take a better look. Brian pulls me back. "Don't let anyone outside see us."

"Why not?" I'm giving him a worried look. "Are we in danger?"

"Only of me losing a perk I just shared with you. Not everyone can just waltz into the courthouse like that. So be careful." Brian makes his way to a window and carefully peers out with one eye.

I start to laugh. "Are we in a spy movie?"

"More like a war movie. Take a look at the diner." Brian is shaking his head as he pulls back from the window.

I carefully peek through the window. The sky above the diner is filled with black smoke. Orange flames scream from every side as the fire battles to stay alive against the firefighters' assault. The front facade is gone, leaving behind only a painful view of the destruction behind. The black and white checkered floor of the Safe Haven Diner is nothing more than multiple shades of dark char and fleeting embers. There are no more dirty windows. The walls and floor resemble something one might see in footage of a war-torn country. The intense heat has caused the old metal tables to appear to be kneeling. The counter is a carbonized ghost of itself. Gone are the red barstools that once lined the old soda jerk counter. The yellowed mirrors and frayed wallpaper are now small flecks of remembrances scattered throughout the carnage. Not a single blade of the vintage metal ceiling fans is discernible. There is no ceiling either. "You're right. It looks like a war zone." Brian has left the window and is standing at the elevators.

The elevator doors open, and the smell of smoke escapes from the inner compartment. "Is it safe to use the elevator? Maybe we should take the stairs."

"We're going to the fourth floor. Besides, the fire isn't in this building." Brian steps into the elevator and holds the doors open, gesturing for me to get in.

We exit the elevator into an empty corridor. "Come on, let's get to the conference room. I want to go over my closing argument with you. I also want to prepare you for what Barrens might say, so you don't have any reaction." Brian's pace is brisk. It's like he's trying to get away from something.

"Brian, I need a moment before we start. That was much worse to see than I thought it would be." I sit down on a bench in the corridor.

"Jordan, take all the time you need. I'll be inside."

Brian's choice not to sit with me is out of character. I get up and rush to the courthouse suite. I open the door. He's crouched down, cautiously leering out of the window.

"Brian . . . Brian."

He quickly stands but doesn't turn around. "Sorry, I dropped my pen. Wow, that's a lot of smoke."

I see the pen sitting on the table. "Yeah . . . it is. Do you want to sit down and go over your closing argument?"

He slowly turns around. His face is pale and sullen. "Sure, yes.

Please sit." He rubs his face and eyes. "All this smoke is irritating my eyes."

"I know it's none of my business, but I am a doctor. I can tell. And we haven't lied to each other all this time." I think it's better to touch him at this moment.

There is a heavy lament from Brian as his shoulders drop. "Sorry, I've seen this type of destruction before. I was in Iraq many years ago. I saw what bombs can do. What fire can do. So, for me, the reaction is twofold." His voice is low and strained. Another deep sigh. "The first is for the loss of the diner, which, like most of my colleagues, is like losing a close friend. The second is Iraq. I'll never forget that. I've learned to move past it, and I cope by focusing on something else." He is not making eye contact.

Brian suddenly shifts his attention and begins removing papers from his briefcase. "I want to read my closing statement to you, so you understand the direction we are going. If there is anything that you feel isn't correct, let me know." Brian is all business.

"Brian, can I ask one more question before we start?"

"Of course, just not about Iraq. I don't speak about that part of my life." There is no doubt that this is not open for debate.

I already know not to go there. "Will they rebuild the Safe Haven Diner?"

"I hope so. But rumor has it that old man Stockland doesn't make much money from the diner. It's more of a love affair that keeps it going." A somberness carries his words.

"What about the attorneys?"

"What about them?"

A tenuous smile peeks through. "Couldn't all of you chip in and rebuild the diner? It's given all of you so much, maybe it's time to give back."

Brian has that way-off-in-the-distance look that he's always tormenting me about. He chuckles. "Jordan, that's a nice idea, but you see how we fight. I don't know if we can all be on the same side. Let's get back to work."

We spend the next forty-five minutes going over the finer points of Brian's closing argument. Every detail is a laborious debate of point and counterpoint. Brian's passion for the law, and all the minutiae that swirl through it, could keep him going for hours or even days.

Watching him is entertaining, but I need a break. "I need food and some coffee."

Brian stops at this comment and is about to address my request when there's a knock at the door. "Brian, are you in there?" Erin's voice becomes clearer as she opens the door. "I've been trying to reach you on your cell for the past half hour."

Brian says, with just a little too much glee, "Sorry, we were knee-deep into my fabulous closing argument." I roll my eyes.

Erin looks at me and half laughs. "I know how he can get."

"Ha ha. What can I do for you?"

"Judge Harris's clerk called. Because of the fire and limited access to the building, court has been postponed until this afternoon."

"How did you get into the building?" Brian is standing with his hands folded across his chest.

"I have perks too." Erin pretends to give a sheepish look. There is nothing sheepish about her.

I burst into laughter. "Back way in?"

Erin looks at Brian. "It was three years before you showed me that."

Brian quips, "Necessity rules."

I stand between them like I'm preventing a fight. "Can we get something to eat?"

Brian continues the playful banter by rubbing his belly. "That's an excellent idea. I wish someone else had thought of that." Brian turns toward me. "When this is over, I might give you the senior position at the firm."

"How long have I been working for you?" Erin drops a brown paper bag on the table. "Egg and cheese on hard rolls; three of them. On the company card."

"What, no coffee?" Brian says with a snort.

"Oh, they're sitting on the bench in the corridor. I couldn't open the door with them in my hands." Erin turns and opens the door; Attorney Barrens is standing there, holding a tray with three to-go coffee cups.

"I thought you might want these sooner or later. I'm just waiting for you to open the door. My hands were full, and I too couldn't open it." Barrens feigns a smile. "You might as well invite me in."

"Not a good idea, and you know it," Erin responds quickly and with a bit of arrogance.

"You heard her." Brian doesn't take his eyes off the Prosecutor. "But I'll tell you what, we'll invite you to the victory party. No hard feelings or that BS that goes with it. Or, would you like us to wait until after you and Judge Harris finish with your posttrial party for two?"

Barrens takes the poke in stride. "I'd like a 2013 Perrier-Jouet Champagne, and you can have Erin serve it to me."

Erin's steps closer to Barrens. Brian diffuses the situation, "Okay, okay, enough fun. We'll see you in court." Erin closes the door in Barrens's face.

"Don't let him get to you, Erin. He's a—" I step forward, but Brian stops me from finishing the sentence.

"No, he's not. He's just trying to knock us off our game like we did to him yesterday. You might not think it, but outside of the courtroom, he's a decent guy. Unfortunately, the heat has been turned up on him. You know what they say about flowing downstream."

Erin sneers at Brian as she moves to the window and pretends to look at the rubble below. Brian starts to laugh. "He took the coffee with him. Guess we'd better pay better attention in the courtroom today."

I join Erin at the window. "At least the flames are out."

Erin turns to her boss. Her voice is still gnarled. "Brian, kick his ass."

Brian remains silent and walks to another window, then returns to the conference table. He says nothing and begins thumbing through files and folders. The egg sandwich remains on the table in front of him, only one bite taken.

Erin finds a reporter's feed on her cell phone and shares it with me. Brian makes no effort to watch.

It was Hellfire in Haven today. The damage is unimaginable. Nothing remains but the charred skeleton of the one hundred-plus-year-old diner. For those of you who don't know about the establishment, its nickname was the Safe Haven Diner. It was called this because lawyers could go there and everything was off the record. Reporters, like yours truly, dared not venture in. I hear the food was mediocre at best, but the sanctuary it provided was priceless. The cause of the fire is unknown at this time, and by the looks of the place, I'm not sure they'll ever really know. We'll update you as soon as we know more.

Erin turns down the sound. We sit there quietly eating. Brian continues to shuffle papers and busy himself by reciting his lines aloud. Erin and I look at one another.

I text her: *PTSD.* She gives a single nod in agreement.

CHAPTER 38
BOXES AND WHISTLES

Courtroom Five feels claustrophobic compared to its big sister. The fire has kept my fans and the court junkies away. The gallery is nearly empty, except for a few reporters sitting in small clusters.

I glance around. "I understand that a fire might keep the looky-loos away, but the reporters too? Isn't it their job to be in the danger and report?"

Brian explains, "Closing arguments are like the seventh-inning recap at a baseball game. The announcers give all the highlights of the game and maybe some trinket of insight. Nothing new is shared."

Apparently, Brian is a big baseball fan. I never really followed the sport.

Erin quips, "He thinks he's the ace starter and the star closer on the team."

I nod in agreement, but I'm not sure what either term means.

Brian pretends he's slapping a ball into a mitt. "I don't just think that, I know that. If I didn't, we'd be in big trouble right about now."

Erin spits back, "You gonna adjust your junk now, ace?" Our laughter causes unwanted attention from those in the gallery and from Barrens, who sits alone at the prosecutor's table.

Brian leans over towards Barrens. "Champagne's on ice." Barrens shakes his head but doesn't reply.

"All rise for the Honorable Judge Constance Harris." The return to Courtroom Five also means the return of the bailiffs and the court reporter. Surprisingly, there is a sense of being home.

Judge Harris is straight to the point. "Mr. Barrens, are you prepared to give your closing argument?" If the burning of the Safe Haven has any effect on her, she is unwilling to show it. The jury looks tired and concerned. I'm guessing they don't want to be so close to a smoldering building.

"Yes, Your Honor." Barrens points to the back of the courtroom where his final two associates have situated themselves. With a single flick of his right hand, both proceed to the front of the courtroom. They are wheeling the Money Box and the Pill Box on rolling carts. Barrens has them position the exhibits in front of the jury box.

"You have to admit, it is very odd that a woman, raised in an upper-middle-class family, with a bright future as a doctor, decided to open her practice in a financially challenged neighborhood whose drug problem is one of the worst in the state. Why did Dr. Carey do all this? She stated it was because of a broken healthcare system that was unwilling to help her patients. I ask you to consider this question. Was Dr. Carey the only doctor to have patients who fell victim to her so-called broken healthcare system? The obvious answer is, of course, no. So then, why is Dr. Carey the only one to use these two boxes?"

Barrens paces back and forth from the jury stand to the boxes to the front of the defense table. Each time he passes near me, there is an urge to hit him. Brian warned me that Barrens will paint me as dark and evil as he can. He is doing a good job.

"Dr. Carey's financial woes are well proven. Besides the money her practice owed, she has student loans that will cripple her for decades. I give Dr. Carey credit. The Money Box was ingenious. The people in that neighborhood are hardworking and have pride.

They don't like owing money. Dr. Carey understood this and took full advantage of it. The Money Box provided the neighborhood with an easy way to pay in cash at a discount. She then took the cash and did whatever she wanted with it, and it was all tax-free. Win, win, win. The cash was un*track*able. I coined this word so you, the jury, can truly understand how devious this plan was. The word normally used here is "untraceable." But Dr. Carey is too smart for that word. She gave us a trail to follow. She pretended to place all the money in the bank and then spent it in all the right places. In truth, she only showed us the money she wanted us to see. We heard that the office count and the bank deposits often didn't match. We heard that Dr. Carey made most of the deposits. That's where she slipped up, just like every other criminal. Again, I'll tip my hat to her. She didn't pay off everything at once. Dr. Carey even let a few nonessentials slip into the collection, just for good measure. I should also note that Dr. Carey has not been able to practice medicine for over a year, yet she hasn't taken money from anyone. Yes, if you're wondering, we checked." Barrens stops to take a drink of water. The jury is following his every move. I want to look at Brian but stare at the judge's bench, fighting every emotion that wants to cross my face.

Barrens returns to the jury and places his hand on the Pill Box. "Let's talk about this box. The Pill Box, as it is known, was used by Dr. Carey to collect unused medications . . . why didn't she call it the Medication Box? Because medication wasn't what she was after. Pills were the prize. Dr. Carey took in unused pills, repackaged them, and gave them out. Just like with the money from the Money Box, the pills here were un*track*able. No one truly knows how many pills Dr. Carey took in. Heck, the only ones we really know about are the ones she marked in the patient's charts." Barrens makes air quotes while saying the word "patients." "She could have been the biggest drug dealer in the neighborhood, and no one would have suspected it." Barrens again stops and pretends to examine the boxes. He opens the Pill Box lid. It's filled with pill bottles and loose pills in small transparent bags. "This is what the box would look like if it were filled with the pills Dr. Carey was taking in."

"Objection! Your Honor, I understand that objections during a closing argument are not costumery, but Mr. Barrens is putting on theatrics that you have already warned us about. Also, no evidence or witness testimony has been presented during this trial suggesting that Dr. Carey was selling or profiting from the medications. Lastly, the medications and their presentation in the box are pure fabrication. Everything was photographed, and a pre-trial agreement was made not to bring the medications into court." Brian stands with both hands pointing to the Pill Box. "Filling the Pill Box with random pills is evidence tampering! Your Honor, please."

"Sustained. Bailiff, please close the boxes. Mr. Barrens, you may keep the boxes in the room, but you may not open them again, nor will you continue with any further statements that Dr. Carey was illegally or legally selling the pills. The jury is instructed to disregard Attorney Barrens's last remarks as well as the contents in the Pill Box." Judge Harris no longer stays detached as a nearly silent "Hmm, hmm, hmm" slips from her closed lips.

Barrens carries on for another thirty minutes, explaining how my calculated moves broke dozens of laws. He tells the jury that they have no choice but to return a verdict of guilty on every count against me. Everything Barrens says after opening the Pill Box is irrelevant. *If I can't forget the picture of all those pills in that box, how is the jury supposed to?*

"We will take a fifteen-minute recess." Judge Harris bangs her gavel and leaves the courtroom. The jury exits the courtroom, murmuring, while the associates loudly praise Barrens for giving such a convincing argument.

Brian stands and turns to walk toward the exit. I'm working hard to keep the thought of spending the next ten years in prison.

Erin hisses in my ear. "Jordan, get up. Now."

The walk to the suite is a blank. All I can see and hear is the box filled with drugs and the head juror saying the word guilty.

"Jordan!" Brian is almost standing over the top of me. "I told you that Barrens is desperate. He's playing dirty, pushing on every edge. Don't worry, I have this."

"How? How do you have this, Brian? Tears stream down my face uncontrollably.

"I can show the jury you're a good person, a good doctor. If, for some odd reason, it goes the other way, Barrens has just given us grounds for a solid appeal. I know you don't see it now, but he opened so many doors for us with that stunt."

Brian sits down next to me. "I know it looks bad, but it's not. Just ride this out to the end with me."

Erin rushes in. I hadn't even noticed she didn't come back with us. "I just spoke with Judge Harris's law clerk. He said the judge is furious with Barrens, and she is considering a mistrial. He said Barrens tried to slip in new evidence during his closing argument, and the judge, being a stickler for the law, wants to call a mistrial."

Wiping tears, I look at Erin. "I don't understand."

Erin sits down across from us. "Closing arguments are basically your last chance to tell the jury that you proved your side of the case. You can't introduce anything new. Most judges might allow you to stretch the boundaries a bit, but Barrens went way past the line."

Brian places a hand on his chin, then quickly scribbles on a yellow legal pad. "Erin, can you talk to your law clerk buddy and get him to convince Judge Harris not to declare a mistrial?"

Erin's shoulders rise. "Sure, I think so."

"I thought we wanted a mistrial?" I place my head down on the table when I hear the door click shut. "I feel like I'm going in circles."

"I'll explain. All our cards are on the table, and Barrens will have time to build a stronger case if we have a mistrial now. Judge Harris has the right to give what's called a direct verdict. That means she can rule on the case, and the jury will never get a chance. Thanks to Erin, we know what the judge is thinking. I can use that to our advantage, if we need it." Brian packs the yellow pad into his briefcase. "Let's get back to the courtroom."

The walk back to the courtroom is as much a blur as the one leaving it. *Did I break the law? Am I really a criminal?*

Brian stops me just before we enter. "Don't show any cracks in there. After the next sixty minutes, you'll feel better. I promise."

"I hope so . . ."

Brian releases a forced smirk. "Remember, I'm the star closer."

It seems the word of Barrens's performance has reached the outside world, thanks to the few reporters who showed up earlier. The gallery is almost full of reporters, sketch artists, and free-lancers, all trying to get that scoop that will catapult them to the top of their world.

The Money and Pill Boxes are still stationed at the front of the courtroom. *How easy it would have been to sneak in and steal them during the break.* Barrens has me thinking like a criminal, and not a good one. The place is literally crawling with police officers.

Barrens et al. are sitting at their table, engaged in quiet chatter and adding an occasional over-the-top laugh while looking at me. I'm not fazed by it. Actually, it has the opposite effect. "Brian, you're right. They're worried."

Brian scrolls through the pages of his legal pad. I look over at it; only the first page has writing on it. The rest of them are blank. "Don't smile or say anything. Look worried but not too worried."

Erin walks into the court seconds before the bailiff is about to start his cadence. From the seat at the end of the table, she gives Brian the faintest of a nod.

Judge Harris again bypasses the opening ceremony and the pleasantries. "Mr. Freeland, please give your closing argument."

"Yes, Your Honor. Thank you." Brian walks over to the boxes. He knocks on them and bends down as though they might speak to him. Then he lets out a whistle. Judge Harris raises the gavel slightly off the bench. Brian gives her a nod of compliance and turns his attention to the jury. "Imagine if they could talk. I'm sure if they could, we wouldn't even be here. Sadly, they can't. I didn't know using a box became a crime, and I'm a pretty good lawyer."

The jury and gallery give a mild chuckle. Even Judge Harris tries to hide a grin.

Brian whistles again. " I'm going to be one very busy lawyer." Laughter rolls around the courtroom again.

This time, Judge Harris does bang her gavel. "Move it along, Mr. Freeland."

Brian tips his head to the judge and continues. "We all know this is not true. Just like we all know that the charges against Dr. Carey are not true. There has been no solid proof that Dr. Carey stole money, dealt pills illegally, or, for that matter, legally. She didn't evade taxes or do anything wrong. There has been a lot of posturing and conjecture on behalf of the prosecution, but no proof. 'What proof was given at this trial?' we might ask. That's a simple question to answer. Witness after witness admitted that Dr. Carey didn't do anything wrong, but that's not the answer we're looking for. The real answer is that Dr. Carey is a caring and devoted doctor. She was willing to put her entire life on display, to risk everything for her patients. Everything you and I cherish and, at the same time, take for granted. The prosecutor is correct when he says that Dr. Carey gave up a fancy office and a very comfortable life. But, he's wrong about the why. And deep down we know that too." Brian strolls back over to the boxes without saying a word. The entire courtroom holds its breath.

"We have shown that Dr. Carey accounted for every dime she spent, every pill she gave away. Yes, gave away. Please listen to that carefully. Dr. Carey gave the medication to her patients for free. The experts you heard from don't know Dr. Carey. To them she is a name on a piece of paper filled with a bunch of other data to be scrutinized. The patients who got up on the stand, or who came to this courtroom, they know Dr. Carey. Think about it, they came to support the doctor who just moved into their community, just came into their lives." Brian whistles for a third time. "That's the proof; the answer to that simple question. Did Dr. Carey make mistakes? Yes, she did. But were those mistakes intentional and did she break the law? Only by a stretch of the imagination in the prosecutor's mind. Dr. Carey made those mistakes fighting for patients, not for herself. She never thought twice about herself. Even during the trial when she met Stella Thorne on the street. Dr. Carey knew the danger she might face and she risked it anyway. When you're deciding what Dr. Carey's fate will be, remember Charles Spinelli dying with dignity, remember Henry Robski begging to die. Remember Dr. Carey, who fought for them and hundreds of others like them, like you. You must find Dr. Jordan Carey innocent here today. If you don't, you will send a clear message into the world. Other doctors will stay in the shadows. Good doctors will be afraid to step up, and more good patients will suffer. I'll leave you with one last thought. If you needed a doctor, wouldn't you want one willing to fight for you like Dr. Carey? Thank you."

There is a hushed cheer from the gallery. Brian has given them the show they came to see. Judge Harris stares at the gallery, who settles instantly.

"Thank you, Mr. Freeland. At this time, I will instruct the jury. Ladies and gentlemen of the jury. It is imperative that you only weigh the permissible evidence that both sides have produced in this trial. You must decide if the prosecution has proven its case beyond a shadow of a doubt on each count. I have read the laws involved in this matter to you. Each of you has expressed that you understood them. I now ask that you return to the jury room for your deliberation. If you have any further questions, please have the bailiff bring them to me in writing. I thank you in advance for your efforts." Judge Harris gives a slight rap of her gavel, and the jury stands to exit.

Now it's a waiting game. Brian was right, I do feel much better.

CHAPTER 39
FAVORS AND VERDICTS

My first thought is to tell Brian and Erin that we should go across the street for a quick bite. The automatic response strikes me, and then the reality of the situation hits. Barrens is perched along one of the corridor walls as we exit the courtroom. "He still thinks that he's going to find something on me." I step toward him. Erin grabs hold of me.

"No. He wants to talk with me." Brian makes eye contact with him and points to the courthouse suite.

Inside the suite, Brian fires first. "What dirty trick do you want to try now?"

"It's not what you think. I'm not offering a deal. This one is going to play out whatever way it does. I need something else." Barrens takes a long pause and looks at Erin and me.

Brian replies. "They stay."

Barrens raises both hands in agreement.

"Well, am I supposed to guess, or are you going to tell me?"

"Brian, can we not do this dance? I'm asking for your help. When this trial is done, I'm going to need a good attorney to represent me in front of the bar. Judge Harris has lodged a complaint. Actually, several complaints. I need a good attorney. More importantly, I need one that I respect." Barrens extends his right hand.

Brian places his hands on his hips and walks around to the opposite side of the conference table. "Look, as you might have already thought of, the bar will reach out to me. As your attorney, it would be a conflict of interest. Wait, you want to hire me so I can't testify against you. What happened to you? When did you forget the law and start just looking for ways around it? You want the State Attorney's seat one day, and you can't have any blemishes, especially now. Why don't we say I declined your request, and you walk away now?"

"Brian, wait." Barrens is pleading. "We both know I bent the rules a great deal in this trial. You and I have gone up against one another dozens of times in the past, have I ever acted this way? Wouldn't you say it was totally out of character for me?"

"You can't step that far over the line and expect nothing is going to happen. Isn't that the whole premise of your case against my client?"

Erin opens the door. Brian shifts his eyes to it.

Barrens steps through the door. Erin slams it. "What a piece of sh—"

"No, just another old friend fallen into darkness." Brian rubs his head. "Erin, take Jordan down to the lobby coffee shop and grab some food and a coffee for me. I could use a minute alone."

Erin and I stand in a long line at the lobby coffee shop. "Is he going to be okay? How could Barrens put him in a spot like that?"

"I don't know." Erin looks around to see if anyone is listening.

"He, uh, was told to win, no matter what," a strange voice from behind us stutters.

Erin and I turn around. It's one of the original juniors. "Off the record, what did you say?" I ask.

He speaks freely. "On the record, off the record, who cares. I'm probably going to get called in to testify. That means I'm losing my job. So, what's the difference?"

"Keep it off the record. I'm not getting involved." Erin looks around again, then pulls us out of line to a secluded corner of the lobby. "Okay, what are you talking about?"

The junior lawyer explains how Jake Zane told Barrens he had to win my trial if he wanted to become the next in line for State

Attorney. Zane added that if Barrens lost it, it could cost Zane the election. The junior also says that Zane threatened to fire Barrens if he caused everyone another black eye. Erin and I leave the junior lawyer standing in the corner and head for the suite. The elevator to the fourth floor seems to take forever. Erin is standing in place, tapping her left foot; I point to her foot. She stops. The elevator doors open; Erin is almost at a jog down the corridor.

"Weren't they friends? Why didn't Barrens just come clean?"

Erin stops. "What would Brian have done with that information? If he doesn't say anything, he's complicit. If he does, he's a rat. Yes, that's a thing among attorneys." Erin sits down on the bench. "Shit! Now I know, and now I'm complicit." She starts heading back to the elevator.

"Where are you going?"

"Just wait there. Don't move."

Erin returns minutes later. She moves at a much slower pace. "Jordan, none of this ever happened. You have to swear to me you will never tell anyone, not ever, no matter what. It will get a lot of people in trouble. It could get me disbarred."

"Um, okay . . . I swear."

Erin hugs me. "Good. Now act natural."

We return to the courthouse suite. "Where's my coffee?"

"Um." I turn to Erin.

She leaps in. "They were out."

Brian frowns. "What about your food?"

I answer, "The line was too long. Before you ask, we overheard someone ahead of us ask for coffee. That's how we know there wasn't any more."

Brian scrunches his face. "Okay . . . I think." He goes back to playing on his phone. I peek over at Erin. She harshly points to a chair. I sit.

About an hour later, there's a knock on the door. "Attorney Freeland, you in there?"

"Yes, come in please."

A large bailiff is standing in the doorway. "The jury has returned with a verdict. Judge Harris wants you to come back to court." Without any further conversation or any acknowledgment, the bailiff turns and walks back down the corridor.

Reporters jockey for a space closest to the door. This is the grand finale. None of them wants to miss being the first to tell the world of my fate.

The three of us take our seats at the defense table for the last time. Barrens and his crew are also seated. The respect for each other, the unwritten attorney's code, and the outside-of-court friendship are all gone.

The familiar "All rise," which I hope I never hear again, ushers in Judge Harris. The jury settles. We stand and wait to hear what I'll be doing tomorrow.

"Madam Foreperson, has the jury reached a verdict?" Judge Harris speaks in her usual, unaffected timbre.

"Yes, Your Honor, we have." The thin, aging woman responds as she hands the bailiff a single sheet of paper.

The bailiff then hands it to Judge Harris. "Thank you, bailiff." She studies the page for only seconds, then refolds it and hands it back to the bailiff, who returns it to the sender.

The Judge recites the first charge. "What say you on the charge of tax evasion?"

"We, the jury, find Dr. Carey not guilty."

"What say you on the charge of drug trafficking?"

"We, the jury, find Dr. Carey not guilty."

"What say you on the charge of fraud?"

"We, the jury, find Dr. Carey not guilty."

"What say you on the charge of dispensing medication without the proper licensing?"

"We, the jury, find Dr. Carey guilty." A collective gasp arises from the gallery. None of the jury members are willing to look in my direction or even hold their head up.

Brian is quick to respond. "Your Honor, I would like the jury polled on the last count, please."

Judge Harris shuffles the pages she has sitting on her bench, then stands. "That will not be necessary." She takes a long, deep breath. "First, I would like to thank the members of the jury for their hard work. I have heard and reviewed all the facts and testimonies in the matter. I have taken into account the numerous actions and the lengths both sides have gone to prove their case. I find that certain actions have made it difficult for the jury members to rule on the last charge without prejudice. It is within my power to overrule any and all guilty verdicts, and I have chosen to enact a judgment of acquittal regarding the last guilty verdict. Dr. Jordan Carey, all charges against you have been dismissed. You are free to go. The jury is also dismissed." Without any further words, Judge Harris bangs her gavel and heads out of Courtroom Five.

The gallery erupts with the sound of clapping and the rush of shoes against the floor as the scoop-getters race to make their mark on the world. I stand there stunned. It hasn't yet registered in my mind that I'm free. Brian leans over and bear-hugs me, his great whites almost bursting out of his mouth. Erin makes her way behind me. My attorneys engulf me.

After the initial celebration, I sit down behind the defense table for the last time. Tears cascade down my cheeks. I want to say they are tears of joy, but they're not, they're tears of relief. My attorneys allow me to have my moment as they pack up. Brian reaches over and opens the wooden gate that separates the gallery from the rest of the courtroom. Three figures are following a large bailiff. His Hulk-like frame obscures them from me. As he steps aside, I can see their tear-filled faces.

"I didn't know you were here." My throat is hoarse and my tears are now from joy.

"How could you, with all those reporters? We could barely see anything." Joseph Carey pulls me close and holds me like he's never letting go. Mom repeats the act but is too filled with emotion to even speak. She silently kisses my face, repeatedly.

Andie waits for her turn and then smothers me. Her hug is so tight that I'm not sure I'll survive the love. "Andie, let go. I can't breathe."

"Just shut up, please." Andie's sobs start all four of us crying again.

Barrens reaches across the open space between the two tables and extends a hand. "I won't be filing an appeal. We're done here."

Brian shakes his hand but says nothing, not even a smile. He spins back to my family and me. "Let's get something to eat and a drink or two. I seemed to have missed lunch today."

CHAPTER 40
THE VERDICT

BRIAN PULLS me to the side. "We won the war, but we lost some battles along the way. Your license is gone. I'll file an appeal, but honestly, I don't think you'll be able to practice medicine again. You're young, and I'm sure you will find something else to do." His voice is gentle.

"Thank you, Brian. I know what you did cost you much more than you were paid. I don't know if I can ever make it up to you. Like you said, I probably won't practice medicine again."

Brian hugs me again. "You don't owe me anything."

I look at him and Erin, who rejoins us. "I'm not sure what comes next after this ordeal, but I know I'm tough enough to handle it."

We wait a long time for the courtroom and the corridor to empty. As we walk out of Courtroom Five for the last time, I pat the door frame and thank the old girl for doing a good job. She has stood there for countless decades, and I'm not sure anyone has ever thanked her.

Erin pushes the elevator button, and I ask them to wait a moment. I race down the corridor to the courthouse suite. I open the door; there is a new group huddled around the conference table. "Sorry, Can I just have one sec?" Without waiting for their response, I thank the suite for its help and service. This gets odd looks from the new occupants. I don't care.

. . .

I grab Brian by the arm. "I'll make a brief statement to the press when we hit the courthouse steps."

"Today, the unruly crowd will not back down." Brian looks me in the eyes. I think he's sizing me up to see if I'm ready.

"I'm good, Brian." He gives me those big pearly whites.

Microphones project from every direction. Questions are hurled at me hundreds at a time. Brian crosses in front of me. He's still my champion. "Please settle down."

"What was it that made the jury go in your favor?" The chaos begins again.

Brian raises his hand to ask for quiet. "The truth of the matter is that Dr. Jordan Carey is a good doctor and an even better person. The jury and the judge saw this truth, and they acted accordingly." Brian's words are as elegant as they are powerful. "Before I let Dr. Carey speak, I would like to make an announcement. As we all can see, the iconic landmark behind you has fallen. While as reporters, you may have been banned from the place, as laypersons, you were always welcome. For attorneys and those wishing a spot to rest and recharge, the Safe Haven Diner was just that. I would like to announce that I will be spearheading a campaign to rebuild the Safe Haven Diner just as it was before. Maybe with cleaner windows." There is a roar from the crowd. "I ask that all of us pitch in whatever way we can to make this possible." From behind us, the clapping is heroic. I turn to see the bailiffs, attorneys, security, cleaning crew, and even judges unified in support of the rebuild.

Brian steps aside and I step forward. Questions fly again. And Brian again, quells the mob.

I look at Brian, who signals me with his outstretched hand to give my audience a few words. Like Nathan, I want my fifteen minutes of fame.

"I've endured a great deal of scrutiny, both in there and out here. In the last two weeks, I have grown a great deal. I used to be afraid for my future, but not anymore. Just like the members of the jury and Judge Harris, I know that what I did was just. My actions were well-intentioned, whether or not they were well thought out. The one thing I've come to realize is that my fight is not over. It is just starting. First, I will fight to regain my medical license. I created a positive change for a small handful of people. But that's not enough. I have a community to serve, and I can only do that one way, as a doctor. With the help of my attorney, Brian Freeland, and his team, we will try our best to get my license reinstated and I will practice medicine the way it was intended. I will find new and better ways to make sure that those I treat will be able to get the medical care they need and deserve. Patients are looking for a true champion, and I want to be that champion. As I move forward, I will surround myself with experts who care as I care. Together we will find a way to set new standards of care."

"Okay, that's enough for today. Thanks for your support. As Dr. Carey said, we will now begin preparing a case to have her medical license reinstated. Dr. Carey will practice medicine again, and she will stay within the confines of both the law and the medical system. She will continue to provide the best care possible to her patients." Brian gives a forced smirk as he gently shuffles me from the steps. He and Erin walk me to the curb and into a waiting car.

"Damn it. Why did you cut me off?"

Erin moves in close to me and speaks softly. "Because you were giving the licensing board all the ammunition they'll need to prevent you from getting back your license. You callously confessed to future wrongdoings."

"Jordan, let's celebrate the court victory today and worry about your, our, next move later." Brian's goofy thumbs-up motion defuses the tension.

I grin. "You're right, we should celebrate."

Brian tells me he has arranged for my parents and Andie to meet us at The Verdict, another haunt of the legal community. According to Erin, winning attorneys take their clients there to celebrate before unleashing them back into the world.

Brian adds, "And to soften the blow of how much they owe."

Erin snarls, "Not in your case. Right, Brian?" He agrees.

Linda and Joseph Carey are hopping up and down, like they're about to see a celebrity walking down the red carpet. They ravage me with thousands of kisses.

"Thank you. Thanks. All right. Where's Andie?" I ask.

Dad replies, still holding onto me, "She's inside making sure we have a table."

A handful of reporters are snapping photos of the entire greeting. Brian waves them off. A few more camera flashes flare in my direction. Mom is taking her own keepsakes. I try not to look embarrassed.

Erin opens the front door to The Verdict. From the street, I can see that all the lights have been turned off. "Brian, is the place open?"

He remains detached. "Jordan, get in. I can only hold off the paparazzi so long."

This distracts me just long enough. I rush through the open door. The lights immediately come on, and the space is filled with so many familiar faces. Patients, fellow doctors, and neighborhood people, even Mr. Borlin is here.

He shakes my hand vigorously, "Roz says she's sorry she couldn't make it. Oh, and congratulations. She's doing well, recouping at home."

After an exhausting round of hellos and thank-yous, I stand in front of the table of honor and once more offer my gratitude to everyone there.

Stella, Ellie, Inez, Samuel, and Billy are sitting at a table to my left. I make my way over to them. "I don't know how I would have made it through all of this without all of you.

Stella reaches into her purse and pulls out a full bottle of rye. "We do."

I blush, and Samuel puts his arm around me. "No worries, Jordan, I don't have dreadlocks." We start to laugh.

Rebecca and Clara walk up behind me and hug me. I sigh in relief. "I'm so glad you're here. I'm sorry for putting you through this. As soon as I get my license back, we'll be—"

Rebecca interrupts. "Jordan, that's not happening. You're moving on to something bigger. I can feel it."

Clara takes her turn. "Your time in that office is done. That's one of the reasons we're all here. You did so much for this group, and they love you for it, but it's time for you to go."

Tears fill my eyes. "Wherever I'm going, you two are coming." They smile.

I finally see Andie, who is moving frantically around the room. "No."

"Yup, my last one for the next two years. Think of it as a . . . 'see ya later' gift."

I wave my arms in the air. "How did you have time to put all this together?"

She moves in close. "That's my secret power."

After a few drinks, Brian is as merry as the atmosphere itself. He clangs his glass with a fork several times and everyone hushes. "As is tradition after we attorneys win, we end up here. Jordan, you truly are a good person. Despite all your efforts to lose this case . . ." Brian places his paw-like hand on Erin's shoulder and looks at her, ". . . we pulled it off anyway."

"Attorney Freeland, both me, and Linda, Jordan's mother, that's her sitting right there, cannot tell you how much you and your team mean to us. Thank you for all you have done. Andie. Andie, you know that Linda, Jordan's mother, and I love you like a daughter.

You put together the money for Jordan's defense. Without you, we wouldn't be here today. Thanks for putting this together too. And Jordan, your mother, Linda, and me, we know how hard this was on you. You were such a trooper, honey." Dad raises his glass to his lips and drains the last third of the wine.

Mom staggers to her feet. "We have one more thing to be thankful for. Andie, we love you just like Joseph said. And we are thankful that you are well on your way to kicking that nasty drug habit. We are here if you need us."

"Mom!"

Andie places an arm around my mother, looks at me, and smirks. "Thanks, Linda. I know I can always count on you."

I slink over to Brian. "I thought you invited Barrens to our victory party?"

"I did." He snorts and, from under the table, produces a bottle. "2013 Perrier-Jouet, just in case."

CHAPTER 41
PONDS VERSUS OCEANS

A LITTLE OVER a month has passed. Brian and Erin have been working on a compelling argument to get me reinstated. They've compiled dozens of patient and peer affidavits, legal briefs, and who knows what else. The possibility of not getting my license back forces me to see where I fit in the world. I have no answer as of yet.

Andie left two days after the end of the trial, and I moved into their home shortly after that. My landlord was glad to let me out of the lease; I was just falling further behind on the rent. I miss Andie. Our goodbye was quick. Neither of us wanted to endure the painful face-to-face for long. I'm sure Andie has made new friends. We'll be sisters forever, but even sisters grow apart.

I am on my way to meet with Erin for drinks and to discuss the final touches of my appeal. She's now solely in charge of my licensing case. I'm sure Brian still asks for updates; he can be a micromanager. We are meeting at an outside café. Leon's and The Verdict just don't seem right.

"Hi, Jordan. I hope this table is okay." Erin's smile is not quite as big as Brian's, but it's still a welcome sight.

"Yes, this is fine."

"Why don't we get the business part out of the way quickly? I wanted to tell you that I sent everything I prepared to the licensing board about a week ago. Is there a problem?" Erin sees the questioning look on my face.

"Yes, I thought we were meeting today to finalize the appeal.

And, don't we get to meet in person with them to tell our side?" I'm trying not to sound desperate.

"Jordan, the first step is to give them the chance to change their original decision. If they don't, then we can request a formal hearing. Let's not jump the gun here." Erin has a way of calming me down that oddly works, and infuriates me on an entirely different level.

"Fine."

"How have you been doing with the downtime?"

Erin and I have become friends, but she maintains a distance to keep it professional. "I have good and bad days. The good days outnumber the bad as the weeks move forward."

"Have you spoken with Andie?"

"Yes, but the calls are getting shorter. I think she's picking up an English accent." We both laugh.

"Are Mom and Dad doing well?"

"Yes, they are doing fine. Erin, is there something you're not telling me? I feel like you're stalling."

"Fine, I want to share an idea with you. But you have to keep it to yourself."

"Another secret. By the way, what did I swear to on that bench?"

"Okay, but only because I need you to say yes to this one."

"Hold on." I look all around us.

Erin starts looking around too. "What are we looking for?"

"Just checking to see if Barrens has a private investigator watching us." I tap her arm.

She shakes her head. "I scared the crap out of that first-year flunky. Not really proud of it, but I did. Anyway, I told him I would file a conspiracy case for trying to drag me into it. And if that didn't work, I would file a defamation suit against him. For good measure, I told him that even if neither worked, his name would still be mud, and he would never work as a lawyer again."

“That worked?”

Erin brushes her fingers across the front of her jacket. “It’s all about the acting and the tone of your voice. It also didn’t hurt that he was so green and already scared.”

“Okay, I swear to this one too.”

“Jordan, this is the last case I will handle for Brian. After we left your party, Brian and I had a long conversation. It was very apparent at the party that I was never going to escape from under his shadow, so I’ve decided to do my own thing. Brian tried everything he could to make me stay.” Erin reaches over and gently closes my open mouth.

“I thought you would someday replace Brian.”

“That’s what he thought too. But he shades too much sun. I think I found a new calling. Your trial showed me that there are a lot of things wrong with our legal and political system. Too many people aren’t represented or are harmed by some of our laws.”

“So, you want to run for office?”

“No, I’m nobody, I have no clout, no name recognition, no following. This is where you come in.” Erin takes a large sip from her water glass as she waits for me to catch up.

”Me? How do I fit into all of this? I’m confused.”

“Jordan, what I’m about to share with you is going to be painful for you to hear. Just remember that what I want to propose is a much bigger opportunity.” Erin has once again taken my hand in that soothing way she has.

“Wow. Now I really don’t know what to expect.”

Erin starts off cautiously. “Jordan, your speech on the courthouse steps was picked up by every local and state news station. It was a sensation. It made people sit up and take notice. Use whatever cliché you want. Some of those people who sat up and took notice were on the licensing board. Those same people said we needed to make an extremely convincing argument to change their minds. You admitted, on the record and to the public, that you’ll continue to push medical boundaries. Brian tried to make a save. It didn't work. Jordan, I don't think you're going to get your license back."

"But you don't know that for sure!" Inadvertently, I'm almost at a full shout.

"Jordan, I kind of do. We can fight it and ask for a hearing, but it may be just a waste of time, and it could hurt you in the bigger picture of things to come." Erin hands me her cloth napkin.

I'm too angry to cry. "Erin, when will I learn? I've overstepped again, and again I'm paying the price."

"That leads me to the opportunity part. I'm leaving Brian's firm because of you." A Brian-esque smile emerges.

"What are you talking about? Erin, I don't want that kind of responsibility."

"Jordan, you have the people's ear now. They want those boundaries we just spoke of moved or changed, and I think you're the one to do it. Someone must be a voice that is loud enough to be heard. Going back to private practice is the small pond. You're meant to fish in an ocean."

"Enough with the metaphors; they're not helping."

"Jordan. I think you should run for office. How does State Representative sound? And I want to be the head of your legal team. I've been studying the law on this since about midway through your trial. I saw, see, something in you. You're a fighter who fights for the right reasons. You saw the courtroom's reaction when you stood up for yourself. People love an underdog, and you're the underdog fighting for all the other underdogs."

"So, I don't return to private practice; instead, I run for the State Representative? And you think we can do this?" I look around the table.

"Now what are you looking for?"

"Just making sure we haven't had any alcohol, and this is all part of a drunken stupor."

"We haven't, and it's not. Don't worry, I'll be there to guide you and keep you in line. You have to agree to listen to me when I'm trying to save you from you." Erin drops a crisp new business card on the table with her name in the center of it. She then unfolds a piece of paper that she has sitting next to. It's a mock-up of a poster. "Jordan, you can change things from there."

"Erin, is this a joke? Did you and Brian cook this up?" I let the idea sink in.

"No. You'll always be a doctor wanting to help your patients. If you win, you could have the power to help make positive changes for more than just a small neighborhood. Ponds versus oceans. Think about it."

I fold the flyer and stuff it into my jacket pocket. "I will, but not now. Can we talk about something else besides my future?" We spent the next hour talking about things that don't matter. Things that keep me away from the fear of the rest of my life.

Erin stands at the curb as I pull away in an Uber. The driver, not Samuel, passes Borlin's Rx. Stella is exiting the pharmacy. I open the window and wave. She smiles and holds out a steady right hand, opening her palm to reveal a prescription bottle.

I pull out the flyer. "State Representative Dr. Jordan Carey. I like the sound of that."

The End